PRAISE FOR

The LOST HISTORY *of* DREAMS

"Waldherr's gripping debut mystery takes its inspiration from Gothic romance classics like *Wuthering Heights*. . . . This novel is an unexpected delight that grows steadily more compelling as its pages fly by. Waldherr plays with Gothic tropes, from the plot devices of misty moors, unexpected fires, and uncovered letters to the gendered conventions of tragic romance. The novel builds into a surrealist, haunting tale of suspense where every prediction turns out to be merely a step toward a bigger reveal."

—*Booklist*

"*The Lost History of Dreams* is a dark, shimmering gem of a novel, glittering with love lost, secrets kept, and long-buried truths revealed. Wonder, memory, death, and passion haunt every page of Kris Waldherr's powerhouse Gothic debut."

—Greer Macallister, bestselling author of *The Magician's Lie* and *Woman 99*

"There is a Scheherazade-like structure to Isabelle's tale, and the haunting beauty of the love story makes Ada and Hugh come alive as characters. As in many Gothic stories, the moldering old house that represents family tragedy is a fitting, creepy backdrop to the mysteries of the past. Waldherr avoids cliché in her rich descriptions and hints of supernatural presence that never cross into melodrama. Additionally, while most Gothic tales offer only darkness and tragedy, a surprising amount of light and joy imbues the ending here. Fitting, perhaps, for a novel that uses stained glass as a symbol for heavenly possibility, even in the face of death."

—*Kirkus Reviews*, starred review

"In this accomplished debut, Kris Waldherr transports the reader to the fascinating world of Victorian England and its tradition of postmortem photography with a deft hand. An atmospheric tale of lost love, family secrets, and an inquiry into how our own histories define us, I relished every poetic page. Mesmerizing, lyrical, and deliciously brooding."

—Heather Webb, international bestselling author of *Last Christmas in Paris* and *Meet Me in Monaco*

"An atmospheric and hypnotic love story that not even death can end . . . a sensual, twisting Gothic tale that embraces Victorian superstition much in the tradition of A. S. Byatt's *Possession*, Diane Setterfield's *The Thirteenth Tale*, and Emily Brontë's *Wuthering Heights*; the mystery is slyly developed, while the love story is tastefully titillating."

—*BookPage*

"Kris Waldherr's *The Lost History of Dreams* is very aptly titled, as reading this novel feels indeed like entering into a dream, one from which I have yet to fully awaken. With beautiful prose and poetry, Waldherr weaves a darkly seductive Gothic tale of love, art, death, and obsession. You'll want to keep reading this one late into the night."

—Alyssa Palombo, author of *The Spellbook of Katrina Van Tassel*

"[A] tense, atmospheric, and sensual Gothic thriller."

—BookTrib

"In *The Lost History of Dreams*, Kris Waldherr delivers a novel of haunting mystery and passion reminiscent of *Wuthering Heights* and Byatt's *Possession*. Layered within the pages of this gorgeous Gothic tale is a story of several loves, each masterfully wrought in dazzling, poetic detail that will leave the reader longing for more."

—Crystal King, author of *Feast of Sorrow* and *The Chef's Secret*

"*The Lost History of Dreams* plunges the reader into a sumptuous feast for all the senses. Through the perspective of a very Victorian yet empathetic male protagonist, Waldherr cleverly depicts the confining roles women of the era were forced to play. This creepily delicious tale will rob readers of their sleep as it asks and answers its own question: '"How can there be so much beauty in this world amid so much sorrow?" The only solution was to create more beauty.' With this novel, Waldherr has done exactly that."

—Clarissa Harwood, author of *Impossible Saints* and *Bear No Malice*

"Kris Waldherr's *The Lost History of Dreams* is an exquisitely crafted literary Gothic. With its labyrinthine twists and turns, it evokes the dark mysteries of the classic Victorian ghost story in all its brooding, atmospheric glory. A riveting, addictive read. Sarah Waters fans will be entranced."

—Mary Sharratt, author of *Ecstasy* and *Daughters of the Witching Hill*

The LOST HISTORY *of* DREAMS

The LOST HISTORY *of* DREAMS

A Novel

*

KRIS WALDHERR

ATRIA PAPERBACK
New York London Toronto Sydney New Delhi

ATRIA PAPERBACK

An Imprint of Simon & Schuster, Inc.
1230 Avenue of the Americas
New York, NY 10020

First Atria paperback edition February 2020

ATRIA PAPERBACK and colophon are registered trademarks of Simon & Schuster, Inc.

For information about special discounts for bulk purchases, please contact Simon & Schuster Special Sales at 1-866-506-1949 or business@simonandschuster.com.

The Simon & Schuster Speakers Bureau can bring authors to your live event. For more information or to book an event, contact the Simon & Schuster Speakers Bureau at 1-866-248-3049 or visit our website at www.simonspeakers.com.

Interior design by Kyle Kabel

Manufactured in the United States of America

10 9 8 7 6 5 4 3 2 1

The Library of Congress has cataloged the hardcover edition as follows:

Names: Waldherr, Kris, author.
Title: The lost history of dreams : a novel / Kris Waldherr.
Description: New York : Atria, 2019. |
Identifiers: LCCN 2018025501 (print) | LCCN 2018032731 (ebook) |
ISBN 9781982101039 (Ebook) | ISBN 9781982101015 (hardcover : alk. paper) |
ISBN 9781982101022 (pbk. : alk. paper)
Subjects: | GSAFD: Historical fiction | Love stories
Classification: LCC PS3623.A356735 (ebook) | LCC PS3623.A356735 L68 2019 (print) | DDC 813/.6—dc23
LC record available at https://lccn.loc.gov/2018025501

ISBN 978-1-9821-0101-5
ISBN 978-1-9821-0102-2 (pbk)
ISBN 978-1-9821-0103-9 (ebook)

For Edward and Joyce Miller,

with gratitude and love

Eurydice, dying now a second time, uttered no complaint against her husband. What was there to complain of, but that she had been loved?

—Ovid, *Metamorphoses*

Every love story is a ghost story.

—David Foster Wallace, *The Pale King*

PART I

DREAMS LOST

*

February 1850

London

The Annunciation

Excerpted from *The Lost History of Dreams* by Hugh de Bonne, published 1837 by Chapman & Hall, London.

Whilst the life inside her grew so round
The dream was lost as it was found.
Such was it thus : Aft their vows
Orpheus slept espoused
Silenced as the One Who Ends
Came 'mid Helios to transcend
Amor's gilt clad arrow.

Yet in the morn, Eurydice found no sorrow :
Her eyes clamped mate, her devotion bright.
Cried she : ''Tis love, not sun, that draws the light,
And Thou, my Spouse, shall be my fame.'
She knew not when her annunciation came
Amid Moon, not Sun. For no serpent smites
Along the ground. Instead, it bites
And leaves no sound.

*

I.

Robert Highstead's workday ended with a letter thrust inside his pocket. Before that, it was spent in a second-story parlor in Kensington, squinting into a camera at a corpse.

Through the camera's viewing glass, Robert watched a young woman lying as if asleep, her hands cupped against her breast like she'd been called to cradle a dove. She appeared upside down on the viewing glass as though floating. It was a pose Robert had witnessed hundreds of times in the past three years: the serene smile upon the lips, the closed eyelids, the awkwardly draped shawl across the shoulders that a loved one took upon herself to orchestrate. A last display of care before consignment to the grave. The only variant today was a small book, *The Lost History of Dreams*, by an author Robert had never heard of. The volume was splayed across the woman's belly, as though she'd just set it down to rest her eyes.

The thin cry of an infant revealed the cause of the woman's demise. From the blood-stiffened linens thrown in a heap against a limewashed wall to the slack-shouldered midwife napping beside the wash basin, Robert understood the woman had labored long and hard. "The noblest of sacrifices," he'd told her sister and husband, to help them grasp whatever comfort they could. Their muffled sobs gave hint to the ineffectuality of language. The winter air inside the parlor was weighed with the tinge of iron despite the geraniums set on the window ledge, the ice beneath the coffin boards. Not that it mattered—after all, Robert had work to do. He needed to be in Belgravia in two hours for a thirteen-year-old consumptive whose family yearned for a last portrait while she could still acknowledge their presence.

Robert unlatched a long wooden box to remove the silver-coated copper plate for the daguerreotype. He'd already buffed it to a mirrorlike sheen before exposing it to iodine and bromine fumes. As he reached toward his camera, his eyes tripped to the clock on the mantel as he thought of his wife. She hadn't come home the previous evening—a not uncommon occurrence in their three years of marriage. Nor did it help that this was the third corpse he'd daguerreotyped since breakfast. Though Robert was accustomed to such sights, today it felt too much.

The widower, who was dressed in the modest clothes of a merchant, approached Robert, the newborn in his arms bawling. "She . . . she was lovely," he said, his eyes reddening.

Robert tutted between his teeth. "I'm so sorry." The more often he repeated the words, the less currency they seemed worth. He set the frame containing the plate inside the camera with a slide that felt as visceral as anything he'd experienced of late.

"Now the camera is ready," he announced, ignoring the slight stench already rising from the corpse; the ice wasn't helping. "The process will take little time, sir. Less than a minute."

The widower pressed a palm against his eyes. “I appreciate how quickly you arrived. Very good of you. My sister claims you're the best daguerreotypist of this sort.”

“I promise to use all the skills of my art, sir.” Robert's heart lurched with sympathy; at least he still had his wife, wherever she was. *She always comes back.* “If there's anything else I can do to offer comfort . . .”

The widower's eyes fixed on Robert with a wet desperation. “Can . . . can you make her look as she did when she was alive, Mr. Highstead?”

“Ah, I understand! The daguerreotype will record your wife so your daughter—”

“Son. We're naming him Charles. After her.” The widower indicated his wife's corpse with a tight nod. “My wife's name was Charlotte. Those who care for her called her Lottie.”

“Then your son Charles will have something by which to recall his dear mother's life.”

Robert next took out a thick binder from his satchel. “If you'd care to look at our Catalogue of Possibilities,” he said mildly, setting it before the widower. The leather binding was gilded with the motto “Secure the shadow 'ere the substance fade.” The catalogue showed a journeyman's ransom of items to spill shillings on. The silver-bordered frame bearing a capsule for a lock of hair. The velvet-lined glass mounts. The alternate views of the departed. Images of the family gathered around the corpse, faces pinched from the effort of not shifting for the camera. The stillborn babies supported by black-cloaked figures.

“Are they alive?” the widower asked.

“Sometimes,” Robert replied. He possessed little pride for his ability to pose an infant in a mother's lifeless arms without the exposure blurring. A few drops of Mother Bailey's Quieting Syrup worked wonders, though he hated how it affected the child. Yet there was something about his employment Robert couldn't turn from. Something compelling. He told himself it was because he was offering comfort by transforming loss into proof of memory. Sometimes the daguerreotype seemed like sorcery itself, especially when he saw the image emerge from the plate like a ghost from the ethers. But it was more than this.

“For an additional fee, the image can be hand-tinted,” Robert added, pointing at a colored daguerreotype. Pink-hued gum arabic over silver foil. Flesh over bones.

Once coins were exchanged and bills of sale signed, Robert began the delicate process of daguerreotyping the corpse. He steadied his breath as he stared through the glass. He took the lens cap off with a flash of his palm, letting light record shadow on the plate. He ignored the widower's sobs, the tearful last confessions of love. After all, they weren't directed for his ears, but to those who could no longer hear. As Robert counted down the seconds of exposure, he anticipated what he would find when he developed the daguerreotype. For he knew in each person's image he would discover the lost history of their lives: the scars, the wrinkles, the dreams never fulfilled. Or, worse, the lack thereof.

And then a messenger had walked in and thrust the letter into Robert's pocket.

"How did you find me?" he'd asked the messenger, a towheaded boy of no more than fifteen. But the messenger had no answer, for he was already out the door.

The letter remained unopened for the remainder of Robert's afternoon. But it was not forgotten: he'd found himself unable to daguerreotype the consumptive in Belgravia, the first time he'd ever not shown for a client.

Instead of taking a carriage after he'd received the letter, Robert used his disturbance as an excuse to walk toward Clerkenwell. Toward home. He hoped the exercise would calm him. The simplest thing would be to read the letter. To learn the worst. He couldn't. Not yet.

He detoured along Oxford Street, though it took him out of his way. Even on a frigid February day, Oxford Street offered the distraction of shop-lined pavements crowded with silk-clad pedestrians. Such was the effect of Robert's step—he dragged his left leg to compensate for the weight of his daguerreotype traveling case—that some paused in his wake. Robert understood their interest wasn't because he was particularly handsome. With his thick pale hair and fair skin, his were the type of looks better described as sensitive than arresting; even now, three years after he'd left Oxford, he resembled the scholar of history he'd been. It was because Robert understood that even they, strangers to him in every sense of the word, *knew* there was something about him. Something somber. He noted their attention, but he'd grown used to it in the same way a butcher ignores the flies buzzing about his shop. After so much time daguerreotyping corpses, Robert understood death hung off him. Sometimes he imagined it possessing a physical form, like a martyr in a Flemish painting. Other times he fretted he smelled of decay, though he washed his hands nightly in carbolic acid followed by castile soap. This regimen left the skin on his hands reddened, but he couldn't bring himself to forego it.

By the time Robert approached Theobald Road, the shock of the letter still hadn't worn off. He walked quickly, bypassing narrow lanes snaking up into fog-draped indistinction. His pace only slowed once he turned left on Grays Inn Lane at the intersection where it met Laystall Street. His boarding house.

He ascended the four flights of stairs to his room, ignoring his landlady's solicitous greeting. He didn't bother to ask whether his wife had returned home; he knew Mrs. Clarke never noticed Sida's comings and goings. Anyway, for once Sida didn't dominate his worries. Mrs. Clarke's orange-striped tabby followed him upstairs, mewing plaintively. The cat understood Robert was good for a saucer of milk, but not today.

Once his door was shut, Robert settled the traveling case onto the floor in the room.

The room was enough for his needs. It contained a bed, a milk-painted dresser, a table the width of his lap for meals, and two wicker chairs. A long worktable held a glittering stack of silvered copper plates he'd begun polishing with pumice powder and oil; his business required a constant supply. Quarter plates, which measured about three by four inches, were Robert's favorite, for they required only his compact Richebourg daguerreotype outfit. He didn't like to work with daguerreotypes smaller than this—too hard to view without a magnifying glass. He possessed a camera expressly for this purpose, but preferred not to carry it along with the quarter-plate one. However, if business improved, he planned to invest in a newer American-style full-plate camera. As for the room itself, its walls were angled. No art could be hung on them, which perturbed Sida, who liked to draw, but the view from the windows was compensation. They looked out on chimney pots and muddled skies, where birds collected at dusk. On clear days, he could even spy St. Paul's to the south. When it grew foggy, Robert swore he could see coal dust suspended midair. The dust would enter his room, lining the plates in grey even after he closed the windows. Regardless, he preferred the windows open despite coal dust and the occasional errant crow at dusk.

Tonight the room was empty of crows. It was also empty of Sida.

Robert sank onto their bed, uncertain if he was relieved or disappointed she wasn't there. If the letter's sender was as expected, it might upset her more than him.

Relieved, he decided. *Better she not know. She'll return. She always does.* Yet he feared this time would be different.

What troubled Robert most about Sida's absences wasn't the possibility of her betraying him; he knew she was too devoted for that. Nor was it loneliness; Robert was the sort of man who found as much companionship in a book as he did in humanity. It was that he never understood the perimeters of her comings and goings.

When they were together, Robert knew his marriage was a fair trade. Apart, it was difficult to think of anything save Sida's unpredictable ways. He often wished he could stay home to watch over her. He'd bring her pomegranate seeds and mint tea, red wine and gentle kisses. He'd provide her with peace. But this could never be. Though Robert was the son of landed gentry, he'd abandoned his land right after they'd married.

The letter reasserted its hold. He glanced anew at the door. What if Sida showed? To distract himself, he'd read. Ovid's *Metamorphoses* would do. While at Oxford, he'd written an acclaimed history of Ovid's world. His second book, a biography of Ovid, had been slow work: the poet had spent the later part of his life in undocumented exile.

Still, the comfort of old obsessions called. He shifted the book onto his chest and read in Latin: *Eurydice, dying now a second time, uttered no complaint against her husband. What was there to complain of, but that she had been loved?*

The words blurred before his sight. Sida or no, the letter would not be ignored.

He drew the letter from his pocket like it was a snake. It was postmarked Belvedere, Kent. Where he'd grown up. It was addressed in a hand he knew well, though he hadn't seen it since his marriage. His brother's.

"Shit," he said.

Just then the door creaked open. He let the letter slide from his fingers.

Sida's form was silhouetted against sunlight from the landing. She was wearing a blue-grey silk gown, the one she'd married him in. The sleeves were unusually full about the shoulders, a style she was fond of. He ignored the dark stains marring the bodice; they hadn't been able to launder them out. Robert's eyes passed hungrily over her. Sida looked as she ever did: petite, fine-boned, doe-eyed. Her ebony hair was unplaited about her shoulders, damp from an unseen rain. The moisture brought out the gleaming curls of her hair, which reminded him of a Titian Madonna he'd shown her at the National Gallery, the first time she'd ever viewed art in a museum.

"You're back," he said, hoping she wouldn't notice the letter on the floor. "I missed you."

Sida smiled in answer, letting her Kashmir shawl drop as she approached him. The shawl was one her father had brought from India; he'd been a lascar who'd married an English woman when the East India Company had brought him to London. Sida had been employed as a seamstress when Robert first met her. Later he learned her uncle had forced her into service after her parents' death, but he hadn't cared. His brother had.

He opened his arms wide. She slid into them, the gesture easy. *This* was what he'd needed—not money, not family favor, nor universities at Oxford. *This* was why he lived in this fourth-story room where birds trespassed at dusk.

How light she felt in his arms! How soft! It no longer mattered that his days were spent daguerreotyping the dead. Besides, he was good at it. Instead of writing about history, he was capturing it on a silver-lined plate for generations to come. As for Sida, what did it matter she wasn't as she'd been before their marriage? Neither was he. All this was proof they were fated to be together. They'd never be parted.

"I love you," he murmured. "Only you."

Robert raised himself above his wife on their bed, ignoring the letter below. Whatever was in it couldn't be more important than her. The candle beside the bed cast shadows along her cheek, accentuating the bones beneath. He wove his fingers into hers, his skin pale against her dusky hand. He grew aroused, but didn't dare venture further. Instead, he rested his cheek against her breast, his hand on her waist. Her bodice was soft with moisture.

As the room darkened with the shadows of winter, husband and wife lay together on their bed, head to head, eye to eye, Robert's breath the only sound in the room before Sida's eyes lit on the letter.

II.

It is not an average day when a gentleman is asked by his brother to daguerreotype a deceased cousin. The day is even less average when the gentleman in question has never heard of this cousin.

Once Sida spied the letter, Robert could no longer ignore it. She'd forced him to read it. *"You can't avoid the past, Robert,"* she'd said, her lips pursing as she prepared for what might be.

His brother, John, had written on a sheet dated the eighth of February 1850:

> *From methods too ungentlemanly to set in words, I have learned of your return to London and your uncommon occupation. Though I'd intended to leave you undisturbed, I now have urgent need of your services for our cousin, Hugh de Bonne. I am uncertain of the logistics of such an endeavor on your end. Regardless, I implore you to arrive on the eleven o'clock coach the morning of the tenth. If you send word confirming your arrival, I'll have Durkin meet you with the carriage.*
>
> *If you or your wife ever bore me affection, I beg you not to ignore my request.*

Robert hadn't sent word, so no one met him at the coach stand. He'd walked the two miles to his family home alone, the handle of the traveling case containing his daguerreotype outfit pulling at his hands. He was grateful for the walk, for it enabled him to gather his thoughts. *Death changes everything,* he mulled, *yet nothing.* When he'd eloped with Sida, it hadn't been his intention to never speak with his brother. Nor did he bear him ill will. Their estrangement had happened as many do, wrought from good intentions and solidified by discomfort. By the time he'd abandoned Oxford for London, Robert had convinced himself the estrangement was for the best. Now he didn't know what he believed.

The manor house his family had occupied for only two generations was as Robert had recalled: an imposing presence built of red Georgian brick and white granite. The fields surrounding were the same too: separated by hedgerows, stone walls, and hegemony. There was a lovely garden hidden behind the house, one planted by his mother soon after his father had acquired the estate. Robert assumed this hadn't changed either though both of his parents were gone. The air was so sweet, so pure. So different from the fetid fogs of London. Robert opened his mouth and sucked in air. It felt soft as honey against his tongue, as sweet as summer grass. This he'd forgotten.

A bevy of large black crows darted out of the hedgerows at Robert's approach, raucous and rude. Once he reached the portico, he set the traveling case and tripod down and smoothed his best black overcoat. He surveyed the brass knocker for a good long minute. His face looked pale and strained in its curved reflection.

A moment after he'd pulled the knocker, the oak door was opened by a plump woman whose face was creased with wrinkles. Mary, the housekeeper. She'd aged since he'd last seen her; her flesh had crumpled around brown eyes once considered fine in the village. He'd never been especially fond of her, but he'd appreciated her loyalty. She'd taken over the household upon his mother's death when he was nine, and hadn't wavered since.

"Master Robert?"

The door halted midway, Mary's face caught in what appeared an attempt to smile. Her expression gave Robert the sense he'd become a ghost visiting the living, rather than the flesh and blood tied to this house.

"You didn't expect me." Robert also attempted to smile, but failed. "Am I so greatly altered?"

She shook her head. "You look the same. Perhaps leaner. Greyer. I just never thought to see you again after . . . after your marriage." Her tone grew odd. "Master John said you weren't coming. I'd heard they found you in London, that your brother hired a detective. I didn't believe it, after over three years."

"Has it been so long?" He knew exactly how long it had been.

"April 1846. Everyone still speaks of it. Three months after your brother returned from India. After your father's death."

"Indeed. May I come in?" With his equipment beside his feet, he felt like a tinker begging for a meal. "I'm here to daguerreotype my cousin."

At last Mary relented to open the door. She even bobbed a curtsey after casting a wary eye at his trunk. "Shall I have Durkin bring it to your room? I assume you'll be staying the night."

"Best I take it—it's fragile. I'm only here for the day."

Robert stepped over the threshold of his family home for the first time since his marriage. The long dark hallway was as he remembered. Narrow. Cold. Crowned by tall ceilings paneled in dark wood and gold-flecked wallpaper, all markers of plenty. How removed he'd grown from his birthright. Even if he wasn't the eldest son, he'd still been raised like a prince in a fief. He'd been expected to live a gentrified existence, to devote his life to scholarship and ease. To marry an heiress, not a penniless seamstress.

"This way," Mary said. "To your brother's study."

He followed the housekeeper, cradling his case and tripod. Mary continued to sneak gapes over her shoulder.

"'Tis a wonder to see you, sir."

"And you." Robert's nerves thrummed. "Perhaps you should announce me first."

"Master John is out with his dogs. I don't know when he'll return."

"Then it's best you take me directly to my cousin."

To daguerreotype him. Robert's stomach tightened, surprising him.

"He's laid out in Master John's study."

"Thank you, Mary." Perhaps there were mourners already congregated there, partaking of funeral cakes and ham, though Robert doubted it; the house felt too still. No crape over the mirrors either; some believed this prevented the departing soul from being trapped in the glass.

Mary stopped before the door of John's study. "I'll leave you to it, sir."

Robert bent his head inside. The study looked considerably different than the last time he'd been there three years earlier. Though the study had then held a coffin too, the room had been adorned with the trappings of authority and exoticism: a long mahogany desk scented with sandalwood, marble busts copied from ancient ones, silk tapestries from faraway lands. Now the only items of furniture inhabiting the study were the desk and a chaise draped in purple moiré. The chaise had been in his mother's bedroom; Robert had a distant memory of lying on it when his head ached, her French perfume enveloping him like a song. It was before this chaise that his cousin's open coffin rested across a pair of saw horses.

This was his cousin. His cousin who was dead.

Though it made little sense, Robert stepped toward the coffin as though not to disturb.

The last time he'd been in John's study, the coffin had been made of plain pine; Robert had insisted on it, yearning for simplicity. The coffin was also smaller, built to house the corpse of a young woman. This time, the coffin was constructed of dark lacquered wood swathed in deep purple velvet. The color of royalty. It was deep enough that his cousin's corpse remained hidden. This was a relief to Robert—he wasn't ready to view him yet. What had been his cousin's name? Hugh? Wasn't it a French name? For some reason, he resisted remembering. He'd never even heard of him until yesterday. Regardless, he had work to do.

Robert wiped his brow and set down the tripod and the heavy wood case containing his daguerreotype outfit. He unbolted the leather straps; the buckles and slides reminded him of the livery on a horse's head. He lifted the boxes containing the silvered copper plates, the bottles of chemicals and pigments. Finally, he removed the camera itself. It was a large box bound in honey-colored wood and glass. *Boxes within boxes. Locked and contained.* However, once he set his camera on the tripod, he forgot where he was, the task he was to do, shifting from family member to daguerreotypist. It was easier than he'd imagined, like putting on a hat before going outside.

Robert examined the corpse. Hugh looked as he'd expected: like the corpse of a man well past the middle of his life. He was thin and tall, his auburn hair dulled by white, his hands ropey with veins and bone. No one could argue he wasn't dressed elegantly, his ensemble unlike anything Robert had ever seen his wife sew. Hugh wore a well-tailored dark-hued frock coat. Beneath it, a black velvet collar was attached to his linen, which was fastened by an elaborately bowed necktie; his trousers were cut of the same fine wool as the coat, as though to match. Hugh reclined in the coffin, one long arm curved across his chest, as though overcome by surprise when his heart stilled.

"What did you die of?" Robert whispered. "Where did you die?"

Hugh revealed no sign of disease beyond approaching threescore years. Nor did he bear the stench of decomposition; the subtle scent of almond indicated he'd been embalmed in arsenic mixed with spirits of wine. The high color on his cheeks suggested carmine had been added to the mixture. Embalmed or no, Hugh's closed eyes had already sunken into his face. He must have passed about two weeks earlier and in another land; a small brass plaque set inside the coffin latch was engraved with a Geneva address. Hugh had traveled far to come home.

Inspired by the grandeur of Hugh's coffin and clothes, Robert would use his finest supplies. A gilding of gold chloride after fixing the plate with mercury. This would grant the daguerreotype the appearance of warmth—something his cousin's body now decidedly lacked in death.

Once the camera was positioned, Robert surveyed his cousin upside down on the viewing glass. Even after opening the drapes, the light was low. In such a case, Robert would move the corpse into a more advantageous pose. He'd even use a teaspoon to adjust the focus of their eyes, but the thought of this repulsed him—even if he'd never met him before, this was his cousin, not some stranger. In all of Robert's dealings as a daguerreotypist, he'd grown to think of death akin to a train pulling away—his job was to help the survivors wave goodbye. Now, after viewing his cousin's corpse, he was reminded death was a door slamming shut. Especially as he recalled that small pine box three years earlier.

A deep shudder rose from within him.

What to do?

The answer came unbidden: *We do what we must.* He'd take a portrait of his cousin's face in repose, cropped closely. A longer exposure would compensate for the low light. Once he developed the daguerreotype, he'd leave before his brother discovered his presence. He'd be done with his past—or as much as was possible.

Robert tucked his head beneath the black cloth covering the back of the camera. Reached for the silver-coated plate for the daguerreotype. Stared into the glass finder one last time.

His wife's face stared back at him.

III.

Robert dropped the silvered plate. As soon as it clattered to the floor, Sida disappeared; Hugh's corpse returned. Not that it mattered—Robert knew no one could see her but him. He'd had three years since Sida's death to become accustomed to her ways: the silent arrivals in the dark of night, the glimpses of her blue gown in tangled crowds. This time, though, he knew he'd imagined her. The proof was in the circumstance: the last time he'd been here, it was to bury her. Her ghost rarely showed outside their home. In the few occasions Robert had ventured beyond London, she'd never followed. He was still desperately short of sleep. His memories were affecting him.

Robert stepped away from his camera shaking his head, his hands. Anything to pull himself from the past. Yet the memory of that humble pine box remained, as tangible a presence as the corpse of Hugh de Bonne. Sida's stilled body within the coffin. Her dark eyes staring out. The carmine dabbed upon her cheeks to disguise the bruises . . .

He glanced over his shoulder, yearning for his wife's presence. Wishing she still lived. "*Robert,*" he imagined her murmuring, "*you must trust I'll never leave you.*"

Dead cousin or no, Robert had to go. Now.

He thrust the plate box, the camera into the traveling case. He didn't bother to take any care, precious camera be damned. Glass cracked, a vial of varnish slopped over his trousers and stuck to his skin. He ignored the mess. All he wanted to do was to find his way back to London. To Sida. He'd been a fool to leave her. His stomach twisted recalling how she'd clung to him after they'd read John's letter, color leeching from her face before she'd faded into the shadows. *"We'll never be parted,"* he'd sworn. And then he'd gone and abandoned her for a cousin he'd never even heard of before. What sort of husband was he?

Once the case was buckled, Robert dragged it toward the door. Before he passed into the corridor, a plethora of hounds rushed into the room. The dogs nipped at Robert's heels, sniffing his shoes, circling and barking. Robert swiped at them with his free arm. The hounds were followed by a tall man dressed in voluminous silk robes. The scent of musk, smoke, and horse sweat overtook almonds.

"What the deuce is going on?" the man bellowed in a deep voice. "Robert? Is that you? You came!"

Before Robert could respond, he was enveloped in an unavoidable embrace. His only brother, John, had returned.

"I must go," Robert said once he'd extracted himself. "I've urgent business."

But John wouldn't be put off. He pulled Robert toward him, dragging him into the corridor, beyond the gaping servants who'd gathered to eavesdrop. His brother's grasp was surprisingly strong—Robert supposed that's what came of all those mornings riding to the hounds.

"Don't leave, Robert. Not yet," he begged, his heavy silk dressing gown encasing Robert like a fly. "God, you look rough. We haven't seen each other in three years. Not since Cressida . . ." John's expression was embarrassed at best. "Well, you can't leave without visiting Mother's garden. Can you?"

"You want me to daguerreotype a chapel?" Robert said to John. "I thought this was about our cousin."

A half hour later, the reunited brothers strolled the winter-ravaged garden, surveying the herb beds, the briars—it was still too cold for snowdrops and crocuses—while John's hounds coiled about their ankles yelping at the frozen world beyond. Gravel crunched beneath their feet. Every so often, one of the hounds would dart off to piss on a hedge that looked exactly the same as it had during Robert's last visit. Robert did his best to ignore them; he found dogs to be overeager at best, unpredictable at worst. They even tried to lick the broken skin on his hands. The walled garden revealed the influence of their mother, who'd turned what had been a wilderness of abandoned rose beds into a refuge famed throughout the county after their father purchased the estate. All of a sudden Robert missed her with an acute longing. She would have appreciated Sida's love of beauty.

John replied, "Trust me, it's not any day you'll view a chapel such as this. It's rumored to be one of the most exquisite places in the world, like the Taj Mahal on a far more intimate scale." As boys, Robert and John had marveled at engravings of the Taj Mahal; it had spurred John's fascination with India. "The chapel is constructed almost entirely of glass. Set in a wood on the moors of Shropshire. Hugh de Bonne commissioned the chapel for his wife. Been locked since her burial inside it over a decade ago. He wants his corpse to be daguerreotyped beside her there. A final request."

A day earlier Robert had never even heard of Hugh de Bonne. Nor had he ever heard of someone building such a memorial. "I had no idea."

"I know, I know—it's a surprise to me too," John explained, bending over to comfort a hound who had an unfortunate encounter with a thistle. "Hugh was a poet. He's quite famous, though I wouldn't know." John's interests were limited to hunting, hounds, and travel. He also possessed a business acumen that had brought him wealth in India. John continued, "Neither Father nor Mother spoke of him, though I recall Mother mentioning we had a poet in the family by marriage through a French relative of Father's. I thought this was a euphemism for something disreputable. Hugh's last book was *The Lost History of Dreams*. Considered his masterpiece. Don't suppose you've read it."

"No." Robert recalled the deceased mother in Kensington, the book resting on her chest, the leather binding embossed in gilt letters. *The Lost History of Dreams*—the title was visible even after he'd developed the daguerreotype. His agitation pushed any wonder away. "I prefer the classics."

John heaved a sigh. "I know. Ovid. The eternals. You fit in well at Oxford, brother of mine. I must admit your new vocation was unexpected.

It was interesting explaining to your friends what kept you too occupied to acknowledge their attentions."

"Who complained to you? Someone from Oxford?"

"Would you write them if I told you? Are you working on your new book at least?"

"I've been busy. Death doesn't rest." Robert found his eyes seeking the road toward London. Toward Sida. "Get on with your story, please."

"Very well. It's a long tale I must relate." John tightened his heavy fur coat, which he'd swapped the silk for. "I should warn what I'm about to say may distress you. The reason we never were told about Hugh wasn't because he was a poet—success at art will silence any critic—or because our relation wasn't through blood. It was because of whom he married."

Robert willed himself to respond. "He married an orphaned seamstress."

"No. He eloped with an orphaned heiress named Ada Lowell." John's face darkened in a manner that belied his jovial tone. "Ada and Hugh's marriage was unfortunate. Cursed, you might say."

Robert shoved his hands into his pockets, cold. "As some might call mine?"

John flushed nearly as red as his silk scarf. "I had no disdain of Cressida. It was her family I feared would prove an unhappy connection. It brought me no satisfaction to be proven correct."

Robert's impatience twisted toward remorse. How could he explain to his brother that Sida had never really left him?

"Tell your story then."

"Very well. After they eloped, Ada became with child while they were living deep within the Black Forest—God knows how they ended up there. Her doctor wrote Father to help them return to England."

"Father didn't respond."

An ironic half smile. "Father's not here for me to ask, Robert. Anyway, it mattered not: in 1836 Ada died in childbirth, the baby stillborn. Afterward, Hugh disappeared, though not before he wrote *The Lost History of Dreams* and built the glass chapel for Ada. I knew nothing of this until last week when a letter arrived addressed to Father from Hugh's solicitor. It accompanied this."

By now the brothers had arrived at the stile separating their mother's garden from the fields and cottages beyond, where the gravel path gave way to dirt. John used the opportunity to pull an envelope the size of a pamphlet from his coat pocket.

John offered the envelope to Robert.

Robert couldn't resist. Though the envelope was thin, it was heavier than expected and constructed of brown paper. Discoloration lined the top of it, where a flare of sun must have fallen for years. Robert knew with a certainty the envelope had been stored face out in a glass cabinet, where it had remained untouched for years. *It's an envelope with a history. An envelope containing secrets.* He suddenly had the sense of being inside a story where an object can change a life. Or ruin it.

"What's inside?"

John's tone was solemn. "A last letter from Hugh concerning his estate."

Robert stroked the envelope in as furtive a gesture as he could manage. The brown paper felt smoother than expected, like unseen hands had caressed it. An assertive flash of sepia-colored handwriting crowned the front:

To be delivered upon my death to:
Miss Isabelle Lowell
Weald House, Kynnersley on the Weald Moors, Shropshire

"Who's Miss Isabelle Lowell?" The name was familiar, like a thread of a conversation that couldn't be recollected.

"Isabelle Lowell was Ada's niece," John explained. "Hugh bequeathed her the glass chapel and Weald House, which had been Ada's family home."

"Have I met this Isabelle Lowell?"

"No. Nor have I." John spoke as though ticking off items from a list. "Hugh's solicitor wrote that Miss Lowell is a spinster. She was desperately devoted to Ada, who was like a mother to her. Took her death hard. You'll need to approach her carefully—she probably hoped to see her uncle again one day. You're to inform her of her inheritance, give her this envelope from Hugh, and inter his corpse inside the chapel beside Ada. Hugh's solicitor wrote she possesses the only key for it, but has kept it locked all these years out of respect for Hugh's wishes."

"Is that all?"

"Not quite. To prove you've fulfilled his final request, you'll need to persuade Miss Lowell to allow you to daguerreotype his corpse in the chapel." An awkward pause. "She's to pose beside him to prove she's been notified of his death."

"What makes you think she'd be willing to do this?"

"Hopefully Miss Lowell's joy at finding herself a landed gentlewoman will make her amiable to her uncle's demands."

Robert thrust the envelope back. "Shropshire is nearly to Wales."

"I'd hoped you'd do this as a favor to me, if nothing else. Until the terms are fulfilled, Hugh's estate legally remains my responsibility."

"I have an occupation. I'm relied upon." The truth was Robert feared leaving London for so long. What if Sida left for good? "I'll give you the name of another daguerreotypist."

John set his hands on Robert's shoulders. "It's a delicate situation. We need a family member. Someone to intervene quickly—so far no one has learned of Hugh's passing." His voice dropped. "Do you know what happened when Lord Byron died? No one could decide where to bury him because of the scandal of his life—no Poets' Corner, no Westminster Abbey. By the time his burial site was settled, thousands of people thronged his funeral procession, and people queued for four days—four days!—to view his body."

"You're suggesting this might happen with Hugh." Robert's tone was disbelieving.

John's warm gaze sought Robert's. "I don't think you comprehend the situation, brother of mine. Once others become involved, chances are Hugh will end up buried apart from Ada."

Robert tried not to feel affected. But he was. As the brothers walked, he took in his childhood landscape: the fields of wheat latent with decay, the rows of oaks straining toward the blustery grey sky. Rolling stone walls, rough with mortar and moss. He was surprised how eternal it felt. More crows poured forth from the field beyond, their cries echoing in the cold. "It's like they're anticipating Hugh's funeral," John muttered, swatting at one. "I should hunt them just to reduce their damn numbers." It was all as Robert recalled and yet somehow different.

The hounds ran into the woods after a rabbit just as the brothers approached a cottage beyond an allotment. Robert's heart gave a little thump of recognition. The cottage was set beside a slender stream and looked the same as when he'd last visited: the rough-hewn timber and plaster construction, the tangle of blood-red roses creeping along the walls even in winter. His eyes prickled with a peculiar heat as he recalled the fig and apple trees, the rows of beans and melons twined over willow stakes, the mill spilling with water. Now the small vegetable plot and fruit trees marking the front of the house looked abandoned from more than the season.

"This had been Cressida's home?"

John presented the statement as a question, but he knew. Everyone knew.

Robert nodded, his throat tightening. If he closed his eyes, he could still see Sida the first time he'd come upon her at the tailor shop in the village, bent over her sewing. *"She's Eurasian—you can tell by her eyes and skin,"* John had announced; even then he was fascinated with India. *"Half-caste. Don't see many outside of Town."* But there was something beyond Sida's appearance that had drawn Robert back the following day. When he'd returned, a sketch was set on the table beside her, a drawing of a mourning dove. It was the loveliest thing he'd ever seen. *"Who drew this?"* he'd asked. *"Not you,"* she'd teased. Her voice was warm. Welcoming . . .

John's voice turned as soft as the silks he favored. "You must miss her so."

Robert jutted his chin toward the cottage. "Who lives there now?"

John gestured into the air with his hands. "Does it matter?"

Her aunt must have abandoned the cottage after the scandal. Sida had loved its garden with a desperation, perhaps because it was the one place her uncle never ventured. When she wasn't sewing, she'd sketch there, the tip of her tongue caught between her lips in blissful concentration.

With this, Robert's thoughts turned to his fourth-story room in Clerkenwell, where he prayed she awaited. An odd panic fell on him. If he didn't leave in that moment, he'd lose his wife like Orpheus in his Ovid.

Robert made an extravagant show of examining his pocket watch. "I must depart. If you could return to the house . . ."

John stared at his mud-covered boots. "I'll have Durkin take your camera to the coach stand."

"I appreciate this." He couldn't even muster the energy to warn how fragile the equipment was.

"So you'll leave me responsible for Hugh's estate?"

Robert didn't answer.

"Will I ever see you again, brother of mine?"

In lieu of a reply, he offered John his hand. Estrangement was easier than loss.

"This is goodbye, Robert?"

"For now, John."

At last John accepted his hand. The handshake turned into an embrace, one that seemed to encompass all of their collective regrets. He doubted he'd see his brother again. Nor would he return.

Once they broke away, Robert stole a last glance at Sida's garden. He envisioned her waving to him as she was before their marriage, her blue gown fluttering against her limbs in the wind, her sable hair tumbling about her cheeks as she ran from the garden. Beauty amid the cruelty . . .

Goodbye to that too.

Just as he turned toward the road, John called out. "One last thing . . ."

Robert looked back.

"I'm only going to say this once, Robert. Just this one time," John said, his words surprising Robert with their passion. "You of all men should understand—Hugh only wants to be reunited with his wife. To go home to her. Nothing more. Nothing less. Can you really deny him this?"

The Glass Chapel

Excerpted from *The Lost History of Dreams* by Hugh de Bonne, published 1837 by Chapman & Hall, London.

As the Poet waited 'neath domed glass
Whilst the clocks chimed forlorn for noon
His fists stopping those who might trespass
With dreaded words he dared impugn.

'It cannot be,' he wept. 'She whose skin
Was white as snow from winter's blight—
She whose lips were red as roses. Poison
You say? Nay, it cannot be! Such spite
Lives not in this kingdom.' (Alas, 'twas so.)
Then he cried : 'Break the glass, but not to plunder!
Let Eurydice rest protected from her foe
On a bed of diamonds—a chimera of wonder—
A home for her soul.'

And thus the chapel in which they'd wed
Became a house where worms were fed.

*

I.

There was no one there. Six hours on a coal-spewing train from Euston, another three on a coach from Shrewsbury to the coach stand, which turned out not to be the warm, inviting inn Robert had hoped for. Instead, he found himself at the intersection of two spindly country lanes at the base of an isolated incline. A large oak, far wider than any he'd ever seen, marked the crossroad like a sentinel. Beside the oak, fields glistened with frost. Beyond that, nothing.

"Kynnersley on the Weald Moors," the coachman announced, already reaching to unlatch Hugh's coffin cart from the back of the carriage. John had gone to considerable expense to arrange for Hugh's transport, even hiring a private carriage to meet them at the railway terminus in Shrewsbury.

"Are you certain?" Robert asked, his breath pluming in the cold.

"Quite certain."

Robert peered out from the coach. Though it couldn't be more than half past three in the afternoon, the sky was weighed with an ominous gloom. It only contributed to his mood. Already he missed Sida with a yearning tainted by anxiety. She'd been waiting on their bed when he'd returned from his brother's and had sobbed when he'd informed her of his task. *"I'll return to you as quickly as I can,"* he'd promised.

Robert climbed down from the coach, careful not to slip on the frozen ground. Ice shattered like glass beneath his heels. The envelope concerning Hugh's bequest pressed against his ribs; to protect it, Robert had tucked it beneath his waistcoat next to his linen shirt. He'd memorized the address by heart: *Miss Isabelle Lowell, Weald House, Kynnersley on the Weald Moors, Shropshire.* Every time he'd shifted in the coach, the paper grazed his flesh.

The coachman asked once he'd unlatched the coffin, "Is someone to meet you, sir?"

"From Weald House. A Miss Lowell. Do you know her?"

He offered a dismissive pout. "I'm not from these parts."

Robert squinted into the distance. The sky would be completely dark within the hour. A rumble of thunder sounded.

"Is there somewhere I could wait that's less isolated?"

"Naught here in Kynnersley. Closest place with a public house is Wellington. That's five miles from here"—the coachman pointed his whip at a distant point—"if you walk down that path through the moors. I'd take you but I need to return to Shrewsbury before the rain starts. Supposed to be nasty. Might even turn to sleet by morning."

"I'll wait here then." Better this than wandering alone through the moors at night dragging a coffin and his camera.

"I expect you haven't much choice." The coachman held out his hand for a tip just as a faraway slash of lightning cut the sky. "Anyway, I think I see someone coming. Perhaps it's for you."

"You just want to be off," Robert said, bitterness infusing his attempt at humor.

The coachman settled his hat over his brow as he side-eyed Hugh's coffin. "Can you blame me?"

Once the dust from the departing coach settled, Robert stared into the distance. The coachman was right: someone *was* coming. A low rumble shook the ground. A chaise-cart, a two-wheeled carriage such as a governess would drive, approached pulled by a single black horse. Robert could make out the dull gleam of dark cloth across the carriage hood. Brass livery.

The chaise shuddered to a stop before him, the horse neighing in protest. A flash of bright teeth presented from the shadows beneath the hood, accompanied by a whiff of tobacco smoke.

"Mr. Highstead, yes?" a rough voice called.

"Yes?"

"I'm Owen Rhys, the groom. Miss Lowell sent me from Weald House to fetch you and Hugh."

Owen jumped down from the chaise. To Robert's surprise, Owen's deep voice belied his youth—he appeared no older than eighteen. His eyes and hair beneath his broad-brimmed felt hat were dark. Welsh heritage, Robert supposed. He was reminded how close Shropshire was to the border of Wales.

Owen pointed to the coffin. "I assume that's Hugh in there."

"He is," Robert answered; he'd closed the casket himself.

"I'll take care of him." Owen stomped out his cigarette, the smoke lingering, before he fastened the cart holding the coffin to the carriage with a thick chain. He pointed to Robert's traveling case and tripod. "That yours too?"

"I'll take them. They're fragile."

Once they were underway, Robert peered out from beneath the carriage hood, unable to see anything beyond trees and mist as they traveled. The sky was gloomy with storm clouds. Hopefully it would clear by morning so he could daguerreotype the chapel and be on his way.

Robert asked, "How far are we from the chapel Mr. de Bonne built?"

Owen's mouth quirked. "You mean Ada's Folly?"

"Is that what it's called?"

"Mainly. We'll pass it soon."

A moment later, the groomsman brought the chaise to a halt. "If you want to take a gander at Ada's Folly, it's over there, behind the grove of oaks. But hurry—think I heard thunder."

Robert climbed down from his perch, his boots sliding on icy leaves. He squinted into the dusk. He saw naught but a winter forest shorn of leaves. Tree limbs entwined like arms forbidding entrance. Below, a carpet of mist. And then at last, he saw Ada's Folly, or the roof of it anyway: an arc of clear glass floating behind tree branches. It resembled a bell jar, if a bell jar could be large enough to cover part of a forest.

It was a wonder. A miracle.

His pulse speeding, Robert stepped toward the glass dome, nearly tripping on the tangle of tree roots crossing the forest floor. Ada's Folly was much smaller than he'd expected, not much larger than a cottage; John's description had made it sound far grander of scale. The chapel was octagonal of shape. Below the dome, milky glass covered the exterior of the stained glass, hiding the chapel's secrets to outsiders. Ivy crept up its walls, as if nature were in the process of reclaiming the chapel for its own. This was a place that had been abandoned. Forgotten. As though it were too exquisite for the world to bear.

Robert found he couldn't speak. Couldn't look away. Owen lit another cigarette, flicking ashes into the leaves beyond.

"I remember when Ada's Folly was built. I was a small child. My father said he never imagined such places existed."

"Your father saw inside it?"

"No. Only heard talk."

"He met Hugh then?"

"Not that either, Mr. Highstead. My mother did see Miss Ada once at church."

Robert's curiosity rose. "What was she like?"

"Beautiful. Light, but not of looks. Just the way she had about her. Mum said she mainly remembered her voice. It reminded her of bells."

Suddenly Robert sensed Ada's presence from across the years, as though she'd arrived to welcome her husband home. He imagined her silvery voice. Her radiance. Spurred by this visceral emotion, Robert wished he could break open the chapel door to daguerreotype Hugh beside Ada's grave. To see what no one living had ever seen. But this would not have been honorable. Nor would it fulfill the whole of Hugh's last request; he wondered how Miss Lowell would respond to posing beside a corpse.

Owen pointed at the rapidly darkening sky. "Storm's about to start."

A second later a splatter of water beat against the coffin; a tawny owl let out a hoot; a flash of lightning struck. And then the rain began in earnest.

Yet Robert couldn't look away from Ada's Folly. This time it wasn't temptation that rooted his feet. It was a sense of futility. Even if he obtained Isabelle's consent, how would he ever capture this glass chapel, this folly, this *thing*, in a daguerreotype? Beyond the technical considerations of light and shadow, it was so much more than he'd expected.

It wasn't a chapel bearing a corpse he'd traveled all this way to daguerreotype. It was a history: love, loss, and everything in between.

Robert's first exposure to Weald House wasn't of a house. It was of a dog.

Just as the chaise carriage rumbled past the gate to the estate, a large black retriever leapt toward their cart, barking madly in the rain.

"Down, Virgil!" Owen yelled. "Dammit, boy." He said to Robert over his shoulder, "Excuse me, but the dog don't listen. He's so old it's a miracle he's still around."

Once they reached the dry stable, and the coffin was settled in an empty stall ("We can move it later into the parlor," Owen explained), the dog hewed close to their side, his long pink tongue lolling from his mouth.

"He was Hugh's dog?" Robert asked, taking a step back when Virgil shook water on his legs, just like his brother's dogs. At least this one didn't try to lick his hands.

Owen reached for a lantern hanging on the stable wall. "No, he belongs to the house. Dunno where he came from. I don't even know how he got his name." He pointed beyond the stable, where the rain still spilled. "House is just over there, through the garden. Watch the beehive—'tis hard to see in the dark. Hurry!"

Water plastered Robert's hair to his face, his overcoat against his back, as Owen led them to a thick-planked door. The servants' entrance—Robert had seen many of these during his time working as a daguerreotypist.

As soon as Owen swung the door open, Robert was blasted with heat and light. Once his sight adjusted, he understood he was inside the kitchen. The room was dominated by a long table set before the fireplace, around which a pair of servants sat. They paused eating what appeared to be an undistinguished beef stew, their faces raised expectedly toward Robert. There was a thick-waisted older woman, her grey hair hidden behind a yellowed linen widow's cap. The cook, Robert decided. Next to her, a girl of perhaps sixteen dressed in a grey dimity frock, her eyes widening with challenge beneath her gold hair. She was pretty, and knew it. Surely she was the housemaid. She twirled a curl about her finger. "You're late for tea, boy." Owen flushed crimson before replying, "Did you miss me, Grace?"

"Ah no, but Virgil did," she teased. "Give him a kiss."

The three servants erupted in warm laughter—a laughter that distinctly excluded Robert.

"Hugh's cousin is here," Owen announced. "Mr. Highstead."

Robert took his hat off. Rainwater fell from the brim, pooling about his feet. "So sorry. I'll clean that."

"No need, sir. I'll get it." The older woman rose from the table unsteadily. She wiped her mouth against a corner of her gravy-stained apron, revealing uneven teeth. "Mr. Highstead, how rude we are! Come, sit! I'm Mrs. Chilvers, the housekeeper—well, I also cook since we're short of help. It's true then? You're his cousin?"

"Yes. Through my father by marriage," Robert supplied, sweating from the heat of the kitchen. "Please, no need to curtsey, madam."

"Some food? You must be famished after your journey."

Before Robert could answer, the golden-haired girl—he recalled her name was Grace—called out, "You're really here with Hugh?"

How familiar they were, calling his cousin by his Christian name like they'd known him intimately, instead of as their employer.

"I fear it is true—Hugh de Bonne has passed and I have arrived bearing his mortal remains," Robert answered in his most professional tones. "I regret bringing these sorrowful tidings."

Owen said, "That's what Miss Isabelle said your brother wrote. She was so upset she locked herself in her room for a full day."

"Are you to take possession of Weald House then?" Mrs. Chilvers asked, wary.

"No, no. Miss Lowell was chosen as Mr. de Bonne's heir," Robert reassured. "I'm only cousin to Mr. de Bonne through marriage—I never had the privilege of meeting him in this life. That said, I pray I can fulfill his last wishes as he desired."

"Aren't you fancy?" Grace rejoined.

A collective giggle ran around the table. Robert's cheeks prickled with warmth. This was no lecture hall in Oxford with scholars, or parlor in Belgravia crowded with the bereaved. Even so, he could tell this was a house in mourning as surely as if he'd come across a crape bow on the door. He'd seen enough during his employment to recognize the signs: the disarray, the hushed tones, the excited yet lackadaisical servants, as though the house were trapped beneath a stilled clock.

"Come now, Mr. Highstead," Mrs. Chilvers said. "No need to share words intended for another's ear. I'll take you to Miss Isabelle." She gathered a candle from the mantel. "I suppose there's no point putting off bad news."

Like Mary at his brother's house only a day earlier, Mrs. Chilvers moved with a surprising haste despite her bulk. Propelled forward by the anemic glow of her candle, Virgil the dog followed them, his claws clipping on the dulled wood floor.

"So strange to think of Mr. Hugh's coffin down in the stable," she said. "I must admit I was staggered when I heard you'd be bringing him here from London. 'Tis a far way to travel."

"Not as far as Mr. de Bonne has come," Robert said. As they passed through a labyrinth of darkened corridors, he inhaled the scent of mold, took in shadowy corners cloaked in neglect. One long wall caved with moisture, its plaster crumbling beneath the weight of gravity. Perhaps Weald House would be shown to better advantage under daylight.

"Mr. de Bonne passed in Geneva," he added.

"So your brother wrote. A heart attack in his bath, no less. Bathing can be so dangerous." She pointed down a passageway lined with crimson velvet curtains. "This way, sir."

As they walked, Robert made out that the estate was oriented around what had probably been a one-room farmhouse; this room had metamorphosed into the kitchen, presumably to take advantage of the overlarge fireplace. The rest of the house sprawled out from the kitchen: a reception room, drawing room, a pantry, all reflecting a time when Weald House was inhabited by more than three servants and their reclusive employer. Now these rooms lay abandoned like limbs whose muscles had atrophied from lack of use.

"Sorry it's so dark," Mrs. Chilvers said. "Candles are quite dear these days. I must admit I was surprised to hear of your existence, Mr. Highstead. I hadn't known Mr. Hugh"—Mrs. Chilvers addressed him by a title, unlike the others—"had any relations. He never spoke of any while he was here. Well, beyond Miss Isabelle, of course. Though she was only through Ada. Hence, I'd assumed—"

"I was his heir?"

Mrs. Chilvers nodded. "You'll be staying three nights at least?"

"I'd hoped only one." From a corner of his eye, Robert spied a long-eared wood mouse caught in a trap.

"There's room enough to stay as long as you'd like, though most of the house is unused these days. We only use the west wing, so you'll be there. Third floor. I'll have Owen lay a fire for you. The east wing has been closed up since Miss Ada's marriage. Not even a stick of furniture in them—well, now I'm gossiping . . ." Her words trailed off in ominous omission as they approached a wide stairwell curving up into more darkness. "Miss Isabelle dines in the library. She's there now."

"Do others reside here?" Perhaps Isabelle had a companion to keep her company in this isolated place.

The housekeeper shook her head, stifling a yawn. "Miss Isabelle is a solitary sort. She mainly dwells upstairs, away from Mr. Hugh's study."

"And where would his study be?"

"There." Mrs. Chilvers pointed with her candle down toward a corridor below the stairwell; the walls appeared in better repair. "Just beyond the front entry. It's the door with the brass plate. Well, we *had* to do something. The pilgrims come."

"Pilgrims?"

Mrs. Chilvers nodded solemnly. "They call themselves 'Seekers of the Lost Dream.' *The Lost History of Dreams* and all that. Once Mr. Hugh disappeared, they flocked here for some sign of him. 'Twas Miss Isabelle's idea to let them tour his study so they wouldn't disturb Ada's Folly. But the pilgrims still ask about it anyway."

"Because Mrs. de Bonne is interred here?"

"That and because of Mr. Hugh's poetry. Still, the tours help."

"So you have random people—Seekers of the Lost Dream, if you will—just show at Weald House?"

"Yes. I know it sounds mad, but the pilgrims are easy enough to identify. One even dyes her hair red in honor of Mr. Hugh—far darker color than yours, Mr. Highstead, though yours looked a bit ginger in the light. Most wear cockades of raven feathers surrounding a rose."

"Why on earth would they do that?"

"From a poem he wrote, 'The Rose and the Raven.' Supposed to be about Miss Ada and their baby." Mrs. Chilvers halted on the landing, her mouth grim. "I don't want to think what they'll do once they learn he's dead. They'll probably wail and rend their clothing."

They turned down another corridor, where piano music drifted toward them. A Beethoven sonata. Whoever was playing was quite accomplished.

Robert asked, "Is that Miss Lowell?"

Mrs. Chilvers nodded. "She practices every night. Must have finished her tea."

Whether it was the music or that she'd run out of words, the housekeeper finally fell into silence. Robert was grateful. The unexpected emergence of beauty infused him with courage. The truth was the closer Robert grew to meeting Hugh's niece, the more his apprehension rose, though he was uncertain why. If Isabelle refused his request to daguerreotype Ada's Folly, he'd just return home to his wife. Hugh, however, would have to be interred far from Ada. John would have to understand, despite the inconvenience of managing the property.

At last Mrs. Chilvers halted at a closed door. It looked no different from any other they'd passed: dark wood with chipped varnish.

"Here we are. The library." Her voice dropped. "Be gentle. Miss Isabelle is sure to take whatever you have to say hard. Understand?"

And then she knocked on the door.

II.

The piano music came to a halt, leaving an unresolved chord dangling. "Come in," a weary-sounding female voice responded from inside the library. "You can take my plate."

"I'm not alone, Miss Isabelle," Mrs. Chilvers explained, her cheek pressed against the door. "It's Mr. Hugh's cousin, a Mr. Highstead. He's just arrived."

"Oh. So soon."

A long pause. A clash on the keyboard. The chord restarted and grew into an impassioned arpeggio.

Robert girded himself, his courage from the music forgotten. This was really no different than his job, he told himself. When he daguerreotyped those corpses, it had been easy to dispense with the homilies and kindnesses. But he'd never been related to the grieving parties. Until now.

Mrs. Chilvers raised her voice over the music. "Do you want Mr. Highstead to return?"

"No, no . . ." The piano silenced. "It's just that I'm . . . I'm not really dressed for visitors, mind."

"Miss Lowell, we can speak at your convenience," Robert interjected, hoping his reassurance would win him favor.

Mrs. Chilvers whispered, "She's usually not one for vanity." She opened the door, gave him a little shove. "Go."

Once the housekeeper shut the door behind him, Robert was confronted with the unctuous odor of mutton. Because the room was nearly as dark as the hall, it took him a moment to identify where the smell originated: slices of the meat were arrayed on a porcelain plate beside a loaf of bread. Both mutton and bread were untouched. His stomach growled, reminding him he hadn't eaten since Shrewsbury.

"If you'd like some port," that same female voice said from the shadows, "it's on the table, Mr. Highstead. Just beyond the food Mrs. Chilvers forgot to take."

His eyes strained in the dim gloom. Where was she?

"That's very kind of you, Miss Lowell."

Robert turned his attention to the rest of the library. Isabelle would be seated at the piano, if only he could find it. How could anyone read music with such little light? She must have played the Beethoven from memory.

The library was a long, narrow room with tall windows lining one side; if it contained books, they were hidden in shadows. Though the drapes were open—a hint of cold drifted from the bared glass—night had curtailed the sky into blackness. On the farthest wall, a coal fire faintly glowed amber beneath a coat of grey ash. A large mirror glimmered above it.

"Where are you?" he asked at last.

"Behind you, Mr. Highstead. By the door."

Robert turned. The piano, a spinet, was set tight against the wall. A wraithlike figure was silhouetted before it. Hugh's niece.

She pointed from the piano toward a glass decanter set beside her uneaten meal. For the first time, Robert viewed something tangible of Isabelle: a bony wrist, bleached of color, jutted below her lace cuff like a talon emerging from feathers.

"Port?" she offered again.

"That would be welcomed," Robert conceded. However, it wasn't port he wanted, though he'd never admit his hunger. It would be too crass.

He poured himself a glass and took a cautious sip. The port tasted brash with acid.

"Sit there, Mr. Highstead. By the fire. Where I can see you."

Her hand pointed to a red leather chair adjacent to the fireplace; he hadn't noticed it earlier.

"Thank you, Miss Lowell."

From his seat beside the fire, his view of Isabelle Lowell was no better. She remained shrouded in darkness, which made his task seem all the more terrible, like inflicting a wound on a rabbit trapped in a bush—though he couldn't see the animal, the blow would be lethal. He'd need to be careful. Gentle, as Mrs. Chilvers had implored. He took another slug of port for courage.

Robert adopted his most compassionate tone. "It saddens me to meet you under these circumstances. I have arrived with unfortunate tidings."

"So your brother wrote," she rejoined. "My uncle Hugh. Dead. Tell me, is this true?"

"I fear so."

He paused to let his words settle. He heard a sharp catch in her throat. Even unable to view her face, he knew what Isabelle was experiencing: shock. She'd probably denied the veracity of the letter until his arrival bearing Hugh's remains. He also knew that, in a moment, she'd begin to cry. He'd seen this before too many times and in too many ways since he'd become a daguerreotypist.

"Miss Lowell," he said, adopting a tone as mild as milk. If he calmed her before she grew too far gone, he might circumvent a complete collapse. Then he'd be able to press for Hugh's last request without delay—with luck, he'd be on his way home before noon tomorrow. "Or may I call you Miss Isabelle, since we're family through Hugh?"

"Miss Lowell will do," was her short response.

Her breathing became heavy. Irregular. She was going to weep. He knew it.

"I'm so sorry," he said. "I wish there was some way I could help—"

"Hugh can't be dead! He can't be!" And then she wailed, just as Robert feared. Her wailing went beyond anything he'd heard before. It was a desperate, primal sound, emerging from deep within her, like something a woman would make in the depths of childbirth, or an animal under threat.

Without thinking Robert extended his arms in sympathy. It was a gesture he'd offered many times to the grieving, a quick pat on the back to acknowledge their loss. How strange, though: unable to view her face, he felt as though he were offering comfort to a shadow.

Before he could reach Isabelle, she rose from the piano bench and began to pace. Her profile was silhouetted by the glow of the dying coals.

"Oh God," she sobbed. "What's to become of me? What shall I do?"

She wrung her hands, occasionally parting them to pull at her fingers. Even in the low light, the tendons and veins of her hands looked especially prominent. Musician's hands. If he were to leave Weald House at that moment, he'd have no knowledge of Isabelle's appearance beyond those twisting, bony hands.

"I understand this is a shock. I hope it will be consolation that your uncle cared to make you his heir," he said gently. "I'm so sorry."

"Sorry?" she snapped, heaving for air. "Is that all you can say?"

Isabelle turned toward him—and at last her face was illuminated. Though he knew it was rude, Robert couldn't stop gaping.

Isabelle Lowell was not what he'd expected her to be. He'd assumed she was close to his age, but her hair was white and thick and pulled tightly behind her ears, akin to how he imagined the enchantress Circe would appear from his Ovid. Yet Isabelle wasn't elderly. Her unlined face bore a moonlike countenance, which contrasted against her sharp thin form. Her cheeks were high with color. She was terrifying, but not because her features were disharmonious. Far from it. Her eyes were large and of a color some would call grey, her mouth sensitive within that broad pool of a face. It was because her face was taut with hopelessness, as though life possessed no sweetness and never would. That nothing mattered.

Robert turned his attention to Isabelle's clothing, as if this would tame his intimidation. Her purple gown was of a style popular over a decade earlier, featuring shirred sleeves alternating with puffed crests. She was still in half-mourning years after Ada's death. And now Hugh was gone. Even if Isabelle hadn't seen her uncle in years, he'd stolen her last hope from her.

"I'm so sorry," he repeated. "If there's any way I can be of assistance . . ."

For some reason, his words unleashed something in Isabelle. "Assistance?" A bitter laugh. "You're only saying that because you want something from me, now that Hugh is gone."

"I don't want anything from you," he lied.

"But you do! You do!"

She erupted in a new fluster of tears. How fragile she appeared, how distraught! Robert felt like the coldest, most venal person to walk the earth. Here she was, suffering with sorrow and loss—and she was right. Even now, he was thinking of Hugh's daguerreotype in the chapel, his brother, and his return home to Sida.

"Please, Miss Lowell," he said in his mildest tone. "I understand Mr. de Bonne's death is a shock. That you cared for him."

"Oh fie on you! You're like all those who come to this house all these years, waiting and hoping for my uncle's return, and caring naught for my aunt, like those pilgrims. Hugh never even really lived here—this was Ada's home. It bears Ada's history. Not Hugh's! Not that anyone seems to care . . ."

As Robert listened to her tirade, he couldn't decide how to respond. Hugh never even really lived here? Mrs. Chilvers hadn't mentioned this when she spoke of him. Nor did Isabelle seem that distressed by her uncle's death. None of this made sense. Robert drank the rest of the port in a gulp. It didn't help that the alcohol was snaking through his veins, heightening his confusion. His fists clenched at his side. He yearned to shake her, to startle her into silence so he could think in peace.

He interrupted, "I was under the impression Mr. de Bonne considered Weald House his home."

She waved his explanation away like a gnat. "Hugh spent a total of two weeks here before the chapel was finished. Two weeks!" She drew a breath, her eyes wet and swollen. "And now you arrive bearing his corpse like a king returning from exile. I'll never have any peace!"

Robert raised his hand. "It's late, madam. I didn't come here only to speak of Mr. de Bonne's death. I have other news."

Somehow these words distracted Isabelle. He sensed her anger slow into a curiosity tangible as honey dripping from a knife.

Encouraged, he continued.

"I have a bequest for you."

She blinked. "What did you say?"

"A special bequest. For you."

From his waistcoat he drew out the envelope John had given him. Isabelle's eyes widened like a child at a birthday party.

"For me? From Hugh?" Again she looked as though she'd weep.

He nodded. "All the way from London in the middle of winter. My brother said it was very important." He lowered his voice to calm her; he'd learned this while soothing the bereaved. "Would you like to know what's in it?"

Isabelle drew the envelope from his hands. When she finally spoke, her voice was tremulous.

"You already know what's in here."

"I do." Robert met her gaze. "It concerns your inheritance of Weald House and the glass chapel in the woods."

"Ada's Folly." Isabelle's tone was hollow.

"Ah yes. Ada's Folly. I've heard it's called that."

Isabelle sank into a chair before the fire, grasping the brown paper envelope tight against her bosom like a baby. Her purple gown puddled about her legs, as though she'd lost control of her limbs.

After a deep breath, she broke the envelope's seal.

"It's Hugh's handwriting all right," she said, pulling the pages close to her face. "I'd recognize it anywhere. Plus he used only brown ink. An affectation of his. Among others." Her hands shook as she turned the papers over as she read. Once she finished, she set them back inside the envelope on her lap and stared into the fire.

After some moments, Isabella muttered, "There's a poem. His last one."

"That must make his bequest all the more precious."

Do it now. Tell her about Hugh's last request. Robert began to sweat, but not because of the port.

"I'll leave you to your reading, Miss Lowell. I hope you find comfort in it."

Gratitude softened her lips. "Thank you, Mr. Highstead. I . . . I misjudged you. I've been unkind."

"This is a difficult time. I'm pleased to be of service."

The vein on Robert's neck began to throb. *Ask her now.*

He cleared his throat. "Before I retire, there's one last thing . . ."

Isabelle looked up, her face blotchy. "What would that be?"

"It's an unusual request." His voice sounded weak. Wheedling. "It regards Ada's Folly. The chapel I understand you possess the only key for."

"Yes?"

He forced himself to meet her gaze. "His request is very simple. Mr. de Bonne would like his earthly remains interred in the chapel beside your aunt. It's part of the terms of his bequest to you." He couldn't find the nerve to explain about the daguerreotype.

Isabelle snorted. Still, her aspect remained benign. "That's not possible. It's to remain locked."

"If I understand correctly, the chapel has remained locked all these years only out of respect for your uncle's wishes." He pointed toward the envelope in her lap. "But now this has changed . . ."

To Robert's surprise, any sympathy he'd gained fled Isabelle's face. "That's why you're here! You nearly tricked me with your kindness. You *did* want something, just like the pilgrims—"

"Not for me. For Hugh."

"I thought you came here to bury him in the churchyard. Not to disturb my aunt's resting place."

"He built the chapel—it's his right. He also requested a daguerreotype of his corpse before the interment as proof—"

"But he's been dead for over two weeks!"

"I can assure you your uncle's remains have been embalmed." He didn't dare confess Hugh required her presence in the daguerreotype. "If it makes any difference, I'm employed as such, and can assure the utmost discretion and professionalism."

She shook her head. "A daguerreotypist! Your brother wrote you were a scholar. Your story grows more and more sordid. What sort of gentleman are you?"

Robert's voice rose. "I *am* a gentleman. Everyone deserves proof of memory—daguerreotypes offer this. And I was a scholar. A writer—"

"A poet like Hugh? Lord help me!"

"No, a writer of history. I'd published a book, one about Ovid. I was writing my second at Oxford until my marriage three years ago."

She wagged her finger. "*Now* I understand. You were disinherited because your family didn't approve of your wife. You had to take employment that paid in pounds, not prestige. You want to make amends to your family."

He lied. "Surely you can understand my situation."

"Then you traveled here with false hope. Hope, Mr. Highstead, is the most unsatisfying of meals. It grants the appearance of substance but melts like ice in the mouth. It would have been wiser of you to choose another path than to come here on such a fool's errand."

"I did not intend to offend," Robert said, thinking desperately. He pulled at his collar, which had grown too tight. "As executor of your uncle's will, my brother is required to give you Mr. de Bonne's bequest. Until it is fulfilled, the estate remains my brother's responsibility. He had hoped you could indulge a dead man's last wish. If not for the sake of family, then for your own welfare."

"Mr. de Bonne was my most beloved aunt's husband. An uncle by marriage, not blood. That scarcely makes you family, sir. As for his last request, I doubt the courts would care much."

Robert bowed. "Perhaps we can revisit this tomorrow, Miss Lowell."

"No need, Mr. Highstead. You'll leave in the morning with my uncle's corpse. You'll have to bury him elsewhere." She nodded in dismissal. "We shall not meet again."

She threw the envelope containing Hugh's last poem into the fire. Despite the low coals, it burst into flames.

"There," she pronounced with satisfaction. "The matter is done."

III.

Robert couldn't sleep that night. It wasn't the thought of Hugh's corpse downstairs in the stable, or that he was away from his wife. Nor was it that he was in a foreign bed, or that he'd be leaving this same bed in a few hours to travel in the cold with a coffin. Neither was it his hunger, or that he still felt unsteady from the port. It was because he couldn't still his mind from turning over all that happened since his encounter with Isabelle Lowell.

After Isabelle dismissed him, he scarcely noticed Mrs. Chilvers's ceaseless chatter as she showed him to the guest chamber. He'd expected he'd feel relief to be leaving Weald House so soon. Wasn't this what he'd wanted? To return posthaste to his ghost wife? As for his brother, he'd find a way to work around the terms of Hugh's bequest in spite of Isabelle; he was clever like that. Instead, John's last words in their mother's garden reverberated even after Mrs. Chilvers had bid good night. *"You of all men should understand—Hugh only wants to be reunited with his wife. To go home to her."*

"Nothing to be done," Robert murmured to the walls in the bedchamber. "John will have to understand."

The room was little better than the rest of Weald House. Though the linens seemed clean on the narrow hard bed, the walls were scored with peeling plaster dusted with mold. He supposed only so much could be done with so few servants. Still, an attempt had been made to welcome him.

The pitcher was filled with fresh water for washing, the towel scented with dried lavender. Someone had placed on the nightstand a stack of books, a candle, and a hand mirror.

Robert shut the door to his room and opened his daguerreotype traveling case to make sure nothing had spilled during his journeys: the bottles of mercury and silver salts, the sodium thiosulfate, the spirit lamp for the fuming box. Reassured all was as it should be, he loosened his collar from his neck. A new growth of beard scraped against his fingers; he hadn't shaved that morning in his ambivalence to leave London. Though he'd brought his shaving-tackle with him, he couldn't be bothered.

His collar at last detached from his shirt, Robert folded his jacket and overcoat over the rail of the chair. Finally, he removed from his waistcoat pocket a miniature watercolor portrait of his wife's eye set inside a brass watch fob. It was the only image he possessed of her.

Once upon a time, Robert would spend long summer afternoons bent over his desk—his first book had just been published to acclaim and he'd been eager to finish his second before returning to Oxford that fall. One morning, a note fell out from his journal. *Meet me on the heath at noon,* Sida had written. *Your book will wait. This day won't.* Unable to resist, he found her waiting for him just beyond the stile, her sketchbook in hand. "*I've an hour before I'll be missed,*" she'd explained. Soon they were meeting there regularly to conduct their courtship in secret.

The afternoon of the watercolor miniature, Robert had begged her to draw herself standing beneath their favorite willow tree—"*I could bring a mirror,*" he'd said—but she'd refused. "*What if someone discovered the drawing? Then we'd never be able to meet. I've a better idea. I'll paint my eye, and only that—no one will recognize it as mine. After all, the eyes are the window to the soul.*" He'd been moved by her offering; eye miniatures were a tradition dating from the previous century, created as private tokens of devotion. She'd painted herself with a surprising accuracy: the coal-dark iris flecked by gold, the slender arch of her brow. When she'd finished, she'd reached for his hand and smoothed his fingers open—his skin then had been unmarked, protected by kid gloves and privilege. She pressed the watercolor into his hand and their lips met hungrily. They'd sunk together onto the soft moss, whispering secrets they'd never confided to anyone.

Once Robert set Sida's eye miniature beside his pillow, he washed his face, relieved himself in the chamber pot, and undressed. He arranged himself beneath the covers. Blew out the candle. And this was when his thoughts especially began to circle like flies on a carcass.

Try as he might, he couldn't stop remembering the anger—no, *hatred*—Isabelle had shown when she'd confronted him over his intentions for Hugh's corpse. Yet he couldn't blame her. He *had* arrived wanting something. If the sin was in the desire rather than the act, he was everything she'd accused. He had wanted something from her, just like the pilgrims.

As the hours passed, Robert stared into the dark. He considered holding the miniature of Sida. Finally, he gave up. He lit a candle and reached for the stack of books left on the nightstand. He ignored the King James on top and opened the thickest volume. It bore Hugh's name on the spine. He felt that thrill of anticipation that occurs when encountering a new book. Books were easy, unlike people. Writing them, however, was another matter.

The title page read rather loftily:

The Collected Letters and Ephemera
of Hugh de Bonne

Edited and Translated by George Douglas

Published 1847 by Chapman & Hall
London

The pages were numerous. The text was small. The book would have been difficult to read even if he wasn't in a candlelit room. Robert couldn't turn away.

A tingle rode up his fingertips as he turned to the frontispiece, where at last Hugh was revealed to his eyes while he lived. The engraving of his cousin presented what Robert had already noted in his corpse: thick hair, a sensitive cast to the brow, which bore a thin scar along his left temple Robert hadn't noticed before. A light-colored coat with a thick fur collar, probably of beaver, was set across his broad shoulders. Atypical for the era, Hugh wore a full beard; his corpse had been clean-shaven. There was a sensuality to his lips, a fullness, that suggested an appetite for sensation as strong as Robert's yearning for emotional control. He gave an involuntary shudder. How strange that an engraving of a man in the full of life should disquiet him more than his dead body. Regardless, Robert found himself paging through the book, insomnia forgotten.

Hugh's editor had chosen the route of inclusion rather than exclusion: there were nearly two thousand numbered documents spread out over seven hundred pages. Some were notes no more than a sentence long. Others were missives that continued for several pages. The book was organized in chronological order. They began with Hugh's first attempts at poetry as a boy of eight (*Il était une fois un garçon de Marseille . . .*). His juvenilia included notes to his nurse regarding his tea, letters to French authorities regarding lost relatives, and translations from Latin. The last year covered was 1837—the year before Hugh disappeared after finishing the glass chapel and publishing *The Lost History of Dreams*. Before this came letters to tailors requesting updates on Parisian fashion, notes to publishers about typefaces, and even laundry lists (*starch only, please: five Waistcoats, one embroidered, two brocade, two broadcloth; three Cravats, finest silk . . .*).

As Robert read, he had the sense of viewing a man's life reduced to words. Black ink on white paper. Sentence after sentence. The grey minutia of daily routine flashed with occasional color: a review of a poem cycle, a receipt for stained glass, a list of fairy tales for inspiration. These items of interest would inevitably be followed by yet another bill or list.

The hum of tedium was deafening until Robert arrived at the year 1834. *To Miss Ada of the Doves*, Hugh's note had begun:

> *I pray your indulgence for this letter. I am hoping you could relay the following message to your guardian regarding your cote in the rose garden. (I trust the cote was built as recommended, and that the dove still abides.)*

This marked the first of a dozen courtship letters from Hugh to Ada. To Robert's disappointment, they were surprisingly lean of sentiment—he wasn't sure what he'd expected, but it wasn't this. The phrase *locus amoenus*—Latin for "pleasant place"—was repeated within them, employed by Hugh to describe his devotion to Ada. Robert recalled Ovid had written ironically of the *locus amoenus* in the *Metamorphoses*, presenting it as a deceptively beautiful setting that drew the victim toward destruction: Orpheus to the Furies, Narcissus to the reflecting pool. Was the glass chapel such a place? At first glance, it had appeared enchanted to Robert. Not cursed.

There was little else revealed in Hugh's letters to Ada beyond this poetic intimacy: no flowery renditions of love's euphoria or remembrances of the first blissful brush of a hand. Little wonder the pilgrims had no notion of Ada's life: it was all about Hugh. Yet as Robert read the letters, he had the sense Hugh had written them with the expectation that someone would read them one day, like throwing a bone to a dog to distract him from the roast. Robert had seen this before in his research at Oxford. The historian's challenge was to find the story in what was absent. Insomnia or no, his mind was too fatigued for that.

Robert was about to throw the book aside to attempt sleep again when he arrived at a letter dated the year before Ada's death.

He read the letter slowly at first, like treading ice; then quickly, like inhaling water after a parched night.

Letter 1579
Dr Friedrich Engelsohn to unknown recipient

20 December 1835

My dearest sister—

As promised, I have been writing you daily since leaving home, as if we are continuing our usual conversations with each other. Though I have yet to receive a letter from you, I tell myself yours have not found their way to me because winter has fallen here in the Black Forest. Some say that nothing will arrive until the snow ends, that we should think of ourselves as crocuses suspended beneath ice, waiting for our lives to recommence with spring.

Tonight, though, I am writing for a reason besides our daily communion. I am writing because I need your help. The disturbance of my mind is such that I cannot sleep despite it being after midnight.

I will write exactly what occurred, as though you were there beside me, so you may comprehend my distress.

This evening, just as I was finishing my hours at the surgery, and just as another snow storm had started its inevitable assault, a gentleman arrived. The gentleman was tall, almost to the point of intimidation. He was forty years of age at most—his russet hair was sprinkled with grey. His face was one I liked instantly: he had a strong nose that spoke of integrity; his eyes were lively and bright, connoting intelligence. Fine lines about his mouth suggested he possessed a sanguine temperament. His hands were long and sensitive. Snow covered his thin wool greatcoat, which looked of high quality. His German was hesitant and laced with the cultured accent of another land. He had a refinement about him that drew me, friendless as I have been here these past months.

That afternoon, though, the gentleman appeared weighed by worries—his face was blanched of color, his brow furrowed. What had brought him to this God-forsaken place, which so many yearn to leave?

"You must return tomorrow. The doctor has finished for the day," I heard my housekeeper tell the gentleman.

"I won't leave," he replied, clutching his walking stick. "My wife is dying."

At this, I opened my door and presented myself to the gentleman. How could I not after such a desperate statement?

We immediately departed. Outside the surgery, the snow was heavier than I expected. If this wasn't determent enough, the sky was darkening with alarming rapidity. For the sake of expedience, I insisted we take my carriage, which has runners for the snow. Within a half hour his cottage emerged from a grove of oak trees. By then, the snow was so thick I could take little note of the forlorn abode beyond its construction of timber and plaster.

And it is here I must relate the strangest part of my tale, my sister. Once we'd stomped the snow off our boots at the threshold, the gentleman said, "Forgive me for not introducing myself, Herr Doktor—you have been so kind to come so far on a snowy night with a stranger." He inclined his head. "My name is Hugh de Bonne."

"The poet?"

When he nodded, I considered if I was imagining things. Never in my life had I expected to meet Hugh de Bonne, especially under such circumstances! Surely you recall my admiration of his poetry, and how I'd written him last year after reading his Cantos for Grown Children. *His publisher answered he'd departed England after his marriage—and here this same Hugh de Bonne stood before me, his beloved wife near death. I'd imagined him living in Paris in a gilded hotel, or enjoying the patronage of royalty in a palace. Not residing in a hut few would choose save out of desperation.*

However, there was no opportunity to speak of this, or to wonder at its peculiarity. Herr de Bonne rushed me to his wife, exclaiming gratitude all the while.

It took a moment for my eyes to adjust to the gloom inside the cottage, for the sole illumination came from their fireplace ("to allow my wife's eyes to rest," he explained). I made out the slight curves of a petite woman lying on a pallet beside the fire. She appeared some years younger than Herr de Bonne. I could tell she had been exceptionally beautiful before illness had overtaken. The texture of her alabaster skin was as fine as that of a fairy-tale princess. Her dark hair glistened over her shoulders, though tangled with fever. She was so emaciated as to appear ghost-like.

"Ada," Herr de Bonne tenderly addressed her. "I've brought a doctor. Beloved, can you wake?"

Frau de Bonne moaned softly as I approached. "Who are you?"

"I am one who is here to help." I addressed her husband: "How long has she been in this state?"

"Six weeks, though her illness progressed gradually. She's already delicate of health—the cold weather does not agree with her—but she's grown much worse. She frequently vomits. She cannot eat. She barely sips tea. She cannot stand for dizziness. I fear . . ."

And here the great poet was overtaken by sobs. Such was the state of his wife that she only sighed. It was then I noticed the subtle distention of her abdomen. My first thought was one so obvious I feared embarrassing the poet.

My examination of Frau de Bonne proceeded without incident. Herr de Bonne informed me his wife was twenty-two—just a year younger than myself. During my examination, Frau de Bonne turned to retch into a bucket. "I cannot seem to stop." Her teeth were discolored from stomach acid, proof she'd been sick as her husband claimed.

After much apologizing, I asked her to open her wrapper, which was sewn of the finest silk I'd ever seen. She blushed from modesty, but acquiesced. Her breathing was labored, her sputum thick, which was likely due to lack of fluids. Her ribs fanned beneath her flesh. Her womb was enlarged. When I palpated it, a subtle fluttering answered.

It took me little time to realize what was ailing Frau de Bonne, which was as suspected. To quantify my findings, I asked: "When was your last cycle?"

"I can't remember. Two, three years. I rarely experience them . . ." Again, she blushed. "My poor husband! What shall he do?"

I asked her to dress, more disturbed than I'd ever been by a patient's condition. How strange to find evidence of life amid the threat of death!

Since there was nowhere for me to turn as Frau de Bonne dressed herself—remember, my examination took place in their sitting room—I trained my eyes toward the ceiling. To my dismay, I saw several wire cages hung along a dark beam; I hadn't noticed them in my fear of finding Frau de Bonne close to death. Each cage was occupied by birds: sparrows, a raven, swallows, even a pair of white doves. This discovery enticed me to examine their cottage beyond the shadows. There was no way around it: their cottage was squalid. Every spare surface was covered with possessions, though there seemed no reason to it. Pottery adjoined stacks of papers and pots of ink beside forgotten mugs of tea. A piano piled with sheet music, the keys covered with dried rose petals.

Once I recovered from my shock, I noted a maid who was little more than a girl. I scolded her for not cleaning as she should. In response to my impassioned words, the birds chattered and fluttered, sending a rush of feathers from their cages. I plucked a black feather from the floor. "Anyone can see this is not a healthful environment, Herr de Bonne."

"My wife claims the bird song soothes her spirit," he explained. "You have yet to tell me your diagnosis, Herr Doktor. Please."

"Your wife is not dying," I whispered. "She is with child."

He did not believe me at first. After I convinced him thus, he exclaimed, "I never expected such an occurrence."

"It's not a simple matter," I explained, my heart breaking for him. "What I am about to say is very difficult. It is now the middle of December. From the size of your wife's womb, the baby will come to term in about five months' time. I must implore you to leave here as soon as the snow permits to go to a city where there are physicians who specialize in your wife's condition. It pains me to admit this, but I do not have experience for such a delivery. Between her narrow hips and her illness, your wife is too frail to withstand the rigors of labor. By this stage of her pregnancy, her nausea should have lessened. This suggests there is something else sickening her. You must leave here as soon as the snow allows. If you remain here . . ."

What I wanted to say I could not from a strange fatalism: Your wife and child will die.

To my dismay, Herr de Bonne ignored my insinuation. "We won't go. We can't."

"If it is a matter of financial considerations," I began delicately.

"It's not." His tone was resolute.

"But your wife requires assistance! Is there anyone I can write regarding your situation? Someone in your family perhaps?"

The maid spoke up. "Herr de Bonne has a cousin. A Bertram Highstead who lives outside London. He has an estate. Two sons, one named Robert. Write to Highstead. He will bring them home to England."

"Hush!" his wife scolded the maid. "This is our home now."

The couple dismissed me. Before I departed, I gave Frau de Bonne some bicarbonate of potash to ease her nausea, and two bottles of laudanum to her husband, who'd requested it for insomnia.

And that is the main of my story and the whole of my torment, my sister. After many hours of fretfulness, I realized only you can help. Now that you are situated in London for the winter, I implore you to inquire regarding a Bertram Highstead and his family. You must inform them of their cousin's dolorous situation.

I await your reply most anxiously—

—your loving brother Friedrich

Robert set down the book at last. To come across his name in such a manner—he didn't know what to think. He felt as though he'd encountered an alternative version of himself. A doppelgänger. None of the letter's content should have been a surprise—hadn't John told him as much about Hugh and their father? Regardless, Robert was shaken. Disoriented. As if he'd traveled to countries far beyond Shropshire. Beyond time.

To settle himself in his body, Robert flexed his hands and cracked his knuckles; the reddened flesh stung, but the sensation was welcome. It reminded him he was alive in his body, not in a book. That no matter what had happened to Ada and Hugh and their baby, there was naught anyone could do to help them. Not even him. For a moment, he felt truly regretful he hadn't been able to convince Isabelle to inter Hugh in the chapel.

And yet Robert didn't feel fully present: when he looked at the quilt covering his lap, a dark feather lay there. It appeared to be from a raven. Though someone must have used it as a bookmark, it still seemed a sign. Of what, though?

Before Robert could decide, a sudden sound distracted him. A scratching from the corridor.

"Who's there?"

The scratching grew louder. Closer. Sharper.

"Hullo?" His voice sounded unsteady in the darkness.

Another thump.

Before Robert could stop himself, he grabbed his trousers and tugged the door open.

A dog sat there—the same black Labrador that had greeted his arrival. His tail was tucked around his legs.

"You," Robert whispered, setting a fire iron he didn't recall grabbing against the wall. "Virgil, right?"

In response, Virgil sprang to his feet, panting. He barked once and circled frantically. And then Robert saw: a thin stream of urine puddled from beneath the dog's hindquarters.

IV.

The passage to take Virgil outside was long and confusing. Once Robert pulled on his boots and overcoat, the dog led him down one corridor and into another before turning onto a third. He seemed to know the way, which was fortunate because Robert didn't; he'd been too upset by Isabelle to take note.

Once downstairs, Virgil had trotted past the archway announcing the kitchen. Down another corridor, where a grandfather clock pointed toward two. Then, to Robert's surprise, Virgil bounded into the corridor leading to what Mrs. Chilvers had claimed was Hugh's study.

Robert's steps slowed.

The dog wasn't the only one there. Just outside the door, a slight young woman was silhouetted before a small gas lantern. A dark shawl covered her form.

"Virgil!" the young woman scolded in a hushed voice. "Bad dog!"

There was a caress of affection in her tone that made Robert like her. Who was she? The housemaid. He recalled Owen calling her Grace.

Robert pulled back about the corner, silencing his breath. From his vantage point, he watched Grace draw a bone from her pocket. She'd expected the dog to appear.

Just as Robert was about to warn the dog needed to relieve himself, Grace looked up and down the corridor. She opened the door to Hugh's study and entered, leaving the door open behind her. The dog followed, the bone hanging from his mouth.

Robert watched to see what would happen next.

A moment passed. Another.

The clock struck two.

They did not return.

If Hugh never lived there save for two weeks, what could the study contain? Too curious to resist, Robert tiptoed down the hall and peered inside the room. Long translucent curtains billowed out from the back of the room, where two French doors were left open to the winter night. Grace had gone outside. This he had not expected. Yes, he reasoned, it may have been nothing more than taking the dog out. But why walk through Hugh's study instead of the kitchen, which was closer, or even the front door? Even Robert, a stranger to Weald House in every way, recognized Hugh's study as sanctified space.

His heart hammering against his ribs, Robert slipped through Hugh's study toward the French doors. A stiff breeze set papers to rustle as he passed. The rain must have stopped, for the moon had risen, casting an uncanny light over long tables shadowed with books, tall statues, overstuffed chairs, and a piano. Artifacts of Hugh's life, presumably displayed to appease the pilgrims' hunger.

The moon guided Robert toward the French doors and into the world beyond. Once outside, he found himself alone in a walled rose garden, dormant with winter he hadn't noticed upon his arrival. Wasn't there a beehive somewhere? He'd have to be careful. Where had Grace gone? He turned until dizzied, eyes narrowing in the dark, thorns raking his shoulders.

A muffled bark sounded to the left. Some twenty feet away, Grace's lantern bobbed in time with her footfall. Dog and girl clamored into the woods, their forms shadowed beneath tree limbs. They were heading toward Ada's Folly—they had to be. But why?

Robert felt possessed as he followed them at a discreet distance. He had no yearning to confront, only witness. Tree limbs snapped against his cheeks, leaves crackled beneath his step. The bitter wind made his eyes sting, his lips chatter.

Perhaps it was his agitated state, but what appeared far by carriage seemed near on foot. Sooner than he'd imagined possible, Ada's Folly rose above the trees like something conjured from a fairy tale. The moon gilded the glass dome, glittering from the last of the rain. Viewed in the night, the chapel Hugh had built looked even more fantastical, more impossible than Robert remembered. In that moment, he forgot about Isabelle's anger, Hugh's corpse, and his ghost wife. Instead, he felt the presence of the divine, as he did when encountering something too wondrous to believe, like when he'd first met Sida. Hugh loved as he loved. That was enough for a man in this life. Wasn't it?

But then Robert remembered where he was, whom he was following.

He crouched behind one of the larger oaks. Grace approached the chapel, Virgil still lolling at her side. There was a purpose to her every movement that bordered on stealth. Whatever she was doing, she'd done it many times before.

She set the lantern on the ground beside her feet. Robert leaned forward to see better. A sudden wind blew dust into his eyes, the pain sharper than thorns. He clasped a hand over his mouth to muffle an expletive.

By the time he recovered, they were gone. But he couldn't turn back. Not yet—whatever he'd witnessed in Grace seemed to be providence. All of a sudden the burning need to look inside the chapel, to view what no living man or woman had ever seen, overtook him. To view Ada's grave after reading that letter. Robert's breath caught in his chest in a manner nearly sexual in its pleasure. It felt as visceral as love, as tangible as bread. Yes, this was unwise. Yes, this went against everything Isabelle Lowell decreed. Yes, it was night. Still, he couldn't turn away.

His eyes made out an archway hidden beneath veils of ivy. The door. When he approached, he saw the lock was coated in rust and ice. A soft clucking sound drew his attention. When he bent to investigate, a blur of white darted from the ivy.

Doves. They must have been nesting in the eaves.

Once they'd cleared, Robert tried the chapel door. The iron handle was obscured by a bouquet of dying roses someone had nailed above it. As soon as he turned the handle, ice soaked through his glove.

Locked.

An odd disappointment fell upon him. He shouldn't have hoped. But the top of the chapel was clear glass. The moon was full, now that the storm had cleared. There would be some light to look inside—not enough to set the stained glass afire in all its glory, but enough to see something.

Robert glanced around one last time. No Grace or Virgil. His hands reached for the most convenient branch (here, the thickest tendril of ivy). It was still wet from rain. His feet pushed against the ground. Launching himself up, *up!* toward the heavens.

Though it had been years since he'd climbed anything beyond a set of stairs, all of his days climbing trees as a boy came back to him. The ease was exhilarating. As he climbed, ivy rustled beneath his body. His muscles stretched and strained.

Once he was about ten feet from the ground, the ivy thinned, allowing him to view the lead tracery marking the stained glass windows. He let out a long *Oh!* as he brushed the glass, so smooth and cold. It was milk-hued, probably to set off the colors within. Though there was little to see, the knowledge that *this* was what the pilgrims had traveled to view rose in Robert, and he'd touched it. Pride—no, triumph—flooded his chest, granting him courage to climb farther.

Above the glass walls, a ledge of grey stone rimmed the chapel's perimeter, marking the start of the glass dome. Breathing hard, Robert's cold-numbed fingers curled around the ledge. How high up he was! He'd never climbed so far, not even as a boy. A strange unease twisted his stomach. For one mad moment, he imagined Grace returning with Isabelle. Hugh staring down at him from whatever world lay beyond. Ada too with her baby.

He forced his gaze up. Toward the rain-cleared sky. The moon was so large. The stars so bright. He could even see a hint of Weald House's roof, tendrils of smoke rising from its chimney pots.

He pulled himself up those last few feet toward the top. Pressed his cheek against the edge of the glass dome. Stared down into the chapel.

Nothing.

The glass dome was thicker than he'd expected. Less fragile. Emboldened, he pulled his torso against the cold glass for a better view. It fogged from his breath, then cleared.

A long alabaster bench. A shimmer of color tracing a white marble floor. Blues, greens, reds glowing like jewels, even beneath the diffuse light of night . . .

Just as his face beamed into a smile, a crack sounded beneath his belly. The glass. It was giving way.

Terror rose in him, as tangible as the moisture seeping his skin. He saw himself on that hard marble floor, his neck angled unnaturally. His blood spattering the white stone bench. He'd breathe his last in a place where no one would ever find him—after his argument with Isabelle, he couldn't imagine her deigning to unlock the chapel.

He scuttled from the cracked glass. Pressed his toes against the edge of the chapel eaves. He could feel the dome curving and giving, shaking, shivering like a living thing rebelling. Any moment it would shatter into thousands of pieces. He'd be deposited inside the chapel dead and bloodied. It served him right. He'd been a fool to take such a risk.

"Mr. Highstead! Is that you?"

Grace's voice sounded far away. Panicked.

Robert inched to the edge of the chapel dome. His fingernails scraped stone. A cluster of doves rose from the ivy, their wings brushing his face. Once they cleared away, he saw the housemaid below on the ground. The dog beside her. Her arms overflowing with roses. She dropped them.

"What are you doing there?" Grace's eyes grew wide, her mouth a perfect O of alarm. Virgil began to bark wildly.

"I'm uncertain." Wind hissed past his ears.

His toes slipped from the ledge. He swung his foot toward the ivy. Twined it around his ankle. Leaves scattered into the wind as the tendril broke.

"Come down now! You'll be killed!"

"I'm trying," he said.

He reached for the ledge. His legs dangled.

Grace screamed. The dog howled. The wind blew.

Among the Dead

Excerpted from *The Lost History of Dreams* by Hugh de Bonne, published 1837 by Chapman & Hall, London.

> As the Poet passed through Death itself
> Pale-shadowed spirits escaped from darkest graves,
> Black-eyed dogs approached with fangs like knives,
> All led by cruel Chronos who devours all else
> Until he found Persephone, queen o' those caves
> Where no Life abides. Her sharp words drew his fear :
> 'The Dead may be silent, but they have much to say
> For those with ears to hear. Will you listen, Orpheus?'

*

I.

When Robert next opened his eyes, he was lying on a shabby bed surrounded by shadows. Once his sight adjusted, he saw Mrs. Chilvers leaning over him, mouth gaping and eyes wide. She was dressed for sleep, her rumpled face overtaken by a heavily laced cap. Her front tooth was more chipped than he recalled.

"You're here with us at last, praise God! Can you sit, sir?"

"I'm uncertain," Robert replied. Images flooded his mind as his head began to ache and his ankle sing. *Glass shattering beneath his weight. Stars dazzling him. Doves fluttering. Grace's mouth as she screamed. Virgil barking like a hound of hell . . .*

He'd climbed Ada's Folly in the middle of the night. It was the second most foolish thing he'd ever done.

Robert pulled himself up, ribs shrieking with pain. Moths beat against the dark window glass. The room he inhabited looked more akin to a mud hut than Weald House. It was so small that it scarcely contained the furniture it held. Besides the cot, there was a small table set with two crude chairs. A few books on the mantel. A shallow grate provided an anemic fire. A stiff breeze blew into the room despite the closed door and window. The scent of almonds wafted on it, too subtle to be detected by anyone but him; the embalmer must have been overly enthusiastic, anticipating Hugh's travels.

"I'm in the stable house," he said.

Mrs. Chilvers nodded. "In Owen's room. In case you'd broken any bones, they decided it best to bring you here—"

"They?" he interjected.

"Me." Owen's voice chirped from behind Robert. "I found you collapsed by Ada's Folly." He took a step toward Robert and smiled a trifle nervously. His eyes were ringed in purple shadows as he dragged on his ubiquitous cigarette despite the housekeeper's presence. "Pure luck I happened on you. I'd taken the dog out for a walk—soiled himself, bad dog."

"But Grace was with the dog," Robert said.

Owen widened his eyes, warning him to silence. "That's not what happened."

Mrs. Chilvers asked, "How would you know this, Mr. Highstead?"

He lied, "I heard Grace outside my room."

Now Grace stepped forward, her bright hair dazzling. Her face was swollen from tears; she must have panicked when he fell.

"Not possible." She giggled desperately, fiddling with a curl. "I fear you're not in your right mind."

"You've quite the bump on your head," Mrs. Chilvers said.

"I know what I heard," Robert protested, feeling slow and confused. Did he crack the dome? Or had he imagined this?

Grace's voice rose. "I couldn't have been with the dog. I was sound asleep when Owen fetched me. Miss Isabelle gathered you. She told me to stay here with you while she fetched Mrs. Chilvers."

"Miss Lowell did *what*?" Surely Robert misheard.

"She helped me carry you here," Owen said. "Said it was a miracle you were alive, and thought you'd broken bones."

"We haven't found any thus far," Mrs. Chilvers interjected. "The skin on your hands looks scraped up though."

His overwashed hands. He grimaced.

Grace said, "Miss Isabelle was ever so strong and brave. I feared you were dead!"

"She knew what to do, praise God." Mrs. Chilvers nodded so vigorously that her night cap was set to wagging. "What happened, Mr. Highstead? Miss Isabelle said it looked like you'd fallen from up high."

"I don't recall." Robert's gaze slid from Grace to Owen to Mrs. Chilvers and back. The air felt thick with lies. For whatever reason, Owen was protecting Grace, Grace was protecting herself. As for himself, he was just as dishonest. What excuse could he give for climbing Ada's Folly? That Isabelle had provoked him by refusing to let him inter Hugh? That he yearned to view Ada's grave after reading that letter? That he wanted to see what no one living had seen? As for the glass dome, perhaps he hadn't damaged it after all. Surely someone would have said something by now.

He finally said, "I recall falling asleep."

Mrs. Chilvers asked, "Are you a sleepwalker?"

"Not previously . . . Ah, now I remember! I was very tired from my journey. I hadn't eaten. I woke up feeling dizzy," he lied. "I went outside to get air. I became disoriented." He offered what he hoped was a sheepish, winning grin. "I don't recall anything more. I suspect I tripped over tree roots."

"That must be it."

Grace's voice sounded very far away as a new array of pain rose from Robert's body, singing like a siren. He felt his mouth slacken. A thick fog circled, competing with the pain in a strange dance he couldn't comprehend.

Within this fog, he heard the door to the stable house scrape open. Isabelle Lowell's sharp figure, dressed in a dark blue wrapper, advanced toward him. She was scowling. A thick black ribbon dangled from her neck. Hanging from the ribbon was an iron key—it had to be for the glass chapel. It was smaller than he'd expected, yet denser. At its thickest point, the key was the width of a pencil. Robert had never seen anything like it.

As Isabelle leaned over Robert, the key swung between folds of her wrapper, revealing the curve of her breast; he was surprised by the first flush of arousal. Whether it was from the sight of her breast, or his body's response to injury, it mattered not.

He fell back into darkness, thankful for oblivion.

It was the pain that awakened him. It was unlike any he'd ever felt. It wept from his ankle, his knee, his ribs, his head. It reminded him of a night he yearned to forget from three years earlier.

Robert opened his eyes. Grey light slanted from the window, revealing morning had arrived. How long had he slept? It seemed like a week had passed since he'd climbed Ada's Folly. The room buzzed, pulsing with sound. Was it rain or injury?

He sniffed the air. Decidedly rain. It must have started up again.

The rain smelled lovely and clean, unlike a London rain, which was usually tainted with sulfur, at least in Clerkenwell. It overcame the trace of almonds from Hugh's coffin in the stall beyond. The rain didn't sound as heavy as the night before, one blessing amid the chaos. Another blessing: no broken bones. He suspected Mrs. Chilvers was right based on his boyhood experience of breaking his arm. No reason for him to delay leaving for London, though he didn't look forward to traveling with Hugh anew.

He raised the blanket to examine his body. He wore only his shirt and drawers. Someone had undressed him. Not Isabelle, he prayed; he remembered his shame at learning she and Owen had carried him from Ada's Folly, his unexpected arousal. There was nothing he could do but dress and leave. He'd probably missed the morning coach, but there'd be another. Soon, he hoped.

Across the room, his trousers were neatly folded, along with his jacket, on a long bench set beneath the stable window. They'd been brushed of dirt.

He was about to force himself from the bed to dress when a soft cough came from behind his pillow.

He craned his head, wincing.

Isabelle Lowell was seated behind the bed on a stool. Her eyes were shut, her head on a pillow wedged against the wall. She must have spent the night there. She coughed again, cupping a hand over her lips. She was dressed in what Robert understood to be her customary garb: plum-hued half-mourning. Her collar was buttoned resolutely high on her neck. Robert grew warm, recalling the curve of her breasts beneath her wrapper, the key dangling in the crevice.

Perhaps sensing his gaze, Isabelle blinked her grey eyes open like a goshawk. Her mouth shifted as though whatever she was thinking couldn't be expressed in polite company.

"Well," she said at last. "Well."

"What time is it?" He drew the blanket high about his chest.

"It's just after seven in the morning. Four hours since Owen and I had to drag you here like a corpse in the middle of the night."

"I'm sorry—"

"You should be sorry. You with your rubbish about taking a walk to get some air! I know what you were doing. You were trying to break into Ada's Folly—"

The stable house door opened without warning, bringing Isabelle's accusations to a close. Mrs. Chilvers bustled in, her cheeks red from the cold, her navy bonnet flecked with moisture. A flurry of wind rushed behind her, followed by rain.

"Oh Mr. Highstead!" she called with her usual flourish of enthusiasm. "I came to see how you were. Miss Isabelle, you are an angel, sitting here all night with him. Are you all right, sir? Sleepwalking! I thought such things only occurred in novels."

Robert was grateful for her interruption. "I am very sorry to have been such a trouble to your household."

"Indeed." Isabelle offered an incredulous shake of her head.

Mrs. Chilvers said, "I'm very glad you weren't killed. 'Tis terrifying to think of such matters!" Her voice dropped with a tremulous air. "Now that I think of it, you remind me a bit of Mr. Hugh in some ways—I heard you were a writer too." She brushed her hand against Robert's cheek; the maternal gesture startled him, like happening upon a warm hearth after wandering in the snow. "Goodness, look at you! You've elflocks."

"Elflocks?" Robert repeated, confused.

"They're the tangles fairies put in your hair while you sleep." She smiled indulgently. "Now you know you're no longer in London, sir. I'd wager a sovereign there are no fairies there."

"Even if such nonsense was possible, fairies didn't tangle his hair," Isabelle dismissed. "His hair is tangled because he fell after climbing Ada's Folly."

Mrs. Chilvers took a steep inhale. "He tried to climb Ada's Folly? He told me he'd fallen in the woods. Whatever for, sir?"

Isabelle answered for Robert. "To break inside it. He's fortunate Owen happened on him after he fell."

"I can explain," Robert began. "I would have never done such a thing if you'd honored Hugh's last request to be interred—"

"Always Hugh," Isabelle interrupted, "as if this excuses your behavior. Not to worry, Mr. Highstead. You'll be interring my uncle soon enough. You'll be leaving with him on the next coach."

"Mr. Highstead is injured. It's raining like Noah," Mrs. Chilvers protested. "He's family, Miss Isabelle. He must stay with us until he has improved—a few days, a week. Then we can sort out the business with Mr. Hugh. If he can't be buried with Miss Ada, there's the churchyard at least."

"All the more reason for my concern." Isabelle's tone was heavy with sarcasm. "Mr. Highstead needs to recover at home, not here in a stable house in the middle of February with a corpse for company. Mr. Highstead needs his immediate family to look after him, not me." She turned toward Robert, a brow arched. "Don't you agree?"

II.

By the time Robert was dressed to leave, it was well past eight in the morning. He cringed as he slid trousers over his legs and tucked in shirttails. Lacing his boots was even worse—it hurt to bend, to move. His ankle barely supported his weight. He flexed his foot; a large bruise, yellowed like a fig leaf in autumn, crowned the whole of it. His ribs were no better. He examined his face in a hand mirror cracked in a corner; for a brief moment, he thought he spied the reflection of his wife's face. *Wishful thinking.* A thin scab snaked across his left temple; someone must have washed the wound to prevent his hair crusting in it. He'd been lucky—from a fall of that distance, he could have been crippled or worse. His bristle was rough against his fingers. Shaving would wait until he reached London. He'd treat himself to a barbershop.

Just as Robert slid his braces over his shoulders, Owen knocked.

"Rain's getting heavier," he said, tucking a book from the mantel into his coat pocket. "Shame you have to leave so soon." A pause. "Sorry I made you look a fool about Grace finding you and all. Didn't want Miss Isabelle to be upset with her walking about at night."

"Does Grace do this often?" Should he ask about the roses? No, he decided.

Owen colored. "I wouldn't know, Mr. Highstead."

"What time is the coach?" This was one morsel of information Isabelle hadn't deigned to share.

"Not till eleven. Plenty time for breakfast. I'll help you to the kitchen."

"Mr. de Bonne?" Robert had to ask.

Owen gave a visible shudder. "Already attached the coffin—Grace helped me."

"Thank you." Robert hoped for a sympathetic coachman who wouldn't mind dragging the cart to Shrewsbury.

In the kitchen, Robert found his daguerreotype traveling case set beside the door where he'd arrived less than a day earlier. The room was otherwise empty of servants. Owen procured a bowl of porridge, stiff from exposure, before pulling the book from his pocket. *Ethel Churchill; or, The Two Brides*, Robert read along the spine before tucking into the food. Every so often, Owen let out a wistful sigh. He only broke his reading to ask Robert, "Didn't you write a book or something? I thought I heard Miss Isabelle speak of it."

"Or something," Robert replied before turning back to the porridge. Despite a dollop of milk and treacle, the cold food was unappetizing. Even so, his stomach growled; he hadn't eaten in nearly twenty-four hours. Virgil clipped over, resting his warm chin against his knee. Robert flashed with irritation toward the dog, though he had only himself to blame for his injuries.

Mrs. Chilvers darted into the kitchen. "Are they here yet?" she asked Owen, her widow's cap askew.

"No," he answered, setting his novel aside. "Do you think any will come? Weather's so pernicious."

She threw her hands up. "Hasn't stopped them before. Did Miss Isabelle go upstairs?"

"Who are you expecting?" Robert asked, the porridge ignored.

"Forgive me, Mr. Highstead. I forgot you were here." Mrs. Chilvers offered a warm smile. "It's Mr. Hugh's study. It's Thursday, the day Miss Isabelle lets the pilgrims visit."

"The Seekers of the Lost Dream," Robert said, remembering their conversation on the stairwell the previous evening.

"Yes, Mr. Highstead. Anyway, they come—"

"To sob and gape over Ada and Hugh," Owen interjected, his gaze turning distant. "It's quite romantic really. They bring flowers, they quote poetry. They pay a pretty penny too—sixpence each."

"You're surprised, Mr. Highstead, aren't you? It's because of them the estate isn't run into the ground. 'Twas clever of Miss Isabelle to think of such though they're a bother." Mrs. Chilvers shook her head darkly. "Now with Mr. Hugh dead, who knows what will happen?"

A bell jangled, setting Virgil to barking.

"That's them," Owen announced, shushing the dog. "Shall I let them in? Grace is ready."

"Yes, go!" Mrs. Chilvers cried over the bell. "How impatient they are! Mr. Highstead, you rest here in the kitchen until your coach. I'll get a hassock for your ankle." She glanced out the window. "Lord, I pray they haven't learned about Mr. Hugh yet." She shouted to Owen, "Whatever you do, keep them away from the coffin! Warn Grace too!"

Robert's curiosity overtook physical discomfort.

"If you don't mind," he said, pushing his porridge away, "I'd like to view Hugh's study before I leave. Can you help me walk there?"

When Owen opened the front door, there were only six Seekers of the Lost Dream pilgrims waiting on the threshold. Even if Mrs. Chilvers hadn't said anything, Robert would have identified the pilgrims as such from their tremulous smiles and enraptured gazes. One of them, a plump woman a little older than Robert, clutched an armful of red roses. Her curls were an unnatural shade of copper beneath her bonnet, which was decorated in raven feathers. Robert wondered if this was the lady Mrs. Chilvers had mentioned: "*One even dyes her hair red in honor of Mr. Hugh.*"

"Can it be?" she gasped, pointing to Robert's wounded forehead as she stepped inside the corridor. "Is this *him* . . . ?"

Robert felt a twinge of discomfort as he realized she'd mistaken him for Hugh. Before he could correct her, the red-haired lady swooned into the arms of the pilgrim closest to her, a brawny gentleman. Once she recovered, she stared at Robert, her soft mouth pouting. "You can't be Hugh de Bonne, though you're tall like him. For a moment when I saw your scar . . . 'Tis same place as Hugh's, on the left temple. But yours is fresh and you're too young. How foolish I feel!"

"If it's any consolation, I'm Mr. de Bonne's relation," Robert explained, though it really explained nothing. "His cousin from London."

"Ah. That must be it." She chanted: "'As the Poet waited 'neath domed glass.'"

A severe grey-haired lady clutching a nosegay answered: "'Whilst the clocks chimed forlorn for noon.'"

A third woman exclaimed, "I know that poem! 'The Glass Chapel' from *The Lost History of Dreams*. What a chimera of wonder it is! 'His fists stopping those who might trespass.'"

"'With dreaded words he dared impugn,'" the gentleman who caught the fainter concluded. "Though I must admit I favor this one:

> 'As the Poet passed through Death itself
> Pale-shadowed spirits escaped from darkest graves,
> Black-eyed dogs approached with fangs like knives,
> All led by cruel Chronos who devours all else . . .'

"Now *that's* a chimera of wonder!" he concluded, gazing rapturously about the hall. "Hugh's abode smells just like it always does—of lemon oil and genius."

"Your first time visiting Maestro de Bonne's home?" a young man addressed Robert; his embroidered silk waistcoat and long fawn-colored hair gave him away as an artistic type.

"Yes," Robert replied, astonished by the pilgrims despite being warned, though they seemed more respectful than ravenous. Isabelle's words returned: "*Hugh never even really lived here.*" How different the entry hall was from the rest of the house! The plaster walls looked recently repaired and were painted in a welcoming sage color. They set off a handsome array of framed engravings presumably harvested from Hugh's books. A small oak table held a glass vase containing red-berried hawthorn branches and black raven feathers. Robert recalled the kitchen with its shabby desperation, the barely habitable stable house. And upstairs in the library—well, that was a whole other tableau, with Isabelle probably sulking beside her piano to avoid the pilgrims.

"When did you first discover Hugh's poetry?" Artistic Gentleman asked Robert.

Robert admitted, "Very recently." It appeared none were aware of Hugh's death thankfully. He grasped the back of a chair to keep weight from his ankle.

"Are you improved, madam?" Owen asked the red-haired fainter. "Yes? Let us begin."

He cleared his throat and began.

"Welcome to Weald House, the estate of Hugh and Ada de Bonne. We—the family and servants of Mr. de Bonne—are honored for your attendance on such a miserable day. If you would follow me, his study is yonder. The rest of the house is not part of the tour, for Mr. de Bonne still has family residing there."

"What about Ada's Folly?" an agitated male voice asked. "Will we at least walk by there? I've come all the way from Manchester to see it."

The red-haired woman had recovered from her faint enough to say, "They never show Ada's Folly—it's most distressing!" Her bonnet shook from the vehemence of her words, making her frustration appear almost comical. Yet Robert felt sorry for her: she mourned. His three years as a daguerreotypist of the dead had honed his ability to recognize the signs. In her case, a crumpled black-bordered handkerchief peaking from the lace cuff of her sleeve revealed her loss.

Owen ignored her interruption. "This way, if you please. Miss Grace Blackmoor will explain all to you."

As they entered Hugh's study, the pilgrims murmured with anticipation, even the red-haired woman. One of them, the older stocky gentleman, offered Robert a hand after noting his injury. Once inside, several pilgrims set flowers on the fireplace mantel, their offerings joining a display of desiccated bouquets presumably left from previous tours. Hugh's portrait engraving, the same one that served as frontispiece in *The Collected Letters and Ephemera of Hugh de Bonne*, stared out above the flowers like a relic.

Grace welcomed the pilgrims, though Robert noticed she didn't acknowledge the red-haired woman; perhaps she feared encouraging another faint. The red-haired woman was now fluttering a raven-feather fan before her face and seemed close to tears. As for Grace, instead of her usual housemaid's dimity frock, she wore a grey merino gown that wouldn't be out of place at a philanthropist's tea. She looked older. Respectable. Not the fey creature Robert had followed to Ada's Folly, lured by impulse and moonlight. Her lashes fluttered as she flashed a smile at Owen. He smoothed his curls and flecked his lips with the tip of his tongue, as though his mouth had grown dry.

"Good morning, ladies and gentlemen," Grace said, avoiding Robert's gaze as she surveyed the pilgrims. "I am Miss Blackmoor. I've lived at Weald House for the past six years. Though I fear I never had the privilege to meet Hugh de Bonne, I have many stories to tell of his life."

Robert waited to see if she'd speak of Hugh's death; she didn't.

"This way, if you please," she continued. "There's room for all."

Robert limped after the pilgrims, who'd settled into an awed silence, into Hugh's study. As he observed them, he had the sense of attending church for a religion he'd never known existed. Instead of the mysteries of Christ, it was the mysteries of art: the call and response of the poems, the artifacts of the raven feathers and red roses. To think all this had existed within his family. He'd had no idea. It was like discovering a room you never knew was part of your house.

Grace said, "We shall begin by speaking of Hugh de Bonne's time at Weald House, which had been his wife's childhood home until their marriage in 1834 . . ."

As Grace spoke, Robert was surprised by how much *more* the study appeared than it had the previous evening. And *more* was the only word for it. Even if Hugh had only lived there for two weeks, under the light of day his study possessed an expansiveness that belied the sheer number of items it contained: the books, the statues, the glass display cases, the chairs—paraphernalia of the poet's mortal existence.

As Robert recalled, the far wall was constructed of tall French doors fragile with glass, an anomaly in an English farmhouse, which tended toward thick walls and small windows. Each door held a stained glass panel rich in detail and color. Though the individual panels were no larger than a small book, they featured a solitary bird caught in flight: a dove in one, a raven in another. Hugh must have commissioned them at the same time as the chapel. With this, the mad spectacle of Ada's Folly called anew to Robert. He'd never daguerreotype it. Never return Hugh to his wife's side. Instead, Hugh would spend eternity among strangers in Kent; his body would rest closer to Sida than Ada.

Robert forced his attention back to Grace, who'd moved on to the book display. From the affectless way her words spilled from her lips, she was like a canary singing for her living who'd forgotten the song's meaning.

"Over here"—Grace pointed to a red leather-bound book—"is a first edition of *The Lost History of Dreams*. His last collection of poems."

The older lady cried, "His masterpiece."

Grace flushed prettily. "That's what many claim. And I suspect that, given you've traveled to Weald House on a rainy day, you've read it. However, this copy of *The Lost History of Dreams* is different from others." Her voice dropped conspiratorially. "Do you know why?"

"Because Hugh de Bonne owned it," Owen said in a flat voice that belied the moist yearning in his gaze.

"You're absolutely correct, sir," Grace responded, winking. She drew the volume from the bookcase, opening to a marked page. "But wait! There's more!"

Robert craned his head over the pilgrims, who fluttered collectively like birds themselves.

"See the notes on the side of the page?" Grace said. "They're in Ada's hand. As she lay heavy with child beneath the shadow of death, she conferred with her beloved husband on these very poems. They were one in art as they were in holy wedlock."

Grace replaced the book and stepped toward a small fur coat displayed on a rack. The coat was sewn of different animals—fox, rabbit, raccoon—and bordered in luxurious white ermine.

"Ada was Hugh's greatest inspiration," she continued. "He gave her many gifts to honor their love. This was a coat Hugh gave her to commemorate their first Christmas as a married couple, which they spent in Paris—that's in France, you know. The coat was accompanied by this note: 'My *locus amoenus*'—"

"*Locus amoenus*?" the artistic gentleman called out. "What in heaven's name is that?"

Grace shrugged.

Robert explained, "It's Latin for 'pleasant place.' Mr. de Bonne probably meant he considered his wife his home. As it should be in a marriage."

"And there you have it. Who knew?" Grace returned her attention to the note. "The rest says: 'Here is something to protect you from everything that might trouble your soul. When you wear this coat, imagine my arms embracing you.'"

A teardrop lingered on the edge of the older lady's nose. Robert's eyes darted to the red-haired lady, whose taffeta skirts were swaying. She was going to swoon again, he was certain. Instead she called out, "Miss Blackmoor! What of Ada's Folly? What do you know of it?"

"Questions at the end, please." Grace pointed toward the spinet. "Behold Ada's piano from Germany. The Black Forest no less!"

She pressed her forefinger against a white key. It was raucously out of tune, but no one appeared to mind.

"Ada sang and played beautifully. As sweetly as a siren, some say. She even had training in composing music thanks to Hugh. Before their marriage, he arranged for her to take lessons in secret."

"Why in secret?" the grey-haired lady interrupted.

"The story is some feared she'd yearn for the stage, following the likes of Liszt or Chopin." A cheeky grin. "Instead Ada did something far worse: she eloped with a poet."

Grace waited for the rustle of laughter that ran across the pilgrims. Even the red-haired lady was appeased; she'd folded away her fan. By now, Robert had the sense they would accept anything Grace told them, even if it involved Ada ascending to heaven accompanied by an angelic choir. Such was the power of story; he'd experienced firsthand at Oxford how a story could seduce a scholar despite the hard presence of facts. This power allowed Grace to transform the pilgrims' obsession with Ada and Hugh de Bonne into something to be sold at sixpence a tour.

"And now I fear I must speak of a very sad event, dear ladies and gentlemen," Grace said. "As many of you know, Ada and Hugh's daughter, Mathilde, was stillborn." She pointed to a glass bell on Hugh's desk. It displayed a black feather and a heart-shaped plait of ebony-hued hair. "Alas, Ada never recovered, but before her death she took comfort in the items displayed here. Does anyone want to venture what they are?"

The grey-haired lady shouted, "The hair belonged to the baby."

"Yes . . . and no, madam," Grace replied, staring intently at the feather. "Yes, it was shorn from Mathilde's head. No, in that the plait includes Ada's hair. She and Mathilde bore the same color hair. But what of the feather?"

Artistic Gentleman called out, "'Tis a raven feather. Like in the poem 'The Raven and the Rose.'"

"Yes, it is indeed a raven feather. But it wasn't found from a bird . . ." Grace's words dipped in volume to heighten the solemnity. "When Mathilde was born, I fear the sorrowful circumstances were as you'd expect. However, when the midwife was washing the baby's dear face for her eternal sleep in Christ, she noticed a raised bump on Mathilde's cheek.

"At first the midwife thought it a boil, though this made no sense—the poor babe barely drew a breath in this world before passing to the next. Then the midwife saw a black tuft rising from the bump. She pulled at it . . ." Grace clutched at her chest. "My lovely gentlemen and ladies, it was this very raven feather you see displayed before you."

The room gasped. So did Robert. Though his mind told him Grace's story was nonsense, the gooseflesh on his neck informed otherwise.

"Now I ask you," Grace confided, "how could a raven feather find its way inside the cheek of an infant? And a stillborn at that? You might say, 'Impossible, Miss Blackmoor!' However, stranger things have occurred in this world. Chimeras of wonder, as Hugh de Bonne wrote." Her finger jabbed toward the display. "This feather proves Mathilde was born an angel! That she was destined to be waiting for her mother in the eternal vale without sorrow!"

Once the crowd settled, Grace clapped her hands to signify a change of subject. "But enough about poor dear Ada and Mathilde. What about Hugh de Bonne? We know he was born in France in 1792 toward the height of their troubles . . ."

By now Robert's ankle throbbed anew. He tightened his hands against the chair, which he still used to support himself. He closed his eyes; Grace's chatter faded into a soft buzzing. He barely noticed when she pointed out Hugh's walking stick ("As a young man, he was wounded in a duel in Chalk Farm—that's in London, you know—and walked with a limp. This is the walking stick he used, which was carved from a mulberry tree and has real gold . . ."), or Hugh's book collection (everything from Audubon's *Birds of America* to a rare edition of *Hours of Idleness*, Lord Byron's first book). Nor did Robert pay mind to Grace's description of Hugh's scandalous past before meeting Ada ("It is difficult to speak of the many ladies whose hearts he broke in London and Paris. The duchess who drowned herself in the Seine. The unfortunate who indulged in too much gin after finding herself with child . . .").

Robert forced his eyes open. The pilgrims were still there, wearing their cockades of roses and raven feathers; Grace's lips were still moving, her words ricocheting against the material proof of Hugh's existence that had made its way to this house where he'd never lived.

". . . This was the last letter from Hugh before his disappearance in October 1838," Grace was saying. "It was found inside this very study after he locked and abandoned Ada's Folly upon its completion. Some claim he found his way back to France. Others believe he traveled to America to find comfort in geography. Most fear he went mad with grief, though I hope not. His last letter to Ada is especially affecting when you consider he wrote it after her death. It's like a prayer set to paper: 'To know a love such as ours is enough in a life,' he wrote. 'I love and you love. And thus it ends. In love.'"

Applause sounded, tentative then hearty. Grace offered a curtsey.

"Thus ends our tour of Hugh de Bonne's study. If anyone has questions, I'd be pleased to answer them." A long pause. "No questions? None at all? Very well. Owen will—"

Before Robert could stop himself, his voice rang out.

"Excuse me, Miss Blackmoor . . ."

Grace turned, offering that bright fake smile. "Sir?"

"My question is about Ada's Folly. I've been told someone has been leaving roses on the door there. Do you know who and why?"

Grace's face stilled like she'd been doused with water.

III.

As soon as Robert saw Grace's response, he regretted his impulsiveness. But he wouldn't recant—any moment now he would leave Weald House, never to return.

"What an impertinent question," someone huffed. The red-haired lady. She fluttered her raven-feather fan anew.

"Roses?" Grace repeated slowly, tugging at a loose strand of hair. "I'm uncertain what you mean, sir. Like a bouquet?"

Robert nodded. "I've been told the roses mysteriously appear in the middle of the night. Do you know why someone would be leaving them?"

"Well, I fear I've heard of stranger deeds when it comes to Hugh de Bonne . . ." Grace's giggle sounded forced. "It's not uncommon for people to leave offerings to honor Hugh's genius. As for whoever left the roses, does it matter?"

The red-haired lady muttered, "Perhaps they wouldn't appear if Miss Lowell opened the chapel to the world."

Before Robert could respond, he felt a tap on his shoulder. Mrs. Chilvers stood behind him.

"Mr. Highstead, it's time to leave. Come."

Robert didn't have the opportunity to say goodbye to Grace or even the dog before Mrs. Chilvers led him out the front door, where the chaise carriage awaited with its grey canvas roof raised against the rain; someone had thoughtfully draped a tarp over the cart holding Hugh's coffin. "You'll need to dash for it, Mr. Highstead," the housekeeper warned. "I haven't an umbrella."

The rain was heavier than ever; Robert nearly slipped in the mud, causing his ankle to ache even more. Once he was ensconced in the chaise, he was surprised to find Isabelle seated beside him, his tripod and traveling case resting at her feet. Her eyes appeared bloodshot from lack of sleep, her cheeks sunken. Still, she'd managed to dress her hair. Her plaits coiled beneath her plain straw bonnet like a nest of albino serpents.

"I'd thought Owen would drive." Robert was too nonplussed to be polite.

"I'd have thought the same thing," she replied coolly, curling her gloved hands about the reins. "Given the events of last night, I decided it prudent to escort you myself."

Isabelle flicked the reins against the horse.

As they traveled, Robert trained his gaze outside the cart at the passing scenery, away from Isabelle. Anything to avoid interaction. Viewed beneath the cover of rain, the winter landscape surrounding Weald House was even more desolate than he recalled. He viewed fallow bogs delineated by thorny hedgerows, long abandoned to any attempt of farming. Stone houses where no chimney smoke rose. Horses and cows lazily grazing in overgrown fields. A short canter later, the fields were replaced by woods, within which he knew Ada's Folly stood. The forest appeared even more tangled, even darker, and more threatening than he'd recalled. He must have been mad to have followed Grace into it. Grace, at least, had the excuse of familiarity to explain her willingness to walk there in the dead of night.

"Not much longer now," Isabelle said, breaking the sharp silence. "The coach stand is just ahead. Hopefully there won't be delays because of the rain. I must apologize for this unreasonable weather we've having, Mr. Highstead."

Her exchange was so peculiar, so unexpected, so downright polite, that Robert nearly laughed. He answered with matching formality. "No need, Miss Lowell. Man cannot control the weather any more than he can control fate."

"Nicely put, Mr. Highstead. Like something a wise vicar would say."

"Thank you, Miss Lowell."

Robert's spine prickled with dread. How long could they continue being so cordial? He knew he should welcome this peaceful impasse as a graceful ending to an unpleasant interlude. Instead, he distrusted her civility.

He recognized the oak tree marking the coach stand. Isabelle brought the horse to a halt.

"No need for you to remain with me," Robert said eagerly. "The coach will arrive shortly. If you would kindly unlatch the cart, I'll manage from here."

Her eyebrows flew up. "In this storm? That would be inhospitable of me. Anyway, you'll need help with the cart and your belongings."

The minutes passed. The air inside the carriage felt heavy with moisture. His ankle was tight inside his boot.

"I think I see the coach," Robert said, who hadn't actually viewed any such thing. "It will be here any second—I'm certain of it."

"I don't see anything," Isabelle said. "Must be running late."

"Well, it *is* raining, Miss Lowell."

She offered a slow smile. "If I didn't know better, I'd say you wanted to get away from me."

Robert sweated beneath his overcoat. "I am grateful to you for your hospitality. I regret all that has occurred. I know I behaved dishonorably. Ungentlemanly. Though I understand it is much to expect, I pray in time you will understand the circumstances leading to my actions whilst beneath your roof. Though I fear it may be too late, I hope you will find it in yourself to forgive and . . ."

Reconsider Hugh's request to be buried with Ada, he wanted to say. It was the least he could do for his brother and Hugh. But he couldn't, much as he yearned. Better to return home with some measure of dignity.

"And what, Mr. Highstead? What did you intend to say?"

"Nothing, madam." Where was the coach?

"I don't think so." Her gaze darted like a bird. "Were you going to speak of the untimely death of your wife?"

Her tone was mild enough, but Robert felt as though she'd slapped him.

"Well?" she prompted.

The only sound in the cart was her even breath punctuated by the patter of rain against the canvas roof.

"If . . . if you will hand me my trunk, I'll be on my way. I'll never trouble you again. I apologize for my behavior while a guest in your home." His words felt thick in his mouth, his throat dry. How dare she!

He rose from his seat in the cart, struggling under the duress of his injuries. Isabelle grabbed his arm, drawing him back. He sank down in his seat. Her eyes locked with his. Try as he might, he couldn't look away.

"I know all about you," she said. "I was warned."

"I'm uncertain what you mean, Miss Lowell."

"Ah, but you do, Mr. Highstead. I know your wife, Cressida, died soon after your marriage. I know you haven't been the same since—"

"That's not true!"

"But it *is* true. Shall I explain?"

Robert's will fell away as her grip tightened on his arm. His world shrank to two things: the cadence of her voice and the renewed weight of his grief. Her words fell on him as persistent as the rain against the roof.

"I know you blamed yourself for her death, though I'm uncertain why. I know this was the reason you left your position at Oxford, why you were cut off by your family—"

"I wasn't cut off. Who told you all this? My brother?" To the best of his knowledge, she couldn't have read about Sida's death in a newspaper—John had done all he could to keep the loss private. No obituary. No articles.

"It matters not, Mr. Highstead. I know the truth."

He choked out, "If you know the truth, why are you telling me this now?"

Isabelle smiled at last. "Because I want you to understand I'm not the fool you took me to be." She released his arm. "Ah, here's the coach at last. I'll see to the cart."

The air was filled with the stomping and whinnying of excited horses, the splatter of wheels in puddles. Robert swung his legs out from the chaise carriage toward the ground. Away from Isabelle. In the minutes since they'd come to a stop, the storm had grown harder still. His eyesight blurred as he stared out at the teeming rain; his grief felt keener than the edge of a knife. Yet what upset him most wasn't her knowledge of Sida's death. It was her accusation he'd gone mad. *"I know you haven't been the same since."* Who would be, after the loss of a beloved spouse? But his upset was more than this. Isabelle's words had conjured his deepest terror: that he'd imagined Sida's return from the dead.

You didn't, he reassured. *Her ghost is real.*

Robert inhaled, willing his fears away. He stared down from the carriage. The muddy ground appeared almost as unwelcoming as Isabelle. *The sooner I leave here the better.* He imagined Sida alone in their rooms. Sida awaiting him.

He heard Isabelle grunt as she struggled with the chain for the cart bearing Hugh's coffin. The rain was a sheet of water, cascading from her shoulders. He knew he should help her, to maintain some show of normalcy even if his ankle was sore, his hands shaking. But he'd be damned if he'd reveal his distress. He'd been so good, so righteous for so long, his life so filled with promise. None of it had mattered. His decency hadn't protected his wife from death. Nor had it kept him at Oxford, or helped him write his damned second book. Neither had it obtained those daguerreotypes of Hugh reunited with Ada inside the glass chapel. It had only brought him to this water-logged place in the middle of a moor where a strange woman jeered him over his deceased wife while questioning his sanity.

Finally the coach stopped before them. A dark-hatted figure cried from the perch, "Coach to Shrewsbury. You here for it, madam?"

"The gentleman is," Isabelle shouted over the rain. "He'll need to change for the train to London. 'Tis a complicated situation though."

She explained quickly about the cart and the coffin as though she were discussing the transport of cattle, not a man's body. They must have come to terms, for Isabelle nodded and handed him a stack of coins with an effusive "much appreciated, good sir."

The coachman climbed down to take Robert's equipment and fasten Hugh's coffin cart. Once these were settled, Isabelle offered her hand.

"Come, Mr. Highstead," she said. "Let me help you to the coach."

And then she smiled for the third time since Robert had made her acquaintance. This time her smile was wide enough to reveal her teeth, which were even and white. Within her smug, satisfied smile, Robert saw the whole of his past three years compressed into one long moment of loss. Somehow this released something in him—something he'd pushed aside in the wake of Sida's return from the dead. Robert's hands clenched into fists, his blood beat in his ears. He'd never felt so livid. But instead of being distressed by his anger, he was grateful. The relief of no longer feeling sorrow was intoxicating.

Isabelle's smile slipped. "Are you well, Mr. Highstead?"

"Better than I've ever been, Miss Lowell." And he truly meant this.

"Come," she coaxed, her hand still extended. "Be careful, the ground is slippery. Wouldn't do to have you fall again. Then you'd be trapped here with me."

"Trapped here with me." He stared anew at Isabelle. God knows he didn't want that. Yet she seemed transfigured with an exceptional beauty, though this made no sense: grief had worked its weariness on her features just like it had on his.

The coachman called, "Is he coming or not? Weather's getting worse. Running late already."

"He's coming," Isabelle answered. Again, that smile—this time it appeared less certain. "Mr. Highstead, the coach shan't wait forever."

Robert swung his feet from the cart. His injured ankle dangled above the mud. So slippery, so dangerous . . .

"Trapped here with me."

The coachman snapped his pocket watch shut. "With this rain, better I go without the coffin. I promise to return tomorrow for it, madam. This mud too—"

"No! The coffin must travel today. The gentleman too." Isabelle's grasp on Robert's hand tightened. "Mr. Highstead, hurry! Have you gone mad again?"

Robert's anger flared even brighter and hotter, turning his senses keen, his sight sharp. His path became clear.

He released Isabelle's hand.

IV.

The coach for Shrewsbury left without Robert or Hugh's corpse.

"You fell on purpose," Isabelle accused, her face flushed with anger as she helped him from the mud. "Because I called you mad."

Robert couldn't argue. Once he'd let go of her hand, he'd taken a strange satisfaction as his leg twisted behind him, his shoulder slamming against the ground. The pain had seemed far away, along with its consequences for his return to London—Sida hadn't even entered his considerations. As he'd fallen, he'd watched Isabelle drop to her knees. Saw rain pool about her skirts, Isabelle's lips shift from that smug smile into a circle of dismay. And he'd been happy.

"I think I broke my ankle," he said.

"The ankle doesn't appear broken," Mrs. Chilvers announced. "Just sprained. We should fetch the doctor to be sure."

"No," Isabelle said. "I'll trust your judgment."

An hour after he'd missed the coach, Robert lay once again in Owen's bed in the stable house, the pain in his ankle softened by the morphia the housekeeper had given him. From the other side of the stable house, he heard the neighing of horses, the lowing of cows; they must have been brought in from the fields. Thanks to the morphia, Robert found he didn't care about anything, not even about his camera; Owen had set his equipment next to the door where anyone could jostle it. Even his abandonment of Sida to remain at Weald House didn't vex as it should. He supposed he could thank Isabelle for this—opiates were more powerful than anger.

"Since the ankle isn't broken, he can leave," Isabelle said; she'd been tapping her fingers against the door frame, as if she could hurry Robert's departure by a display of impatience.

Mrs. Chilvers frowned. "It's not a serious injury, but he needs to remain off the ankle. It'll take him at least three days until he can put weight on it. More if he doesn't rest."

"Three days!" Robert had never heard Isabelle so frustrated. "Are you certain?"

After Mrs. Chilvers left, Isabelle approached Robert.

"I was right about you," she said. "Only a madman would injure himself purposefully over an insult." Her face looked distorted, probably due to the morphia he'd ingested.

Morphia or no, Robert's rage returned full force. "Why did you say that about my wife?"

Isabelle recoiled. "About her death? Well, it's true, isn't it?"

"That was unkind of you!"

"Unkind . . . I consider myself to be very kind considering you attempted to break into my aunt's final resting place in the dead of night." Her eyes flashed with indignation. "Here's how I will be kind, Mr. Highstead. I will treat you as I would any stranger in need of aid. You will remain in this stable. You will be fed, nursed, and sheltered. Once you are sufficiently recovered in three days' time, you will leave here with my uncle's remains, which you can bury as you and your brother deem fit."

Isabelle rose from the chair, her purple bombazine skirts rustling. The sound seemed distorted and distant. Slow.

"Goodbye, Mr. Highstead. You won't be seeing me again."

"Wait!" Robert called out, his voice slurring as he gave way to the opiates flooding his blood. "You must tell me: Who told you about my wife's death?"

She wouldn't meet his eyes. "Wouldn't you like to know?"

Robert was too drugged to protest. He sank into a thick sleep. It was dreamless.

The next thing Robert remembered was someone cooing, "Are you awake?"

The voice was soft, feminine. Lilting. Broad-accented. Her tone revealed an edge of fear accompanied by defiance. The conundrum of emotions was enough to lure Robert out of his drug-induced doze.

He forced his eyes open and focused on a blur of gold hair and blue eyes.

"Grace. What day is it?"

"It's still Thursday. Twelfth of February," she replied pertly. "About five in the afternoon."

"Oh." He'd only slept a few hours. The scent of horse shit overlaid with the tang of almond reminded him where he was. Hugh's coffin. And then he remembered. *Sida. London. Home. Three days until he could return.* He wrapped his hands around his head. What had he done?

Grace sat in the same seat Isabelle had occupied earlier that day. She'd changed her clothes from the grey gown she'd donned for the study tour. Now wearing her maid's frock, she looked a girl barely more than sixteen. Her hands were cupped in her lap. They were reddened from labor. Not as bad as his.

"Here's clean clothes for you," she said, pointing toward a stack of folded fabric on her lap. "I fear yours are quite muddy, far worse than when you fell off Ada's Folly."

Suddenly Robert recalled the glass dome shivering and cracking beneath his weight. He'd forgotten about it in the rush of his departure.

"Did I damage the chapel?"

"I wondered if you'd ask about that." A quick smile. "Just a few cracks along the edge. Miss Isabelle said naught, so I doubt she noticed. Could have been far worse." She handed him the clothes, which were of a rich blue wool save for a black damask waistcoat and cravat. "If you'll give me your clothes, I'll have them cleaned. You can change beneath the covers—I shan't look."

She turned toward the door. Once he'd exchanged one set of clothes for the other, he pulled himself into a seated position against the wall.

"You can turn around," he announced.

"The clothes fit?"

He nodded.

"You feel better?"

"Somewhat." His ribs still hurt when he breathed; he coughed, protesting the cold air inside the stable.

"If you need morphia, bottle's over there on the mantel. I brought you a walking stick too. I thought you'd need it when nature calls."

The walking stick was carved of mulberry wood and tipped in gold—she'd taken it from Hugh's study. He didn't dare ask whose clothes he was wearing.

"How long have you been here, Grace?"

"An hour or so. Miss Isabelle ordered me to watch you until you woke."

"Like a guard?"

"Not exactly." Grace giggled, wrapping a long gold curl about her forefinger. "Imagine me, a guard! She doesn't want to risk you hurting yourself anew."

"How kind of her," Robert said dryly.

"Miss Isabelle is kind—you just don't know it yet." Grace released the curl. "You upset her."

"Perhaps. Thank you for the clothing. I should also thank you for sending Owen to find me last night after I fell."

"Pure luck." Her tone was lighter than her expression.

Robert cocked his head. "I wouldn't call that luck."

A flush spread across her face. "I won't insult you with a lie, Mr. Highstead—I know you followed me to Ada's Folly last night. But that's not why I'm here."

"Besides to guard me?"

"Besides to guard you."

Grace rose and pulled a chair against the door knob, effectively locking the room from intruders. Robert now noticed her hair was unbound about her shoulders, cascading like a river of gold; she'd let it down. Before he could mull this significance, she advanced toward him and unbuttoned her grey merino bodice far enough to reveal her chemise. Her small breasts pressed against the muslin, her nipples erect from the cold. Robert averted his eyes.

Grace sat beside him on the bed, her eyes warm with invitation.

"I need you to remain silent about what you saw at the chapel. Understand?"

Robert's head slowed. "About . . . the roses on the door?"

She nodded. "It's hard to explain. Nor am I allowed to. It's just that someone pays me quite generously to place them there. If anyone were to find out . . ."

"Miss Isabelle would sack you." This must have something to do with the pilgrims.

"Something like that." She placed her right hand on his thigh. Inched it upward. Perhaps it was the aftermath of the morphia, but Robert couldn't find the will to resist.

"If you help me"—her breath was warm against his ear—"I can help you. You want to look inside Ada's Folly, don't you? To daguerreotype it? I know someone who wants to go inside it too."

Robert pulled away. "I can't help you."

"Are you certain?" She met his gaze meaningfully. "Where's your camera?"

Robert pointed across the room. "Over there, next to the door. Inside the wood box."

Her eyes widened. "I hadn't realized how large it was. I can pose for you. Do you want me to set it up?"

"No! I'd prefer no one handle it but myself. It's quite fragile. Expensive."

"Very well. I'll ready myself . . ."

Grace used her free hand to release the final two buttons of her bodice. She pulled at the frayed ribbon lacing on her stays.

He grabbed her hands. "That's quite enough. I don't do this."

"Do what, Mr. Highstead? Don't you want me to pose for you?"

His tone grew cold. "If you knew what I usually daguerreotype, I don't think you'd care to."

She crinkled her nose. "You only daguerreotype churches?"

"No. I daguerreotype the dead. Corpses."

There. He'd said it without evading the truth—usually he used a euphemism such as "preserve a remembrance" or "secure their shadow."

Grace's mouth twisted into a grimace; Robert supposed she was too unworldly to have knowledge of his occupation.

"Why the hell would you do that?"

"Because Mr. de Bonne requested it. Because it brings comfort to those who have lost the ones they love. Because I'm skilled at it. Because it pays."

But this wasn't the complete truth, and in a day filled with falsehoods, Robert found himself craving honesty like air. Maybe it was the morphia, maybe it was a way to distract himself from Grace's unexpected display, but in the end it mattered not: Robert found himself telling her the history of his occupation.

He told Grace how it all began one night in a public house in Leadenhall Market soon after he'd left Oxford. Robert had been seated in a dark corner, drinking a whisky, staring at his miniature of Sida's eye. When a black-clad gentleman had laid a black-clad hand on his shoulder, Robert had welcomed him, wishing him to be Death himself. "Why so sad?" the gentleman asked, sloppy with drink. Robert answered with a passage from Ovid:

> "As wave is driven by wave
> And each, pursued, pursues the wave ahead,
> So time flies on and follows, flies, and follows,
> Always, for ever and new. What was before
> Is left behind."

"Strong words, my friend," the gentleman replied. "Perhaps I can bring you comfort." And then he'd drawn out his Catalogue of Possibilities. "These daguerreotypes preserve the past as memory, Mr. Highstead," he'd explained. "They keep our loved ones close." Robert had looked at the stillborn babies supported by black-cloaked figures, the alternate views of the departed, the family gathered around the corpse. Robert had seen such daguerreotypes before, but he'd thought them unnatural. This time though, instead of being repelled, he'd been intrigued. Not because he wanted to daguerreotype Sida—that narrow pine coffin had already been buried for some weeks—but for reasons he couldn't yet name.

Robert invited the gentleman to sit. He ordered a bottle of whisky and two glasses. The two men spoke, Robert evasively of his marriage and exile from Oxford, the gentleman, with expansive drunkenness, of his business prospects. He'd brought out a deck of cards. "If you pull an ace, I'll teach you how to use my camera; if not, you owe me a ha'crown. Deal?" When he'd splayed the cards across the table, Robert had felt a madness he couldn't turn from. By closing time, the gentleman had lost his business to Robert. Later, Robert learned the business bore debts the gentleman had yearned to be rid of, but it mattered not. Robert had found his vocation.

"You're shocked," Robert said when he finished.

Grace shook her head, but the blood had leeched from her cheeks. "Not shocked—drunk men gambling don't surprise me any. No, I'm confused. Why'd you do it?"

"I wanted to see what it was like to daguerreotype a corpse."

"I still don't understand."

His voice broke. "My wife had died. I couldn't imagine a life without her."

"What of your family? Couldn't they help?"

"I suppose. But I couldn't go home. You see, my wife had become my home." *My* locus amoenus, he thought, using Hugh's words. "I would have done anything to reclaim her. Somehow by taking daguerreotypes of the dead . . ."

I'd keep her with me always.

Unable to continue, Robert dropped his head into his hands. Now he felt worse than ever. Sadder. Angrier. The memory of Isabelle taunting him returned, along with his frustrated yearning for Sida. He couldn't even blame his confession on the morphia. The drug had worn off enough that his ankle throbbed with his every breath.

"My God, Mr. Highstead. What about those who still live?"

He raised his head from his palms. "You mean like Miss Isabelle and her glass chapel? You with those roses and the pilgrims?"

With his mention of the pilgrims, Grace's hand drifted back to her chemise, but the gesture seemed perfunctory. "Wouldn't it be nicer to make a daguerreotype of me instead?"

"I don't think Owen would appreciate that."

She gave a little giggle. "Owen?"

"Anyone can see he cares about you."

"Well, I don't care about him. Not anymore—he's a flirt. Besides, I've got something else planned for my future. Something better than fussing around here while Miss Isabelle weeps over Ada and Hugh." Her voice dropped to a whisper. "You won't say anything? About him or those roses?"

"I won't." He met her eyes. "However, there's something you can help me with. In exchange for my silence, of course."

V.

"I told you that I never wanted to see you again," Isabelle cried when Robert appeared at the library door. "How did you get up here? Someone must have helped you—they'll be sorry when I find out!"

Robert was breathing too heavily to reply. He was also taken aback. When Isabelle opened the door, she'd been holding a goblet of red wine in one hand, a handkerchief in the other. Her face was swollen and blotchy beneath her nest of plaits. He'd interrupted her weeping. Ever so briefly, Robert surged with sympathy. Then he recalled how she'd called him mad at the coach stand. His compassion fled.

"I'm not going to tell you who helped me," was his quiet but stubborn reply.

"Leave! Or I'll scream! I'll have Owen put you and my uncle on the next coach out of here, ankle be damned."

"Scream away then," Robert said, his jaw tight. "I refuse to leave until you tell me how you learned about my wife's death."

Isabelle folded her handkerchief deliberately. She set it inside a skirt pocket, as if her sorrow could be contained in it.

"Oh. That."

She turned to her tea and sat. The meal was arranged like it had been the previous evening, only tonight there was a platter of cheese with sliced ham instead of mutton and bread. She took a long gulp of wine followed by a forkful of meat.

Sensing her strange acquiescence, Robert staggered into the room. He collapsed into the chair closest to her, Hugh's walking stick still in his hands.

"Did my brother write you?"

Isabelle looked over her shoulder to meet his eyes; hers still glistened with tears. "No."

"Someone in Oxford?"

She took another sip of wine. Her hand shook.

"Well?" Robert pressed. "Aren't you going to answer?"

She waited until she'd finished chewing before replying. Her lips looked slick with grease beneath the candlelight before she wiped them with her napkin. Her voice was so low that Robert had to strain to hear.

"What does it matter how I learned about Cressida's death?" She rolled her eyes but he sensed her discomfort. "The truth remains as it was."

"What else do you know?" She couldn't know about Sida's family, could she?

"Beyond that she was dead?" She turned away from his gaze. "I heard she died under unfortunate circumstances. That you weren't as you had been before her passing."

"Mad, you mean." Robert's head grew hot again. Buzzing. "Once more, who told you this?"

In lieu of a reply, Isabelle rose from her meal, wineglass in hand. As she had the previous evening, she began to pace the length of the library, thus granting Robert the opportunity to examine the state of her grey merino gown. This one was nearly as shabby as the purple one she'd donned the night before. She wobbled slightly, as if the ground had gone soft. It was then he realized she was as drunk as a barmaid in Whitechapel.

Isabelle halted to face him. "How did she die? That's the one thing I wasn't told." She tapped her finger against her lips, like a child plotting mischief. "Let me guess. Did she die in childbirth like Ada?"

"No." He fought the urge to slap Isabelle's wind-roughened cheeks.

"Hmm . . . I recall you arrived here wearing black, like an undertaker. You're rather young to be a widower. She must have passed recently. Consumption? A fever? I must admit your situation surprised me when I first learned of it."

First learned of it? *She can't hurt Sida. It doesn't matter.* But it did—for whatever reason, Isabelle's knowledge of Sida's death had rendered him breathless with unease.

Robert closed his eyes to calm himself. Everything compressed to sounds: the dark hiss of winter rain against the shutters, the crackling of fire in the hearth. What he could have told Isabelle about his wife's demise could only be presented in images. The hotel room they'd chosen for their honeymoon, with its red-flecked wallpaper and cheap gilding. The red frothing her lips from internal injuries unknown until then; they'd eloped in spite of the beating she'd received from her uncle. Her cold fingers clutching at her breast, stilled mid-breath. Her bared legs thrust out from beneath her stained blue silk gown; by then, her blood had dried into a splatter of brown spots that bore little resemblance to the force animating a life.

After Sida had breathed her last, Robert had sat there for hours, his face covered by his hands, unable to move. Though the physician told Robert nothing could have been done to save her, it had brought no comfort. It had only renewed his grief. If he hadn't loved her, she might have lived.

But Robert confided none of this to Isabelle—how could he? She'd only call him mad again. Another rush of rage swept over his body: rage that life could be so capricious, rage that this woman mocked him with her grim existence, her resentment toward the pilgrims' veneration of Hugh. Rage that she'd made his time at Weald House so unpleasant. But he said nothing. Instead, he opened his eyes and stared at his folded hands. He'd clasped them so tight that his over-washed flesh had turned bone pale.

"My wife died three years ago." He forced a rueful smile. "I chose not to taint your sorrow with mine. After all, sorrow shared is sorrow multiplied."

"I see," she said dryly, setting her empty wineglass on the table. "Did they teach you to say that in Oxford?"

Robert's smile tightened. "Among other things."

Isabelle turned back to pick at her food.

"Aren't you going to say anything? Or are you too drunk?"

Her fork clattered against the plate. "You bastard! I'm not drunk. I'm sad. If you're whom you claim to be, with your never-ending mourning for your wife, you should understand. You should have compassion."

"You should have compassion too! You're not the only one grieving."

"You never back down, do you?" Isabelle flung her arms open. "Next you'll be haranguing me about Hugh's corpse and Ada's Folly."

"Very well. I'm not going to leave here until you let me daguerreotype him beside his wife."

"I knew you'd say that. You're just like the pilgrims, gnawing at a thing until you give way so they'd let you be. I suspect you're like them in other ways too." Her voice wavered. "They adore Hugh's suffering over Ada's death. The tragedy of his love for her. Like you with your— "

Despite his ankle, Robert lunged for Isabelle. She ducked nimbly away.

"I loved my wife more than anything in the world! Your uncle Hugh is dead. You inherited his estate. You can turn the pilgrims away anytime you like. Isn't that enough satisfaction?"

"No," she replied.

What Isabelle did next astonished Robert far more than her knowledge of Sida's death. Like Grace an hour earlier, Isabelle unbuttoned the collar of her bodice. Instead of revealing her chemise, she drew what he assumed was the key to Ada's Folly—he hadn't imagined it dangling between her breasts in the stable house. She fondled it, her fingers pale against the dark iron. The key seemed to absorb light from the room. Robert resisted the urge to grab it.

Isabelle met his eyes. "Weren't you a historian?"

"Before my marriage." Robert's neck prickled. "I'd written a book about Ovid."

Her tone turned pensive. "I've a brilliant way we can suit both our needs, Mr. Highstead. We'll make a trade."

Robert frowned. "I don't understand."

"A trade like people do in a shop. However, instead of trading shillings for goods, we'll trade what we most want. An exchange. It's really quite brilliant. I wish I'd thought of this earlier—it could have made our time together more productive." She leaned toward him. "Would you like to hear more?"

After a moment, he nodded.

"Very well . . ." She let out a long breath. "I'm not entirely without mercy. I comprehend your desire to bury Hugh beside Ada, and your need to prove his final request has been met. Hence, I'll give you the key to the chapel. I'll allow you to daguerreotype him there, and bury him beside my aunt—well, as soon as your ankle allows."

"Truly?" Robert didn't believe her.

"Truly."

She placed the key to Ada's Folly on the table between them. Tapped it once with her forefinger.

Wary, Robert leaned in. "What do you want in return?"

"I have a story to tell you."

How drunk was she? "What sort of story?"

"A story about my aunt Ada. You see, everyone knows about Hugh—the letters, the books, his study. The poems, the passions. But no one knows about Ada."

Robert scratched his head. "That's all? You want me to listen to a story?"

"The main of it. You'll also write her story down using all your skills as a historian. Then you'll publish it for me."

"Why not write and publish it yourself?"

"Because I'm not much of a writer, and you're a scholar who's been published. Because no one would believe me otherwise."

As she spoke, her face softened with sorrow, illuminating an unexpected motivation for her exchange. She wanted her aunt to live anew through her words, just as he'd yearned for Sida to live again when he'd become a daguerreotypist.

"I understand very well," Robert said, his chest tight.

She offered a grim smile. "I should warn you my story may take some time."

His sympathy soured. "How long?"

"Five nights, Mr. Highstead."

"Five nights! I haven't the time—I need to return to London." He pictured Sida alone in their room. Sida abandoning him. "Three nights. By then my ankle will have improved."

She waved away his words. "Five nights is what's required. We'll meet here every night at seven o'clock. If this doesn't suit . . ."

Isabelle rose from the dais.

"Wait!" Robert called. "I didn't say I *wouldn't* accept your offer. But given all that's occurred between us, why should I trust you'll honor it?"

"I can't think of a single reason. But I can think of many why you should accept my offer." She ticked off each on her fingers. "You'd rather not transport Hugh's corpse back to London. You yearn to make amends to your brother for your unfortunate marriage. You also want the satisfaction of fulfilling Hugh's final wishes and relieving your brother of his responsibilities toward me and this estate. If that's not enough enticement, I'll also reveal how I found out about your wife's death."

Robert wouldn't concede so quickly. "As part of our trade, I'd need you to pose beside Hugh's corpse inside the chapel as proof you were notified of your inheritance."

She blanched. "Wouldn't it be easier for me to sign a document?"

"Your uncle's terms. Not mine."

She shook her head. "This is an offer, not a negotiation. But that reminds me: as one of our terms, I'll need your camera—"

"My camera! It's expensive. Fragile."

"I don't care, Mr. Highstead. I need assurance you won't attempt to daguerreotype my uncle in the chapel before I finish my story." Her eyes swept over his ankle. "Let us be honest. You've proven as untrustworthy as I have, but I'm prepared to offer proof of my pledge. I'll even write up our trade as a document, which we'll both sign and consider binding."

She held out her hand. "Agreed?"

Robert stared at her hand. He hadn't written anything since Oxford—he couldn't bear to. If it had been one night, he'd find a way to manage.

But five? *Leave. Return to Sida before it's too late.* Then John's last words before he'd left Kent returned: *"You of all men should understand—Hugh only wants to be reunited with his wife. To go home to her . . . Can you really deny him this?"*

As Robert wrapped his fingers around Isabelle's, he fought the urge to recoil.

"Done! Until tomorrow night, Mr. Highstead."

"Tomorrow night, Miss Lowell."

He staggered to his feet, leaning on Hugh's walking stick. Just as he reached the door, Isabelle's voice rang out.

"One last thing, Mr. Highstead . . ."

Robert turned back, his ankle unsteady. As he waited for her to speak, the hem of her gown swayed, her head drooped. For a moment, he imagined her collapsing from the combined forces of alcohol and resentment. However, Isabelle was only gathering strength for a last riposte.

"I understand you saw the pilgrims this morning with their cockades of roses, clutching their copies of *The Lost History of Dreams.* They believe themselves blessed by their understanding of Hugh's last book. His last sacred offering of art and genius, inspired by Ada's death and all that. But there's one thing they don't understand about Hugh's poetry. One thing I do.

"You should know that *The Lost History of Dreams* isn't about dreams or 'chimera of wonder,' as the pilgrims claim. Nor is it about love. It's about the ambitions and hopes that plague us in life, which we end up regretting." She shot Robert a meaningful glare. "Now go."

VI.

Outside the library, Robert staggered down the corridor, his knuckles straining against the walking stick. He had no idea how long it took him to make his way downstairs. All he knew was how many steps it had taken: twenty-four down the stairway into the main hall, which he managed by grasping the runners as though they'd keep him from drowning. Next came sixty-five steps along the corridor into the kitchen, where Mrs. Chilvers offered a chair and a bowl of stew. He accepted both gratefully, along with the glass of ale she set out.

The housekeeper must have sensed his disquiet, for she didn't gossip for once. Try as he might, Robert couldn't stop shaking from anger. With every word Isabelle had uttered about his wife's death, he'd felt as though she'd stripped back layers of his soul, exposing his deepest secrets to light. He'd forgotten his love for Sida, his desire to do right by his brother, to Hugh. In that moment, Robert knew without a shadow of a doubt he hated Isabelle.

He asked for another glass of ale, his hands unsteady. *He hated.* If there was any time to drink, it was now.

Robert's meal was interrupted by the arrival of Grace, who refused to meet his eyes as she passed through the kitchen. She was followed by Virgil, who offered a friendly wag of his tail.

"Help Mr. Highstead, Grace," Mrs. Chilvers called out. "He can barely walk."

Grace did not turn around—so much for their agreement. She bore a new red ribbon in her curls, probably a bribe from one of the pilgrims. "I'll manage," he assured Mrs. Chilvers. And then he staggered off toward the stable, resting his weight on Hugh's walking stick as though he were a man of ninety instead of twenty-nine.

The food must have strengthened him, for Robert didn't find himself counting his steps to the stable. Hugh's walking stick was a good one: sturdy and of a length compatible with Robert's height. It easily navigated through the icy mud-slopped ground outside Weald House. Even so, once he arrived at the stable room, he collapsed onto Owen's bed, his forehead dotted with sweat.

It took him a moment to notice the traveling case containing his camera was missing. He immediately understood what Grace's errand had been, along with her reason for avoiding him. A folded sheet of paper lay in the center of the floor, accompanied by a new journal with pencils.

Robert cursed beneath his breath as he opened the letter.

Dear Mr. Highstead, Isabelle had written in a spidery hand. *I promise to take good care of your camera. Enclosed are the terms of our exchange. If you agree, please sign and bring it with you tomorrow night.* Another piece of paper followed the first, presumably the contract.

He crumpled it without reading, tossing it to the ground. How dare Isabelle take the camera from him without notice? Treating the fragile equipment like it was rags to be sold for ha'penny a pound?

His hands fisted. He pounded the bed, an ineffectual revenge. But then a cool, moist breeze caressed his brow. He *knew* what this meant: Sida was there.

For the first time since he'd left London, his chest relaxed, his mouth spread into a grin. She'd never appeared to him outside London—but she'd come to him. She'd somehow found her way. They'd never be parted.

"Come to me," he whispered into the shadows. "How I've missed you."

He twisted toward the coolness, unable to make out his wife's form. Yet. By now, Robert knew what to expect—he'd had plenty of time since Sida's death to grow accustomed to her ways.

It had been four months after Robert's dismissal from Oxford when he first sensed his wife's return; he'd just begun working as a daguerreotypist, had settled in Clerkenwell far from anyone who might know him. One morning when he was shaving he'd glimpsed Sida reflected in the mirror behind him. The gradual manner in which her face emerged on the glass surface resembled how those corpses emerged from the daguerreotype after he'd exposed the plate to mercury.

"*Don't turn around,*" she'd murmured against his ear, the air wet. "*Remember, happy are those who dare courageously to defend what they love.*" This had been the Ovid quote he'd used to convince her to marry him despite her uncle.

Robert had dropped his straight razor, nearly slicing his fingers. By the time he'd collected the razor off the floor, she was gone.

Afterward, he'd attributed his experience to being a product of his yearning and guilt, his reluctance to accept the finality of her death. The camera had nothing to do with his hallucination. It had only encouraged it. After all, hadn't he become a daguerreotypist to better understand her death? To hold on to her? He considered whether his inability to write was a factor—he'd invested so many years, so much ambition into his Ovid biography for naught. In those days he was more dependent on morphia to sleep than he would have wished. He'd also become gaunt from a lack of appetite. He told himself his experience was a solitary phenomenon, never to be repeated.

He was wrong.

Three days later, Sida returned, taking on a greater presence that could not be excused as the product of an unstable mind. He'd feel her cool hand on his thigh as he slept. Her soft lips on his brow, murmuring how she cherished him. She was real—or as real as a ghost could be.

Once Robert understood Sida had found a new life beyond the grave, joy replaced grief. Even so, he struggled to understand the circumstances. Sometimes she'd appear within a crowd as he was leaving a job to walk home, only to vanish when he drew close. Other times she'd disappear for days; just as he despaired of her return, she'd show up beside him in their marital bed, her body clammy with ephemerality and yearning. He spent hours at the library researching ghosts and hallucinations, trying to decipher exactly what his wife had become. His studies in Oxford spoke of lives before death, but not of life after death. Had Sida's soul continued on to another realm, leaving an etheric shell behind? Or was there something darker to blame, having to do with his sorrow that his camera had invoked? After much thought, Robert arrived at an equation a mathematician would appreciate: Love = Presence.

That evening in the stable house, Robert's patience was rewarded. The air soon felt wet with a rain that never came. A moment later, the shadowy presence of his wife stood before him. She looked as she ever did. Beautiful. Kind. Cherished.

"I found my way here, my sweet. It was ever so hard."

Robert pulled Sida onto the bed beside him, his chest releasing at last. He was careful not to embrace her too forcefully lest his arms pass through her. "All that matters is you're here."

"The more you love me, the more I live. You do, don't you?"

"I do. More than anyone in the world."

She gestured toward his temple. *"You're wounded. What happened?"*

"'Tis nothing. It'll heal." He brushed her ebony hair from her beloved face. Kissed her forehead. His lips met wet air.

Robert felt the clocks slow about them. A solitary candle flickered. Outside the stable house, a crow cawed on the roof beyond, its tone desperate. He sensed the bird's wings fluttering like shadows into the dusk. A single black feather falling to the ground beneath it, like that feather he'd found in Hugh's book.

He closed his eyes, yearning to will her into new life through the forces of love and memory. Several times he'd sworn he'd grown close. He'd felt her mouth become more than moisture beneath his lips. A subtle pulse when he'd kissed her jaw against the bluish veins that lined it. This time he couldn't bear to try.

Instead, husband and wife lay together as they usually did, Sida enveloped in his arms, Robert curled behind her, his breath the only sound in the room. Her chest was still as it ever was, her heart silent, her form clammy. Still, she was there, and that was all that mattered.

"Promise you'll never leave?" he said.

When Robert's ankle roused him in the middle of the night, Sida was gone. He didn't despair—she'd return. His face hurt from smiling.

"The more I love you, the more you'll live," he murmured into the air.

He rolled back onto the bed and reached for the morphia.

The Window of the Soul

Excerpted from *First Poems* by Hugh de Bonne, published 1831 by Chapman & Hall, London.

'We are so afraid of living
That we live as though dead,'
Fret the young Pilgrim whilst he tread
On step toward the Path unending
Ne'er denoting the Pain ensnaring
Whilst his solace went unfed
Subsumed toward a greater dread.

'What is Death but time granting
Life new wings?' proclaimed Queen Joan,
Great of age and crowned by Kings.
''Tis the Window of the Soul
For those Lives are short of Springs.'

And so Pilgrim knelt to royal Crone,
His heart becalmed by sage Tidings.

*

I.

On the first night of Isabelle's story, Grace fetched Robert from his stable room at the precise stroke of seven. "You know why I'm here," she announced.

"I do," Robert answered. With little to do all day but wait, he'd prepared himself for his encounter with Isabelle as much as he could. Despite the joy of Sida's arrival, his anxiety rose at the prospect of writing another book, even if it was a dictated one.

To calm his uneasiness, he'd written John, explaining he'd injured himself; hence, daguerreotyping Hugh in the glass chapel would take close to a week. He considered asking whether he'd informed Isabelle of his wife's death, but decided against it. He'd rather assume John had, for the other possibilities were too distressing. Robert also read further in the book of Hugh's letters, and managed to obtain copies of Hugh's books, including *The Lost History of Dreams*. If he was to write about Ada, it would help to know more about Hugh.

Once the clock drew close to six, Robert donned a second set of clothes Grace had brought to replace his mud-splattered ones. Though he hadn't shaved, he'd combed and oiled his hair. His face appeared new beneath the thick fuzz covering his cheeks and neck. He appeared older too—several new white bristles dotted his chin. He'd never grown a beard before. It seemed lazy, unfashionable. Anyway, when Sida was alive, she complained if he went too long between shaving.

The clothes fit Robert as though made for him. Unlike the previous set, these had grey-checked trousers and a double-breasted frock coat lined in crimson satin. It was a fine coat, though à la mode from years earlier—the waist was cut narrow, the sleeves tighter.

"French seams, silk lining," he imagined Sida announcing wryly if she'd been there. *"These are the clothes of a man who is confident of his worth. He knows their cost, but doesn't want to flaunt his wealth. It would be too vulgar. Thus their luxury is hidden within the lining, which cost more than most make in a year."*

Robert examined the label.

Couturier M. Courtois, aux Montagnes Russes, Paris.

The clothes had been Hugh's—Robert was convinced of it. Though they shared no blood, his cousin had been tall like him. Lean like him. It had been difficult to tell from his corpse, but now he knew. He crammed the journal and pencils Isabelle left into his pocket. After a moment, he set Sida's miniature beside them.

"Wish me luck," he'd whispered into the air once Grace knocked. "Remember I love only you."

"Come in!" Isabelle called from the other side of the door. At the sound of her voice, Robert's muscles tensed. He forced himself to turn the knob.

Inside the library, the overbearing scent of beeswax assaulted Robert's nose. A dozen candles lined the fireplace mantel, an extravagant abundance. In addition, two whale oil lamps were set on the long table where Isabelle took her meals. Robert had the sense she was overcompensating for the darkness that had left him stumbling during their first meeting two nights earlier.

Finally able to view the library in full, his eyes trailed around the perimeter of the room in the same way a warrior takes in the lay of the land before a battle. The spinet piano was where he recalled, beside the door to his left; now Robert noticed the cheap varnish, the ruched black velvet covering the instrument's legs from modest eyes. Beyond the piano, giving lie to the room's name, was one solitary wall shelved with books, their leather bindings coarsened with either neglect or overuse. Above the fireplace, a large mirror bore the tattered visage of a crape bow. A last wall was hung with tapestries: thickly muscled satyrs chasing unicorns, and wimpled maidens peering out of the tails of their eyes while they drew water from meandering streams. These tapestries fluttered in the cool air, granting them the uncanny appearance of life.

Just beyond the tapestries, Isabelle was seated like a queen on a dais beside the fire, her white hair coiled about her temples. Whether it was the light or happiness at the prospect of Ada's story being revealed at last, her expression was softer, less threatening, though Robert knew to distrust this impression. His cousin had also let off her half-mourning at last. She dressed in an indigo blue that made her sallow complexion appear to glow. Robert was surprised. Isabelle Lowell did not appear a harpy. However, neither did she appear a woman to be trifled with.

"Evening, Miss Lowell." He wondered where she'd hidden his camera.

Isabelle tipped her head in greeting after taking in his clothes and walking stick without comment. "Is your ankle better?"

"It's improved." He gripped Hugh's walking stick all the tighter, determined not to show any weakness. He'd let off the morphia, fearful of dulling his senses for Isabelle's story.

To steady himself, he stared at a tall portrait of a young ebony-haired woman. The painting dominated the wall farthest from them. Her eyes were soulful and radiant. Her wide lace sleeves sloped off her shoulders, suggesting the fashions of some twenty years earlier. A nut-brown sparrow sat on her raised hand. She looked too pure-hearted for the world, like someone who'd give bread to the poor out of joy rather than obligation. An angel even. Viewing that portrait reminded him of the first time he'd seen Sida six years ago, that he'd encountered someone who was an extension of God's inherent goodness. Robert stared. If the painting was of Ada de Bonne, it was difficult to see much resemblance to Isabelle beyond light eyes and broad cheek bones.

Robert tore his gaze from the portrait. "Is that your aunt?"

Isabelle nodded. "Painted in 1832, when she was eighteen, two years before she met Hugh. Four years before her death."

And then Robert thought of Hugh's corpse in the stable, the scent of almonds rising amid the flies buzzing and horse shit. The pilgrims circling Hugh's legacy, unaware of his passing. Five nights Isabelle swore she'd take to tell Ada's story—even if Hugh was embalmed, it was still a risky proposition. He should be buried beside Ada. Not resting in the company of horses and cows.

"Shall we begin, Miss Lowell?" The journal for her story felt bulky in his pocket beside Sida's portrait.

"Sit, Mr. Highstead."

She pointed to an olive-green chaise adjacent to her. Robert recognized the battered upholstered piece from the downstairs drawing room—she'd had it brought up for him. This kindness bothered him. It was easier to consider her an adversary.

Once he was arranged on the chaise, Isabelle took a sip of tea. No wine tonight.

"Before I start my story, I want to remind you of the terms of our contract. You are not to interrupt. You are not to contradict. You are not to comment. You are only to record what I say." Her tone was brisk, though Robert sensed unease tingeing it.

"Understood." He had little other choice.

"Did you bring something to write with?"

He pulled out the journal and one of the pencils she'd left him. Another tingle of nerves overtook him.

"Did you sign the contract?"

Robert drew the paper out from inside the journal. He'd smoothed the crinkled sheet to camouflage how much she'd upset him.

"Thank you," Isabelle said mildly.

She folded the contract into quarters before placing it inside a silver box on the mantel. Like a shopkeeper with an exchange; Robert half expected her to give a ha'penny in change.

Once she settled back in her chair, she spoke.

"Do you believe in ghosts?"

Robert gave a little start. She couldn't know. No one could see or hear Sida but him; the few times she'd shown in public, she'd drawn no notice.

"I believe the only thing that haunts us are our regrets." His tone was aloof.

She laughed softly. "That is an unsurprising sentiment coming from you. But I digress—I ask about ghosts because the story I'm about to tell is a ghost story."

This Robert had not expected. "Because of your aunt?"

"No. Because I believe love stories are ghost stories in disguise."

Robert folded his arms. "I don't follow your logic."

"It's quite simple. In speaking of love, we speak of intangible things. Like ghosts." Her tone turned uneasy. "Thus, that which we love haunts us with possibilities, with denied yearnings like a ghost. The closer we approach, the more they elude."

Robert still didn't understand, but he pressed his lips tight. He had no desire to prolong her story—under such circumstances, he could imagine her claiming to need more than five nights. Regardless, Isabelle fell into a silence so profound that he heard the wind rise outside, the shutters clang against the grey-stoned house. A flash of pain, of sorrow, colored her expression, unexpectedly softening her mien. Would she ever speak?

She raised a hand to her mouth to stifle a cough before reaching for her tea. Her throat was dry.

"Well then," she said once she'd taken another sip of tea. "Shall we begin our ghost story? It starts in this very house."

II.
The First Night's Story

All houses have a story to tell, Isabelle began. Some houses are akin to fairy tales, as many claim of Ada's Folly. Other houses are structured like poems, with rooms devoted to beauty but lacking in function. However, only a few houses offer ghost stories. They're built to be trampled by sorrow and loss. And that's what you'll find deep within the very walls and doors of Weald House: a ghost story begun from love.

Our ghost story begins before the first time Hugh de Bonne came to Weald House, and found all the intangible desires of his life—yes, the ghosts he sought—take on flesh in the personage of my aunt Ada. It begins before Ada learned of the flaw in her history that signified true happiness could never be. Indeed, our ghost story goes all the way back to Ada's parents, Lucian and Adelaide Lowell, whose lives prepared my aunt for the love Hugh would bring. You see, Lucian won Weald House in a hand of whist one cold night in November 1809 after finessing what had been deemed an impossible trump off of Sir Walter Sloane, whose family had owned the estate for generations.

It mattered not Lucian was only a boy of nineteen. Nor did it matter he was only the gardener's son. What mattered was that Sir Walter had underestimated Lucian, who was madly in love with Adelaide, the spinster daughter of the house ten years his senior; she'd made the mistake of brushing her lips against his downy cheek after she'd drunk too much wassail at Christmas four years earlier.

After that kiss, Lucian was despondent. Undereducated as he was, he was clever enough to know that gardeners' sons didn't marry the daughter of the house. The only property he owned was a hoe and a rake. The only knowledge he possessed was the planting times for Shropshire soil, and how to lure crows from trees. None of this stopped Lucian from yearning for Adelaide the way flowers yearn for rain.

He'd dally on the path between Weald House and his home, hoping to spy Adelaide driving her cart and pony. He stopped sleeping in on Sundays in favor of church. Instead of the mysteries of Christ, it was Adelaide he sought to worship. Lucian would arrive early to sit as close as he could to the Sloane family pew, praying to glimpse her bared wrist when she reached for her hymnal. When this grew insufficient, he'd feign faints to view the lace of her petticoats when she knelt in her devotions.

After six weeks of this, Lucian stopped plowing the field. After six months, Lucian grew thin as a shadow. And then one day he simply disappeared. No one questioned where he'd gone, for there was no time for it: because of the war with France, many had run off to seek their fortunes, leaving their loved ones behind to fulfill their duties.

Four years later, Adelaide had forgotten everything about the gardener's boy she'd kissed save he reeked of apples. Therefore she did not recognize Lucian on that February night in question when he arrived at Weald House attired like Beau Brummell himself. After an embarrassed introduction, he claimed to have become lost in the countryside en route to Wellington. Adelaide simpered like a girl when he kissed her hand. She giggled when he revealed his copy of *A Short Treatise on the Game of Whist*. (Unknown to Adelaide: Lucian possessed another pamphlet by the same author, this one on probability theory.)

"The book is by a Mr. Hoyle," Lucian explained in his most bewildered manner, "but I don't understand half of it. I was on my way to town to partake in a game with some very fine gentlemen who were to instruct me." He sighed the longest sigh possible. "'Tis not to be now, alas."

"Ah, my father plays whist! And he has two friends here for dinner at this very moment!" cried Adelaide, who didn't care if the handsome stranger was the devil himself as long as he didn't leave. "How fortuitous!"

"Very fortuitous indeed," Lucian replied. "Do you think it possible your father would be at leisure to suffer my company on a cold winter night? My name is Lowell—I doubt he remembers me."

Yes, her father was at leisure. No, he did not remember.

Several hours later Weald House had passed from Sir Walter to the gardener's son, who'd learned much during his four years away, which he'd spent in the army as well as places beyond. Suspicion was cast, but because whist was a gentleman's game, it was conceded that cheating could not be involved. Accompanying the property deed was the hand of Adelaide, whom Lucian had shyly pressed to marry ("to avoid uprooting her from her home," he claimed). Initially Walter refused to consider Lucian's suit at all, but Adelaide had grown strong-willed during her long years of spinsterhood—if her father was drunk enough to gamble away her security in a card game, she'd be damned if she was going to accompany him to a spider-filled cottage on the moor.

A month later, the two were wed in a ceremony Sir Walter refused to attend. The bride wore her favorite satin gown with a fine net overlay and clutched a bouquet of anemones despite them being out of season. The groom wore the Beau Brummell tailcoat with breeches that had impressed Adelaide that first night. After the wedding, these clothes were relegated to the back of the wardrobe, along with the airs he'd acquired while away.

Lucian never touched another card deck, for he had no need—he'd won all he'd ever desired now that he'd gained Adelaide. To his delight, their marriage was all he longed for. Because she was so far above him in every way—an angel, he called her—he worshipped her in the manner he'd desired all those Sundays at church. And worship her he did: Adelaide had hair black as night; Adelaide had skin white as stars. Most miraculous of all, Adelaide loved him in return, the gardener's son who'd managed to win her through a hand of whist. Her years alone had taught her that love given purely was worth tenfold over a per annum of two thousand pounds.

The couple spent their mornings lying on their bed bathed in light even on rainy days. Their evenings were filled with simple pleasures: hearty meals, good music—Adelaide possessed the voice of an angel—and endless conversation.

Adelaide and Lucian. Lucian and Adelaide. No one else existed in their world but the other. But even the most blissful union cannot avoid disappointment. Despite Lucian's most assiduous worship of Adelaide, her womb remained barren of fruit. Alas, this led to the creation of Weald House's first ghosts.

Adelaide had married the gardener's son initially because she yearned for children—love was an unexpected consequence. Though she'd grown up surrounded by brothers and cousins, the years had called them away to places she only knew of from Sir Walter's map book in the library: London, Edinburgh, Paris, Milan, Rome. As time passed, their letters had dwindled, leading to isolation for poor Adelaide. Yes, Sir Walter could have sent her abroad, but she was his last child at home and the image of her late, much-mourned mother, with the same long ebony hair and white hands. Until that fateful whist game, Adelaide had resigned herself to a solitary existence nursing her father's gout. But now that she was a wife, hope rose hot and furious. A baby to suckle at her breast! A child that would reflect the devotion she bore for Lucian!

Each month her hopes were dashed when the inevitable arrived. Each month her tears were plenteous enough to water the garden Lucian had once borne responsibility for.

By the time three years of marriage had passed, Adelaide had turned ashen-cheeked, her hair shot with white.

"What am I to do for you?" Lucian asked one night—by now their shared evenings had become forlorn of song and conversation. "If you stay this way, you will die—perhaps not a death of the body, but a death of your soul. I can live without a child, but I cannot live without you."

"I cannot live without you *and* a child," Adelaide replied. And then she spoke the words that made her soul pang with fear. "There's one thing we have yet to try, beloved. I've heard it whispered in the village that if you plant a rosebush under the full moon . . ."

Her words drifted into an anxious silence. After all, she was suggesting what some called superstition, and others called worse. A century earlier maids had been burned for similar charms; even now, in the enlightened year of 1812, Adelaide feared for a servant to overhear her words. But she could speak to Lucian with her eyes. And speak she did.

Lucian met her eyes. Lucian understood. After all, he'd been raised a gardener's son.

That next full moon, Lucian didn't plant one rosebush. He planted *twenty*, all of which he'd managed to cultivate from the finest stock Shropshire could yield. He gathered the bloody rags from Adelaide's last round of courses, which he'd swiped from the laundry. He planted the rags beside each rosebush, and covered them with mulch. By then it was the end of February, and it had been a fair February too: warm and sunny yet moist with the promise of an early spring.

Lucian knew the rosebushes would flourish under such circumstances. And flourish they did: by the time the roses bore their first blood-red flowers in June, Adelaide's stomach protruded enough that the servants gossiped she was carrying twins. They were wrong. She was carrying triplets—two boys who were strangled by their cords, and a girl. Before she breathed her last, Adelaide named her daughter Ada.

Thus were three ghosts added to Weald House's history.

Upon receiving news of Adelaide's death, Lucian took one look at his daughter. When he saw Ada bore her mother's milky skin and dark hair, he knew he'd never stop mourning. He ran to the rose garden screaming until his lungs gave out. He yanked the bushes by their roots, twining their long briars about his arms, thinking all the time how these arms would never embrace his beloved again, that these hands would never caress her dear face. He welcomed the sharp sting when the first thorn punctured his flesh—pain was easier than sorrow—and then wrapped the rest about his chest and neck, twisting them tight. When his blood soaked his shirt, he trampled the soft, fragrant blossoms beneath his heels until all that remained was their perfume. He sowed handfuls of salt into the soil to ensure nothing would ever grow. And then he left, vowing never to set foot in Weald House again. Five years later, his corpse was found on the moors beneath a cluster of crows.

Before his disappearance after Adelaide's death, Lucian wasn't completely senseless in his grief. He'd written two letters. The first was to his solicitor in Birmingham. The second accompanied the deed for Weald House:

> *As of today, the Seventh of October in the Year of our Lord 1813, I am Dead of Soul and soon shall be Dead of Body. In Anticipation of this Event, I pray you honor the Claim of my Sole Descendent, my Daughter Ada to all of mine Estate. Whoever finds these Documents shall serve as her Guardian until she reaches Her Majority on the Sixth of October 1834, until which you shall be Compensated with a per annum of Two Hundred Guineas.*
>
> *I pray you protect Ada well, and let her know her parents loved too well.*

And so Weald House collected its fourth, but not final, ghost.

It was the scullery maid, Margaret, who found the letter and served as Ada's first guardian. Though Ada was a scrawny infant, the sixteen-year-old Margaret did her best to provide her with a decent wet nurse and affection. The promise of wealth made Margaret senseless as a doorknob; by the time Ada reached her third birthday, the maid was found drowned in a wash bucket of suds—she'd knocked herself unconscious while dousing her hair with perfume. Ada's next guardian fared slightly better. Wilhelm was the elderly butler who liked children well enough but found Ada lacking in vigor—she'd turned from a scrawny infant into a puny child prone to sniffles and aches. To remedy this, Wilhelm took her for long walks on the moors no matter the weather. This led to his undoing when they were caught in a freezing sleet one January afternoon. A month later, he'd succumbed to the pneumonia that many deemed the inevitable fate of old age.

By then, Ada was eight years old—old enough to remember Wilhelm's kindness, and that his snowy hair smelled of fried onions and tobacco—and I was barely three, for I'd just been brought to Weald House after my parents, who'd been distant cousins to Lucian, passed from cholera. Though

I was too young to understand, I know Ada mourned Wilhelm as much as a child is capable. By then she'd learned the tragic history of her own parents—alas, Adelaide and Lucian were only a grave stone to be visited in the Kynnersley churchyard. However, Wilhelm had left her with more than he had taken. He had taught her to read, opening the world to her. Being of German descent, he had given her a copy of the *Household Tales* by the Brothers Grimm in spite of the belief that these coarse stories were not meant for children. Regardless, this book taught Ada that families were not comprised of a solitary girl with a toddler and servants in a large dark house haunted by ghosts. Wilhelm also introduced her to the classics of Ovid and Virgil, which revealed a sunlit abode to Ada beyond the moors.

By the time Ada reached her fourteenth year, I'd witnessed her go through six guardians, most of whom never lasted beyond a year. Even then she seemed hewn from stardust and sorrow. Most mornings Ada's face was the first sight I'd see when I awakened; she'd be seated at the foot of my bed with a mug of warm milk. Though our family ties were as cousins, she insisted I address her instead as aunt. "Because I am older than you," she explained. We'd spend rainy afternoons sewing clothes for my dolls, and evenings reading from Wilhelm's books. She was patient. Kind. Clever. I loved her like the mother I wished I'd had.

As for Ada's guardians, though their fates varied, each brought gifts to her, like a fairy at a christening. From Madame Clarice, the widowed piano teacher in the village, Ada discovered she took after her mother with a talent for music. (Madame Clarice was forced to return to France when Ada was twelve.) Verity the cook and her husband, Maurice, taught Ada to garden, thus leading to the resurrection of the rose garden—turned out Ada was the gardener's granddaughter after all. (Verity and Maurice passed when Ada was fourteen after Verity poisoned the soup by mistaking one mushroom for another; luckily Ada had refused lunch because of a queasy stomach.) From Reverend Smallsworth, the rector who'd yearned for Ada's two hundred guineas to become a missionary in India (where he promptly dropped from dysentery), Ada gained a pet sparrow. She'd discovered the baby bird beneath a rosebush one morning where it must have fallen from a nest. Smallsworth taught her how to care for it, which led to another gift for Ada: a friend.

The sparrow became Ada's most constant companion besides myself. It remained unnamed—after all it was a feral creature, just as some claimed Ada to be—and slept on a perch beside her bed. During the day, the sparrow remained near Ada, hopping from one hand to the next. Though I was fond of it too, its loyalty was to Ada, not me. It was just as well, for soon after I turned nine, I was sent to school, leaving Ada alone at Weald House save for servants and guardians.

You must imagine Ada at this time in her life. She was beautiful, a gifted musician, and the wealthiest girl in her shire, for before his disappearance, Lucian had appointed a solicitor in Birmingham named Watkinson to manage Ada's affairs. Because of her peculiar situation, Ada was judged in need of masculine guidance. In addition, the constitutional weakness Wilhelm had sought to remedy had intensified with age. Ada was akin to expensive porcelain, and as fragile. She spent too many days on her chaise recovering from mysterious ailments. Given how unpredictable her guardians had proven, a husband was deemed more reliable to bring structure to Ada's life. Hence, marriage was recommended *tout de suite*, even before her majority was reached at twenty-one.

When Ada turned eighteen in 1831, Watkinson arrange for a portrait to be painted, a full-length oil revealing Ada at her most luminous, with her long dark hair and pale face, accompanied by her sparrow on her hand. The portrait was titled *La Fille Solitaire—The Lonely Girl.* I was home for school holiday while she posed; I recall the scent of linseed oil in the library, her embarrassed silences when the artist flirted with her. Afterward, I imitated the artist's obsequious manner to make her laugh. Once the portrait was exhibited at the Royal Academy of Art, suitors arrived at Weald House as plenteous as those who called on Penelope during Odysseus's absence. Their attentions accentuated Ada's isolation, for she understood they only wanted her beauty and fortune, not her heart. None of these fancy gentlemen saw her for who she was: a girl who'd spent her life alone and sickly. Instead, she was a princess trapped in a house on the moors. She was to be rescued. Conquered.

Ada refused all of their proposals.

A year later, she turned nineteen. By then the frenzy over the portrait had calmed, and Watkinson again tried to find her a husband, this time arranging for a series of soirees with gentlemen who would have married her sight unseen because of her wealth. During these endless dinners with their courses of soup, fish, cheese, and empty compliments, Ada used breaks in conversation to slide beneath the table, hoping no one would note her absence. Later, she'd confide to me, "At least the soup was good." If a suitor was forward enough to call at Weald House, Ada found other ways to resist.

She'd make a show of offering tea and then free her sparrow in the drawing room, taking silent pleasure in the havoc wrought. No one returned.

And so the wealthy orphaned girl who lived in the house on the moors remained unwed and unloved by all save for myself. However, Ada was not unhappy: if longing was memory, and memory invited ghosts, she was never alone. On rainy days, she felt the presence of her mother seated beside her on the piano bench, like the benign spirit conjured by Aschenputtel's hazel tree from Wilhelm's book. Other times, Ada sensed her father in the rose garden, his scarred hands smoothing the soil where she'd trod. Of all her guardians, the only one who ever returned was Wilhelm, who'd been as close to a grandfather as she could have wished. She'd smell his onion-laced breath, the pungency of tobacco. And, if I am to be honest, sometimes I sensed him too.

Ada resigned herself to a life of contemplation with her music and sparrow. However, it was already too late: soon after her twentieth birthday, she was well on her way to becoming a ghost herself. Love will do that to a girl.

III.

Robert's hand halted, unable to bear the feel of the paper against his skin. Isabelle's words made him too aware of all he'd lost. The paper in the journal was an expensive textured stock, but he took little pleasure in it. His handwriting looked unfamiliar. Distant. The memory of his abandoned book returned. *"Happy are those who dare courageously to defend what they love."* Ovid. Poetry. Sida . . .

Isabelle's low throaty voice interrupted his reverie. "You've stopped writing. Is there a problem, Mr. Highstead?"

The pencil snapped in Robert's hand.

He glanced down with a start: a thin scratch traversed his palm. Isabelle recoiled with something that would be called concern in another woman. But she wasn't another woman—she was Isabelle Lowell.

"You should wash that," she said, reaching for his hand. "I can ring for water."

"It's nothing." He pulled away; he'd be damned if he'd reveal any weakness. Anyway, he didn't dare say more, recalling the terms of their contract: *"You are not to interrupt . . . You are only to record what I say."*

Robert pulled his cuff over the scratch and drew another pencil from his pocket. "Shall we continue, Miss Lowell?"

"Where did I leave off, Mr. Highstead?"

"You'd said 'Love will do that to a girl.'"

This time as Isabelle spoke, Robert noticed her words seemed less confident than when she'd begun.

* * *

The morning Ada fell in love with Hugh de Bonne started off as a usual day. It was a Tuesday in early March, the weather not dissimilar to that when Lucian had planted those rosebushes for her mother twenty years earlier: moist and sunny and warm. The snowdrops had already finished, but the crocuses and anemones were still plentiful.

Ada awoke in her room, which adjoined the rose garden downstairs. It was not a day I witnessed, for I was at school; regardless, I know of it as though I was there. Once she found her way to the dining room for her usual morning tea, Ada was joined by her current guardian, a plump-cheeked, high-bosomed widow bearing the unexpectedly grand name of Missus Dido, a lady from the village who'd reluctantly agreed to the position because she had married her three daughters off brilliantly; hence, she needed the guardian's per annum to pay off their respective Seasons. After Missus Dido presented her obligatory lecture du jour about the role of a landed heiress in society ("to aid the less fortunate, to marry to improve her position"), Ada retired to the library, where her piano awaited. After three hours of ecstatic practice—her usual when she was feeling well, plus she was working on a tricky Beethoven sonata—she had more tea in the kitchen with the cook, with whom she was very fond of playing cards, especially *trente et un*. Finally, Ada fetched seed for her sparrow, who was beckoning to go into the rose garden.

It was the sort of day that made Ada feel as though nothing bad could ever happen, though so much already had. She inhaled the moist air, anticipating the arrival of spring, as she gathered a handful of blood-red anemones. And what a sky! It bore nary a cloud save for a grey swirl that seemed to shift according to an unfelt wind. Rain would come soon, she decided. Best to take advantage of the weather while it lasted. It was still early enough in the season that the roses remained dark-thorned and leafless.

Covering her morning gown with naught but a shawl, she ran into the meadow beyond the rose garden, her sparrow flying beside her, the anemones scattering from her hands. That last morning before love entered her life, Ada's soft leather boots flew against the wet grass, so supple from melted snow, her heels slipping in a way that was vaguely pleasurable because of the unpredictability. Her limbs felt uncommonly strong for once. Yet as she ran, she had the sense she was running from the adulthood encroaching upon her, for Missus Dido's lectures had wormed their way into her against her will.

Ada had scarcely settled in her usual seat, a grey stone bench beside a yew tree inside the rose garden, to toss seed to the sparrow. In many ways, she was still like a child despite her age. But that day her hand stilled for reasons she could not name.

A shiver traced her spine as she looked over her shoulder.

A man stood in the meadow she'd just run through. He was too far away for his features to be distinguishable. Regardless, she could tell he wasn't from the village. The wasp waist of his coat and checker-patterned trousers looked of the city. (Ada had learned much from her suitors.) There was something about the man's posture that suggested the taint of another place. He walked with his head cocked toward the sky, as though pulled by an invisible thread. His stride was quick though uneven. As he drew closer, Ada saw he bore a walking stick.

Ada pursed her lips. Another suitor. It had been some months since the last one. Well, she'd show him.

She straightened herself on the bench. She whistled to her sparrow. The bird settled on her shoulder, nipping at a strand of hair that had come loose from the plaits she slept in.

"Who's there?" she shouted.

Silence. Perhaps the gentleman hadn't heard, with his head in the clouds.

"Hello!" she tried again. "You're strolling on private land, sir."

Still no sign of acknowledgment. And then it happened, the moment that would change Ada's life forever.

The gentleman's head whirled toward her. "Shush."

She stood, sending her sparrow into the air. "This is not a right of way, sir."

"Shush," he said again.

And then their eyes met across the garden just as he stepped toward her.

He wasn't as old as she first judged, perhaps fifteen years her elder. His hair was the color of an oak in autumn, coiffed longer than worn in the village. It was softly waved about his brow. Though clean-shaven, his temples revealed a smattering of grey and a faint scar. He was harmonious enough of feature, though he bore sensitivity within his hazel eyes as well as a brash confidence. For some reason this infuriated Ada.

She cried, “How dare you—”

He waved her off, pointing at the sky. “Did you see that?”

She looked up. Light dazzled her eyes. “I don’t see anything.”

“It’s beginning now.” The gentleman’s voice was honeyed, as though from a faraway land; again, she decided he didn’t seem quite of this world. Her stomach fluttered like it had been invaded by moths. “You’re fortunate to be here. This is a rare event.”

“How so?” Her anger cooled as her curiosity quickened.

He pointed upward. “That cloud? The grey one?”

She rolled her eyes, but the gesture felt half-hearted. “It’s going to rain.”

“It’s not what you think,” he said, grinning as though clutching a secret. “You’ll see soon.”

Despite her intentions otherwise—she’d thought to flounce inside for Missus Dido—Ada sank back on the bench. Her sparrow returned to her shoulder. She shifted when the gentleman sat beside her, his chest rising and falling in silent expectation.

How beautiful it all was! How alchemical! They sat there for some moments, watching the sky darken and the wind pitch as though the world was coming to an end in the most fantastical manner. Ada squinted into the distance, shivering. Yet she was not afraid. How could she be, with the trees quivering with subtle rhythms, the air pulsing with life? The handsome stranger seated beside her? She had the sense of waiting all her years for this impossible moment, that Fate had wrapped its fingers tight into her arm, and would drag her along whether she allowed or not.

“I’ve traveled miles to see this,” the gentleman said in a tone hushed with wonder. “It’s like watching souls in flight.”

“Souls?” Ada tightened her shawl. Her sparrow hopped to her lap.

He nodded solemnly. “Well, birds are the embodiments of souls.”

“This makes little sense.” Ada wasn’t fanciful in that way despite Wilhelm and his books.

“How do I explain this?” He shifted his walking stick from one hand to his other. “I’ve read Egyptian tombs were decorated with ibises to guide those who had passed into the next world. In ancient Rome, priests believed they could predict the will of the gods by watching birds in flight. Papists still consider the holy spirit to appear in the form of a dove." He stared into the distance. "Perhaps it's pagan of me, but I quite agree. Birds act as the eyes of the world. Like souls who see everything." He stood, shaking his lame leg. "They're nearly here."

"Who is?" Ada had to shout to be heard over the gathering din. Her sparrow flew off, alarmed.

"*Columba palumbus*—wood pigeons. I've never seen them migrate in such a mass before. Come!"

The gentleman grabbed Ada's hand and yanked her to her feet; she didn't pull away. Shadows fell, heavy and relentless. The sky grew leached of light as though a solar eclipse was upon them. And then she saw what he'd spoken of: thousands upon thousands of pigeons, all far larger than her sparrow, who now seemed a puny vulnerable thing just as Ada felt herself to be, all gathered as a mass in the sky.

It was terrible. It was wonderful. Grey and ebony and striped of feather, the pigeons drew together then apart, amorphous of shape as they performed ever-shifting, ever-changing groupings. Ada felt the gentleman's warm presence beside her. The press of his hand against her palm.

The wind from the pigeons' flapping wings whipped Ada's cotton skirts against her legs, her shawl from her shoulders. She could not see where her sparrow had flown to, but there was no time to look: the first pigeon dipped down, fluttering about her face, and then a second. Though they did not alight on her—the birds were far too plump for that—Ada flailed her arms in panic.

"Oh!" she cried. "Oh!"

"They won't harm you. I'd wager they're going to land over there," the gentleman hissed over the roar, pointing to a large oak with his stick. "Come! I'll protect you."

He set his arms around her shoulder, guiding her into the meadow in time to watch the birds' arrival. The gentleman was right: the pigeons settled on the oak tree in clusters of ten and twenty, one above another and beside each other, cooing and clucking, their feathers shuddering like molten pewter as they shifted to make room for more. They appeared a shimmering mass of life, as unsettled in rest as they had been in flight. Now Ada saw there were dozens—no, *hundreds*—of pigeons on every branch. Her breath caught in something that went beyond wonder. How would the tree bear it?

The answer to this question came as abruptly as the birds' arrival. A giant crack sounded. The thickest branch of the oak splintered off, overwhelmed by the weight of the wood pigeons. But the branch did not drop to the ground. Instead it did something far more astonishing. Ada watched, open-mouthed, as the branch lifted into the sky, pulled by an army of pigeons. Their claws dug into the bark. The branch flew higher, closer, darker. But even the valiant effort of seemingly thousands of wings could not defeat gravity. An unearthly cry spread across the moors as the branch crashed to the ground, crushing hundreds of birds beneath it.

The last thing Ada recalled was the echo of her scream. When she next opened her eyes, there was blue sky above her. Spots danced before her eyes, grey and black and white. They certainly weren't wood pigeons. She was gasping for air.

"I'm so sorry." The gentleman—she'd recognize his plummy voice anywhere. "She seemed fine, and then . . . Well, it was a shock." Who was he speaking to? Not her, that was for certain. "I feel quite terrible. I should have insisted she take shelter inside, knowing what was to occur."

"Thank you for your concern, sir," Missus Dido replied. Her tone was as supercilious as ever. "Your attendance is no longer required, Mr. . . ."

"Mr. de Bonne," the gentleman said. "Hugh de Bonne."

"You're not from here." Interest colored Missus Dido's voice. "You're French, aren't you? An aristocrat perhaps?"

"French by birth. I've resided in England for most of my life, though I've no family of my own. I was on my way to Herne Bay."

Missus Dido fluttered her lashes at him from behind her spectacles. "You're awfully far off course. That's all the way south in Kent."

"I was following the pigeons as they returned from their migration. This lady is your daughter?"

"No. I'm Miss Lowell's guardian, Missus Dido Martin. She's an orphan. Her parents—"

Breathless or no, Ada couldn't listen to another recitation of her unfortunate past. Knowing Missus Dido's salacious love of detail, she'd describe Adelaide and Lucian's ill-fated love before inching her way to Ada's present with details of every doomed guardian along the way.

"Excuse me," Ada wheezed, fighting a fresh round of coughing. "H-help me."

"She's awake!" The gentleman, whom she now knew bore the aristocratic name of Hugh de Bonne, helped her upright, murmuring soothing sounds all the while. He handed her his handkerchief, which she used to cover her mouth as she coughed. Spots of blood blossomed against the fine white linen like anemones in the snow, but Ada barely paid mind. She recalled the tree limb, how enormous it looked when it rose into the sky. The darkness towering over her like a fist . . .

And then she looked into Hugh de Bonne's eyes. She recognized something in him she knew in herself, though she did not know what it was called then.

This glimpse of familiarity was forgotten as she remembered.

"Where's my bird?"

Missus Dido said, "Come, Miss Ada. Let us help you inside."

"Where is it?" She whistled. The effort made her dizzy.

"Was it a sparrow?" Hugh asked, his eyes warm with sympathy. Later, he'd tell Ada that he'd never felt so protective of anyone as he did of her in that moment.

"Yes. I'd tamed it." More coughing as she struggled for breath. "I've had it for several years. It's the sweetest thing . . ."

Hugh's eyes darted into the rose garden beyond the meadow. Toward the stiffened mass of bloodied brown feathers trapped inside the briars.

Ada howled, for she understood her oldest fear had come to light: her sparrow had left her, just as her parents had left her, and so on along with her guardians. Even if she married as Watkinson pressed, she'd always be alone.

"I'm sorry, Miss Lowell," Hugh said. "So very sorry." He took his handkerchief from her to wipe her tears.

He gave a start at the blood adorning the linen.

"She's cut her mouth, Missus Dido. Let me bring her inside."

Missus Dido whispered, "It's not that, Mr. de Bonne . . ."

"What is it then?"

She shook her head. "I shan't speak of it here. Once we're inside, I'll give her draughts. That'll settle her."

As Hugh and her guardian spoke, Ada felt very far away: there she was, lying in the crocus-covered grass on the first nice day of the year after seeing a marvel that was never to be repeated in her life. And now her sparrow was gone, and she could not stop sobbing or coughing.

"This is her residence?" Hugh asked Missus Dido. "I'll carry her."

"Yes, sir. There's a door beyond the rose garden to her chamber."

Once Hugh handed his walking stick to Missus Dido, he draped Ada over his shoulder. She felt his heart pulsing against hers, his arms resting along her spine. How warm he was! How welcoming! Without thinking, she curled her fingers with his for the first time, but not for the last.

Once she was in her bed, Ada didn't refuse Missus Dido's offering of laudanum. Hugh remained by her side. As the drug took hold, Hugh and her guardian's conversation wove into a braid of buzzing too distant to unravel. Ada still wept for her sparrow, but something new came over her—something unexpected. She felt a kinship with Hugh de Bonne, mad as it was. It made little sense with all that occurred, but there it was. Lying there, she still sensed his touch radiating from where her body had pressed against his. He'd felt strong. Concerned. Ada already knew more than she wished of the world's ways because of her inheritance. Her suitors had arrived bearing flowers and promises she knew to distrust. Even the kindest of her guardians was only there because of the per annum.

For the first time in her life, Ada sensed she'd met someone who'd give to her rather than take. The knowledge surprised her, like opening a door to a room she never knew existed.

A wild happiness grew within her, as tangible as water, and as warm as fire. It twisted up like a tree twining toward the heavens, the roots digging deep within her soul. She'd never felt such a thing before—not in all the years with her guardians, nor during the months where suitors had courted her for her fortune, or in the hours she'd spent alone with her sparrow at her piano. She loved.

But then Ada heard the words that made her realize complete happiness was not to be trusted. Try as she might, she could never avoid the ghosts surrounding her.

"I've noticed your ward," Hugh whispered to Missus Dido, "is a consumptive. Does she know?"

IV.

With this, Isabelle spoke no more. Robert looked up from his journal to find her seated just as she had been at the beginning of their audience: her white hair coiled about her head, the hem of her indigo blue dress draped along her feet. Her long hands trembled as she reached for her teacup, set beside her on a small round table. Finding the cup empty, she refilled it from a silver teapot that was probably a remnant from earlier days, when Weald House wasn't overtaken by ghosts and loss. As she drank deeply, Robert sensed she yearned to contain her emotion.

He glanced up at the clock above the mantel: he'd been listening to her for just over an hour. More importantly, he'd been writing all that time. For some reason, once he'd snapped the pencil, something thawed in him. Though the words he'd set down had come from Isabelle's mouth instead of his brain, he'd become lost in the transmittal of words to paper. He'd forgotten how it felt, how alluring the act of writing could be, how encompassing. While he was writing, he'd even forgotten the disappointment of his abandoned book.

While Isabelle had related Ada's story, Robert had grown far from his injured ankle, Hugh's corpse in the stable, his yearning for his ghost wife. Even the loss of his camera didn't distress like it had. He'd sensed the years fall away, the rose garden at Weald House blooming anew with spring's bounty, the birds fluttering like a storm. He'd even felt the presence of Ada as though her portrait across the room had become flesh and bone. Yet he was troubled. "*Only a few houses offer ghost stories*," Isabelle had said. If he hadn't known better, he'd think she was taunting him.

Four more nights to go. He was uncertain if he was exhilarated or uneasy.

Robert raised his gaze to Isabelle as she sipped her tea. Her silence felt charged. Volatile. He didn't dare break it, remembering their contract.

Isabelle drained the teacup, set it down. She met Robert's eyes with a frank sorrow that startled him; again, he was surprised by sympathy. He waited for her to speak, to give some sort of signal.

Was he to leave? Or had she more to say?

Without another word, Isabelle glided out of the library.

"Thank you for helping me downstairs," Robert said to Owen a half hour after Isabelle's abrupt departure; Owen had come upon Robert still seated before the fire, uneasily rereading what he'd written of Ada's story. Robert had smelled smoke, glanced up to find Owen leaning against the door clutching a book.

Robert added, "I supposed it appeared strange, finding me alone in the library."

"Be careful," Owen warned on the stairs, pointing to the darkened landing, his cigarette glowing like a firefly. "Not so strange. I'd seen Miss Isabelle in the rose garden, wondered if you'd gone back to the stable. I looked, saw you weren't there. Anyway, I wanted the next volume of this."

This time Owen was reading *Francesca Carrara*; Robert recalled his mother weeping over the novel as a child. He said, "I'm grateful you came. The stairs are tricky even with a walking stick."

"I can imagine." A long drag on his cigarette. "Have you seen Grace about?"

So that's why Owen had gone to the stable to look for him. "Not since seven."

"Oh." Owen released Robert's arm. "You make it on your own from here?"

Robert had no chance to answer before he was abandoned on the landing; he grabbed the balustrade, nearly losing his balance. Luckily, Mrs. Chilvers heard Robert's uneasy shuffle. "Mr. Highstead! Come, I'll help you downstairs, sir."

Back in the stable house room, Robert was disappointed but not surprised Sida wasn't there. "She'll return," he told himself. Hugh's coffin remained amid the horses and cows, surrounded by a fresh supply of hay. However, a corpse wasn't company; the hours of the night loomed ahead.

After spending the evening hearing Ada's story, Hugh's story called anew. Robert paged through *The Collected Letters and Ephemera of Hugh de Bonne*. No mention of Ada's consumption. Nor was there of Isabelle, though that wasn't surprising—as Isabelle was a relative of Ada's, the editor had probably deemed her unworthy of inclusion in Hugh's papers.

A letter by Hugh dated the year after Ada's death tugged especially:

> *I am still awaiting word from you regarding the blue glass I ordered five months ago. It is imperative it be sent immediately—until its arrival, I shall have no peace of mind. I do not comprehend your delay. Have not I paid you generously? Granted you extra time? Offered to smooth over any transportation difficulties that might arise, given that you are shipping the glass from Sèvres?*

With this, the glass chapel pulled anew at Robert's imagination. That night with Grace and the dog, he'd been so close to looking inside it. To witnessing Ada's grave. His regrets were cut short as his ankle began to moan its familiar song of pain. He considered the morphia bottle across the room. *Not yet.* Still, he'd be more comfortable if he readied for bed.

Balancing on one foot, he folded Hugh's clothes in a pile. He couldn't resist smoothing the pricey wool, as if he could sense the poet within the fabric. He splashed his face. The icy water in the wash basin was bracing. Calming. He couldn't bring himself to shave the new growth on his cheeks. Too weary.

Now easier, Robert propped his leg on the sole bed pillow and returned to Hugh's letters.

> *Yes, I understand that cobalt necessary for the glass is the rarest shade to obtain, but you had given me your word as a gentleman it would arrive by the end of May. Until it arrives, I cannot commence work on the glass chapel I am building. The chapel must be the most beautiful place ever to be built. A poem of a building. A locus amoenus . . .*

The remainder of the letter disintegrated into ravings more appropriate to a lunatic than a poet.

Hugh was mad from loss. Just like Isabelle.

The thought arrived unbidden like a ghost. Isabelle was guilty of the very thing she'd accused Robert of. And then he realized: she hadn't mentioned herself once after describing Ada's first meeting with Hugh. Was this an oversight? Or intentional?

All of a sudden Robert could read no more. Morphia and sleep would help.

He drew out the miniature of Sida's eye from beneath his pillow to give it a goodnight kiss before blowing out the candle. But then, as though invoked by his yearning, the air turned cool and wet as his wife's shadowy form materialized beside him on the bed.

He felt his chest release, his heart sing. She was all that he needed. All that he loved.

Tonight, Sida reclined on her back, her toes pointed toward the ceiling. Her position reminded Robert uncomfortably of that woman he'd daguerreotyped in Kensington the day he'd received his brother's letter. At least she'd finally let off that stained blue silk dress in favor of a grey merino gown.

She stretched her arms his way. "*I missed you today, my sweet.*"

"I missed you too." Robert pressed his lips against her cold moist brow. "Lay with me."

She curled against him on the bed. Hugh's books jutted against their bodies, but he didn't complain. How insubstantial she felt, as elusive as morning mist. She rested her cheek against his shoulder, her body against his; he was careful not to shift lest she dissolve into him. A soft murmur rushed from her lips. It smelled faintly of almonds. He ran his finger along her neck, wishing for things to be as they were before her death. How painful it was to love someone so much at times! Still, she was there—that was all that mattered.

Silence fell upon the stable room save for the soft whinnying of horses, the shuffle of jackdaws in the eaves. The solitary beat of Robert's heart.

And then he heard it. Piano music. The notes drifted into the stable on the air, as tangible as if he was standing outside the library door. This time, it sounded like Isabelle was performing Liszt or someone similarly furious. A waltz.

She was still awake.

In this, Robert found a strange consolation. He'd disturbed Isabelle as much as her story had disturbed him.

V.
The Second Night's Story

That evening, Isabelle swept into the library nearly an hour after Robert had been sent for. Once she arrived, she settled on her dais; tonight she'd returned to wearing purple mourning. The portrait of Ada with her sparrow stared down at them, remote in its warmth. Robert picked up his pencil and journal. Though his nerves had lessened from the previous evening, he'd brought the eye miniature of Sida again.

Isabelle began without preamble.

* * *

From where I ended our story last night, I suspect you think this was when Ada learned death would claim her as his bride. But you'd be wrong, Mr. Highstead—remember, all ghost stories are love stories in disguise. So tonight I shall speak of love.

The following morning, Hugh returned to Weald House, arriving at a time when Missus Dido had stepped out to go to the village. He brought with him a white dove in a gold cage. Ada felt improved enough to receive him in the drawing room, ignoring the impropriety of it. Her heart pounded when he met her eyes after his bow. Had she imagined loving him? Was it a reaction to her poor sparrow's death?

No, she decided, considering him anew. No.

Once Hugh settled on a chair, he placed the cage on the card table near her.

"An offering," he said. "I must apologize for what transpired yesterday."

To hide the moisture threatening her eyes, Ada hid her face against the chaise. She loved him. And she was doomed. Overhearing Hugh state the truth of her consumption had the air of inevitability. No longer could she deny the evidence surrounding her since she was a baby: her weak lungs, her night sweats, and irregular fevers, even her thinness, which she'd considered a disinterest in food rather than the product of disease. Suddenly the stubborn pursuit of her suitors turned sinister—they'd understood she'd die young and leave them wealthy.

The poor bloodied body of her sparrow flashed before her. Vulnerable. Alone. Like her.

Ada said, her face still buried against the chaise, "You needn't do this, Mr. de Bonne."

"I know some things cannot be replaced. Still one tries."

Ada heard the metallic click of the cage being opened. A flurry of wings. She squeezed her eyelids tight until her skin puckered like muslin. Still the tears threatened. To discourage them, she pressed her fingernails hard into the fleshy mounds of her palms.

"Will you not even look at the dove?" Hugh asked. "You must admit she's so beautiful."

For a moment she wished he'd said, "*you're* so beautiful," instead of "*she's* so beautiful." Her suitors would have used the opportunity to flatter her.

The ruffle of more feathers fluttering.

"Should I leave, Miss Lowell?"

"No, no," was her muffled response from against the cushions. *Never leave me*, she thought. She didn't voice this, for what did she have to offer but sorrow? While she didn't know Hugh de Bonne well, she felt this deeply—her inheritance was not his aim.

"I'm glad to hear this, Miss Lowell. It would be hard to depart Shropshire, thinking of you so sad and alone."

"I'm accustomed to being alone, Mr. de Bonne."

"Being accustomed doesn't make it any more welcome. I've been alone most of my life. It can be a burden."

Ada raised her head from the cushions. "Alone? A gentleman such as yourself?" She shook her head as she took in Hugh's immaculate dress, his debonair air. Though his clothes were of good cut and quality, the brushed wool was faded in places. "You appear acclimated to the crowds of London or Paris, not the moors of Shropshire."

He set the dove on his shoulder and stroked her pure white feathers. "One can be in a crowd and still be solitary."

"True." Ada watched the half-moons indented in her palms fade to white. "Thank you for the dove, Mr. de Bonne." She forced herself to add, "I bid you good day."

Please stay, she wanted to say.

"Very well then . . ." Hugh set the dove back inside the cage. "Before I go, I should explain how to care for her. It's best to have someone build a cote, so she'll have room to fly."

"I know how to take care of birds, Mr. de Bonne." Her tone was unexpectedly short, but that was better than sad.

"I've insulted you. Forgive me, Miss Lowell."

She forced a smile. "There is nothing to forgive."

He picked up a book she'd abandoned on the settee, examined the spine. "You read German?"

"A little. Fairy tales. A gift from one of my guardians."

"Now gone?"

A resigned nod. "They're all gone—well, except for my current one obviously. I'm bad luck for them. I've had nine guardians since my parents passed. My first guardian drowned. Another had dysentery in Asia. To be fair, not all meet untimely deaths. Some abandon me. My favorite was quite old when he passed—he's the one who gave me the book and taught me German. So it's not all misfortune."

"No wonder you're alone." His lips quirked as he traced a finger along the keys of the spinet. "You play?"

In lieu of a response—she'd grown weary of language—Ada rose from her chaise. Once she'd settled herself before the piano, she launched into the sonata she'd been practicing, pouring the whole of her self into it. Her actions surprised her, but there was little about this day that had not been surprising.

As she played, she recalled all Madame Clarice had taught before she'd departed for France; they'd worked together on this sonata, the second one of the Beethoven Third Opus. *"Just because it's in C major, don't be misled by the charming first movement, mademoiselle,"* she'd said. *"The andante in the second is where you'll find your soul. Your sorrow."* What a thing to say to a young girl! But at last, Ada understood. It had taken the loss of her sparrow, the appearance of Hugh to teach her this.

Once the final chord faded into air, Ada's hands fell to her lap. The ticking of the clock had never sounded so loud. Now the playing of her piano seemed as forward an act as sitting unchaperoned with a gentleman, or admitting she read fairy tales in German. Or falling in love with a stranger met on the moors.

Unable to bear the silence, she glanced at Hugh.

His eyes were wet.

"How did you know?" he said at last.

"Know what, Mr. de Bonne?"

"About my past. Your music spoke of it." He shifted next to her piano bench. "Forgive my forwardness, but this is extraordinary."

And then Hugh launched into his life history, one he'd never shared before with a living soul.

He told Ada of the Revolution and its aftermath that had plagued his native land during the early part of this century. He told her that, though he'd left France for England as a child of seven, he remained guilt-ridden by the knowledge that he was most likely the only one of his immediate family to elude death. He told of how his father had succumbed to fever in prison, his two sisters of malnourishment, and his mother at the guillotine—she'd had the forethought to hand him off to a distant relation en route to the scaffold, saving his life. The woman into whose arms he'd been thrust was a spinster English cousin, Henrietta Highstead, who'd been foolhardy enough to visit Paris during the worst of it; she'd been inspired by the ideals but oblivious to the price. Henrietta had to wait three long years before she could return to England with Hugh, during which period they'd survived by migrating from farm to farm like birds. Once in England, it became clear Henrietta had taken him out of the desire for attention rather than any maternal instinct; she treated him akin to a lapdog, granting him a life of luxury without substance. Henrietta died of influenza soon after he turned eighteen, leaving him set but not settled. He'd traveled for years, unable to find a place of rest. His memories were scant of his mother. He bore less of his father. As for his two sisters, he recalled long warm summer nights playing children's games in their garden, which seemed a veritable Eden.

He concluded, "I am a man without a home. I belong nowhere, have no immediate family. But for a moment while I was listening to you . . ."

He fell into a weighed silence.

"I'm sorry," Ada said.

Before she could stop herself, she placed her hand on his cheek. It was a forward gesture, but one she couldn't resist. He'd lost those he'd loved, just as she had. He was alone, just as she was. The thought of Watkinson returned, bent over his books in Birmingham as he wrangled proposals from Ada's suitors.

"How good you are," Hugh murmured, his breath warm against her hand. "So kind."

Their eyes met.

The moment was interrupted by the arrival of Missus Dido, who bustled into the drawing room still wearing her best silk bonnet before putting on her spectacles. Ada drew away, her cheeks hot.

"Whom have we here?" Missus Dido said, smoothing the curls at her temples. "Mr. de Bonne! I apologize for not being at home to you."

Hugh rose from the chair and bowed. "I should not have been so presumptuous to call, but my concern for Miss Lowell outweighed my desire for propriety."

"Where did the dove come from?"

Ada spoke up. "Mr. de Bonne brought it."

Missus Dido flailed her hands but did not look displeased. "It's rather large to remain indoors. And dirty too—doves are unsanitary creatures."

"I suggested to Miss Lowell that a cote be built. Perhaps in your rose garden?" Hugh bowed again. "I've taken too much of your time."

"What a handsome gentleman," Missus Dido said once Hugh had left. "I swear he quite made me feel like a girl—I do think he was flirting with me! He's ever so modest, but I'm sure his family must have been royal before the troubles. Yet he's so peculiar with his talk of birds and such."

Her manner turned thoughtful. "I should send a dinner invitation. Did he say how long he'd remain here? Is he staying in Wellington? Perhaps the Bell Inn or the Bull's Head?"

No, he did not say how long. Nor did he say where. How fretful Ada felt! She wished she hadn't played her piano for Hugh, or caressed his cheek. Had she imagined his love for her? As for the dove, it only reminded her of the loss of her sparrow.

"No matter," Missus Dido said, patting her curls. "Mark my words, he'll return."

Hugh did not return.

However, that wasn't the end of it. Three weeks after the wood pigeons' migration, a letter arrived for Ada. Instead of a seal, the correspondent had fastened the letter with pin pricks, as though he'd run out of wax. The handwriting was insistent. The ink was a rich sepia, the paper fine.

To Miss Ada of the Doves, Hugh had written:

I pray your indulgence for this letter. I am hoping you could relay the following message to your guardian regarding your cote in the rose garden. (I trust the cote was built as recommended, and that the dove still abides.)

I have located a companion for your dove. (Hence, I address you with 'doves' plural rather than singular.) Perhaps the cote is large enough to accommodate two? More pertinently, I pray you ask Missus Dido whether I may be so forward as to send it—I would hate to overstep propriety. I think often of that sonata you played that day, and how very moving it was.

You may address her response to me care of the Royal Pier Hotel, Herne Bay, Kent. I plan to remain in my present location through April before heading to Town.

I remain your most humble and hopeful servant—

H. de Bonne

VI.

Approached from the west, the seaside resort of Herne Bay resembled little more than the hamlet it originally was. Set on a gentle elevation overlooking the coast, Herne Bay remained undeveloped until the building of a pier, a hotel, and a promenade several years earlier. These new structures encouraged paddle steamers to bring ladies and gentlemen by the boatful along the Thames from London, thus turning the hamlet into a desirable destination for those who wished to holiday without going abroad. All agreed Herne Bay's vistas were picturesque, its accommodations hospitable. Best of all, the air was fresh and clear and good for invalids. Ada had used the sea air as an excuse to convince Missus Dido to holiday in Herne Bay immediately after Hugh's letter had arrived. "Perhaps I shall improve there," Ada had told her guardian, unwilling to confess her yearning for Hugh. "We can remain through April. I'll bring my dove."

A week into their month-long stay, Ada was sitting in the tearoom of the Royal Pier Hotel, stealing sugar cubes without Missus Dido's notice—Missus Dido had become shockingly oblivious to her charge once they'd left Shropshire. It was the first time either had ever traveled beyond Birmingham. London seasons or no, Missus Dido had never experienced anything more exciting than the sheep shearing festival held every spring in Wellington, for she'd sent her daughters to stay with cousins. The smell of the water, the sound of the tide, even the shore birds peeping along the sea—these were all new to her. Ada, however, was disconsolate. Hugh had departed the Royal Pier Hotel two days before their arrival. She felt foolish, but she couldn't convince Missus Dido to return so soon. After all, the journey from Shropshire had taken several days and much expense.

"Oh, isn't it so lovely here!" Missus Dido cried that April morning. "We should view the Clock Tower today. We can hire a donkey to take us."

"I'd rather rest in my room," Ada replied. The truth was her lungs had worsened in Herne Bay—her night sweats had returned, turning sleep into a distant hope. (Or was it heartbreak that made her sleepless?) Besides stealing sugar cubes, this was another of her games with Missus Dido: she'd pretend that all was as it should be. Instead of saying, "I feel ill," Ada would claim, "I'd rather rest"; instead of "I am sick with love," she'd say, "The sun feels hot." To pass the time, the two had spent endless hours putting together jigsaw puzzles. Their latest had revealed the dome of St. Paul's, which they'd visited in London on the way to Herne Bay.

"You were wakeful all last night again, weren't you? I told you to take laudanum—"

Missus Dido's words halted into a jittery silence followed by a giggle. Much to Ada's chagrin, Missus Dido had proven to be an irredeemable flirt away from Weald House; she'd had no one to pay her mind there save the elderly groom. Turned out the widow didn't care for being widowed, and had hoped her brilliantly wed daughters in London would have settled her with a new husband by now.

"What is it?" Ada forgot about the sugar cubes hidden in her napkin.

"There's a gentleman staring at us. He's quite dashing too. Older, I think. Distinguished. Oh, how nearsighted I am! 'Tis hard to make out much."

Ada turned away, her cheeks coloring. "Put your spectacles on then."

"Too late! He's walking toward us!"

Missus Dido checked her reflection in the back of a spoon, patting her drooping ringlets. She offered Ada a sideways glance before smoothing her charge's thick ebony hair for good measure. Ill or no, Ada was still as striking of appearance as she had been in that infamous oil portrait. If anything, her unstable health had accentuated her otherworldly beauty, causing men and women to turn to gape whenever she passed.

Overcome by shyness, all Ada saw was the gentleman's hands, which were gloved in dove-grey kid. They were curled around a walking stick. When she raised her eyes, the gentleman dashed off his top hat, which was in a matching grey silk.

By the time the hat was returned to his head, Ada's fate was set.

"Mr. de Bonne," she breathed. "I was unaware you were here."

"We are so pleased to see you! We'd heard you left Herne Bay." Missus Dido's voice was flecked with invitation like frosting on an overly sweet cake. "Miss Ada, curtsey!"

Ada could only stare into Hugh's eyes. He was exactly as she recalled: the sorrow weighing him, the warmth of his accent, the softly curled auburn hair. She recalled playing her piano for him, the dove, her sparrow. Loss and gain entwined as one. She'd come to Herne Bay in hopes Hugh might court her. Now that he stood before her, had she imagined loving him?

No, her heart answered. *No*.

"I suspected it was you, Miss Lowell," Hugh said pleasantly. "How very unexpected! Did you receive my letter regarding the companion to your dove?"

"We did indeed. The dove traveled with us, Mr. de Bonne. What a coincidence we should all be here at the very same time!" Missus Dido said, bending the truth.

"It is! And to think I might have missed you—I was in London for several days." He pulled out a white wicker chair. "Life can be so peculiar in a good way. If it's not too forward, may I join you?"

Ada nodded shakily before attempting to rise to her feet, thinking the act would clear her head. It was no use: her last memory was the rattle of sugar cubes dropping from her napkin onto the tiled floor.

Yet again she fainted before Hugh de Bonne.

Ada's next memory was of Missus Dido's lilting giggle. The sound pursued her, snaking about her head like the loop of a noose. After two weeks isolated with her guardian in a hotel, even the most tolerant of charges would have grown snappish.

To bring the giggling to a close, Ada willed her eyes open.

She was lying on the white wicker daybed in her hotel room. Hugh was there, his face close to hers. He was holding smelling salts.

"You're still here," Ada whispered to herself.

"She's awake!" Missus Dido cried tremulously. "Thank heavens!"

Even after her guardian rushed to Ada's side ("Oh Miss, we were ever so worried about you!"), Ada did not shift her gaze from Hugh's face.

"I hope this isn't too scandalous," he said, "but I carried you here. You didn't stir the entire time, if that makes the experience less troubling."

"It's true!" Missus Dido swore, a rise of pink splotching her cheeks as she bent over to offer Hugh a view of her overfull bosom. "I was here too, if that soothes your mind."

"Oh," Ada said. But the word was so much more than the sound it made. In that syllable, Ada signaled to Hugh her approval of his presence even if she had not offered a single smile.

Encouraged by that low sole syllable, Hugh took the seat beside her daybed. Missus Dido's eyes darted from one to the other, her mouth tight.

When Hugh finally spoke, his voice was so soft that only Ada could hear. "What have you done to yourself since we last met?"

The question was simple but contained multitudes of meanings. Was he commenting she appeared older, though less than two months had passed since they'd last met? Or that the hold of illness was more overt? Though Hugh's tone was as light as she recalled, Ada decided the latter—his concern was revealed in his tight brow.

"I'm just tired, Mr. de Bonne," Ada answered, wishing she knew how to flirt.

"Regardless, shouldn't your guardian send for a physician?"

"Oh, I'm used to such things," Missus Dido simpered. "Miss Ada is a sweet child."

Ada resisted the urge to slap her.

Hugh laughed. "So twenty-year-old ladies are now considered children, Missus Dido. Or twenty-year-old consumptives are."

Missus Dido's eyes widened. "We don't say that, sir." But Ada was relieved by his honesty—she'd had so little of it in her life. Now that she understood her consumption for what it was, it astonished her how long she'd been deceived. Her disease had always been referred to by various euphemisms such as "her delicate lungs" or "fragile health" or "sensitive nature." Knowing the worst had set her oddly free.

Ada felt a smile travel along her lips. She pulled herself up, conscious of Missus Dido's sharp gaze. For once, her guardian wasn't giggling.

"I thank you for your concern, Mr. de Bonne. I feel much better now." And she did.

"That's good, Miss Lowell, for I have an invitation for you."

What Hugh said next neither Missus Dido nor Ada could have anticipated.

Hugh explained that the journey to Canterbury Cathedral would take not more than an hour from Herne Bay. "I'm not a pilgrim, like in Chaucer's day. I yearn to view the stained glass—I've read it's wondrous," Hugh explained to Missus Dido. "If Miss Ada could join me, that would give me pleasure. Alas, I'd planned to be unaccompanied tomorrow, so I only hired a phaeton unable to seat more than two."

"But she'd be unchaperoned!" Missus Dido protested, her dark eyes bulging. Ada hid her grin.

Hugh offered Missus Dido a bouquet of daffodils he'd somehow procured. "There'd be a driver—if anyone ever gossips, inform them I took Miss Lowell to church to pray. One can't get more proper than that." He winked at Ada before playing his final card. "Someone as attuned as you to your charge's well-being surely understands her health can only improve with an outing. Sea air can be so moist, Miss Dodo—"

"Dido," Dido protested, an edge to her tone. "Like the ancient queen. Royalty."

"Oh, I'd thought like the bird," Hugh smoothly said. "I must say you do look peaked from responsibility. A lady of your quality has certain . . . sensitivities. I suspect you wouldn't mind a day to yourself. We'll return before tea."

The following morning, once they were in the carriage, Ada felt her chest release, her head lighten. She hadn't realized how much the constant presence of Missus Dido constrained her. Even before her guardian had relented ("as long as you dress warmly and wear a veil"), it had surprised Ada she hadn't hesitated in agreeing to Hugh's plan. She'd never been alone with any man in all her life, not even those relentless suitors. But she'd never loved before. How comfortable she felt in Hugh's presence! How calm! Even her lungs didn't worry her as they usually did.

"Thank you," she said simply.

"I vow to take the best care of you," he said.

As soon as they turned inland from Herne Bay, the salt tang in the air turned sweet, tinged with hyacinths and bluebells. Ada sensed something green and fecund. Something she refused to entertain. Though she'd told Missus Dido she'd rest all the way, she couldn't resist opening the window to poke her head at the world passing by. The air was soft as velvet, as warm as a caress. The sun winked through the green canopy of trees. But then the wind caught at the brim of her best silk bonnet.

"Oh! It's gone!" she cried, as the bonnet tumbled down the road out of sight; it was one Madame Clarice had left behind. However, this was a minor inconvenience: Hugh ordered the carriage to a stop, and located the errant bonnet in a patch of cow parsley.

He tucked a blossom of the creamy weed inside the blue ribbon crowning the brim, and tucked the veil away. "A flower for a flower."

As he passed her the bonnet, Ada yearned for his gloved hand to brush against hers. She didn't replace the veil. Nor would she later, to Missus Dido's annoyance.

Too soon for her liking, they arrived in Canterbury. Perhaps because it was one of the first fine spring days, the city was more crowded than anything she'd ever experienced, even when they'd arrived in London for the Thames paddle steamer. Canterbury's winding cobblestone streets were dense with dark-timbered shops—Ada had never seen so many gowns, hats, books, and ribbons for sale. Nor had she ever heard such a calamity of cries. The stench of butchered meat threaded up her nostrils. The cathedral loomed above this fleshly cacophony, poking the clouds with towers that seemed to absorb all light.

"This way," Hugh said, ordering the driver to settle the phaeton once they'd reached Christ Church Gate. "We shan't be long."

As soon as they entered the cathedral, Ada's mood soured. Was it the noise of Canterbury? The crowds? No, she knew what it was. She was too young for him. Missus Dido was right: she was little more than a child. She set her jaw, recalling how Hugh had avoided touching her hand when he returned her bonnet.

"Isn't the stained glass celestial?" Hugh said, raising his arms toward the light. "There's no longer anything like this in France. Most of the stained glass was smashed during the Revolution. If this isn't sad enough, the remaining windows at Notre-Dame and the Sainte-Chapelle have since been removed and placed in storage. Heaven knows if they'll ever be replaced."

"I've never traveled to France. Nor do I expect to."

"Forgive me. I'm foolish to speak of such things." Hugh offered Ada a shy glance. Now that they were away from Missus Dido, his mask of bravado slipped; she sensed the young man he'd been a decade earlier. "I'm thankful you were able to accompany me. It's the least I can offer, considering our shared history."

"So that's why you invited me, Mr. de Bonne." What had she expected? He felt guilt because of her sparrow. His promise of the second dove had yet to materialize. His interest in her music was politeness. His attention was nothing more than pity.

"I invited you for your company, Miss Lowell. Beauty is better shared." He pointed down the aisle. "Let's step beyond the nave. There's something I want to show you."

They passed silently through aisles of flickering votives, the stained glass casting long bands of color across everything. The cathedral was filled with supplicants murmuring and shuffling along the stone floors. In a corner nave, a raven had somehow found its way in, and perched atop a column. Every so often, it would fluff its wings and fly wildly across the nave, cawing as though to protest the presence of humanity amid the divine.

Ada looked up toward the windows. Hugh was right: the glass *was* celestial. Brilliant blues, reds, and greens. Majestic saints and earthly sinners. Once her eyes had drunk their fill, she shifted her gaze toward a row of tall ironwork cages. They enclosed private chapels and reliquaries from a distant past. From what little religion she'd had, Ada knew she should distrust them as the papist icons they were. But her unhappiness was more than this. It was how she'd sensed Hugh's interest shift away from her once they'd entered the cathedral. She yearned to rush outside, toward the sunlight and blue sky, away from the raven, the colored glass, even Hugh himself. She even missed Missus Dido—good blunt Dido with her overbearing care and flirty manner. Nothing was hidden in her, not even her irritation when Hugh changed her name from Dido to Dodo to amuse Ada. (In the carriage, he'd teased, "You must take good care of her, Miss Lowell. If your guardian follows the paths of your previous ones, I fear she'll grow extinct.")

Ada pouted beneath the cathedral's stone vaults. "I'm cold. I'd like to leave."

"Almost there." Hugh pointed to another dark cage of ironwork. The raven promptly settled inside it. "Here it is!"

The ironwork cage surrounded two long sleeping figures carved of marble. They lay beside each other on a raised pallet, adorned in crowns and mantels shimmering with gold leaf and red enamel.

"The tomb of Henry IV and Joan of Navarre," Hugh announced. "I'd read it was here."

Ada's fingers curled around the ironwork bars, ignoring the raven so close. The cage was a prison for the dead. She blinked, eyes stinging, thinking of the fate looming before her once her disease had its way. While some consumptives survived to live full lives and even have families, Ada understood this wasn't to be for her. The pursuit of her suitors had made this too clear.

She said, "I wonder if someone will build me a stained glass tomb after I die."

"Is that really what you want, Miss Lowell?"

Though Hugh's tone was gentle, the tears threatening Ada since they'd entered the cathedral began in earnest. "Perhaps it'll be set in a cathedral like this. After all, there's nothing sadder than a dead girl, or more sacred, especially when she has an estate."

He tutted. "I'd wager you've some years left, Miss Lowell—your color has improved now that you've some air. You're not the first to experience struggles. Four hundred years ago Joan of Navarre lived to be nearly seventy despite hers."

Ada forced a laugh. "Was she a consumptive too?"

"Worse." Hugh paused for effect. "She married two kings. Some might consider that worse than death." He pointed toward the male marble figure. "Henry here was her second husband. If I remember my history correctly, Queen Joan even survived an accusation of witchcraft."

"Did they try to burn her at the stake?"

"I'm shocked, Miss Lowell—you appear too angelic to know of such things. I shall have to tell your guardian so you may repent."

"Repent . . ." Ada laughed oddly despite her wet eyes. "I have nothing to repent for, for I've done nothing with my life. I will leave nothing behind with my death, nothing that matters—not even my piano matters. I have no faith, Mr. de Bonne. The only thing I know is I am going to die."

And that I love you, she thought.

"Strong words from one so young, Miss Lowell."

She met Hugh's level gaze. "I've shocked you."

"No, no . . ." His voice softened. "I'd like to believe death contains a logic the living cannot comprehend. That the dead surround us. That those who truly love us never truly leave. They care for us in their way."

"That's easy for you to proclaim, given you have years before you."

He turned away, his shoulders tight. When he spoke, his tone was cool. "Health is no guarantee of a long life."

She gasped, recalling how he'd lost his family while a boy. "I'm a fool. A self-pitying fool. You should pay me no mind." She pointed at the tomb of Joan of Navarre. "Is there anything else you wish to tell me about your Queen Joan?"

After a long moment's silence, he said, "I wrote a poem about her. A sonnet."

"Poetry?"

He nodded. For the first time since Ada had made his acquaintance, he seemed as vulnerable as when she'd played her piano for him. "It's my true passion. My vocation, if you will. My first book was published just over a year ago. The sonnet is from it. Would you care to hear? It begins with a pilgrim seeking solace."

He recited softly:

"'We are so afraid of living
That we live as though dead,'
Fret the young Pilgrim whilst he tread
On step toward the Path unending . . ."

By the time Hugh reached the poem's final line, Ada had forgotten she'd ever lived in a house on the moors populated by ghosts. Perhaps it was because she was dazzled by being in a setting far grander than any she'd ever been. Or perhaps it was the sonorous rhythm of Hugh's voice. No matter—she'd remember this moment for what it was: the moment she began to dream of something beyond the death she was ordained to meet.

Outside the cathedral, there was an artist offering watercolors for sale on the lawn. Crude as the art was, Ada recognized a portrait of King George and another of Liszt, whom she'd seen engraved on her sheet music. The artist was aged of years and desperate of mien. When he smiled, his teeth were rotted beneath his grizzled beard.

Ada was about to offer the artist a tuppence when he addressed Hugh. "Portrait of your beautiful lady, sir? Something to mark your visit to Canterbury so you'll never forget?"

"How much?" Hugh asked.

They shook hands after a short haggle that Ada couldn't quite comprehend. Before she could demur, she was set on a stool. The legs were uneven.

Hugh said, "Tilt your head away from the cathedral, Miss Lowell. Like you're returning home after a pilgrimage." He addressed the artist. "Does this work for you, sir?"

"Well enough," was the artist's judgment; he appeared eager to please Hugh.

"How long must I sit here?" The stool wobbled beneath her weight.

"Not long." As Hugh adjusted the blossom of cow parsley back into her bonnet, his fingertips brushed her flesh. Ada thought she'd swoon. "Don't move. Don't blink."

She sat there long enough for the sun to move behind a cloud. Once the old man laid down his brushes—by then the cathedral bells had tolled eleven—he gave Hugh the watercolor. Her eyes could make little of it save a brushstroke here and there.

"Is this what you want?" the artist asked. Hugh nodded, exclaiming with glee before handing over the promised shilling and then another with a degree of ceremony that delighted Ada as much as it unsettled. This was Hugh's way, she realized, to treat everyone the same whether they were beggar or king. Even her.

Hugh brought the watercolor to Ada. "There! How lovely it is!"

Ada examined Hugh's face to see if he was jesting. "He only painted my right eye, Mr. de Bonne."

"Yes. A perfect likeness!"

"But you paid for a portrait, not part of a face." Ada shook her head, though she felt unexpectedly pleased. "You were far too generous, Mr. de Bonne. He looks like the sort who'll spend it on drink anyway."

"Not so. He painted only what I requested."

"An eye?"

"And only your right eye. Nothing more. It's not as grand as that oil portrait at your house, but an eye miniature is a tradition I like very much." And then he quoted his poem, delighting Ada. "After all, the eyes are the window to the soul."

VII.

The eyes are the window to the soul.

Robert's pencil stilled against the paper, his engrossment in his task gone. "Could you please repeat what you said, Miss Lowell?" He resisted the urge to touch the miniature in his waistcoat pocket.

Isabelle raised a brow. "Am I speaking too quickly for you, Mr. Highstead?"

"It . . . it's not that."

He drew a shaky breath. Had Isabelle really just claimed that Hugh had a miniature of Ada's eye painted? Surely he'd misheard her.

"Very well." Her tone was laced with impatience. "I'd said that Hugh told Ada, 'After all, the eyes are the window to the soul.'"

Robert's stomach tensed. *"I know all about you . . . I know your wife, Cressida, died soon after your marriage. I know you haven't been the same since . . . I know you blamed yourself for her death . . ."* It all returned to him in a rush; he'd set it aside in the pleasure of his writing, her words.

Isabelle continued on, oblivious. "When they returned from Canterbury, Missus Dido was in a state when Ada spoke of the eye portrait—"

Robert's heart pounded. "Stop."

"Why?" Isabelle arched her spine and yawned, the gesture unexpectedly sinuous. He recalled the curve of her breast beneath her wrapper; again, he felt that unwelcome pull toward her. "I'd think you'd be eager to hear Ada's story, given our bargain. Have you grown weary?"

"Not weary, Miss Lowell. Confused . . ."

"The eyes are the window to the soul." With that single sentence, Isabelle had turned his only physical representation of his wife's existence into a weapon to be deployed.

There was no way she could know about the portrait of Sida. It was a small thing. A private thing. He'd been careful to keep it either in his pocket or beneath his pillow while at Weald House . . .

Unless she'd gone through his possessions when he was unconscious after his fall.

"Ada had an eye miniature?" he said at last.

She nodded. "I know it's strange Hugh only chose to have her eye painted, but he was fond of puzzles and such. I'll speak more of this later in my story."

"If this is true, then I don't know what to think, Miss Lowell." A coincidence was more troubling than if she had spied on him.

"Think? You're not to think, Mr. Highstead. You're to write." Isabelle frowned in a manner that, to Robert's eye, appeared genuine. "Don't you want to hear how tonight's story ends? I haven't even gotten to the best part." She glanced up at the clock, which only showed eight. "It's run down again—Grace must have forgotten again. I have no idea how much time's passed."

"It hardly matters." Robert recalled Sida's joy in painting her eye. His joy when he'd received it that day in the woods. *"After all, the eyes are the window to the soul."*

"An hour? Four? No wonder you're restless. Hmm, poor Virgil has left, probably in search of someplace to relieve his bladder."

"It's not that, Miss Lowell . . ."

Robert forced himself to rise from the chaise, clutching the fireplace mantel for support. His ankle was stiff with pain, though better than the previous evening. He wished it was recovered enough to let him pace just as he'd seen her pace that first evening, as though this action would enable him to understand how such a coincidence could be.

"What is it then, Mr. Highstead?"

He drew a deep breath. "I'm having a hard time comprehending your story given certain . . . discrepancies."

There. That word, *discrepancies*, as ineffectual as it was, would have to do, despite how strongly he ached to understand the overlaps between his marriage and Ada's story. To reassure himself Isabelle hadn't spied on him.

"I trust you're not accusing me of falsehood. Remember the terms of our contract."

"I haven't forgotten."

He fell back into the chaise. How to proceed? His chin pressed against his hands, which didn't feel as raw as they usually did. He'd again forgotten about his unshaven face; the unfamiliar sensation disoriented him as much as Ada's story.

He let out a long breath. "It's this, Miss Lowell. I'm questioning . . ."

"You are not to question, Mr. Highstead!"

"But I *must* question . . ." He'd have to appeal to her pride. "If I'm to publish this book for you, you must consider my position as a scholar. You want me to assist you in writing a book that will honor your aunt's life. As your history now stands, Ada's story has no proof. No provenance. No one will believe it."

Her head cocked. "Wouldn't my word be enough?"

"No. A history requires more than one person's testimony—people make up stories all the time. It's only by comparing differing accounts we can arrive at the truth." Robert continued without thinking. "Here, I'll give you an example of what could happen if your history has no provenance. When I was in Oxford, there was a historian who was writing a biography of the poet Ovid—"

"A poet like Hugh." Her tone was dismissive.

He gritted his teeth. "Yes, a poet like Hugh. But I'm speaking of Ovid's history, not his poetry." His voice dropped. "Anyway, in this historian's case, his biography of Ovid was problematic because it lacked correlation. Though Ovid had written about his life in his poetry, very little was recorded after he went into exile on the Black Sea." A deep breath. "It mattered not: the historian became so enthralled with what he *believed* had happened—with needing to *know* what happened—that he shaped what he conjectured about Ovid into a narrative so compelling, so seductive, that the historian forgot he had no proof. No provenance." Robert's throat tightened. "It didn't help that the historian had suffered a most grievous loss at that time."

Isabelle met Robert's eyes, all rancor gone. "What happened?"

"What you would think." The memory was still exquisitely painful. "The historian ended up ridiculed by his peers, his previous successes forgotten.

He abandoned his book—a manuscript that had occupied several years of his life. Never wrote again . . ."

Robert shifted on the chaise, aware he'd revealed more than he'd intended. To avoid Isabelle's eyes, he stared at the portrait of Ada—how lovely she'd been!—before stretching his hand to pet Virgil, who'd returned from wherever he'd gone. For once he didn't mind the dog's presence.

"Very well," Isabelle said slowly. "I accept your point, Mr. Highstead. What constitutes proof?"

"Primary sources. Letters. Artifacts. Birth certificates. Death certificates. For example, I've noticed you're not referenced in your uncle's collected letters. Nor is Ada's consumption. Some could claim this contradicts your account."

For once, Isabelle looked shaken. "You shouldn't believe what you read in books, Mr. Highstead."

"I don't. Hence, I question. Here's another question others might ask: You lived with your aunt, did you not? Yet you've rarely mentioned yourself since you began your story."

Color rose on her cheeks. "I've spoken only of my aunt's experiences to save time—after all, I'm telling of her life, not mine. Remember I was sent to school when I turned seven."

Robert flipped through the journal. "By which guardian?"

She nodded tightly, avoiding his eyes. "Reverend Smallsworth. He wanted me to have a proper Christian education, and didn't have time to mind both myself and Ada. Ada was his priority. Not me."

"That was the guardian who'd died of dysentery in India?"

Another tight nod. "Until Ada's marriage, I returned to Weald House for holidays. Summers. Ada told me secrets she confided to no one else."

Robert leaned in. "And after her marriage?"

Isabelle's voice rose. "She wrote me letters. Piles and piles of them."

"You possess these documents?"

"I burned them upon her death to protect her privacy."

"And now you want to betray her confidences with your book."

She flinched. "Only because of the pilgrims."

"Then you've destroyed proof of Ada's story."

Isabelle's chin jutted. "The truth is what it is."

"It's not that simple, Miss Lowell." Robert warmed to his subject. "In addition, there's the matter of your story. You haven't revealed anything

I couldn't have surmised from your uncle's letters and the pilgrims save for Ada's consumption. It's an oft-told story: a man loved a woman, they courted, they wed. Though the story ends sadly, thus far there's nothing to warrant special attention."

"You haven't heard the rest of Ada's story yet! There's much no one knows of her life. I do!" Isabelle wrung her hands, reminding Robert of the first time he'd seen her in the library: the bony wrists, the twisting fingers. "Anyway, it doesn't matter whether I can prove my story, or what you think of it. I know all about Ada. I know! There's always a third person who serves as witness, a third who sees all. I was this for Ada—her third. The eye that sees into the soul."

With this, something in Robert snapped. She'd made up Ada's eye miniature. She was spying on him. Taunting him.

"One last question . . ." Robert had to ask, though he could barely force the words out. "I'm curious about that miniature of your aunt's eye. I assume you still possess it, given your devotion to her memory. May I see it?"

"I'm insulted by your distrust." She stood from her dais, her skirts swaying. "Good night, Mr. Highstead. We shan't meet tomorrow."

Robert could feel the heat rising to his face. "We had an agreement! Five nights for your story—this is only the second night. I need to bury my cousin!"

"I didn't promise the nights would be sequential. Tomorrow is Sunday. We'll reconvene Monday at our usual time."

"Miss Lowell, I cannot wait an extra day—"

She raised her handkerchief to silence him. "As I stated, we will speak again Monday night. I will spend Sunday in rest and contemplation. As should you. And remember, I have your camera." She met his eyes meaningfully. "If I were you, I'd be more respectful of our agreement in the future."

Robert hardly noticed his injuries as he made his way back to the stable room. The first thing he did was to reach for the miniature of Sida in his waistcoat pocket to find a better place to hide it. His hand came back empty.

Isabelle couldn't have stolen it. Could she?

"No," he said in an attempt to calm himself. "You dropped it. That's all."

He lit a second candle for more light—he couldn't see anything beyond the length of his arm in this damn dark place. He pulled the stool out from beside the bed to look beneath it.

Not there either. He resisted the urge to yell, to shout. His stomach curled. Now his ankle was burning from overuse. He knew he should sit. Rest. He couldn't.

"What happened, my sweet?"

Sida materialized before him, but Robert could take no pleasure in her presence. "I lost something," was all he could say.

He ignored his wife, too distressed to rest. He could hardly return to the library to search for the miniature at this hour—it must have fallen out of his pocket. Then he remembered Isabelle had claimed Ada possessed a similar miniature of her eye. If he found it, that would confirm her story. Perhaps he'd feel less vulnerable.

Robert pivoted toward the door.

"Where are you going?"

He forced a reassuring smile. "I'll be back soon."

Before Sida could protest, Robert stumbled out of the stable room into the main house. He groped his way toward Hugh's study.

The door to the study was unlocked as he'd hoped. Inside, a slant of moon illuminated the room from the rose garden, where Ada had sat so long ago with her sparrow. Robert went from display to display, his fingers trailing along the surfaces. He felt the signed first editions, the manuscripts, the glass bell with the raven's feather from Mathilde's cheek, the fur coat Hugh had given Ada.

Just as he found his way to Hugh's desk, a rush of cold wind fluttered the hem of his jacket. The French doors were ajar.

Isabelle stood outside in the rose garden, her back turned to him as she paced back and forth, as he'd often witnessed in the library. Her posture was as straight as ever, her shawl clutched as tight. Yet he sensed a hesitation in her aspect he'd never viewed before. There was something about her. Something he couldn't turn from. In that moment, she looked as haunted as he was.

Unable to leave, Robert pulled himself behind the door. Just beyond the rosebush, he made out another figure, a slight pale form. Grace. She winked, raised a finger to her lips. No matter. His eyes were all for Isabelle.

He watched Isabelle approach the bench overlooking the yew tree. Watched her bury her face in her hands as she sank onto the bench. The gesture surprised him. He hadn't considered her capable of gentleness. And it *was* gentleness she displayed—the slow dip of her hands against her face, the release of her breath. For once, instead of a goshawk, she reminded him of a dove, with her soft white hair gleaming beneath the moonlight, her swooning movements.

She was kissing something small in her hand. The oval-shaped object was no larger than her palm. It glinted metallic in the night.

The miniature of Ada's eye. The one she'd spoken of—it had to be.

When Robert finally returned to bed, Sida was nowhere to be found. "I'm sorry," he whispered into the air. "I shouldn't have left you. Should have been more attentive. You know I love only you." It took him some time to settle himself to sleep. Once he lay down, he located the miniature of her eye. It had been tucked on the nightstand beneath the journal bearing Ada's story—he must have overlooked it.

"A coincidence," he told himself yet again. "Only that."

Still, he felt more troubled than he cared to admit, as if Ada and Hugh had been conjured by a cruel god to remind Robert of all he'd lost.

Tea and Acrimony

Excerpted from *Cantos for Grown Children* by Hugh de Bonne, published 1834 by Chapman & Hall, London.

The house was bricked with sugar'd blight
And hid 'mid oak and tall pine. The scents
Of sweets needled their hunger. 'Come in! I invite,'
Cloyed a voice from inside. 'Where are your parents?
Children, come! Have you yet taken teas?'
'Ah, you tease,' Sister swooned. 'My stomach seizes
At such smells! 'Tis too long since I've ate my fill.'
Sister smiled and grabbed Brother's hand. 'Shall we then?'
'No!' Brother hissed to Sister. 'You shan't accept!
    That woman is one to fear—
    A Seductress of children ;
    An Enchantress of souls ;
    A Circe seeking swine ;
    A Witch without morals.'

*

I.

The following morning, Owen and Mrs. Chilvers arrived while Robert was still in bed. Since he was to remain in the stable house, he couldn't be bothered to rise, though he'd dressed in another set of Hugh's clothes. It was one thing to be lazy, another undressed.

"Breakfast," Mrs. Chilvers announced, revealing a plate of fatty bacon, a bowl of porridge, and a soft-boiled egg in a cup accompanied by tea and honey instead of sugar. The food at Weald House was generous but bland at best. The housekeeper seemed a dazzle of warmth compared to Owen, who leaned against the smoldering fireplace flicking matches against the grate, glaring at Robert. Robert couldn't blame him—he'd displaced Owen from his bed, sorry as that bed might be. After their exchange on the stairwell, he suspected Owen had been using the stable for assignations with Grace.

"Come, let me help you to the table," Mrs. Chilvers invited. "I'd thought by now Miss Isabelle would let you sup with us in the kitchen."

"I'll manage. Thank you for breakfast," Robert said.

He staggered into the chair before the table. Flatware and china jangled as Mrs. Chilvers set the tray on the table. Once this was done, she perched on the edge of the bed, her broad palms resting on her thighs. She was wearing her nice black silk gown, the same one with the Belgian lace fichu she'd donned Thursday for the pilgrims' visit. Her eyes darted to the coffin beyond—Robert supposed she'd set Hugh's corpse out of mind until now—before she signaled to Owen to shut the door.

Robert cracked the eggshell with a spoon. "More Seekers of the Lost Dream this morning?"

She smoothed her skirts. "Oh no, I'm dressed for church, Mr. Highstead. We're to leave in a half hour. We usually walk. Owen will take you in the cart because of your ankle—Miss Isabelle said you're to go too. I'll bring an overcoat for you. Yours is quite ruined."

"What if I don't want to go?" He'd thought Isabelle couldn't bear to see him. Had she sighted him spying on her? Not that, he decided; she probably didn't want to leave him alone in the house.

"And why wouldn't you?" Owen said, lighting another match; this one he blew out before dashing it to the floor. "Have you another plan for the morning?"

"Calm yourself, Owen," Mrs. Chilvers scolded. To Robert: "Ignore him. He's just upset over . . . oh, never mind!" She rose from the bed. "I'll see if the others are ready for church. I may join you in the carriage. 'Tis chilly out. Oh, before I forget, a letter from your brother came late yesterday—only saw it this morning."

Once Owen turned his back, Robert tore the letter open. A thin piece of newsprint fluttered to the floor. Hugh's obituary from the London *Times*. It was dated the day Robert left London.

Scattered phrases grabbed Robert's attention.

Hugh de Bonne, our generation's Orpheus, was discovered deceased in his bath late last month in Geneva . . . Mr. de Bonne had been the author of The

Lost History of Dreams . . . *never recovered from the tragic death of his wife, Ada, and their only child, Mathilde . . . Surviving family members include Miss Isabelle Lowell of Kynnersley, Shropshire, heir to his estate and sole blood cousin to Mr. de Bonne's wife, and the Highsteads of Belvedere, Kent. A private burial will take place in Shropshire at the family's discretion. It is presumed Mr. de Bonne will not be laid to rest inside the stained glass chapel built to hold his wife's remains, which remains locked as it has been since her burial . . .*

Too anxious to continue reading, Robert set the obituary aside to scan John's letter, which must have cross-posted his.

Brother of mine,

By the time you read this, I trust you will have arrived safely in Shropshire, and were able to speak to Miss Lowell regarding her inheritance. Have you yet laid to rest our Cousin Hugh inside the glass chapel? (I dare not ask of the daguerreotype and Miss Lowell's participation.) If not, I must press you to return immediately so we may bury him in our family plot. Alas, that which I most feared has come to pass, as you will see from the enclosed obituary. From here on, we must aim for nothing more than to protect Hugh's earthly remains from those unwilling to honor his Last Wishes. As to the estate, it shall remain my burden until I can persuade Hugh's solicitor otherwise—I've no desire to cheat Miss Lowell of her inheritance.

I urge you to hurry home with all haste—I regret involving you in this.

Yours in haste,

John

PS: Another regret I must confess: I confided about Cressida's passing to Miss Lowell. I'd hoped this would aid Hugh's suit by gaining you sympathy. In retrospect, I pray nothing has been said that might cause you further pain.

"Bad news?" Owen asked. Another match lit and flicked.

"Something like that."

Robert shoved the letter and obituary into his pocket. The gesture did little to ease the weight on his chest despite learning of John's indiscretion to Isabelle. Hugh would never be reunited in the glass chapel with his wife. Never go home.

"When's the next coach to Shrewsbury, Owen?"

"Tomorrow morning at eleven."

"None at all today?" Robert's head pounded anew.

"None." Owen smiled for the first time all morning. "Never any coaches on Sunday—"

His gloating was interrupted by a sharp female voice shrieking outside the stable. "Help! I've been stung! Bees!"

"Grace," Owen said, running toward the door. "She must have bothered the hive."

By the time Robert limped to the door, the worst was over. Just beyond the stable gate, several bees buzzed in a manner more desultory than dangerous. Grace lay ashen beneath an oak tree clutching a long black shawl. To Robert's astonishment, Isabelle was cradling the girl in her arms.

Isabelle ordered Owen to fetch vinegar and tweezers from the kitchen. "You poor girl, why'd you disturb them? They were settled for the winter."

"I was telling 'em"—a shaky breath—"about Hugh's death. No one told the bees . . ." Grace fingered the black shawl. "Someone told me I must tell them or—"

"Who told you this?" Owen demanded, taking Grace's hand from Isabelle; he'd returned with the vinegar at last. Grace pulled her hand away, but only after she'd thrown a sly look Owen's way. "Highstead? Or another fool?"

"'Twas something I heard." Grace's eyes darted about the garden. "I thought . . . I feared . . ."

"Hush child," Isabelle said, dabbing the welts on Grace's cheek. "Hush."

II.

The church at Kynnersley was down the road just over a mile from Weald House. It was a humble church, red-stoned with a squat bell tower. It rested atop a gentle hill dotted with snowdrops, the first sign of spring. Robert knew he should find encouragement in this small sign of life. He couldn't: upon closer examination the hill surrounding the church contained a cemetery. Grave stones, some dating from as early as the sixteenth century, laid pressed into the grass all the way to the ivy-draped stone walls.

Owen deposited Robert at the church gate with a grunt, leaving Mrs. Chilvers to guide Robert up the path toward the side apse. Hugh's mustard-colored overcoat, with its beaver collar and padded shoulders, draped heavily across his frame; Robert had immediately recognized it from that frontispiece to Hugh's book of letters.

"Ignore Owen," Mrs. Chilvers said again, patting Robert's arm. "He says he overheard you speaking to someone last night in the stable house. From the sounds of it, a woman. He insists she was Grace."

"Grace?" Robert retorted, staring at his feet. The path to the church was paved with cobblestones eager to catch the tip of Hugh's walking stick. "That's impossible."

"That's what I said, Mr. Highstead. Or may I call you Mr. Robert? I do feel quite protective of you, with your injury and such. I told him it was impossible too."

Robert stumbled. Owen had overheard him with Sida.

Mrs. Chilvers tightened her grasp on his arm. "Oh, do be careful!"

"I should have been." Whenever his landlady overhead him speaking to Sida, he'd excused himself with the claim of reciting poetry.

"Anyway, he's in a snit. Just thought you should be aware. If you would be so good as to assure him, but pray don't tell him I said anything. Ah, here we are!"

They approached the apse, a small alcove crowded with more people than Robert imagined the village held. The mass of humanity seemed to daunt even Mrs. Chilvers, who tutted and fluttered her hands against her heart. A swell of organ music escaped through the open doors, competing with jackdaws complaining from the eaves. From the corner of his eye Robert saw Grace dart across the graveyard with Owen in determined pursuit; a smile flickered across her face before she hissed, "Let me be! I told you I don't want to speak with you." She appeared well recovered from her bee stings.

By the time he and Mrs. Chilvers shuffled into the church, all the pews were filled save the first one. "The family pew," she explained. "Can you make it up the aisle, Mr. Robert? Heavens, there's more people coming. I think they'll have to stand soon."

She staggered, nearly bringing Robert down with her.

"Oh sweet Jesus!"

Robert grabbed her arm to save her from falling. "What is it?"

Mrs. Chilvers pointed down the aisle.

Robert followed her hand toward a sea of black-clad people. Each wore a cockade of raven feathers circling a single blood-red rose. They sat with their heads high in anticipation. They'd crammed the pews of the small church from front to back, leaving a few villagers dressed in their Sunday best squeezed between them. Whether you called these black-clad people pilgrims or Seekers of the Lost Dream, the effect was the same. They reminded Robert of a fox hunt held soon after his mother's death. How the spectators had stood waiting in the icy dawn for the dogs to drag out the cornered prey. Though Robert was only a boy, he'd hated every single moment of it, especially the applause at the end when his father lifted the bloodied fox above his head. At the display of carnage, a cluster of sparrow hawks had swept over the crowd. Afterward, Robert found the fox picked clean to the bone; he might not have recognized it save for its white-fluffed tail, which remained obscenely pristine.

This memory remained with Robert as he made his way down the aisle with Mrs. Chilvers, especially when he saw that not all pilgrims were seated. A woman with bright auburn hair stood to the side of the aisle; Robert recalled her from the tour of Hugh's study. She looked older than he remembered, closer to forty than his age. The tepid light pouring through the stained glass illuminated her stubborn chin and weary eyes. She'd been weeping. Her eyes widened as she took in Robert wearing Hugh's overcoat. Suddenly self-conscious, he smoothed his hair beneath his hat, wishing he'd shaved. The sorrow he'd sensed in her during the study tour now seemed replaced by something darker. Desperate. He could see it in her posture, which was as rigid as a Christian martyr. Like she was waiting for something. Or, worse, some*one*.

"Where's Miss Isabelle?" Mrs. Chilvers asked as Robert led her toward the front pew "They must have learned of Mr. Hugh's passing, God help us."

The obituary. His brother had been right.

"Come," Robert said in his most soothing tone. "We're in a house of God. A sanctuary."

"Won't matter." The housekeeper craned her neck. "Miss Isabelle isn't in the pew—we should warn her. Do you see her?"

Robert glanced over his shoulder toward the doors. "She must be outside. I'll go."

Mrs. Chilvers's grasp tightened. "Too late."

Isabelle Lowell stood in the heart of the aisle like a bride betrothed to loss rather than love. She was clad as ever in mourning—a deep purple gown peeked out beneath a shabby black bombazine cloak—with her ivory hair pulled tight beneath her straw bonnet. If she took any notice of the pilgrims, she revealed no sign save her nose flaring as though she smelled something foul.

The organ silenced. Conversation ceased. The only sound in the church became Isabelle's heels on the cold tiled floor. It was a disquieting sound. A familiar sound, reminding Robert of the tap of Hugh's walking stick as he'd dragged himself from the library the night of their bargain.

"Perhaps it would help if we sit," Mrs. Chilvers said, her gaze locked on Isabelle. "Where are Grace and Owen? Of all times for them to go missing!"

The housekeeper slid into the pew, Robert beside her. By then Isabelle was nearly down the aisle.

The red-haired woman strode from her post by the church wall, halting before Isabelle. Heads turned as one toward the pair.

"Good day, madam," Isabelle said, offering a smile. (Robert shuddered, recalling the few times he'd witnessed that smile.) "How *good* of you to worship at my aunt's church. I hope it offers you succor."

And then, to Robert's wonderment, Isabelle stepped around the red-haired woman, continuing down the aisle (*tap, tap, tap!*) as though the pilgrim was only a neighbor she'd happened upon at church.

"Come back here!" the red-haired woman shouted. "Don't you dare ignore me, Isabelle Lowell!"

Isabelle looked over her shoulder. "I hardly ignored you."

The two women locked eyes.

"When were you going to tell us of Hugh de Bonne's death? Today? Tomorrow? A year from now?" The red-haired woman's voice echoed all the way to the rafters.

Isabelle's smile faded. "It's evident there was no need for me to inform you. As for my silence, I'd hoped for privacy to mourn."

"Mourn?" The red-haired woman took another step toward Isabelle, her petticoats ruffling. "Mourn! What about those who esteemed him most? Who drew comfort from his poems?"

A jackdaw cawed. Robert's heart thudded.

"I expect you've already buried him, Isabelle Lowell. You probably laid him to rest without honor far from Ada, given that the chapel is still locked," the red-haired woman cried. "Don't deny it! We all know you care naught for Hugh or his art. Haven't you proven as much these years with your refusing to open Ada's Folly? And now you've inherited the whole lot—we'll never see the glass or visit Ada's grave!" She broke into sobs. "It's a travesty, I tell you. A travesty! And you know why, Isabelle Lowell. You know why! Do you want me to tell this entire church?"

"You've said enough. Go in peace." Isabelle's voice was unsteady.

"Go in peace . . ."

The red-haired woman drew so close that the hem of her gown touched Isabelle's. She puckered her mouth and spat.

Even the pilgrims gasped.

The saliva landed on Isabelle's cheek. As she pulled out her handkerchief to wipe her face, the red-haired woman collapsed sobbing to the church floor as the congregation erupted into shouts, screams, and shrieks. Mrs. Chilvers fell into a swoon beside Robert. Somehow Owen emerged from the side apse, gathered the housekeeper in his arms, and fanned her face with a hymnal, affording Robert the opportunity to spring to his feet (though stumble would be a more accurate description). Just as Mrs. Chilvers's eyes fluttered open and Owen guided her to her feet, the organ began to play a panicked tune that sounded decidedly nonsecular and someone screamed. Then Robert was on his feet, ankle or no, staggering toward Isabelle Lowell just as the mass of black-clad pilgrims lunged her way.

"Let me be!" Isabelle's panicked voice rose above the pilgrims, entwining with the organ in a mad cacophony.

Somehow Robert was running toward Isabelle, though God knew how, with his ankle throbbing amid the screaming and confusion. His blood surged in his veins; his head was light, just like it had been the night he'd tried to rescue Sida from her uncle. And then somehow Isabelle was in his arms and he was lifting her away, her bonnet falling from her head but held on by thick black ribbons. The bonnet dangled dangerously about Isabelle's throat—Robert feared someone grabbing it, snapping her neck.

"I have you," he breathed into her ear. "You're safe."

Isabelle was warm. Fragile. He'd protect her. How could he not? Yet part of him understood it wasn't Isabelle he was addressing—it was Sida. In that moment, it was as though he'd been transported to three years earlier before they'd married. There he was, lifting Sida's bloodied body away from her uncle, yelling at her aunt to get a constable. "You'll never hurt her again," Robert shouted before he'd punched him. "I'll keep her safe." His vow hadn't mattered—her uncle had been too fast and too strong. But this time the outcome would be different. *Must* be different.

He shouldered a pilgrim away. Isabelle's head curled against his chin, beneath his nose (he would have never expected her hair to be perfumed, and a floral scent at that), and her arms looped around his neck. Her handkerchief somehow fell from her fingers into Robert's hand. He struggled as he stuffed it into his pocket—he'd leave nothing behind for the pilgrims to scavenge.

And then he was carrying Isabelle down the aisle and out the vestibule into the churchyard, though he'd later have no coherent memory of this. He'd only recall his hat falling off and the pilgrims gasping, taken aback by the revelation of Robert's scar and Hugh's bright mustard coat.

As soon as he carried Isabelle outside into the cold sunlight, Robert saw Grace bearing an armful of roses. Isabelle saw her too—Robert felt her torso stiffen against his. Grace dropped the roses, and her hand crept to her mouth before she ran off down the path toward God knew where. Then Owen was beside him, taking Isabelle from his arms: "I've got her, Highstead." Once Isabelle was on her feet, Owen hastened her toward the chaise carriage, which awaited at the church gate; Mrs. Chilvers was already seated in it.

Isabelle grabbed the reins. Mrs. Chilvers clutched her shawl. Robert watched them drive off down the narrow lane faster than he'd imagined possible, the horses whinnying in protest against the crisp February air.

And then it was over. All that remained was dust rising from the carriage.

III.

Robert looked around. He was alone. Where had the pilgrims gone? His ankle throbbed. The reality of his situation fell upon him: he was alone in a graveyard over a mile from Weald House with a sprained ankle.

Robert staggered to a tomb, wishing he hadn't lost Hugh's walking stick.

"Shit."

A thin female voice interjected, "Strong words outside a house of God." Her accent sounded vaguely foreign.

Robert turned.

A stately black-clad woman draped in velvet and bombazine stood less than an arm's length from him on the cusp of the graveyard. He made out a pair of sharp dark eyes behind her thick black veil. Mourning dress. Full at that. Steel-grey curls. Where had she come from?

He inclined his head in lieu of a bow. "I beg your pardon, madam. If I'd known you were nearby— "

"I wasn't, sir. I was over there"—she pointed to a distant corner of the graveyard bedecked by ivy—"when I heard shouts. At my age, I avoid church services unless they're necessary."

"I take it you witnessed what happened."

"Enough to understand you're without transport. And from the unsteadiness of your gait, this"—she offered Hugh's walking stick—"belongs to you."

"Where did you find it?"

"On the tomb over here. I saw a pretty girl with blond curls set it there before she ran off. There's also a hat. I presume that's yours as well?"

Robert accepted both with a thanks. "Perhaps you know of a carriage for hire?"

"Better." A somber smile behind her veil. "I've a carriage of my own. My cottage is just across the road. I'll even give you tea before I send you on your way."

"Marcus, we've company for tea!" the lady in black called as she led Robert to a chair in her sitting room. The room was dark and narrow but smelled of beeswax and lemon. It was a welcoming smell, orienting Robert in his body after the suddenness of all he'd experienced at the church. "I've the young gentleman from London. From Weald House."

Robert gave a start. "How did you know?"

"People chatter. You're Hugh de Bonne's relation."

"Robert Highstead at your service, madam. And you are?"

She must not have heard his question, for she remained silent as she removed her bonnet and veil. Once they were placed on her mantel, she asked, "The disturbance was over Hugh's funeral?"

"Among other things. How did you know?"

"It's not surprising." She peeled off a pair of black silk gloves, revealing a black jet ring beside a gold band on liver-spotted hands. "Everyone feels strongly about Hugh de Bonne, especially now that word has escaped of his passing."

The low upholstered chair Robert settled in offered a full view of her sitting room, of which one wall was covered in floor-to-ceiling shelves. Half of the shelves contained books, their titles indistinct in the shadows. An array of framed art and daguerreotypes filled the remainder, each decorated with black crape bows.

"Mr. Highstead, do you take lemon or milk in your tea? Lemons are a luxury this time of year, but I insist on them for health."

"Milk, please." Robert looked up at her. "Whom do I have the pleasure of attending?"

She turned in marked dismissal. After two attempts to obtain her name, it would be rude to press further; he'd have to think of her as the mourning woman.

"Milk with the tea, Marcus!" She rang a small brass bell. To Robert: "Marcus will drive you home when we're finished. He's my only servant, but he's loyal. He's been with me since my husband passed five years ago."

A distinct sense of unease crept along Robert's spine. After five years, she should be wearing half-mourning if that. No matter. He'd drink the tea and accept her carriage. He had no other choice.

He pointed to the crape bows. "My condolences for your loss."

"They're not for my husband." She bit her lip and looked away. "My loss is your loss."

"How so?" Robert's neck prickled.

"Are you not cousin to Hugh de Bonne?"

God help him, she was in mourning for Hugh. "You're a pilgrim."

She arched a brow. "No, Mr. Highstead, I'm not a Seeker of the Lost Dream or whatever nonsense they're calling themselves these days. Though I'm more acquainted with them than I would wish." She glanced down the hallway toward where Marcus had yet to appear. "Tamsin Douglas can be quite formidable."

"Tamsin Douglas?"

"The lady who accosted Miss Lowell, if I am to trust the commotion I overheard."

"The woman with the red hair? She seemed disturbed of mind." Robert wouldn't mince words. After her display at the church, his earlier sympathy had soured into wariness.

"I don't know if Mrs. Douglas is disturbed as much as she's grief-mad," his hostess opined. "Her son was stillborn, just as Hugh's daughter had been. And then her husband died unexpectedly—they'd been exceptionally devoted to each other. She'd equated her loss with Hugh's, but many do after reading *The Lost History of Dreams*. Now that she's learned of Hugh's death . . ." She gave a little shrug. "It is unfortunate Mrs. Douglas's grief fuels vulgar displays rather than charitable acts. The irony is Miss Lowell once considered her a friend—yes, I know, 'tis unexpected. They'd had a falling out three years ago over Ada's chapel."

"You witnessed this?"

"Not personally." She flushed. "Again, people chatter. They're like those doves around Ada's Folly, billing and cooing to no effect." The mourning woman sank into the chair beside his. "Anyway, 'tis for the best you're here. I'm so very, *very* pleased to make your acquaintance at last. We'll have tea and a chat, and I'll return you to Weald House in time for dinner." She pointed to a hassock upon which someone, presumably herself, had needlepointed the words *Hope, Love, Faith* in purples and greys. "Pray rest your ankle, Mr. Highstead. I'm amazed you were able to carry Miss Lowell considering your injury. From what I could see, you appeared quite heroic."

"I suppose it was the shock of the situation." He hadn't even noticed the pain at the time. "You're acquainted with Miss Lowell?"

"When she was a child." She set a pair of half-moon spectacles on her nose. "Ah, now I can see you properly! Hugh de Bonne was your uncle?"

"No, cousin through marriage."

"Then Miss Lowell is your cousin as well."

"I suppose a distant one."

Her eyes filled behind the thick lenses. "Even if you share no blood, you truly are the image of Hugh when he courted Ada. Oh, I know your hair is far lighter, and your chin sharper. But you've longish hair parted on the side like his, a similar height. A similar sensitivity. Between your limp and that scar, the clothing—I recognize Hugh's waistcoat, yes?—the effect is quite transporting."

Her rhapsodies were interrupted when the aforementioned Marcus finally shuffled in bearing a teapot on a long tray accompanied by a tall glass bottle, half a seed cake, and other implements of hospitality. His face was far more wrinkled than the mourning woman's, but his frock coat was of the latest cut from London and sewn of bright green velvet. Expensive. Robert had recently daguerreotyped someone in Mayfair wearing a similar garment; afterward the man's sons had squabbled over who should inherit it.

The mourning woman gestured toward the bottle once Marcus left the room. "Have some elderberry cordial, Mr. Highstead. It's medicinal. You need it after the shock you just received."

Robert relaxed. This was a reaction he could understand. "You're very kind, madam. Tea is sufficient."

"Cake?" Before Robert could demur, she'd cut a large slab and set it on a plate. "You really should try the cordial—I brought it with me from Geneva."

"It's not necessary, madam."

The mourning woman adjusted her spectacles before pulling her chair closer to Robert. Her bombazine gown smelled as fusty as it looked; the grain of the fabric shimmered like water.

"That is so interesting about your relation to Miss Lowell," she said. "Did you know her before Ada and Hugh wed?"

Robert stirred sugar in his tea. "I only met her for the first time this past week."

"You knew her parents?"

He set his spoon down. "No."

"Then you had no knowledge of Isabelle Lowell's person until this past week. Never interacted with anyone who'd met her."

"This is correct. My brother sent me to Weald House to inform Miss Lowell of her uncle's death. Until then, I was unaware of her relation. However, I was unaware of Hugh as well." In an attempt to swerve the conversation from the personal to the universal, he added, "I must admit I am still dumbfounded by what occurred at the church. Wouldn't you agree?"

"Yes, it was quite loud even in the graveyard. Very disturbing . . ."

Her papery lips spread into a smile, baring yellowed teeth.

The clock ticked. Robert stared down at his tea.

The mourning woman broke the silence. "One might say your visit is most fortuitous, Mr. Highstead."

Robert looked up. "Fortuitous?"

"Very." She flicked cake crumbs from her sleeve. "You see, there's a matter you may be able to assist with. It's a small matter . . ."

"How small?"

A girlish giggle. "Very small indeed. Regardless, it's a matter that has troubled me even before Hugh's passing." She made the sign of the cross.

"A matter that has led me to return to England for the first time since my marriage fifteen years ago."

Robert said impatiently, "I suspect you're about to tell me your small matter has to do with what occurred at church with the Seekers of the Lost Dream."

"Not directly." Her teacup clattered against the saucer. "What I want to say is difficult. First off, I have no doubt that Miss Lowell is a good woman—everyone agrees she saved Weald House from ruin after Mr. de Bonne's disappearance. I also have no doubt she holds Ada de Bonne in the highest esteem. But . . ."

The mourning woman's lips pursed as though she couldn't bring herself to say what she'd intended.

"But what?" Gooseflesh crept along his arms.

"It troubles me to admit this, but . . ."

There was that troubling word *but* again.

"Just say it, madam," Marcus called from the next room. "No need to be so delicate."

"Very well then." The mourning woman met Robert's eyes at last. "Mr. Highstead, Miss Lowell may not be whom she claims."

IV.

"I don't understand," Robert said, slumping back in his chair. He pointed toward the cordial, no longer shy.

"She's not who she claims to be," the mourning woman reiterated, pouring the liquor into a tall thin glass. "Just as I said."

"You mean she's a fraud," Robert replied after he'd taken a healthy slug; he welcomed the burn as the alcohol snaked down his throat.

"Those are hard words, Mr. Highstead," she replied; her dark brown eyes were enormous behind her spectacles. "But yes, that's what some claim."

"Who claims?"

"The Seekers of the Lost Dream. Especially Mrs. Douglas. Now that Mr. de Bonne has passed"—again, she made the sign of the cross—"she's demanding access to Ada's Folly to make certain he's buried beside Ada. Of course, she's also eager to view the chapel, like everyone else. She wants to 'break the glass, but not to plunder' and all that."

Robert waved the fragments of poetry away. "Mrs. Douglas has no legal authority." Though he desired the same fate for Hugh's remains, he felt obliged to disagree.

"She claims she does, Mr. Highstead. And she's engaged a solicitor to prove Miss Lowell is an imposter." Whether it was the alcohol she'd imbibed or relief from no longer avoiding a difficult subject, her words arrived tripping on the heels of each other. "Tamsin Douglas and her ilk claim Ada's Folly is a property of artistic importance, like Lord Byron's Newstead Abbey. They think it's a crime for Miss Lowell to refuse them access, that she's selfish and obstinate."

Robert couldn't argue with their assessment of Isabelle's character. Yet he felt oddly protective of her.

The mourning woman continued. "Three years ago Tamsin Douglas tried to purchase Ada's Folly, offering an absurd amount of money to entice Miss Lowell. Miss Lowell refused, using Hugh's disappearance as an excuse."

"But wouldn't this prove Miss Lowell to be as she claims? An imposter would have accepted the money and left, don't you think?"

She pursed her lips. "It matters not. It ended badly."

"Frankly, it's hard to imagine them friends in the first place."

"I suppose to you." The mourning woman leaned in, her eyes bright behind her spectacles. "It's a well-known tale among the pilgrims, Mr. Highstead. Mrs. Douglas was the widow of Hugh's editor. She assisted Miss Lowell in the aftermath of Hugh's disappearance—Miss Lowell ended up responsible for more than just Weald House. Initially Miss Lowell was sympathetic to Mrs. Douglas's losses—who wouldn't be?—but soon comprehended that Mrs. Douglas valued Hugh's poetry and the key to the glass chapel more than their friendship." She shook her head. "But now that Hugh's dead and Miss Lowell's his heir . . ."

"Hence the unpleasantness this morning." Robert rubbed his brow. "But how exactly does any of this make Miss Lowell suspect as an imposter?"

"No one can vouch that Miss Lowell—*this* Miss Lowell—is the one who grew up with Ada de Bonne at Weald House. You see, until the night Isabelle showed at Weald House over a decade ago, no one there had ever seen her before."

The mourning woman paused to pour herself another cup of tea with a hefty dose of cordial for good measure. "It's a peculiar story I am about to tell you. If I hadn't heard it with my own ears from those who witnessed it, I'd believe someone made it up."

The remainder of the tea passed in such strange conversation that Robert was later to speculate whether he'd dreamt it.

"It was late November 1838," the mourning woman began. "Just after the first snow. Soon after Hugh's disappearance upon completing the glass chapel for Ada. That night Mrs. Chilvers discovered a young woman nearly frozen to death in Ada's rose garden. You should have seen her, all skin and bones, along with that shocking white hair! She even had lice and sores from malnourishment. Mrs. Chilvers saved the creature, of course—she'd have died otherwise. Once she was able to speak, she told Mrs. Chilvers she was barely twenty, that she'd traveled all the way from France to speak to Hugh about an important matter.

"And then she said the inconceivable: 'I am Isabelle Lowell.'

"Mrs. Chilvers didn't know her; the housekeeper had only inhabited Weald House after Ada's marriage. The other servants didn't believe her. Isabelle had been a favorite of Ada's, but no one had seen her in years because she'd been sent to school. Most assumed she'd gone into service since she was an orphan.

"The servants wanted to turn her out once she'd recovered. 'How do you know she's really Isabelle Lowell? She's probably an unfortunate seeking to swindle us.' Even then there was so much ado about Hugh's poetry, though they didn't call them pilgrims then—they just called them mad. Mrs. Chilvers argued it went against Christian principles to refuse her shelter. 'Let her stay until Mr. de Bonne returns—he's sure to show eventually since this is his house. If she is whom she claims to be, he'll know her.' But . . . But—"

The mourning woman pressed her lips tight as a seam.

"But Hugh de Bonne never returned to Weald House," Robert finished, steepling his fingers before his face in an attempt to affect a detachment he didn't feel.

The mourning woman nodded, her eyes glistening. "Once Miss Lowell recovered, she just took over Weald House, though no one recalled her. You see, Mrs. Chilvers wasn't the only one not to know Miss Lowell. Nor did anyone else in the village. Not the doctor. Not the grocer. No one." She shook her head. "I recall encountering Isabelle as a girl once or twice during holidays, but she didn't make much of an impression—she was a shy, fey child. I suppose there's some resemblance between her and Ada, but it's been so long and my eyesight is weak even with spectacles."

"I'd been a historian," Robert said, waving away her offer of a second slice of cake. "Questions of identity can often be resolved through a record search. Birth certificates, church records. School rosters. Primary sources."

"I haven't been able to find any thus far, Mr. Highstead. Perhaps the new solicitor I've hired will have better fortune."

"What of extended family? They could vouch for her."

She shook her head. "The Lowells died out after the war—all were farming folk save for Lucian, Ada's father. Nor could anyone find relations of Mr. de Bonne." She locked eyes with Robert. "That's why I was so surprised to learn you were his cousin—I'd truly considered Miss Lowell Hugh's last kin. I'd hoped you could offer resolution. This seems not to be." She shook her head. "It's as if Isabelle Lowell never existed save through thrice-told stories and hearsay."

Robert could bear no more; he felt as though he were suffocating beneath the weight of the past. Tamsin Douglas had sought to exploit Isabelle for her own interests. Isabelle wasn't whom she claimed to be—this explained much of her animosity. Yet he found himself disappointed, though he couldn't explain why. Why should he care? Isabelle had been nothing but repellent during his stay at Weald House. The compassion he'd felt at church was a reflection of the moment. Nothing else.

He pointed to the mantel clock. "I'm expected at Weald House. I appreciate your hospitality."

"I'll have Marcus ready the carriage." The mourning woman offered a knobby hand to Robert. He had the sense she expected him to kiss it in the continental fashion while she assisted him to his feet. He didn't.

Once he was securely upright, he asked, "Why does Isabelle Lowell's identity matter so much to you?"

"Because, Mr. Highstead, I knew Hugh de Bonne. I have an obligation to make sure his legacy is secured. I knew him during his time in Europe even before his first book was published. I cared for him in my way. Not as Ada did, but as one grateful for his art. It was a privilege. I'd been a patron of his even before he wrote *The Lost History of Dreams*. That poem, 'The Raven and the Rose'—I cannot tell you how it comforted me during my bleakest moments." The mourning woman drew a gold frame from a shelf. "Here, I have something precious to show you. Something no one else has seen."

She offered Robert the gold frame as though it were a relic. It contained a greying auburn plait of hair encased in a tiny glass compartment below a daguerreotype—he sold similar frames in his Catalogue of Possibilities. Once the daguerreotype was in Robert's hands, he recognized Hugh's features on the murky silvered plate, but something was off.

Hugh was dead. A corpse.

Robert's tea curdled in his stomach. How different this was from when he'd encountered Hugh's remains in his childhood home. Though he'd taken hundreds of post-mortem daguerreotypes in the past three years, this was the first time he'd viewed someone related to himself in one. He'd only been on the other side of the camera. The observer, not the mourner.

Robert stifled these thoughts, scanning the daguerreotype for some clue to the man his cousin had been. Was Hugh the homeless romantic described in Isabelle's story? Or the saint of poetry and lost love venerated by the Seekers of the Lost Dream? The daguerreotype revealed little: Hugh looked like many of the other corpses Robert had encountered during his employment. His cousin sat in an armchair with a book in his hands, his eyelids shut. Most likely the daguerreotypist had arrived too late to pry the eyes open before rigor mortis set in, but Robert had never shied from such manipulations.

A statuesque lady, veiled in black like an angel of death, stood behind Hugh's chair. Her gaze was adoring.

"You posed for this?" Robert pointed at the veiled figure.

The mourning woman's posture stiffened with pride. "Yes—I arranged for the daguerreotype. I was with him in Geneva before he breathed his last. He would see no one, but he agreed to see me. I'd come all the way from Paris to beg for a poem marking the anniversary of my husband's passing. I convinced Hugh to join me for dinner at my hotel. I recall he ordered the sole, though he scarcely touched it. He looked drawn. Sallow. I didn't dare mention the rumors about Isabelle returning to Weald House. I'd assumed he'd heard, and if he hadn't, I didn't want to distress him, given his state. Instead, I advised him to consult a physician. I'll never forgive myself for not insisting." She dabbed her lashes with a black-bordered handkerchief. "Once I learned the worst, I used my authority to preserve Hugh's likeness for my private collection. I'd hoped for his burial at Père Lachaise in a private tomb beside Abelard and Heloise. Hugh's solicitor intervened before I could make arrangements."

"So you traveled here as quickly as you could."

"I knew someone would show eventually with Hugh." She smiled through her tears. "I've only been here for just over a week. In this time, I've tried to approach Miss Lowell, but she refuses to see me. No doubt she considers me akin to a pilgrim."

Robert returned the daguerreotype, uncertain how to respond. If he told the mourning woman of Hugh's request to be interred with Ada, he'd be granting credence to Tamsin Douglas. But Paris—that wasn't what Hugh wanted either.

"What do you want from me?" he said at last.

"Besides to let me bring Hugh back to Paris? You must speak to Miss Lowell. She should know Tamsin Douglas plans to contest her claim to the estate, and will have her cast out from Weald House." She took Robert's hands, her grip firm. "If Hugh de Bonne is laid to rest in Ada's Folly, Mrs. Douglas will find a way to force the chapel open to any Jane or John with a farthing to spare. There will be displays far worse than what you witnessed today at the church."

"Yet I sense there's something else you desire," Robert said, pulling his hands from hers.

"How clever you are, Mr. Highstead! Just like Hugh." Her tone grew steely. "Persuade Miss Lowell to let me purchase Ada's Folly and Weald House. If we move quickly, a court won't be able to intervene even if she's discredited. I'll protect Ada's Folly from the pilgrims. Preserve it. For art. For the future."

To his surprise, Robert responded, "What of Ada's grave? Perhaps the chapel is best kept locked."

"This won't matter if Mrs. Douglas's suit is successful. Miss Lowell will be turned out without a farthing to spare." She set her palm on Robert's shoulder. "You'll help?"

The memory of Isabelle, how slight she'd felt in his arms while he'd carried her from the church, returned to Robert. He suddenly felt very weary. "Whom might I say is making this offer?"

The mourning woman clapped her hands. "How good you are! Tell her I'm an old friend of Hugh's. The Vicomtesse de Fontaine." A giggle.

"Though if Miss Lowell is whom she claims, she would better know me by my name before I married."

"What might that name be?"

The mourning woman giggled again and smoothed her curls. "Missus Dido."

V.

Missus Dido's carriage was as fettered with mourning as her cottage had been. It was a four-seater brougham decorated with black plumes, purple satin upholstery, and gleaming ebony wood, grand as any Robert had seen during his time as a daguerreotypist of the dead. He hardly noticed. He examined each of the sentences Missus Dido had uttered during their tea, turning them in his mind like they were specimens. Viewed as a whole, they only confused.

"*Miss Lowell may not be whom she claims.*" If this was true, how had Isabelle learned so much about Ada's and Hugh's lives? "*Once she was able to speak, she told Mrs. Chilvers . . . she'd traveled all the way from France to speak to Hugh about an important matter . . .*" What would this matter be? And why would she insist on Ada's story being published now?

Because Hugh is no longer alive to stop her.

Robert stared out the window as the brougham rolled from the village toward Weald House. Instead of passing through fields and woods, which would have afforded a last view of Ada's Folly before his departure, the carriage wove over the moors. Despite the bright day, the moors unfurled with the sullen gold and grey of late winter, different from any landscape he'd viewed before. Unlike the curated fields of Belvedere from his childhood, the moors were wild and open and endless. He made out the soft grey of heather, the ochre of winter grass, and white spots signifying the movement of sheep in the distance. In another month, the moors would reawaken when spring returned: the grass would turn green, the hedgerows bloom. Life would continue in the face of death.

This observation departed Robert's mind as quickly as it rose, for his thoughts whirled like the carriage wheels, distracting him from the heaviness in his stomach. He shouldn't have had the cake and cordial. He leaned his head against the carriage window, relishing the cool glass against his temples.

And then he saw her. Isabelle, or whoever she was.

She stood on the edge of the moor but twenty feet away. Her back was turned from the road, the dog at her side. Or at least Robert *thought* it was her—she seemed a different creature from the sharp-tongued adversary he'd encountered these past evenings, more akin to the woman he'd rescued from Tamsin Douglas and her flock of pilgrims. After hearing Missus Dido's account, Isabelle appeared transformed. Or was it Robert who was transformed?

Isabelle must not have heard the carriage's approach, for she didn't stir. Nor did Virgil.

Robert called up to Marcus. "Is that Miss Lowell?"

"I believe so. We're not far from Weald House now."

"Can you stop a moment?"

Time slowed like treacle as Robert watched Isabelle from the carriage, just as he'd watched her in the rose garden with the eye miniature.

Isabelle looked to be staring out at the horizon. Her arms were raised toward the sky, her bonnet dangling from her shoulders in a strange display he couldn't quite fathom. She swayed, eyes shut as she lifted her head toward the sky. Light streamed over her form. For the first time since Robert had made her acquaintance, her white hair wasn't pinned tightly about her skull. She'd freed it, allowing the thick tresses to fall beyond her waist. Its ivory hue seemed not of this world as it glistened beneath the afternoon sun.

In that moment, instead of reminding him of Ada or a Circe or even a goshawk, Isabelle reminded him of one of the most exquisite things he'd ever encountered: an icon of Saint Catherine by Crivelli he and Sida had viewed at the National Gallery in London while they were courting. The Crivelli was a small painting, intensely detailed in the Flemish Renaissance manner; Sida had explained the art was meant to inspire devotion, not appreciation.

Who are you?

The question rose unbidden before Robert could turn from it.

He recalled Missus Dido's account of Isabelle's mysterious past, how she'd shown up at Weald House after Hugh's disappearance and Ada's death, and that no one had encountered Isabelle in years. Yet as he stared at Isabelle, it seemed it was Missus Dido who was caught in the past, with her daguerreotype of Hugh, her obsession with his legacy. All of a sudden

Robert had the sensation of being caught in the past himself. There he was, with his devotion to his ghost wife, his impossible quest to daguerreotype Hugh inside Ada's Folly. How was he any different than Missus Dido? This realization disturbed him. It felt as dangerous as Owen flicking those matches, or Grace accosting those bees. After Sida's death, Robert had longed for her return with every breath of his being—when she'd appeared that day in his mirror, he'd felt a joy beyond compare. Yet now, standing on the moors staring at the woman claiming to be Isabelle Lowell, his quest to hold on to his wife after her death felt foolish, though he was uncertain why. This troubled him deeply.

He thought of his disgrace at Oxford, his inability to write since then. His burrowing into the land of the dead with his ghost wife and daguerreotypes. He thought of Hugh's pursuit of his *locus amoenus* in Ada, Isabelle's hunger to protect her aunt's resting place against Hugh and the pilgrims, and even John with his desire to be rid of his responsibility to Hugh's estate. Weren't they all constrained by the past, just as he was?

Robert squinted again at Isabelle. At her unbound hair rippling in the wind.

He gave himself a little shake. "Stop being so fanciful. After tomorrow, it won't matter who she is."

But then he remembered her handkerchief, which he'd stuffed into his pocket during the church melee. He'd return the handkerchief, inform her he was leaving in the morning, and request the return of his camera. He'd tell her of Missus Dido's offer, bringing closure to an unpleasant interlude. He'd move into his future, whatever that might be. Yes, his brother would be disappointed, Hugh would never be reunited with his wife, but he'd have done what he could. That would have to be enough.

"Miss Lowell!" he shouted, a strange hope flooding his veins.

Isabelle whirled toward the carriage, a flush spreading across her face. "Is that you, Mr. Highstead?"

Her voice was high and odd as she plaited her hair; he'd startled her along with the dog, who gave a low growl. There was an unexpected openness in Isabelle's gaze, a surprising warmth. Even her complexion looked calmer, her features gentler of mien. In that moment, Robert saw her as she might have been years ago, before she'd become crippled by sorrow and loss. Her lost history, as Hugh had described in his book.

Who are you? he thought again.

An answer to his question came as unexpectedly as his happening upon her on the moors.

Startled by the dog's barking, an army of sparrows fluttered up from the tall grass. They swirled around Isabelle in an array of brown and grey feathers and chittering bird song. As they settled along her shoulders, Robert pulled her black-bordered handkerchief from his pocket. It felt strangely stiff against his fingers.

Blood spotted the ivory linen like anemones in the snow.

PART II

DREAMS FOUND

*

Later That Day

Shropshire

A Coat Sewn of Fur

Excerpted from *Cantos for Grown Children* by Hugh de Bonne, published 1834 by Chapman & Hall, London.

The Forest was cold, the girl was too. That long night
Thru chattering lips she whispered a tale
To help her survive 'til Morning's light—
A tale her Father told : *Once there was a girl*
As white as snow, with lips red as blood . . .

Though her words were hot, the cold was strong
And salt'd tears froze o'er her wan cheeks.
'I shall expire,' she cried. 'O my Father, pray for me!'
But a prayer to one parent is a prayer to all
And bestirred the deepest Forest into Life.

Soon others circled the poor cold girl :
Bear and fox, lion and possum,
A mink draped in gold, a wolf jeweled in pearls.
'Daughter, we're here!' they cried. 'Have no qualm!
We'll warm you like a coat sewn of fur.'

*

I.

Later when Robert was to think upon that moment on the moors when he first considered whether Ada de Bonne still lived, he'd remember it akin to the compulsion that had led to him gambling all he'd possessed to learn how to daguerreotype corpses after Sida's death.

She can't be Ada, he told himself back in the stable house, unable to forget the sight of Isabelle's hair glimmering with sun, her face open with joy, the sparrows along her arms. She'd seemed another woman, not the adversary who'd mistrusted him even before his arrival. He recalled the soft welcome of her arms in the church as they'd wrapped around his neck when he'd carried her from the pilgrims. The scent of her hair. The confusion Missus Dido's words had unleashed. Yet it made sense: If Ada was still alive, she wasn't buried in the chapel. This would explain her panicked refusal to allow Robert to inter Hugh there, or to let the pilgrims view the stained glass.

With this, Isabelle's—or was she Ada?—antagonism rearranged itself into a new history: she *wanted* Robert to leave before he uncovered the truth.

It was mad. Impossible.

His ankle aching, he sat down at the little table where he usually took his meals. His hand sped across the journal containing Ada's story. He wrote:

> *Blood on a handkerchief doesn't always signify consumption.*
> *If she was Ada, wouldn't someone recognize her?*
> *Why would Hugh build a chapel for Ada unless she was truly gone?*

Suddenly he remembered Isabelle had scarcely spoken of herself as she recounted her story. *It can't be a coincidence.* Her words returned: *"I've spoken only of my aunt's experiences to save time . . . I was sent to school when I turned seven."* He'd assumed she was telling her story to preserve Ada's memory. Now none of this made sense.

He wrote: *Who is Isabelle Lowell?*

He underlined the words with a sharp stroke of his pencil. His stomach quivering with excitement, Robert leafed through the journal, rereading the history she'd spun so far. Did Isabelle Lowell even live? Perhaps she'd died years earlier, lost to poverty or worse; Ada had donned Isabelle's identity in the same way he'd worn Hugh's clothes.

Robert tapped his pencil against his chin, flummoxed.

Why would Ada do this? Why would she hide her identity? And then, without warning, a new story unfurled before his imagination: Ada had abandoned Hugh after the death of their daughter, too bereft to remain with him in the Black Forest. When Hugh didn't find her at Weald House, he built the chapel to regain her favor. But by the time Ada returned to Weald House, Hugh had disappeared, leaving her its only key. (Why did he leave? Remorse? Anger? This Robert couldn't figure out.) Nor had Ada ever entered the chapel, if Robert was to believe the evidence. As for taking Isabelle's name, if the pilgrims knew Ada still lived, they'd blame her for Hugh's disappearance and death. They'd make her life a misery. Better to be presumed dead herself. And here she was over a decade later, with her husband dead, her last hope gone, bearing the weight of Ada's story.

Mad. Impossible.

Robert shoved the journal away. This was what had happened with his Ovid biography: he'd made suppositions without supporting evidence. He wouldn't do that again. And then he knew: he couldn't return to Kent the next morning with Hugh's corpse. Not until he knew the truth—or as much as could be surmised from Isabelle's story. But what would Sida think of his decision? His obsession with Ada's story felt a strange disloyalty to his marriage. He still felt awful about ignoring her to look for that miniature in Hugh's study.

All of a sudden Robert could no longer bear it. He had to learn more about Isabelle's past. But who to ask?

The kitchen was uninhabited save for Mrs. Chilvers, who was snoring before the fire, her slackened mouth wet with spittle. ("Did Miss Isabelle say you could tarry here, Mr. Robert?" she said, startled awake when Robert opened the door. "I was informed you were to remain in the stable house.") After a few minutes, she relaxed into her usual garrulous state, even willing to discuss Grace and the pilgrims. ("I have no idea what that girl was up to, Heaven save her. However, Miss Isabelle didn't sack her like I'd expected. Instead, she pretended naught happened. It was very queer.")

Eventually he steered the conversation to Isabelle's return to Weald House years earlier.

"I've been told it was peculiar," he said matter-of-factly. "No one had seen her for some time."

And no one remembers her.

The elderly woman's lips puckered as though she'd tasted something tart. "Who told you that?"

"Oh, someone at church. Not a pilgrim." He added, "You found Miss Lowell in the rose garden, didn't you?"

"That's years ago," Mrs. Chilvers replied, grabbing a bowl of potatoes and carrots to wash. "Not long after I came to Weald House—I truly don't remember much of those days."

Robert wouldn't be deterred. "You were the last person to see Hugh before his disappearance."

"Again, 'twas long ago, Mr. Robert. He was here such a short time. He kept to himself. He was busy with the glass chapel, with laying Miss Ada's remains to rest there."

"You witnessed this?"

"No. By then the glass workers were long gone—they'd come from France—and he refused to let anyone help with Ada's burial in the chapel but old Ned Shephard, who's since passed on." Mrs. Chilvers's words slowed as she rinsed carrots in a basin. "You must understand Mr. Hugh wasn't in his right mind. He seemed to never eat or sleep. Nor did he talk much. We scarcely spoke save when he gave me the key for Ada's Folly. He said it was for Miss Isabelle should she come here. That she was the only person permitted to go inside the chapel." She looked up from the basin. "And before you ask, no, I never used the key to unlock Ada's Folly—I'm an honest woman."

"Forgive me. I wasn't about to suggest this."

"Good." A long pause. "No one save myself even knew the key existed until Miss Isabelle mentioned it to Mrs. Douglas. Which was unwise of her, but what's done is done. Anyway, no need to speak of this. All that matters is Miss Lowell is a good mistress here. If it weren't for her . . ."

Virgil began to whimper, interrupting Mrs. Chilvers. No matter, for Robert could well imagine her unspoken words: *Weald House would have been lost.*

"And now you have me gossiping," she said once she'd let the dog out. She handed Robert a paring knife. "Perhaps you need to be less idle, Mr. Robert."

"My apologies. I should have offered."

Ada's dead. Buried in the glass chapel, he told himself as he peeled potatoes for dinner. It was hard to imagine the Isabelle Lowell he knew malnourished with lice and sores. As for Mrs. Chilvers's account of Hugh and the key, surely the fact that Hugh expected Isabelle to arrive at Weald House weighed in her favor.

"Is Miss Lowell about?" he asked Mrs. Chilvers once he'd finished the vegetables. He'd use Missus Dido's warning about Tamsin Douglas as an excuse to see her.

"Is that wise?" She shook her head. "How strange you are today, Mr. Robert."

However, he did see Isabelle later that afternoon, though the encounter was unplanned. When Robert left the kitchen to wend his way back to the stable house, he heard a rustling from the kitchen garden. He peered over the wall.

Isabelle stood by the beehive. Unsurprisingly, she was dressed in black. The remainder of her attire wasn't anything he'd ever expect. Her arms were covered by long white gloves, and her head hidden beneath a wide straw hat covered by a white veil thick enough to obscure her features.

A soft murmur rose from beneath the veil as she dragged briars from a pile toward the beehive.

"I'm sorry," she said gently. "I know you're angry, but this is to help you. Is there anything else you want to tell me?"

For a moment, he wondered if she was speaking to herself. And then he understood: she was talking to the bees just as Grace had that morning.

Robert watched in silence, fearful of upsetting her or the bees, as she methodically wove briars around the base of the hive, pausing only to survey her work or to speak to them. The thorny barrier must be to dissuade anyone from disturbing the bees. "It's for your own good," he heard her say. "You need peace."

He finally tore himself away, yearning for peace himself. But it was not to be: in the stable house, Robert found a thick green book on the table where he'd taken his meals. A letter was set on top of it.

Gratitude does not come easily to me, Isabelle had written:

> *Regardless I would be remiss not to thank you for your protection this morning at the church. After much reflection I understand I have been unkind—you suffer as I do. I hope this book offers you consolation, and invite you to take your meals henceforth in the kitchen.*

The book was a pricey 1841 edition of Ovid's *Metamorphoses*. The leather binding seemed to welcome his touch, for it felt warm and pliant when he opened it to the title page. Hugh de Bonne's signature slashed across the top margin. He'd written beneath in sepia-colored ink: *Eurydice, dying now a second time, uttered no complaint against her husband. What was there to complain of, but that she had been loved?*

Robert stared at Hugh's inscription for some moments, feeling as though his cousin had reached a hand across the veil of time. But then Robert's elation transformed into an odd disappointment. It took him a moment to recognize why: the signature he'd yearned to see was Ada's, not Hugh's.

II.

Isabelle did not speak of their encounter on the moors, nor of the book and her letter when they met the following evening in the library. But Robert did—he'd spent the day thinking of little else. Despite the comfort of taking his meals in the kitchen and the diversion of Hugh's Ovid, he found himself checking the clock as the day dragged toward seven, scarcely paying mind to Sida's return. "*How distracted you are, my sweet*," she'd said before she'd taken off in her usual way.

"I apologize for startling you on the moors yesterday," he said to Isabelle after offering an awkward thanks for the Ovid. "When I saw you, I remembered I'd found your handkerchief in the church. But then I understood my intrusion."

His tone was careful, as though to avoid upsetting a bird in a tree. Isabelle's hair was again unbound about her shoulders, as though she'd been too weary to dress it. She appeared a different figure than the white-veiled woman he'd witnessed weaving briars around the beehive, or the vision on the moor. He glanced at the oil painting of Ada across the library, at her eyes cast in shadows, her long dark hair. The tenderness he'd felt upon first encountering the portrait now seemed layered with all he'd learned from Isabelle's story: Ada's gentleness and artistry. Her vulnerability. For a moment, he imagined the painted figure bearing light hair instead of dark. Grey eyes, like Isabelle's.

Ada is dead. You only wish her to be alive.

Isabelle accepted the handkerchief without examining it. Her breathing sounded heavier than usual.

"I'd thought you'd returned after the service, Mr. Highstead. I didn't recognize your carriage."

"I had tea with someone in the village," he said carefully. "Someone you might know from your past."

"It seems my past is the same as my future. Here, at Weald House," she said, staring down at the fire while it crackled in the grate. A corner of her mouth lifted. "When I first saw you on the moors, I considered if you were on your way to climb Ada's Folly again."

He swept his hand toward his ankle. "I am quite tamed, Miss Lowell. We have our agreement. I keep my word."

"And I mine," she countered, her old sharpness returning.

"Understood." A deep breath. "I have something I must speak about. This will be unexpected, but there's something I must warn of. It regards Missus Dido and Ada's Folly—"

The speech he'd carefully planned was cut short by a breeze picking up, rustling ashes from the grate. A smattering of dust flew into Isabelle's face. "Oh!" she cried, as she dissolved into a fit of coughing. "Oh, my eyes!"

"You should take better care of yourself," Robert said once she'd calmed. He found himself staring at her hair, her face, her hands. She looked as she ever did, with her tight angular form adorned in grey half-mourning, her preternaturally white hair, her large pale eyes with their dark lashes, her long musician's fingers. Yet everything was different.

She shook her head, moisture streaming down her cheeks. "Why should I take care of myself? No one but pilgrims come here. No one truly knows me now that Ada's gone—not Owen for all his loyalties, not Mrs. Chilvers for all her age, nor Grace for all her cleverness. Ada was beautiful. Ada was loved. What did that get her?" She rubbed her fists against her face, her eyes watering still. "A glass chapel in the woods."

"It must be difficult to view so much of the world as your enemy."

"I don't see the world as my enemy, Mr. Highstead. Only the pilgrims and . . ."

You. She was going to say this—Robert had no doubt.

"I know you consider me an interloper," he said, his tone rising. "Someone who's arrived to bring discord into your life after you've lost so much. I do understand—you and I, we're more alike than not. I've also lost those I love. Not just my wife, but my mother when I was a boy, my father as a young man. It's for these reasons I became a daguerreotypist."

"Which is why you're here." She looked up at last, her eyes swollen from ash. "Our conversations always return to those daguerreotypes of Ada's Folly, don't they? You must be very desperate to regain your brother's favor."

Before he could stop himself, he snapped, "You think that's why I'm here? Because of an inheritance? It's my wife I'm doing this for. No one else. I know what it's like to mourn a spouse and yearn to be reunited with her. If I can grant this to Hugh . . ."

Isabelle's face crumbled briefly. "Oh," she said.

Robert could hear the wind outside rustling against the trees. The crackle of fire in the grate.

Isabelle said, "You must have loved Cressida very much."

"More than you can imagine."

"What was she like?"

Robert knew he shouldn't answer, but he couldn't resist. In a way, it was like making Sida live again.

"She—my wife, Cressida—was an artist. She was wise. She helped me see beauty. She made me care about the world. To take part in it, instead of writing of it for a book." His voice thickened. "She was the kindest person I've ever known."

Before he could think twice, he'd taken out the eye miniature from his pocket. As Isabelle examined it, her brow rose. *Like Ada*, he suspected she was thinking. But that wasn't what she said.

"Such a dark iris. Like that of a Persian."

Robert nodded reluctantly, though he didn't sense judgment in her observation. "Her father was a lascar, her mother English. Cressida was orphaned as a child. Sent to live with her mother's brother who considered her little better than a servant . . ."

Robert's words drifted into silence as yearning overtook him. That August day he'd come upon her by the river surrounded by cattails and dragonflies. She'd offered an apple. "*Pomona*," he'd murmured. The apple was crisp and cool. "*Eve*," she'd answered, taking a bite in turn, defiant despite the bruise on her jaw where her uncle had slapped her. Their lips had met and they'd sunk into the cattails, where no one could spy their entwined limbs. Afterward, she'd said, "*I must go. Yet I can't leave you, my sweet.*" He'd answered, "*Nor I you . . .*"

Isabelle's voice interrupted his memory.

"Mr. Highstead? Are you well?"

Robert drew a deep breath before returning the eye miniature to his pocket. "I've said too much. My apologies."

What had possessed him to reveal the miniature? It only reminded him how he'd ignored Sida that afternoon. Worst of all, he'd grown no closer to uncovering Isabelle's identity. Nor had he warned of the threat to her inheritance.

Isabelle burst out, "I don't mean to be unkind, Mr. Highstead. Had circumstances been different, we might have even been friends—God knows I could use one. It's just . . ."

She dipped her face toward her clasped hands on her lap.

"Ada. Hugh. The pilgrims." Robert trained his gaze on his journal. "I understand." Yet he found he understood nothing at all.

A long moment of silence passed, broken only by Virgil nudging the door open. Once the dog settled at Isabelle's feet, she pointed at Robert's journal. "I must continue Ada's story."

III.
The Third Night's Story

You asked me of Missus Dido and Ada's Folly, Mr. Highstead. Despite Missus Dido's jealousy, you might think the visit to Canterbury Cathedral was when the seeds for the glass chapel were planted. You'd be right, but like seeds sown in frozen soil, they took time to flower. However, if I am to be completely honest in my recounting of Ada's story, I must admit this mattered not. You see, there were other forces affecting my aunt.

Ada was not the same after that trip to Canterbury, when Hugh had her eye painted. If she'd thought she'd loved him before, she now knew without a shadow of doubt that she loved him more than she'd believed anyone could love. Yet this knowledge was an icy splash of water. It wasn't because of Hugh—Ada remained as drawn to him as the day they'd met over her poor dead sparrow. Nor was it because of the portrait of her eye—if anything, she'd taken the portrait as a sign he loved her too. It was because of her parents, Lucian and Adelaide. All those stories she'd been told of her parents and their eternal devotion returned to her. They rearranged themselves into a new narrative: love had led to their deaths as surely as consumption would one day lead to hers. Protectiveness rose in her. If Hugh cared for her, she'd destroy him in time. Ada had never felt so haunted.

If this wasn't enough of a detriment, Missus Dido had uncovered Hugh's history beyond what he'd confided to Ada: the married women he'd seduced, the courtesan who'd drowned herself after finding herself with child, the duel he'd fought in London over a flimsy insult, which had left him with his limp and scar. The scandals. The waste.

"You believe Mr. de Bonne is courting me for my inheritance," Ada said.

Missus Dido clucked her tongue. "I didn't say that exactly."

Regardless, Missus Dido's spiteful words hit their mark. Ada refused to leave her room. Ignored the piano. Refused to come down for meals. Her love for Hugh would become another loss among many.

Sensing her avoidance, Hugh sent Ada the miniature of her eye later that week; he'd mounted the watercolor inside a small brass frame. He wrote: *I have been forward in my attentions. I wish to make amends, but fear I am too late. Regardless, I will remain in Herne Bay hoping for some sign of your favor.* He finally sent the afore-promised dove to join the first one, but he was right: it *was* too late. Ada set the doves in their golden cage outside on her balcony. Still, his letters continued to arrive, some light of tone, others concerned. *I must have wearied you with my talk of queens and kings*, he wrote in one. In others he included poems that spoke of birds and air from a new book he'd written:

Alone, I turn to find her thus:
Her dark hair asunder with nested
Sparrow. Her shoulders artless
Yet garbed with Dove and Ibis.

Ada did not respond. Missus Dido tutted at the arrival of every letter, but insisted Ada read his poems aloud.

Hugh soon replaced his letters with packages. These offerings contained books to tempt Ada's interest, though he had no idea of her interests beyond music and birds. Some were of the classical world to match the Ovid Wilhelm had taught her. Others were of scientific knowledge, such as Audubon and John Walker. None were novels. This pleased Ada, for she was hungry for truth, not illusions—she'd lived with those long enough. He even created a scavenger hunt, where one book led to another, and finally to a letter tucked inside a teapot. Though Ada showed no one what he'd written, her cheeks had stained scarlet.

Encouraged by her spare note of acknowledgment, Hugh sent her geological specimens he'd uncovered during his travels. They were dark and darted with strange shapes. Fossils, Hugh called them; Ada recalled finding similar while on the moors with Wilhelm when she was five. She discovered herself staring at the fossils at odd times: when Missus Dido plaited her hair, or when she should have been asleep. The shapes and colors of these fossils suggested life in reverse; one had to imagine the form that had been trapped in them so long ago, then calcified into loss as they rotted away. The fossils contained a primordial power. She sensed that if one were to look away from them, they'd morph on their own into a fungus that would overtake the room, banishing the pink cabbage rose wallpaper into memory.

Missus Dido offered to speak to Hugh. "I see him every night in the restaurant downstairs," she explained more eagerly than Ada cared. "I can tell him to let you be."

"It's not necessary. I'd like to leave tomorrow," she informed Missus Dido. "Time to go home."

That last night in Herne Bay, Ada breathed regularly to calm herself; her last physician suggested this as an alternative to laudanum or morphia when her nerves became overtaxed. *In and out*, she thought, her diseased lungs straining. Even after removing her stays and donning her nightdress, she still felt distressed. (Perhaps a better word was *disoriented*; Ada found this easier than *overtaxed* or *delicate*. How weary she was of being an invalid!) She forced the window open, welcoming the chill air. In the distance, she heard the lobby clock chime eleven; surely everyone was now asleep. Even Hugh.

It doesn't matter, she told herself. *I mustn't love him.*

Then: *Did Hugh know she was leaving?*

The memory of Hugh in the cathedral returned. His eager voice as he recited his poem. His face beneath the stained glass. His delight in the eye miniature.

What does it matter? she thought. *Nothing matters.*

Ada blew out all the candles save the two framing her mirror. She unpinned her hair, which was as fine as it was dark. Just like her mother's. Her eyes looked especially large and bright, though she hadn't taken any belladonna. Were they like her father's? She untangled her hair, first with her fingers, then moving to the brush. It was a difficult business without Missus Dido's help; she'd sent her guardian away after finding her inexplicably weeping over Hugh's poems.

She blew out another candle, leaving only one. Darkness would help to forget.

Perhaps it was the lack of light, but Ada's hearing sharpened. She heard each stroke of the brush as it caught against each snarl, the rush of the ocean through the window as it beat against the pier. Neptune's Arm, they'd called the pier. A lovely name for something so unlovely. During the day the pier was brash and loud, lined with paddle steamers and people, as hard of aspect as water was soft. Now that it was night, all was silent on the pier but birds. Gulls, cormorants, even crows. She closed her eyes to take them in, imagining their wings caught by air, the rush of wind sweeping toward France. Across the sea. Away.

Her reverie was interrupted by footsteps outside her door. A soft knock.

"I'm sleeping," she said.

"You don't sound asleep," a calm male voice replied from outside the door. Hugh's voice.

Ada opened her eyes to stare at herself in the mirror. She was flushed beneath golden light. Her lips parted in a manner she'd never noticed before. Her eyes widened as if she was anticipating something. But what? *If I love him, we must never be*, she reminded herself.

"Come in." The command in her voice surprised her.

She heard the door open. She heard Hugh take a step toward her.

"Why are you here, Mr. de Bonne?" Her voice was bitter in its imperiousness.

"Because you've been sad."

Hugh stated the sentence like the irrefutable fact it was. Just as Madame Clarice had when she'd described that Beethoven sonata.

Ada didn't bother with a denial. She thought of her piano, how each note marked the passage of time in a way that turned it endurable, how the sound rose from inside it to rise into air. Her fingers clenched, yearning for the keyboard. As if this could distract her from his presence.

"Your Dodo confessed you were leaving tomorrow." His teasing words didn't match his tone.

"I don't want to see you."

"Yet you allowed me in. And you're alone."

Hugh's footsteps drew closer and closer. She didn't dare turn from her mirror to acknowledge him. Nor would she look at his reflection in the glass, as if this would excuse the scandal of being alone with him in her room. She remembered the stories Missus Dido had told her: the women Hugh had seduced, the one who'd committed suicide, the duel . . .

The door clicked shut.

Ada could stand no more. She turned. Her eyes widened and breath tightened as she made out Hugh only a few steps away in the dusky gloom. He was silhouetted against the white-painted door, the carved lintel with its swirls of acanthus oddly delicate above his head. Despite the shadows, she saw he was outfitted like he'd just returned from a walk along the shore; his greatcoat looked dashed with damp, his ruddy hair curling. Ada could smell the salt rising from him, a tang that reminded her of sweat on a horse.

"I know I shouldn't have come to you," Hugh said, "but I was concerned." Another step. "I had to see you, to reassure myself you hadn't taken ill"—two steps—"and that's why you were leaving. I feared if I didn't come to you—"

"We'd never see each other again," Ada finished, her mouth dry.

He nodded, his gaze never leaving hers. Now he was beside her. Perhaps it was the late hour, but Hugh appeared older than she remembered at Canterbury. Tired. He no longer resembled the hero who'd rushed in to rescue her after her sparrow became tangled in briars, or the gentleman offering a mate to her dove. Nor did he resemble the seducer her guardian described. He was a man weighed by loss. A man bearing tangible concern.

For her.

"You must go," she said, her voice catching.

He drew closer, picking up her brush. She grew light-headed.

"Your hair. May I?"

Ada's nod came before she could reconsider.

He gently scooped up her hair from her neck, parting it deftly about her shoulders. She closed her eyes, bit her lip as he pulled a bit too hard with each stroke of the brush against her hair. She didn't stop him. How many other women's hair had he brushed?

Her hair gave way to the brush; she heard it crackle, smooth. "There," Hugh pronounced. "Now you're presentable. Do you want me to plait it? I'm not your Dodo, but I'll do my best."

She nodded, her stomach fluttering with a new warmth. How many other women had he plaited hair for?

But he didn't plait it. Instead, he sank to his knees before her chair, the brush still wrapped in his hand. Ada grew conscious of her feet shoved into her slippers, her bared flesh. His fingers brushed against her ankles.

She trembled with fear and yearning. With a shamelessness she hadn't known she possessed.

He gazed up at her, his eyes warm. He was asking permission. For what, she was uncertain—she was too innocent to know. Despite all those suitors, Ada remained unawakened. Hugh's poem returned to her, the one he'd recited after they'd traveled to Canterbury like pilgrims of old. "*We are so afraid of living that we live as though dead . . .*"

Her heart pounding in her bosom, she ran her thumb against the scar on his brow, his lips. He drew a sharp breath. His lips felt soft, warm. But he didn't kiss her, as she'd hoped. Instead, he swooped down to embrace her ankles as though she were a saint. For him to touch her like this . . . he must feel as she did.

The remembrance of Lucian and Adelaide moldering in the Kynnersley graveyard returned, the sun lacing the soil. Would she offer Hugh sun? Or suffering? But then her hands fell to her sides as he wrapped his arms about her. She clenched the arms of the chair, her fingers pressing into the velvet upholstery. Ada remained silent, fearful that if she gave any sign of encouragement—a breath, a murmur—Dido might overhear them. Or worse, Hugh might leave.

Unable to stop herself, she took his hand in hers, holding it as though it were all she possessed in the world. Her heart raced as she rubbed her thumb against the heart of his palm three times. One time for each of the three words she dare not say aloud. The same words that had doomed her parents.

I love you.

Her gaze locked with his.

Do you understand?

"*I do,*" she thought he answered.

He pulled away, locking his hands against the curve of her hips—"How thin you are!" he whispered—before rising from the floor to settle his mouth on hers.

She closed her eyes.

He tasted saline, like the sea. She imagined she tasted metallic, like her disease. She parted her mouth, astonished by how easily she offered herself to him. That her body had not protested, like it had with those suitors and their attentions. She remembered how it felt to stroke his hand with her thumb those three times, once for each sacred word. How the web of bone and cartilage comprising his palm felt a sacred thing she couldn't explain. The pulse she'd felt rising from beneath the translucent skin.

As they kissed, she felt a moistness—was it her? was it his tongue?—press inside her mouth. She wouldn't stop him. She even sighed. She felt herself open to him in a way she'd never experienced. Yearning for something, though she did not know what. *Her thumb against his palm. Those three strokes*. The yearning heightened the emptiness within her. An emptiness that needed to be filled.

She clenched her eyes shut tighter still. Hugh pulled away. His hand lingered against her cheek, caressing the softness. Frustrated, Ada pressed against his palm, the only way she could think to communicate without crying out her eagerness. Hadn't he understood her? She'd thought he had.

Fearful, her eyes remained closed tight, as if her lack of sight meant there was no substance to their encounter. Nothing to destroy her should he abandon her.

His hand fell from her face.

Ada heard the drape of his coat shift. The creak of his boots against the floor. Was he standing then? He was going to leave her, like everyone important in her life.

Silence passed, heavy. Impenetrable. Ada listened to see what would happen next.

Footsteps. The click of a door shutting.

By the time she opened her eyes, Hugh de Bonne had left her room.

Ada coughed as she took a deep breath. Her hands shaking, she drew the hem of her nightdress down over her feet. She couldn't bring herself to wipe the moisture from his kiss from her mouth, or to stare at her hand that had grasped his. She ignored the last candle on the vanity sputtering out.

You dreamt this, she told herself as she looked around her darkened room, but she knew this wasn't so. In that moment, Ada felt more alive than she ever had.

IV.

Isabelle rose, just as she did at the conclusion of each night's story. But, instead of leaving the library as Robert expected, she began to pace, her finger hooked beneath her chin. Robert's pencil remained on the page. He didn't dare reread what he'd just written; his body felt warm.

Isabelle paused in her pacing, her brow furrowed. "How quiet you are, Mr. Highstead! There you are, night after night, scratching away in such a diligent manner."

"Isn't that what you expect from me?"

"I suppose. Though sometimes I wish you'd interrupt my story."

"Our contract, Miss Lowell," Robert reminded, eager for a reason to remain silent; he shouldn't have spoken of Sida. Nor was he ready to confess he'd be leaving in the morning, or of Missus Dido. As the night had passed, he'd grown weighed by the awareness he'd most likely never see Isabelle again. Never know the truth of her story.

"Fie the contract," she muttered under her breath. "I find myself in need of a walk, Mr. Highstead. Bring the journal with you."

She handed Robert his walking stick and gathered a candle from the table.

Too startled to refuse, he followed her out the library and down the corridor, which was colder than he recalled. Her step was quick enough that her bombazine skirts swished about her limbs, and he struggled to keep pace; now that they'd left the library, she seemed to have gained vigor. Her pale hair glowed against her dark gown, the darkness of the corridor. Robert remained silent. He feared speaking. Feared she'd change her mind and dismiss him; if this was to be their last night together, he yearned to learn all he could.

Instead of taking him downstairs to the rose garden as he expected, Isabelle's steps slowed before one of the velvet curtains lining the walls of the passageway.

"Hold this." She handed Robert the candle, the scent of beeswax wafting in the chill air.

She drew a slender set of keys from her skirt pocket. For the briefest moment, their hands brushed and eyes met, hers revealing an unexpected vulnerability.

"Perhaps it's best to return to the library, where it's warmer," Robert said, concern overruling curiosity.

"I want to show you something," she said. "The east wing."

"Mrs. Chilvers said the east wing was abandoned."

"Mrs. Chilvers hasn't been up here in years."

Isabelle pulled the curtain aside, revealing a hidden set of doors. They were painted in what seemed a forest green; Robert couldn't be sure beneath candlelight.

She twisted the lock. The doors swung open on a huge octagonal room, far larger than any Robert expected Weald House held. Unlike the west wing, which overlooked the woods, the east faced onto the moors—even in the dead of night its rolling expanses unfurled before them, endless and star-filled. Seven of the eight walls held tall windows, most of them cracked in some way; the wind hissed against their glass, persistent and remorseless. The wood floor was undulated from moisture.

"This had been the conservatory?" Robert asked. If it had been, it no longer held any life. What little furniture remained was camouflaged beneath snowy-white sheets.

"A long time ago." Isabelle let out a shaky breath; it plumed in the icy air. "Ada would bring me here as a child on her good days. She loved the view. As do I."

"Who broke the glass?"

"The ravages of time, Mr. Highstead." Her mouth pursed with an unexpected wistfulness. "The conservatory was never used much, but when Ada became ill, one of her guardians decided it was unhealthy and cleared it out." She stared out toward the moors. "Sometimes I come here when it storms, just to watch rain leak onto the floor and know nothing can be done about it."

"Why not?"

She offered a half smile. "Because then Mrs. Chilvers would learn my secret. Everyone should have a secret, don't you think?"

Before Robert could answer, Isabelle took the candle from him and pointed at the white-draped silhouettes.

"There's wicker beneath, a whole set. Fancy too—supposedly Lucian bought it as a wedding gift for Adelaide. Ada used to nap on that settee over there on sunny days. Now, covered in all that white, they look like ghosts, don't they? Though of course, it's a matter of perception—if one was to remove the sheets, the illusion would vanish."

"I suppose, Miss Lowell." He felt a twinge of unease, thinking of Sida.

Isabelle set the candle on the floor, and yanked a cover off a chair. It wasn't as dusty as Robert expected.

"If you can write here, I think the view will help me tell Ada's story. Do you mind, Mr. Highstead? I know it's quite cold."

Robert blew on his hands to warm them.

* * *

In the morning, Ada woke when Missus Dido brought in her breakfast tray. She pointedly ignored her guardian, especially after she saw the letter tucked beneath the pot of chocolate. No pinpricks this time; the letter was sealed with green wax in three places.

Missus Dido looked sharply at the letter, taking in the overcompensation of security. "Another poem from Mr. de Bonne?"

Ada refused to answer.

She held the letter under the table, and broke the seals with a butter knife crowned by crumbs.

Miss Lowell, Hugh wrote—her stomach twisted with a peculiar lightness at the sight of his hand.

> *I must apologize for my behavior last night—you were too kind to receive me as you did. I am writing to assure you I will bother you no more. I must return to London. I pray you give my regards to the doves . . .*

This wasn't all she found inside the letter. He'd also placed her handkerchief, which he must have kept from their first encounter at Weald House when her sparrow met its death.

Once she unfolded the handkerchief, she noticed the dried blood dotting the lace hem. The blood looked as brown as her morning chocolate. As dark as dried menses. It reminded her of those fairy tales she'd read with Wilhelm while a child. How did it begin? *Once there was a girl as white as snow with lips as red as blood . . .* Whether the blood on the linen was from her coughing or from a cut on her lip when she'd fallen, it didn't matter. The blood remained, a reminder of what had transpired and what was lost.

Hugh was gone.

Ada pressed the handkerchief against her eyes, not caring whether her wretched guardian noticed. She recalled Hugh's mouth locked against hers, their hands entwined. The three strokes of her thumb against his palm. Those three unspoken words.

After Ada pushed away the rest of her breakfast, Missus Dido refused to leave just yet. "It's our last morning here, and I want to view the sea a last time. You look peaked—you need air. I won't allow you to say no." Ada suspected the real reason for their outing was a last chance for Missus Dido to flirt with gentlemen who weren't farmers.

They went outside, where a mule-drawn open carriage awaited. Missus Dido tucked the thick wool blanket over Ada's lap as if she were a child. Again, Ada yearned to slap her.

Ada remained sullen as they drove along the wood-lined parade toward the new Clock Tower, ignoring the forced cheer of Missus Dido's commentary: "See how cunningly close they built the Clock Tower to the sea? I heard it cost four thousand pounds. Four thousand pounds! Can you imagine? What I would do with such a sum! Someone told me they're planning to build a chapel down by the pier."

Once they'd pulled up to the Clock Tower, Ada refused to leave the carriage. "I feel weak," she lied.

"Suit yourself. I'll be back in a moment. Then we'll sit over there." Missus Dido pointed toward a bench on the edge of the parade, with a vantage of the sea. "No refusals."

Ada stuck her tongue out at her guardian's back as soon as she disappeared inside the Clock Tower. Now alone in the donkey cart, Ada avoided meeting the coachman's stare. She stifled a cough. She tried not to think of Hugh, of his presence in her room last night. She considered freeing her doves before leaving. She wished she'd brought a book.

The tide was out, leaving abandoned sea creatures in its wake. One crab, caught belly-up, flailed at a seagull attacking it, desperate to preserve its life. The bird's cry was as sharp as the stench rising from a mound of rotting sargassum. Beyond this, Ada's gaze narrowed on a tall figure cloaked in black.

Hugh. He'd lied—he hadn't left after all.

How alive he was, so strong despite his limp; she knew now it had arisen from passion, not accident. This made her love him all the more.

Her heart gave a rude thump. She slunk down against the seat. *Let him be.* Best he not see her. Not speak to her. Again, she thought of her parents in the graveyard in Kynnersley. Yet she couldn't resist peeking over the carriage side, in case she'd imagined him.

There he was, walking along the shore.

"I don't care," Ada said aloud. But she did.

She blinked, her eyes hot. All of a sudden she had a vision of herself from above as a bird would. She lay there in the carriage, a dark-haired girl with dark-rimmed eyes—she'd barely slept after he'd left her room—her body curled against the dark blue cushions, her hands clutching her palms. In that moment, her life seemed comprised of only two choices, one that would tie her to her past and the other to Hugh's future. If she remained in the carriage, her life would remain the same, with naught but illness and death. If she went to Hugh, she'd offer only love and sorrow.

What if he didn't respond?

A gull cried as though sending a message from above.

Then that's fate protecting him.

Ada tapped on the coachman's shoulder, her hands no longer trembling. "Can you help me down, sir?"

Once Ada was set on the ground—she'd winced when the coachman's hands encircled her waist a bit too eagerly—she pointed toward the Clock Tower. "When my companion comes out," she said, offering a shilling—he rubbed his hands at the sight—"can you tell her you took me back to the hotel because I felt ill?"

He nodded. And then Ada turned toward the sea. Toward Hugh.

Her legs felt unsteady, her kid slippers flimsy; she sensed the outline of every rock jutting against her soles, every shell. She should have donned boots like Missus Dido had suggested, but had claimed they'd irritate her ankles.

A few steps carried Ada to the edge of the wooden parade that ran along the coast. Once she reached the edge, she set her legs over the side and pulled her slippers off, dangling them by their ribbons. She hopped down onto the sand after casting a glance toward the Clock Tower. Missus Dido must have emerged, for the mule and carriage were gone. But Hugh was still there. Hugh who'd kissed her. Who'd understood what she'd meant when she'd pressed her thumb against his palm—or so she'd thought.

She called out, "Mr. de Bonne!"

He still looked out at the water.

"Hugh!" She shouted so hard that her throat ached.

Another gull swooped before her.

Turn back, she told herself. *It's not too late. This is fate's will.*

A third gull.

He looked over his shoulder. Toward her.

Too late.

Her heart swelled as though it would burst from her body as she stumbled across the rocky shore, toward the ocean. Toward him.

Hugh watched what Ada imagined was the spectacle of her approaching, her arms thrust out for balance. He later told her that she looked as though she intended to embrace the world, not just him. Whatever Ada's intention, he took her awkward, stumbling embrace for what it was: an invitation to love her.

"I thought you left." That's all she could say once she reached him.

"I only made it as far as the ferry landing."

"Why did you turn back?"

He took her hand in his. Three strokes of his thumb against her palm.

She sobbed with happiness, with terror. He *had* understood after all.

"I know I shouldn't have come to you last night," he said, "but I couldn't stop thinking of you. So lovely. So fragile. I've loved you since I first saw you that day with your poor sparrow—I'd never felt so protective of anyone as I did in that moment." He caressed her pale cheek. "I know I am older than you. I know I have a past that bears no honor. I have no immediate family. No home."

"And I know I have a future that will only bring you sorrow," she warned. "I'm unwell and unable to have children. I'll die and destroy you."

"But you're alive now, as am I." Hugh took a deep, shuddering breath before he gathered her in his arms, kissing her forehead, her neck, her cheeks beneath her bonnet. "I have nothing to offer but poems and birds and love. I will be the ruin of you."

She brushed his hair from his brow. "Perhaps we'll ruin each other then."

He tilted her face toward his, touching her lips gently. A year later, he'd tell Ada he'd tasted death on them; he'd wanted to breathe life into her, as if to bring her back from tipping into oblivion. But by then naught could be done.

V.

The candle began to sputter against the conservatory floor. Robert looked up. Isabelle was shivering.

"Perhaps that's enough for this evening, Miss Lowell."

Isabelle shook her head. "Not yet, Mr. Highstead. But if you're cold, we can return to the library. Here, let me help you up."

Once they were settled anew in the library, Isabelle continued to speak as though there'd been no interruption.

* * *

Ada and Hugh exchanged vows in Calais a scant ten days later, a wedding in which Missus Dido was their only guest. To Ada's surprise, her solicitor, Watkinson, had refused the match because she was underage: *It would be remiss of me to allow you to marry someone of such dubious heritage*, he wrote in a frosty letter. *Nor shall I release the funds for it.* Ever the problem solver, Hugh suggested they marry in France, where Ada's age wasn't a barrier, and contacted a distant cousin in Kent, a Mr. Bertram Highstead, for financial assistance. (Yes, your father, Mr. Highstead—no need to look so startled!) To avoid scandal, Hugh had insisted her guardian accompany them. "I suppose this is for the best," Missus Dido had congratulated Hugh after the ceremony, her eyes mysteriously red. "With her money, you'll be able to write all the poetry you want."

For a wedding present, Hugh gave Ada a coat sewn of furs and a sheaf of poems, which he proudly announced were to soon be published as his second book; they'd been inspired by Wilhelm's fairy tales. "Now the world will know you as I do, my love."

> Soon others circled the poor cold girl :
> Bear and fox, lion and possum,
> A mink draped in gold, a wolf jeweled in pearls.
> 'Daughter, we're here!' they cried. 'Have no qualm!
> We'll warm you like a coat sewn of fur.'

That first night, Hugh knelt beside the bed they were to share as husband and wife; she'd already blown out the candle, and was lying still as could be in her simple ivory nightdress, her hands pressed over her breast, unable to think of anything but what would happen next. Hugh did not stir from his knees for some moments. By then Ada knew him well enough to understand he could not be praying.

"Hugh?" she called out to him in the darkness; the room sounded empty and cold despite the fire blazing in the hearth. Though it was early May, death still weighed the air. "Come to bed."

How strange to say this phrase so matter-of-factly.

"In a moment, my love." He pressed his face against her hand. His cheeks were wet.

"Why are you weeping?" This was their wedding night; they were supposed to be happy. "Are you crying because we've left England?"

"No. I don't care two figs about England—you're my home now. My *locus amoenus.*" Later in their marriage, he'd tell her, *"I was weeping because I fear you are going to die. Because I've married sorrow instead of you."*

But that night Hugh would not explain; he could not explain. Instead, he asked, "Are you cold, my love? You've gooseflesh on your arms. Will spring ever arrive? Come, let me warm you."

He rose to spread the fur coat he'd given her over her form, so still and cool and beautiful on their nuptial bed—

VI.

"I can speak no more of this," Isabelle said, a quaver in her voice.

Robert glanced up, startled, from his writing: the clock in the library showed close to eleven. Between their visit to the east wing and the telling of her story, he'd lost track of time. Upon their return to the library, Virgil had been waiting before the fireplace; now the dog slept curled peacefully at their feet. The fire had grown low, the embers grey. Even so, the heat singed Robert's shoulders. When Isabelle had spoken of Ada and Hugh on their wedding night Robert had recalled Sida during theirs. To his dismay, his eyes were moist. Perhaps it was also the surprising mention of his father funding Ada and Hugh's elopement—Robert had no idea of his involvement.

Robert trained his gaze toward the floor.

"I've shocked you." Isabelle's unbound hair shrouded her face in shadows. "You didn't expect me to speak of their wedding night."

Her voice was so soft, so hesitant, that Robert was compelled to lean in. She was right: he had been shocked. But he hadn't stopped her, even when her voice slowed and she seemed to lose whatever vigor he'd witnessed during their walk to the east wing. Her story seemed a folie à deux they'd engaged in, like a folktale where the mortal was cursed to dance until dawn. How exhausted she appeared! How drained! He'd peer up periodically as she spoke, eager to witness any expression that might betray her identity. Now all he noticed were the purple shadows beneath her eyes, the slackened tilt of her mouth. She'd been possessed by her words as much as he'd been—at least until she'd arrived at Ada and Hugh's wedding night.

Robert cracked his knuckles as he set down his pencil. A strange yearning rose from his stomach. He'd never see her again. Never truly know the entirety of her story.

She must be Ada. How else would she know of such things? I must warn her about the pilgrims before I leave.

He didn't. Instead, he said, "I should have stopped you from speaking. I sat here listening—"

"To a tale that should remain untold." She wrapped her arms around her chest, rocking herself like a child. "I suppose I considered it remiss of me to leave any part out. After you confessed to me of your wife, I suppose I felt I could. I-I wanted you to have everything you need for my book."

"I assure you a history is more than a collection of encounters," was his stilted response.

"I did promise to tell you everything about Ada's life. What of our agreement?"

"There's no need to write something so . . . indecorous."

"But I'm telling the truth about Ada's story—"

"I don't think so," he said, no longer able to hold back. "I think it's your story."

Isabelle rose from her dais, her skirts swaying.

"I feel weary. Forgive me, Mr. Highstead—it must be the hour . . ."

Robert watched her make her way to the door, passing beneath the oil portrait of Ada with her sparrow. Isabelle's pale hair fell below her waist, luminescent beneath candlelight. *Her hair gilded with sunlight, like that Crivelli Saint Catherine. The sparrows settled along her shoulders. The blood on her handkerchief.* He fought the urge to touch a tendril.

Tell her you're leaving. About Missus Dido. Now.

Robert's chest knotted. There was no putting it off.

He cleared his throat to gain her attention. "I'm afraid this is our last night together, for I must leave in the morning. I must request my camera and end our agreement. Now that word is out of Hugh's death, my brother deems it best I bury him in our family plot."

Isabelle turned from the door. "What of your ankle? You were barely able to walk to the east wing."

"I'll manage."

"Oh. I suppose returning is the wisest course." She took two steps in his direction. "And so you'll leave without your daguerreotypes."

He wasn't sure if she sounded triumphant or repentant. It mattered not: with her so close, his yearning to reunite Hugh with Ada seemed from another age—an age that ended the afternoon he'd come upon her on the moors shrouded in sparrows and sunlight.

"It appears so," he answered.

She took another step. He drew a deep breath, still disconcerted by her story. Her presence. He could smell the hint of beeswax perfuming her skin.

The ground seemed to tilt beneath his feet.

She's Ada.

He forced out, "Missus Dido. I must warn you—"

"Warn me?" she said. "I don't want to speak of Missus Dido or any other part of my story. Not now." She cocked her head. "I know our time together has not been tranquil, but I must confess I'll miss you, Mr. Highstead."

An uneasy laugh. "I'd assumed you'd be relieved to be rid of me."

Another step. "It's not that."

"Because I won't be able to finish your book?" He held up his journal. "I'll mark up a few last notes before I go. I'm sure you can find someone to complete it."

Again, Robert felt that peculiar pull toward her. *Isabelle. Ada. No difference.* Though the historian in him wished for more absolute proof than a too intimate knowledge of Hugh's bedroom habits, he had no choice but to be satisfied.

"It's not that either, Mr. Highstead."

"What is it then?"

She wrapped a lock of her white hair around her finger. "What I wrote in my letter. You and I . . . well, we both suffer."

Robert's heart pounded. "I'm uncertain what you mean."

A wan smile. "It's like what we saw in the east wing, with the wicker, the white sheets. In a way, we're both haunted by ghosts, aren't we? You with your wife, myself with my aunt?"

With this, his vision of her gilded with sunlight and sparrows fled, along with his intent to warn her. He shouldn't have spoken of Sida.

He grabbed the door handle and rushed out. She'd have to deal with Missus Dido and Tamsin Douglas on her own. Anyway, she couldn't be Ada de Bonne—he'd only imagined this.

But Ada's story would be told whether or not Isabelle would tell it.

While Robert slept, he found himself in that strange between-land that seems more real at times than waking life. In his dream, he was reunited with his camera, though he wasn't in London. Instead, he was present in Ada and Hugh's hotel room on their wedding night. Robert didn't question why he was there, or what his intentions were, for he was immersed in that unquestioning logic only sleep can bear. For some reason he was convinced that if he could daguerreotype Ada he'd find proof of Isabelle's identity.

Robert watched Ada seated before her piano, Hugh standing behind her. Hugh's hands rested on her shoulders as music swept about them, reminding Robert of when he'd first heard Isabelle playing the Beethoven. A shelf above the piano held an array of daguerreotypes, like those he'd seen at Missus Dido's. Their frames were adorned with small white roses instead of black crape.

The couple paid Robert no mind as he settled his tripod near them. Robert stared through the camera glass as Hugh guided Ada's hands from the keyboard into his. He led his bride to their bed, upon which he'd draped the fur coat he'd given her for their wedding. Hugh kissed her neck as he laid her against the fur. He lifted her nightdress—it was an ivory silk, fancier than what Isabelle had described—to view his bride by candlelight. Her alabaster figure floated upside down on Robert's lens like an angel.

Robert slid the copper plate into the camera's belly.

Hugh slid the gossamer silk from Ada's shoulders. He unpinned her long dark hair and settled the tresses about her pale body. He kissed her jutting ribs, fanning out like a cage over her heart. Her small, tight nipples crowning each of her breasts.

"Ada," Hugh proclaimed, his voice husky with tenderness. "A name that is the same forward as it is backward. A conundrum I will never tire of."

Robert looked away to pull the cap from the lens. He counted the seconds of exposure for the image to take. *One, two, three, four . . .*

Hugh stroked Ada's brow, asking her if she felt feverish. "No, my darling," she replied, meeting his gaze with a disconcerting certainty. Bereft of all her coverings, she appeared a corpse—still, white, pristine. Exquisite. Hugh bent over her, spreading her limbs with his hips. And then the corpse came to life: Ada's colorless eyes blinked wide like a doll's. Yet when Hugh asked if he should stop—to his credit, his concern for her was greater than his desire—she urged him to continue. Her fingers pressed against his shoulders, as though she feared he'd abandon her during this first act of intimacy, leaving her adrift without land in sight.

Robert bathed the daguerreotype in mercury vapors. He varnished the plate once it finished developing.

Once Hugh had finished—Ada had been startled at the sharp cry he'd made at the end—her tears spilled onto the pillow. This time, though, her tears were from pleasure rather than pain. She was happy to be right for once in her life. She'd sensed the possibility of what he could bring her when he'd come to her that night in Herne Bay. That there was something within her body she'd never suspected; a force stronger than disease, greater than death. Whether one called it love, desire, or lust, it existed as tangibly as those ghosts she'd sensed as a child.

Robert took a step closer, pulling his tripod with him. He readied a second copper plate. The couple still ignored him.

Suddenly Ada's hair faded from dark to white. Embers to ash. Ash to snow.

Alarm possessed Hugh's voice. "My sweet, what's happening to you—"

"My sweet, what's happening to you? Did you have a nightmare?"

Robert awoke with Sida's face near his. She'd returned. Was he in Weald House or Clerkenwell? He couldn't tell.

Robert rubbed his eyes. "Something like that."

Ada. Her hair turning white like Isabelle's. Her body possessed by Hugh's . . . To lessen the hold of the dream, he reached for Sida and tried to think of other times. Happier times. That day in the woods, just after she'd painted that eye miniature. How he'd kissed the hem of her gown . . .

A slow smile spread across his face.

"You're still here." Since her death, he'd never woken up beside her; she usually disappeared before then.

"Why wouldn't I be?" Sida rolled on top of him. Her dark hair surrounded him like a cascade of shadows.

Her lips were cold, her fingers too. Any attempt at language fell away as she reached down, cupping his genitals; he'd awakened aroused. *"I love you."* He closed his eyes, shivering at each tug of her fingers against the buttons of his trousers—he'd been so exhausted he'd fallen asleep clothed and without packing. *I'm still dreaming.* Was he?

Her lips brushed against the tendons of his neck. He groaned and met her kiss as though he could bring her back to life through sheer will. Through desire.

Once they'd broken away, she murmured, *"The more you love me, the more I live."*

Their determination to meet at the intersection of life and death seemed to succeed at first. Robert felt his wife's ghost take on a corporality that had never occurred since her death. He'd watched her unlace her stays for him, terrified she'd disappear if he drew too close. When he finally dared to touch her, her skin prickled from the air, her cheeks flushed. Her mouth parted, her rosy lips an O of entreaty. At last all he'd yearned for was before him—his wife, his beloved, turned to flesh anew. Yet he feared injuring her in some way he couldn't understand. What was the protocol for sexual congress with the undead? Unsurprisingly, this wasn't something discussed in Oxford.

"I love you," he breathed into her ear once she was freed of all her layers. "Only you."

"The more you love me—"

"I know," he said, silencing her with a kiss.

He swept her into a tight embrace, pulling the length of her against him, her nipples pressing against his chest. His erection ached. He reached down, caressing the smooth skin of her stomach, her soft cleft. She parted against him. But when he thrust into her, she lapsed back into that intangible liminal state she'd inhabited since her death, leaving Robert's limbs enveloped in a clammy fog. Worse, Sida seemed as confused as he was. As frustrated.

He tried again, pressing against the darkness between her legs. Again, her body slipped through his, dissolving into ether before materializing on the other side of the mattress.

Robert reached for her. "Sida—"

Robert awakened alone in the stable house, his shirt damp with sweat, the only sound in the room his breath.

Ada. Sida. Just a dream.

He lit the candle, took out the portrait of Sida. When that didn't calm him, he splashed his face with cold water. The scab on his temple tingled at the contact. He hadn't seen Sida in over a day. Had she returned to London? Perhaps she'd found John's letter, or overheard him speaking to Isabelle regarding his departure.

Yet, to his infinite shame, his mind didn't dwell long on Sida's absence. All he could think of was Ada with her white hair. Entwined with Hugh. On that coat sewn of fur.

A Cluster of Lies

Excerpted from *The Lost History of Dreams* by Hugh de Bonne, published 1837 by Chapman & Hall, London.

'Jewel or glass? Does it matter?' quoth Charon.
'For in the depths of Hades
All colors become barren
And only gold is bright. That world
You recall is wove of shades—
'Tis but a cluster of lies.'

But Eurydice is brave. Eurydice recites :
'Yellow brilliant as sun. Red as dark as blood—
Blue brighter than twilight.' She won't forget
The seed greening 'neath the mud.

*

I.

Sida was still gone when Robert woke in the morning. Nor was there any sign of her—no shift in the air, no reflection in the mirror. Nothing to be done, he told himself. He'd find her in London—he had to. They'd go back to as they were before he visited Weald House. All would be well.

What if all wasn't well?

He rolled onto his side and stared at the window. Outside, the sky was grey. Inside, he felt the same. His foreboding only heightened when he recalled his dream of Ada and Hugh. Hugh curled over her body. Ada's hair turning to white. Like Isabelle's . . .

"She's not Ada de Bonne," he said aloud.

He'd hoped saying the words would help. Instead, Robert's apprehension grew, as though he'd undermined his marriage by revealing that eye miniature to Isabelle. *She'll be in London.* He wished there was an earlier coach. The sooner, the better. Yet there was something else that kept him lingering: he still hadn't warned Isabelle of the threat to her inheritance. Well, there was one last thing he could do.

Robert made the bed, folded Hugh's clothes—Mrs. Chilvers had finally returned everything but his coat cleaned—and dressed. Once he'd finished packing his belongings, he settled at the small table and tore a sheet of paper from the journal.

Dear Miss Lowell, he began. *It would be remiss of me to depart Weald House without informing you of a particular danger to your well-being . . .*

The sentences came quickly. Despite everything, his stay at Weald House had done his writing good. For a moment when he picked up his pencil, his stomach had churned with that old terror. To his surprise, his concern for Isabelle proved potent inspiration. He even found a way to elegantly parse Missus Dido's questions about Isabelle's identity.

As he signed the letter, he decided, *It matters not if she's Ada de Bonne. Let her go in peace.*

An unexpected serenity fell on him. He'd done all he could. He could go in peace himself.

In the kitchen, Robert's daguerreotype traveling case awaited along with Mrs. Chilvers, Owen, and Grace, who'd just finished with breakfast. He unbuckled the leather straps binding the wooden box. To his relief, the camera inside was intact, as was the fuming box; he'd entertained a fear Owen might have broken them out of spite. He was surprised to find Isabelle's contract set inside. The word *VOID* was written across it in large letters. *I doubt we shall meet again,* she'd set along the margin, *but if we do, may it be under more felicitous circumstances.*

Robert tucked the note into his pocket. Though Isabelle was nowhere to be seen, she was heard: piano music drifted downstairs from the library, a Bach fugue played at double tempo.

"She's in a fine state," Grace said, shaking a fist toward the ceiling. "Been like that since dawn."

"I shan't interrupt her to say goodbye," Robert said, relieved. It would be easier to leave if he didn't see her.

"Just as well. Miss Isabelle specifically told me she wanted to be left alone," Mrs. Chilvers said. "She dislikes farewells."

Owen grunted from behind his novel. "She won't be missing you, Highstead."

"Hush," Mrs. Chilvers scolded. The dog barked.

Robert handed his letter to Mrs. Chilvers. "Please give this to Miss Lowell. It's urgent."

"What is it?" Owen asked, suspicious as ever. Robert half expected him to hit him with his book.

"Nothing to do with you, boy," Grace said in her usual flirty way. Yet there was an edge to her tone Robert hadn't noticed before.

"You're off then?" Mrs. Chilvers offered Robert a distracted smile. "Farewell, Mr. Highstead. Take the walking stick with you—I doubt Mr. Hugh would mind."

She raised her cheek in an unexpected show of familiarity; Robert didn't demur. The kiss he offered was a simple peck, the sort you'd give a dowager aunt after she'd offered a sweet.

Robert held out his hand to Owen. "I know I've inconvenienced you. You were kind to let me stay in your room."

"Wasn't given a choice."

Owen ignored Robert's outstretched hand. To cover the awkwardness, Robert reached down to give Virgil a pat. The dog wagged his tail and whimpered with glee, but Robert didn't mind for once. Dogs were uncomplicated, unlike humans.

"He likes you, Mr. Robert," Mrs. Chilvers said.

He looked up from Virgil. "You won't forget about the letter?"

Grace said, "I'll make sure she doesn't, Mr. Highstead."

And then she winked. Robert pretended not to notice, but the damage was done.

Owen grabbed Robert's arm. "Time to go. I'll drive you—"

"No," Grace said forcefully. "I'm to take him to the coach stand."

"You? Impossible," Owen sputtered. (Again, Virgil barked.)

Grace set her hands on her hips. "Miss Isabelle said so."

"What of the cart with Hugh?"

"Already taken care of—I'm stronger than you think."

The stable boy's face fell as though he'd weep. "I don't believe Miss Isabelle asked you."

Grace's blue eyes narrowed. "Don't believe me?" She pointed toward the ceiling at the fury of music pouring over their heads. "Ask her yourself. I dare you."

Grace drove the chaise carriage the same way she did everything: with a determination that didn't allow deviance from the task at hand. She rushed through the gates of Weald House and down the dirt road, whose bramble-laden hedgerows were budding green. He heard Hugh's cart bump, setting his stomach to clutching. "Be careful! That's my cousin in there!" Grace ignored his warning.

"I did like him once," she said, the horse still racing. "Well, maybe more than that."

"Who? Hugh?"

Grace skidded in the road. Robert clutched his traveling case tighter.

"Hugh? No, Owen," she said, shaking her blond curls. "But that was a time ago. I didn't think him true. Now it matters naught. Naught at all. Even if he loves me more than the earth or more than the sky— "

"Love is complicated. Watch the road!"

The horse reared at a hare. Robert resisted the urge to grab the reins. It would be a miracle if Hugh's coffin made it to the coach stand without damage.

"Indeed, Mr. Highstead. Love is complicated." Grace swiped at her eyes. "Look at Ada and Hugh, even you with your situation. As for Owen, after all this time, how was I to know he'd be jealous of you?" She inhaled, shaky. "Never mind. I fear it is what it is. I shouldn't have lied about Miss Isabelle telling me to drive you, but what was I to do?"

"You lied to protect me from Owen? I assure you I can protect myself."

"Not because of *that.* Anyway, even with your ankle, I know you're strong. That trunk of yours is heavy— " She let out a sob. "Oh, but I did lie. It's so complicated!"

"The pilgrims? Mrs. Douglas? The church? The roses? The bees?"

Grace's silence was answer enough.

"'Tis a mess I've made," she said at last. "A ruin."

Snowdrops gave way to bluebells.

"Why'd you do it? Was it for the money? To leave Weald House?"

Grace bit her lip. "No . . . not at first anyway."

"Was it because you disliked Miss Lowell?"

"Not that either. She's always been kind though she's a strange one."

"Then, for the love of God, why'd you do it?"

Another hare and more trees. The air turned fragrant with pine.

When Grace spoke again, her voice was small. "Would you believe it started because I felt sorry for Mrs. Douglas and her poor dead baby?"

Robert laughed. "No."

"Well, 'tis true! Her situation made me think of Ada, if Ada had survived after all. Can't you imagine how sorrowful she'd be over Mathilde?"

Robert stole a look at Grace, who was staring resolutely ahead. "You surprise me."

At last Grace slowed the horse; he heard Hugh's coffin settle into place in the cart—she'd taken the carriage off the dirt road onto a bridle path leading onto the moors. They approached a bank of willows beginning to bloom purple. He hadn't recalled the path when he'd arrived, but it had been dusk.

"Are we nearly to the coach stand? I can't be late."

Grace let out an unexpected bubble of laughter. "Oh, we've plenty of time, Mr. Highstead. Owen just wanted you gone—well, you understand why."

"I'm sorry to have been such a burden on your household."

Grace shrugged. "Burden, trouble. Naught matters. Not anymore."

At last she brought the carriage to a halt. Robert needed only a glance to know where they were.

"Ada's Folly," he breathed.

The glass chapel stood just as it had when he'd first arrived from London: a solitary enclave framed in ivy and marble, tucked beneath trees. The chapel was wider than he recalled. Taller too. He was lucky he hadn't broken his neck. He strained his gaze toward the glass dome, searching for where he'd nearly fallen through. If the glass bore any cracks, they were hidden behind the marble ledge above the eaves.

It was a wonder. It was a miracle.

"We shouldn't have come here," Robert said when he was able to speak. For some reason, viewing Ada's Folly felt different now than it had upon his arrival. Before he'd made his bargain with Isabelle and learned of Ada's life. It seemed a betrayal, though he wasn't sure why. Strange how emotions could shift because of a story.

"But you're glad we did, aren't you?" Grace asked, handing him his walking stick from the carriage. Her hands were icy.

Robert didn't answer, for the glass chapel felt sacred. Inviolate. He kept his steps soft as he approached it. The grass was still sodden from the rain the night he'd arrived; Hugh's walking stick sank into it. Such was Ada's Folly's effect that even Grace stopped chattering. Once Robert viewed the chapel's doorway, he was glad for his silence, for a dozen doves cooed inside the eaves. The lock on the ivy-draped door remained stiffened with rust though the ice had melted.

A fresh bouquet of roses was nailed to the blue-painted door.

"Your work, I presume," Robert said, bending over to sniff the fragrant blossoms. "How much did Mrs. Douglas pay you?"

"You can't make me feel worse than I already do. I know I've betrayed Miss Isabelle. I know I've made a mess." Grace's face tightened like she was holding back tears. "I've a proposition for you, Mr. Highstead."

"I'm uncertain I want to hear it."

"I think you do. We've an hour until the coach. Enough time to daguerreotype outside Ada's Folly, if that's what you want. I'll even help you—"

"I don't want that."

"What do you want then?"

Before Robert could answer, Grace stepped out of the carriage to approach him. The look on her face reminded him of when she'd tried to seduce him. Determined. Merciless. Fearful.

"Grace, no—"

She laughed wildly. Desperately. "Oh I know you've no interest in me. I know you're in love with someone, though I'm uncertain whether it's Miss Isabelle, or even Ada from her story—"

He stared at his boots, his face hot as though Grace had uncovered his dream of Ada with Hugh. "I love my wife. Only her."

"Don't deny it! I've seen your face after you come from the library."

He met her eyes. "You've been spying."

Grace's voice rose. "There are no secrets in a house with servants. I know you talk to yourself when you're alone. I know you're writing a book for Miss Isabelle about Ada and Hugh. I know you think you're a historian again, though it's easy to write about the past. Why not write of the future?"

"What of the future?" Robert's tone was terse.

"*My* future." Grace wrung her hands. "I need to leave here. Now. Take me with you. I've the tin for it."

"Does this have to do with Owen?"

"I told you, I don't care for him. Not anymore." Her eyes filled unexpectedly. "We're running out of time—you need to decide. Look."

She pressed a heavy sheet of paper into his hand. A hand-lettered invitation decorated with gold leaf.

~ Seekers of the Lost Dream ~

Mrs. George Douglas Invites *You*

NOON *on the 26th of* FEBRUARY

HUGH de BONNE MEMORIAL

to take place at

Ada's Folly

~*~

Be Present as Hugh de Bonne's

Blessed Chapel of Glass

Is Unlocked

for a Private Service to Honor his Legacy

~*~

* WEALD HOUSE *

Kynnersley on the Weald Moors

Robert looked up from the invitation. "This is what's upsetting you? Miss Lowell will never allow it."

"Maybe she doesn't have a choice." She bit her lip anew. "Not anymore."

His stomach plummeted. "For God's sake, you didn't tell Mrs. Douglas about Hugh's coffin?"

"Of course not!"

"What did you do then?"

She grabbed the invitation back and ferociously tore it into pieces. "Nothing at all. Nothing! Do you want your daguerreotype or—"

Something whizzed by Grace's head, landing in a pile of leaves with a soft thunk. A rock.

Robert's head snapped around.

Tamsin Douglas stepped from the willows flanking the stream, emerging from the shadows like a daguerreotype exposed to mercury. Her bright copper hair matched the rose in the raven-feather cockade pinned to her bosom. Her eyes were blotchy. Whether her tears were over Hugh, her lost son, or her husband, it mattered not, Robert decided. She suffered.

"You! Grace!" she huffed as she approached, her skirts swaying. "I've been looking for you all morning. I even considered whether you'd do something desperate like run away." She held up another rock. "I couldn't think of any other way to get your attention."

"You could have just called her name," Robert said, any sympathy doused. He grabbed the rock from Mrs. Douglas. "Give me that."

And then he remembered. The coffin. There it was, in plain sight on top of the open cart, without a tarp this time.

Shit. Robert felt his forehead bead with sweat.

"You must go," he said, approaching Mrs. Douglas to block her view. "Now."

"You're Hugh's cousin, aren't you? I'd fainted before you that day in the study." Her full mouth thinned into an embarrassed smile. "Mr. Highstead, yes? I don't think we've been introduced."

"I'm aware who you are, Mrs. Douglas." Robert pulled himself to his full height as he placed the rock in his pocket. It was sharp. Dense. The size of a chestnut. "You could have injured her, madam."

Mrs. Douglas's chest heaved beneath her black cape as she jabbed a finger at Grace. "Do you know what this wretched girl has done?"

"It doesn't matter what she's done," Robert said. "You've no right of way here. If you don't leave—"

"Don't threaten me, or I'll get the constable on her. She's a liar and a thief! I gave her twenty pounds because she claimed to have the key to Ada's Folly—"

"I didn't exactly say that, ma'am," Grace wailed, flailing her arms into the air. "I never claimed I had the key, only I'd try my best to get it from Miss Isabelle now that Hugh was gone. And I *did* try! Couldn't find it! 'Tis a very different thing. Haven't I done everything else you asked? The roses? The bees?" She shoved her hands into her cloak pocket and pulled out a small pouch. "Here! Take your money back."

"I don't want my money back! I want the key. There's something inside the chapel. Something Hugh wants me and the other Seekers of the Lost Dream to have. I know it! My husband said as much before his death. It's in the poem:

> 'As the Poet waited 'neath domed glass
> Whilst the clocks chimed forlorn for noon
> His fists stopping those who might trespass
> With dreaded words he dared—'

All of a sudden Mrs. Douglas's eyes widened. "Oh sweet heaven . . ."

Shit, Robert thought again. The coffin. She'd seen it.

"It's not what it appears," Robert cried. He rushed toward the cart as quickly as his ankle allowed, but it was too late. Mrs. Douglas had managed to pull her body up against the black lacquer casket. She collapsed sobbing onto it. Even Grace's mouth dropped open.

"Is this *him*? He's in here?"

"No!" Grace and Robert cried as one, dragging Mrs. Douglas off the coffin by her ankles. She kicked in protest, even landing a blow against Robert's shoulder, but was no match for the two of them.

Once Mrs. Douglas had fallen to the forest floor, Grace shrieked and began to run toward the stream as though to drown herself. Just as Robert reached to grab her arm, Grace snatched the horse whip, which had fallen inside a pile of leaves amid the tumult.

"Stay back!" she yelled at Mrs. Douglas, brandishing the whip until it cracked in the air. "Or I fear you'll be sorry!"

Next thing Robert knew, Grace had jumped onto the chaise carriage and pulled him beside her on the seat—she was as strong as she'd claimed—and grabbed the reins. The cart bearing Hugh's coffin strained; the poor horse protested. But then they heaved forth toward the bridle path, leaving Mrs. Douglas behind wailing in their wake with frustration.

II.

"There you are, Grace!" Mrs. Chilvers cried, her widow's cap askew. "And with Mr. Robert too! I was beginning to think you'd run off with him."

The housekeeper had been pacing before the kitchen door when Robert returned to Weald House with Grace trailing behind him. If Grace had driven the governess cart like a madwoman to Ada's Folly, her recklessness as they fled Mrs. Douglas left Robert grateful she hadn't broken their necks. *"You shouldn't have pulled a whip on her,"* he'd scolded while they locked Hugh's coffin back inside the stable. *"Why the hell didn't you take me to the coach stand?"*

"Would you have taken me with you?"

"No. Anyway, she'd send a constable after you."

Grace looked like she'd faint. *"Even in London?"*

"There's constables in London, you know."

"I couldn't think how else to stop her. I imagine she'll show any minute. I'll alert Miss Isabelle. She'll probably sack me, but she'll know what to do." She ran toward the library, the dog barking and following in close pursuit.

"I'm glad you returned, Mr. Robert," Mrs. Chilvers said, ignoring Grace's noisy exit. "Another letter from your brother."

> *If you have not left Shropshire with our Cousin's remains by the time you receive this, I must urge you to do so without delay. An unsettling experience has convinced me to the wisdom of laying Hugh to rest as soon as possible. This morning I received a letter from the widow of Hugh's editor regarding his estate. Mrs. Douglas has made the fantastical claim that Miss Lowell is an imposter . . .*

Unlike John's previous letter, which he'd set on letterhead, this one was scrawled on foolscap. A marker of his impatience and desperation.

Robert threw the letter into the fire. *Ada. Isabelle.* He'd hoped to forget. *Damn Grace.* If she'd taken him to the coach stand as planned, he would be on his way bearing Hugh's corpse to their family plot and then to Sida, instead of standing there with his mind circling from John to Isabelle, from Isabelle to Ada, Grace to Tamsin Douglas in a topsy-turvy roundabout.

"Shit, shit, shit," he muttered beneath his breath.

"You need to sit, Mr. Highstead?" Mrs. Chilvers asked. "Forgive me, I forgot your ankle."

"No," he said, panic rising in him like a fever. What to do? "I'd rather go outside. Fresh air."

Ankle or no, Robert found himself in the rose garden, not quite recollecting how he'd made his way there. The beehive looked unchanged, with its nest of briars about the base, but the sky bore a peculiar brightness because of the clouds swathing the sky; thankfully it didn't look like rain. He breathed deeply, yearning to rid himself of his trepidation. A waft of smoke irritated his nostrils. Owen must have been sulking nearby. Not that Robert cared—he had bigger concerns. He felt as exhausted as Isabelle had looked the previous evening; he recalled her face as she recounted Ada and Hugh's wedding night, how possessed she'd appeared. The story was destroying her. And he was facilitating this.

The bench. He needed to sit. A moment later, he was joined by Virgil. He shifted to afford the dog room to nest beside his legs without pressing against his ankle.

The smoke retreated. Owen had moved on.

Suddenly cold, Robert thrust his hands into his pockets. His fingers wrapped around the miniature of Sida's eye. He prayed she'd be in London, that she wasn't lost to him forever. How beloved she was. How beautiful. His chest felt heavy. Even before he'd dreamt of Ada, he'd betrayed Sida by letting Isabelle view the miniature—he'd never shown it to anyone before. Had he really come all this way to Shropshire to daguerreotype a corpse for Sida, as he'd told Isabelle? He had. And it still wasn't enough.

When will it be enough?

A rush of wind. The back of his neck prickled. A cool breeze. He shoved the miniature back into his pocket, fearful he'd lose it.

"*Robert.*" His name wafted in a voice as delicate as lace. "*Over here.*"

Beneath the yew tree where those wood pigeons had landed years earlier for Ada and Hugh, a shadowy figure stood. Robert's eyes strained. He made out Sida's dark hair, her full mouth. Her blue silk dress with those wide sleeves.

"You're here!" he cried, his face widening into a smile. He hadn't lost her. She'd make everything right again. She had to. Things would be better in London. They'd return as they were. He'd forget about Isabelle and Ada and Hugh.

Sida's eyes appeared shrouded. Heavy. Or was it shadows cast from the tree?

"*Of course I'm here. I can't leave you, my sweet.*"

Robert rose from the bench to approach his wife, squinting into the gloom to better see her. There she was! He reached to embrace her.

"Come to me," he urged. "Closer."

Sida's body grew smaller, denser. Darker. And then she was gone—or so it seemed.

Deep within the yew perched the most exquisite raven Robert had ever seen. Her ebony-tufted head was a curve of harmony. Eyes dark as coal. Feathers gleaming with a cobalt-tinged iridescence, like they'd been woven from nightfall.

"I love you," Robert said, opening his arms for her. "Only you."

"Come to me," he thought he heard her caw. *"Closer."*

He opened his arms wider still.

The raven rose, her wings wide and powerful. She evaded Robert's grasp as she flapped around the roses, her wings fanning his cheeks before she settled anew on the yew tree. Again, she cawed. *"Never leave me."* Robert stepped toward her, his hair rustling from wind. Offered a hand . . .

The raven soared toward the sky and dissolved into brightness.

Virgil started barking as though he'd become a hound of hell himself. "Calm down!" Robert scolded. The dog pulled at his overcoat, still barking.

"Mr. Highstead? Is that you?" Grace's anxious voice cut through the cool air. A drift of smoke followed her. "I've been searching for you."

Before Robert could respond, a fist slammed into his jaw.

III.

Stars burst before Robert's eyes. Sharp. Bright. Loud. Once they dissolved, he saw Owen aiming for his jaw again.

Robert grabbed his hands. "What the hell are you doing?"

"Leave her be, you usurper of love!" Owen shouted. And then Grace screamed and Virgil barked again before Owen pulled away and managed to land another punch, this one on Robert's arm.

"Stop it!" Grace shrieked. "He's not usurping anything, whatever that means!" It was too late: Robert found his hands curling into fists. The fists pummeling Owen's jaw; later he'd have no clear memory of this save the thunk as his right hand slammed into Owen's head. The jolt down his arm to his shoulder as the punch landed. But Robert found he didn't care. Again, like during the church melee, he wasn't there—he was back with Sida's uncle that last afternoon, pummeling him as he pulled Sida away. He wasn't sorry at all.

And then Owen was curled on the ground at Robert's feet, spitting up blood. His eye swelling. His cigarette on the ground beside him, the smoke curling.

Robert stepped back, shaking out his hands, hopping on his feet, ankle be damned. The skin at his knuckles hadn't split, but his head felt light, as though every nerve in his body had been jolted awake.

"Why'd you do that, Highstead?"

"Why'd you attack me?"

"Because . . . because—"

Grace slammed a toe against Owen's thigh. "Because what, boy?"

Owen rolled onto his back, gasping for air. "I've been devoted to you since the first time I clapped eyes on you, Grace. You know that! I was wrong to kiss her, but I thought if I made you jealous—"

"Idiot!" She kicked him again. "What's your excuse now?"

"I heard you with Highstead. You together out here the other night, and then now! You *like* him—I'm no fool. What about me?"

"What about *me*?" Grace shook her head so hard that pins scattered from her curls. "I don't *like* him. Nor do I *like* you right now. The only thing I *like* is the possibility of getting away from this accursed place before all goes to ruin. You're all mad!" And then she stomped Owen's foot with the full of her boot. "Get up, boy!"

"Ow! Why'd you have to do that?"

"Because Miss Isabelle is asking for Mr. Highstead to come to the library—*that's* why I was looking for him. And she's . . . she's"—Grace choked up—"oh, never mind, just come!"

As soon as Robert saw Isabelle he understood Grace's distress.

He found Isabelle lying on the settee she'd brought up after he'd injured his ankle. The library was dark though the sun was bright—she'd drawn the shutters tight, leaving her wrapped in shadows. Like Ada in his dream, Isabelle lay covered by fur; she'd pulled the possum-skin rug usually set before the fireplace all the way up to her shoulders. An assortment of sheet music littered the floor where the rug had been. She'd probably discarded them after playing them that morning during her frantic concert.

Robert's breath caught in his throat. Isabelle was beautiful. That was the only word for how he found her. No doubt it was because he'd equated her with Ada, God help him. (Yet again his gaze shifted between her and that oil portrait of Ada with the sparrow.) All rancor had left her features, granting an unexpected tenderness to her countenance. Her hair was unplaited and reached all the way to her waist. It curled in wild tendrils about her shoulders, like an enchantress from long ago. However, her complexion had grown even more pallid than when he'd last seen her. She resembled a wax figure from a museum, an otherworldly figure he feared to disturb. If she was Ada, she'd survived longer than could be expected for a consumptive, but now the telling of her story was destroying her. Even Grace had witnessed this. He should stop her, turn her back from her story. He should leave, find his wife.

The room was bitter cold. A quick glance revealed the grate was unlit though a fire had been laid.

He rushed over and set a match to the fire. It blazed immediately.

"Is that you, Mr. Highstead?"

Robert turned from the flames; Isabelle appeared cast in gold.

"Yes."

Her chalky lips tipped into a half smile. "Grace informed me you missed your coach. You'll be amused to learn I was distressed by your departure."

"You're ill. I'll send Owen for a doctor."

"No, no," she said, fluttering her fingers in front of her face like she was clearing cobwebs. "I haven't felt well since I started Ada's story. Perhaps that's it . . . once I finish it, I'll feel better."

Robert wouldn't press. "I presume Grace told you everything. Did Mrs. Chilvers give you my letter?"

She shifted into a seated position, muffling a cough. "It's quite a fanciful tale."

"You do understand what will happen if we can't prove your identity?"

A barely perceptible nod. "I knew about Tamsin Douglas, but had chosen to ignore her . . . but Missus Dido! It really was her? I didn't believe it could be. What's she calling herself again?"

"The Vicomtesse de Fontaine. She claims not to recognize you either." Robert paused. "If you have something to confess, I'll do what I can to help."

She jutted her lip out, color returning to her face. "Confess? Like a sinner?"

"That's not what I meant. But we must be quick—I expect Mrs. Douglas to show any moment. Now that she knows about Hugh's death, she's not going to leave you alone until you open the glass chapel."

"I don't care! I won't have anyone disturb my aunt's grave." Now the old Isabelle was back, the one who'd rebuffed him upon his arrival. Still, she asked, "I assume the coffin is locked inside the stable?"

"Miss Lowell, the pilgrims—"

"I *am* Isabelle Lowell! Who else could I be?"

She was lying. She had to be.

"Perhaps we should finish your aunt's story," he said, glancing at the mantel clock. "I have no idea how long we have left."

IV.
The Fourth Day's Story

You've asked me to finish Ada's story, Mr. Highstead, in the hope it will settle the pilgrims' questions about who I am. I am uncertain what proof it may grant—after all, as a historian you surely understand that a story is told with words as well as in silences. The dead may be silent, but they have much to tell—but I digress.

You may have thought the ghosts found at Weald House had been banished once Ada left England. But you'd be wrong. Instead, Hugh used the excuse of their honeymoon to take his bride to Paris in search of his own ghosts. This Ada understood too well—was she not haunted herself?

All was felicitous at first. Hugh found them rooms in a boarding house in the Marais not far from where his mother had been marched to the scaffold. Nearly four decades after the end of the Revolution, France had settled back into an uneasy monarchy that lured all casts of life to Paris: poets, novelists, musicians, courtesans, tricksters, Americans. Due to these uncertainties, the matron of the house examined Ada with suspicion. From the quality of Ada's posture and her accent, she knew Ada wasn't the usual dollymop who took rooms for afternoon liaisons with married benefactors. Ada still looked younger than her age and otherworldly of mien; by then her disease had given her skin a waxy hue that drew stares from all who clapped eyes on her.

"Why are you here?" she asked Ada. "What of your parents? Do they not worry for you?"

Ada spoke French like all good gentlewomen should, for Madame Clarice had taught her a smattering alongside her piano scales. She lied that her parents had perished from influenza, to avoid sharing their history. "I am quite alone in the world," she said, "save for my beloved husband."

Her curiosity assuaged, the good madam accepted the explanation with a tut, even pinching Ada's cheeks for measure. It helped that Ada overpaid generously, though she'd yet to come into her majority.

How happy they were! How blessed! Like Lucian and Adelaide some twenty years earlier, Ada and Hugh spent their mornings lying together bathed in sunlight. During the day, Hugh took Ada to the places that brought him joy as a young man: the Place du Carrousel with Napoleon's triumphant arch, the Tuileries with its serene pathways and graceful fountains. At night, they attended the opera when it was in season; other times, literary salons and plays. Afterward, ears and hearts sated, they ate ortolan on gold-rimmed plates and fruit ices from silver bowls. They drank too much; the alcohol made Hugh snore, keeping Ada awake. They frequented noisy restaurants populated by hollow-eyed aristocrats who'd escaped extinction, feeling a kinship with them no one could comprehend.

While Ada slept, Hugh would write poetry. He obsessed about sestinas and quadrants and iambic pentameter, forcing his emotion onto the page, instead of into life where they belonged. Sheets of paper accumulated like snow upon his desk and along the floor, but Ada didn't mind.

Once they were married, Watkinson had no choice but to release Ada's funds, though not without grumbling. Ada was generous with Hugh, which afforded him to be generous in turn; he'd yet to make much from his books despite good reviews. He bought her a peach silk taffeta dress frothy with lace ("the color of salmon," he said, "like something served cold at midday"), four pairs of velvet gloves. Bonnets blurry with ostrich feathers, a cashmere shawl fringed in silk. An emerald locket she promptly lost in the Seine the night he'd given it. ("The chain must have been weak," she said, laughing off the loss.) He surprised her with zoo visits, music boxes and sheet music. She bought him first editions of Byron and Shelley, a hand-colored copy of Audubon's *Birds of America*, a glass nib holder. A clock which featured a dove instead of a cuckoo. (It rarely kept time.) A silk waistcoat the color of grass after the rain, with matching gloves and hat "to wear when we walk in the Jardin des Plantes." A yellow fur-trimmed overcoat to match the one he'd given her at their wedding. Patent leather boots custom-built to support his weak leg. If they grew bored of ideas for what to consume, they'd walk to the market square on the Île de la Cité and fill their arms with lilacs, roses, camellias, and whatever else was in season, ignoring the precarious wall of cages containing birds and other life forms. When the flowers rotted, they'd simply buy more.

One rainy day Hugh even made a scavenger hunt, like he had in Herne Bay. At the end of it Ada found a love sonnet hidden beneath a church pew. "The sacred amid the profane," Hugh quipped. They ignored the letters Watkinson sent warning of their proliferate spending. (*Farming doesn't bring in the income it once did,* he wrote.) After all, they'd economize once they returned to England. If they ever did—the longer they remained in Paris, the less often they thought of Weald House.

* * *

Robert interrupted, "Do we need so much detail, Miss Lowell?" He pointed toward the library door, half expecting Tamsin to burst in. "Forgive my bluntness, but how will this prove your identity?"

Isabelle shuddered as though waking from a dream. "You're right, Mr. Highstead. Time's wasting." She took a sip of tea. "I'll try to be more concise from here on."

Or you could simply tell me who you are.

But Robert didn't dare say this. What if she refused to continue?

* * *

And so Ada and Hugh's honeymoon in Paris passed, with spring turning to summer, then to fall. October arrived, and Ada turned twenty-one, finally coming of age and into her fortune, which allowed her to ignore Watkinson for good.

Ada and Hugh. Hugh and Ada. No one else existed in the world but each other. However, the ghosts that haunted Hugh would not be ignored.

And then one day, the ghosts returned.

That November morning was the first day they had snow that season. Without warning, fine ice crystals had appeared suspended in the air, a sharp dash of cold. They melted as soon as they touched earth, for it was a sunny day, incongruous in its promise of warmth. Later Ada would wonder if she'd imagined it, a foreshadowing for all that was to be.

By the time the snow arrived it was already time for lunch, which was their usual first meal of the day—she and Hugh had spent all morning lying about in their usual way after too much cognac the night before. Snow or no, Ada dressed in the peach taffeta gown, Hugh's favorite. She called the maid for her bonnet. He called for a carriage.

"Aren't we walking to the market?" Ada asked.

"We're going someplace else," Hugh said, gathering his walking stick; he was wearing his favorite dark green frock coat. "How my head aches! I should take some of your laudanum."

"Where are we going?"

"You'll see." He held a hand palm side up out the window. "The snow's stopped. Anyway, there's no point in waiting."

"Where are we going?"

He refused to answer her questions. He refused to meet her eyes. Regardless, Ada's heart rose. This was his way, to surprise her with an outing. Perhaps they'd go to a matinee, or to buy sheet music. His sullen manner suggested something beyond too much alcohol. Perhaps he'd received bad news from his publisher; he'd just sent them the manuscript for his third book, a collection of bird poems he hoped they'd publish immediately.

Hugh instructed the carriage to drive toward the Île de la Cité, which he liked to call "the beating heart of Paris" in his fanciful way. Ada didn't understand the remainder of his directions, for his voice was low. The winding streets of the Marais soon turned tight and labyrinthine, cased in by ancient buildings crumbling with neglect. How oppressive it was, like a maze leading to nowhere. The day turned dark, the sun a memory.

Ada shivered beneath her cape, troubled by Hugh's persistent silence. Where was he taking her? She didn't dare ask.

The Seine offered a brief reprieve before their carriage was thrust into shadows again. Once they were on the other side of the Pont au Double, they continued farther south before turning west to cross the Seine once more.

After what felt like hours, Hugh rapped on the window, his knuckles taut on his walking stick.

"If I remember correctly," he said, "this is as close as we're going to get."

Ada peered through the carriage window.

They'd halted in front of a small square more crowded than any she'd ever seen in Paris, or anywhere else for that matter. Though the square lay in the center of a formal green park, Ada's overall impression was of chaos.

Her head whipped from side to side as she took in merchants hawking wares, acrobats tossing their limbs into cartwheels, slatternly singers preening for sous, kerchiefed women carrying wide wicker baskets. Uncountable tables heaped with flowers, fruits, meats, and curiosities. A toothless beggar relieved himself against a statue before giving Ada a wink. The cacophony of noise and smells and spectacle made her want to call after the carriage, which had already turned back toward the Seine. Toward Paris.

"We're in Sèvres, my love," Hugh explained. "On the road to Versailles *ville*."

"We're going to Versailles?" She hoped so.

"No. Someplace else." Hugh's expression was inscrutable. "Must be market day."

He said nothing more as he took her arm. Nor did she ask anything more. How cold it was! She shivered beneath the fur coat that had been Hugh's wedding present. Once they'd left their carriage, there was nothing to shield the wind sweeping in from the Seine.

Ada glanced at Hugh from beneath her silk bonnet. His expression had shifted from inscrutable to forbidding. Something was troubling him. Something more than publisher woes.

"This way," he said. His grasp tightened on the soft flesh of her arm.

She was grateful they didn't linger in the square. The pavement was banked by bricked buildings raked up a hill; the landscape was vertiginous behind it, crossed by footpaths leading up to isolated manses bordered by spindly trees. It was one of these footpaths Hugh led her to, steeper than anything she could recall. The moors surrounding Weald House had hills, but they were of the gentle, rolling sort; the sort where you could rest beside a patch of cowslip and stare at clouds if you became breathless. This footpath wasn't like that at all. It mercilessly traversed what felt like the sheer side of a cliff.

Occasionally the path broke into a narrow stair sided by tall granite walls before branching into a dirt road. As she climbed, Ada's crinolines swished and tangled against her limbs. She felt like a fish wrapped in paper. She pressed on, uneasy—Hugh had yet to say a word. For the first time in their marriage, she was intimidated by him.

Breathless, she laid her palm flat against the stone wall. It was cold like a tomb. She felt as though she was being entombed herself. Her lungs tightened.

She stopped to catch her breath, too dizzy to continue. "Where are we going?"

Hugh glanced over his shoulder. "We're almost there, Ada. Just a few more steps. How stubborn you can be!"

Hugh's tone was sharp. Like a stranger's. For a moment Ada's eyes prickled like a child's. Who *was* this man she'd married and shared a bed with?

But then he set his hands on hers.

"I'm sorry," he said. "I know you're not suited for this much walking."

His touch was as warm as ever. Her tears receded.

Up and up they went, one step following the other. And then they were there, wherever it was—Ada knew this because there were no more steps to climb. It was just as well. Her dizziness had grown into distress. She doubled over, her chest catching like a creaking door. *In and out.* Her gaze focused on her boots, on the drifts of red-hued dust and dead leaves lining the road.

Once Ada could breathe, she looked up.

They stood before a tall stone grand *maison*. The mansion bore an imposing entryway, tall banked windows, arched portico, and a red-tiled roof. It once must have been glorious, but no longer. The doorway was hidden beneath brambles. The windows were covered by long planks of rotted wood. The roof must have collapsed years before, for a thick-trunked elm, already leafless with winter, poked through the rubble toward the sky; it had taken root in the ruin below. Three carrion crows shuffled on a high branch, their ebony wings flapping with a predatory protectiveness. The stench of decay wafted in the air.

Ada's gaze dropped from the crows to the roof; from the roof to Hugh, who'd turned his back to her; from his back to his shoulders.

Hugh's shoulders were shuddering.

Ada's heart lurched. She wanted to ask, "Why are you weeping?" She wanted to say, "It's only a house." But in her heart, she *knew* why he was weeping, what the house signified, and why they'd come all this way across the Seine on a cold November day to an abandoned *grande maison* overtaken by trees and crows.

This had been Hugh's first true home.

Ada understood that to say anything would cause Hugh further pain. And so she remained silent, but her silence wasn't fallow. In her silence, she sensed his ghosts. His mother seated beneath roses in the garden. Hugh playing *cache-cache* with his young sisters on endless summer nights. The scent of jasmine. The clinking of silverware against china during long family meals. His father stoking the fire on icy nights. The laughter. The love. All the memories he'd described since their marriage.

Hugh reached out, clutching air. "Gone. All gone."

"I know." Ada's tone was one she'd use to comfort a child.

He rubbed his eyes. "I shouldn't have come here. Shouldn't have hoped."

"You wouldn't have known unless you'd come."

He wiped his cheeks with a sleeve. "Sometimes it's better not to know."

She took his hand. "Let's go home."

Hugh's tone grew unexpectedly intense. "Now you truly know I have no home."

Ada kissed his eyes to ease his tears. "But I'm your home now."

V.

Isabelle's words came to an abrupt halt. "I must rest for a moment." She stifled another cough.

"We've no time." Robert looked up from his journal, feeling akin to Virgil stalking a hare; the closer he came to the truth, the more determined he grew. "What happened after Hugh discovered his home in ruins?"

* * *

Ada led Hugh back to the square where the coach had deposited them. She didn't complain about the catch in her lungs, or the ache in her heart. Instead, for the first time in their marriage, she took care of her husband—and how happy it made her! Every so often, she'd pause to murmur comforting words. His replies were monosyllabic, his face ashen. No matter. They had each other—they'd be each other's *locus amoenus*.

In Sèvres *ville*, they found the streets curiously empty as though the world had ended. The market was over. No coaches were to be found. Before Hugh could despair, Ada suggested, "If we walk toward the river, perhaps we'll find a coach by the bridge."

Hugh said nothing.

They turned down the Rue Grande toward the Seine. The effort of walking countered the chilly air. The sun was already low, the water the color of pewter. In the distance, bells chimed three. The peace embedded in this scene further spurred Hugh's tears instead of calming him. "How can there be so much beauty in this world," he cried, "amid so much sorrow?"

Somehow they found themselves standing before a dreamlike cream-colored palace facing the river—she couldn't recall if she'd led Hugh, or if Hugh had led her. No matter: the palace appeared a remnant of an enchanted age before revolutions and guillotines. An age in which his family's *grande maison* wasn't inhabited by crows and ghosts. The courtyard surrounding held an array of marble figures posed in heroic stances.

Ada read the text carved into the pediment above the main entrance. *Manufacture Nationale de Sèvres.*

"A factory," Hugh said, his cheeks still wet.

"Look, here's another sign. It's also a museum of ceramics."

"Dishes. Vases."

"Let's go in," Ada said. "It'll distract you."

Hugh covered his red eyes. "I can't go in. Not like this."

"No one will care. I'll say you've a cold. At the very least, we can ask where the coach stand is."

The museum foyer was empty as a church on Monday morning. No one greeted them as they ventured from the foyer into a large airy salon dominated by a grand stairway, which twisted toward a domed ceiling painted with stars and fronds in the Roman style. They ignored the stairs to venture into an even larger salon. It featured an octagonal glass cabinet holding a display of vases and bowls, each presented like an offering to the gods. Their gilded paintwork called forth an age when cherubs frolicked with centaurs, and birds plucked cherries from naiads' lips. "Pretty," was Hugh's indifferent remark.

Just as Ada and Hugh stepped beyond the cabinet to examine a display of small bisque figures, someone finally approached, a severe grey-haired madam. Her mouth gleamed with large white teeth and bonhomie. "*Bienvenue, monsieur et madame!*" she greeted before launching into an array of French so rapid that Ada couldn't keep up; she resorted to bobbing her head to avoid seeming simpleminded. Fortunately, Hugh answered Madame slowly enough that Ada understood their conversation.

"*Quoi de plus à voir?*" What more is there to see?

"*Venez avec moi, s'il vous plaît.*" This way, if you please.

Madame led them from the salon through wide corridors into other salons and, finally, into the shop, where they were expected to open their purses in gratitude for their visit.

"What's upstairs?" Hugh asked, pointing at the domed stairway they'd viewed upon their arrival.

"That's where we manufacture stained glass." Madame's tone was dismissive. "Nothing to see."

"Stained glass?" Even Ada could understand this in French. Her lips curved into an unconscious smile as she remembered Canterbury.

"*Oui*. For church windows mainly." Madame fell back into her role as guide, reciting by rote. "Many were destroyed during the Revolution. We are kept quite busy with their replacements."

"I must see it," Hugh said, his sorrow forgotten.

"This is not possible, monsieur—"

But he was already pulling Ada up the stairs.

"Monsieur, that's not part of the *musée*. I must ask you to stop—"

"We'll be but a moment, Madame," he said, winking at Ada. "It's for my English wife." In English he said: "She is difficult. Spoiled. Not to be refused—"

"Very true," Ada added in French. She stamped her foot. "I won't leave unless you let me look!"

"Madame! I must ask you—"

"Only for a moment," Ada amended, overcome by giggles. "*Pardonne-moi*."

They ascended the staircase before they could be stopped, Madame following after them furiously; Ada had never rushed so, but she didn't mind. Surprisingly neither did her lungs. Her feet easily kept up with Hugh's. She even forgot her breathlessness while they'd climbed the hill to his family home.

One flight of stairs, a landing that twisted beyond the dome. Still, they rushed up, Madame's scolding voice at their backs. Ada couldn't stop giggling. Hugh's arms were protective, prepared to catch her should she fall. The steps flew by, wide and cased in marble like those from a palace. They seemed an apt setting for what they were to find once they could climb no farther.

"Oh," Hugh said, blinking rapidly.

"Oh," she said, joining him in wonder.

His arms fell from her as he circled the room. They were surrounded by light. Colored light. Light brighter than anything Ada could have imagined.

Windows covered in color. On one side was a nativity; another, Christ raising Lazarus; and in between, so many others that Ada gave up trying to identify each subject. Marys mingled with Marthas, saints with sinners. The colors dazzled like heaven had burst forth on a clarion.

Hugh's face lifted into the widest grin Ada had ever witnessed. Her heart welled so wide she thought it would burst. Overwhelmed by beauty, by light, she reached for him and kissed him with all of her being, leaving Madame tutting with—

* * *

Robert raised a hand to silence Isabelle. "Shush."

Footsteps sounded outside the library door.

Hesitant. Shuffling.

Once they'd faded away, Isabelle said, "Mrs. Chilvers on her way to bed." She even laughed, a bell-like sound. *Nerves*, Robert thought. *Relief.*

"I don't think I've ever heard you laugh before," he said.

"I know how to laugh. I know what it's like to be happy. I was once happy." She gently tapped his hand, her touch warm. "I must continue with Ada's story."

* * *

Hugh was silent all the way back to Paris, but it wasn't a silence that troubled Ada. It was a content silence. A silence born of happiness. Of peace. She felt responsibility, pride even. She, Ada de Bonne, a consumptive society had only valued for her fortune, a woman many considered would die young and leave no mark on this world, had brought serenity to a bereft man. She watched Hugh open his journal to write. A *poem*, she thought, her heart swelling from her rib cage. *He's inspired.* She recalled the stained glass, how the light had returned to his face once they'd ascended that staircase. Afterward, they'd made a generous donation to the *musée* to appease Madame.

It was only later, back in the Marais, when they were at their usual restaurant at their usual table eating their usual meal of a roast chicken accompanied by their usual claret that Ada realized the influence their museum visit wrought.

Hugh pushed the wine away and ordered coffee instead. Once the coffee arrived, he opened his journal. He slid it across the table toward her.

All Ada saw was a small pencil drawing of what looked like a house. It was surrounded by bursts of words. *Beauty. Fragile. Jewel. Soul.* He'd drawn the house beside a draft for a poem she'd never seen before.

> 'Jewel or glass? Does it matter?' quoth Charon.
> 'For in the depths of Hades
> All colors become barren
> And only gold is bright . . .'
>
> But Eurydice is brave. Eurydice recites :
> 'Yellow brilliant as sun. Red as dark as blood—
> Blue brighter than twilight . . .'

Ada felt her forehead crinkle. "What's this?"

"Guess," he said.

"An idea for a poem?"

"Look closer," he said, pointing at the sketch. "It's for a chapel, a small one made of glass. A *locus amoenus*. Though not my true *locus amoenus*—that's you, my love."

Ada beamed.

Hugh continued. "I'm not much of an artist, so you'll have to imagine the colors, the patterns. But it's all there, like the Muses had tapped me on the shoulder. *Un fait accompli*."

That's what he'd been doing while they were on the train to Paris. Not writing. Sketching. But what a sketch! Crude as it was, Ada was enchanted. Her gaze darted over the page. She made out the arches soaring toward the sky, the willows surrounding it. A glass dome rising like a bubble arrayed by ribs of metal decorated by what looked like jewels. Hugh had even drawn an array of birds nesting in the chapel's eaves—these were indicated by lines rising toward the sky.

"So lovely," he murmured toward the page; the tenderness in his tone reminded Ada of his voice in the morning.

"It's beautiful," she breathed; again her chest caught. "We could build it—no, we *must* build it."

Hugh met her eyes, intense. "That's what I thought."

"In the woods outside Weald House. When we return to England. It will be a wonder."

"A wonder," Hugh agreed. "It would be a chapel like a poem. Besides, I have good reason to build it."

To memorialize his family. Ada immediately understood. In that moment she was never prouder of her decision to marry him despite Watkinson's disapproval and Missus Dido's envy. Not only did Ada love him, Hugh was a true artist—a pure artist. He was able to use his sorrow to create beauty to transform the world. He'd said, *"How can there be so much beauty in this world amid so much sorrow?"* The only solution was to create more beauty. She imagined the chapel rising from the woods toward the grey-clotted sky, an unnatural crop constructed of color and light. The shouts of the workers as they labored. The delicate glass pieces shimmering into form. They'd build it together, he with his artistry, she with her money. It would last beyond their lives, a testament to his poems, their love, especially since they'd never have children.

Ada grasped his hands across the table, nearly knocking the claret onto his journal. How shaky she felt. How hot.

"Oh Hugh, I'm so happy! After everything we saw today—well, I know how distressing it was to find your family home in such a state . . . but with this chapel you can honor your family's memory. Their losses."

At her words, Hugh drew back, the shadows from the candlelight distorting his face ever so briefly. The room turned grey. She felt moisture dot her brow.

"Is it warm in here?"

"My love, what's happening to you?" he cried, his eyes wide.

"I-I don't know."

As if from a distance, she heard Hugh's chair fall as he sprang toward her. Hugh pulled her against him just as her chest began to catch again. Her stomach too. "Doctor!" Hugh shouted in French. "My wife needs a doctor! Get one!" Her lungs heaved as she began to shake. *I'm dying,* she thought. *It's not how I expected it would be.* She'd imagined she'd see her parents awaiting her, Wilhelm too. Some kindness to soothe her away from life. She saw nothing but Hugh's panicked face above hers.

A flare of pain. The room turned a blinding yellow.

Yellow brilliant as sun.

His heart grew loud against her ears, drowning everything else out in the restaurant. “Ada,” she thought she heard. “Never leave me.”

A viscous fluid filled her mouth. Her throat. The tang of iron.

Red as dark as blood.

She tried to speak but couldn’t. She clutched her hands over her chest. Her throat. Her mouth. A splatter of red splayed from between her fingers. Onto Hugh’s favorite blue shirt.

Blue brighter than twilight.

Ada knew it was serious, for the doctor would only speak to Hugh, and Hugh’s eyes were swollen, and he wouldn’t touch her when she offered her hand. He sat on the edge of their bed in their rooms in the Marais for some time before he spoke. He wouldn’t meet her gaze.

“I was wrong to wed you,” he said. “Wrong to take you from your home. Wrong to let you love me.”

Ada began to weep. She recalled how Hugh had scolded her in Sèvres while they’d climbed to his family home. Like he was someone else. Not the man she’d married.

“But I am your wife!” she cried. “Do you no longer love me?”

Hugh wouldn’t answer.

* * *

Isabelle’s voice broke. Robert set down the journal.

“I’m sure this is difficult to speak of,” he said.

Isabelle shook her head, her eyes suspiciously red. “We must continue, Mr. Highstead. After all, I’m nearly to the end.” She glanced anew at the door. “I’ll be quick as I can.”

“Very well, Miss Lowell.”

Robert wrote the remainder of her story without halting. Later he couldn’t recall how Isabelle’s words had found their way from her mouth onto the page. But there they were in his neat handwriting for anyone to read.

The Raven and the Rose

Excerpted from *The Raven and the Rose* by Hugh de Bonne, published 1835 by Chapman & Hall, London.

As I dream, my Past arises to judge
Amid this Limbo abiding on this sweet Earth—
For I was One who once wandered thus
O'er Wood and Moor laid low by Birth
Made too bitter from Darkness and Lust,
My sole low Companions then.
And then—
I awake—I remember—I see—
My *locus amoenus* lying beside me
Again crowned by Roses
And tamed by Ravens.

*

I.
The Fourth Day's Story, Continued

When does an ally turn into an enemy? That was the question Ada asked herself, Mr. Highstead, the day after their return from Hugh's family home in Sèvres.

At first, all seemed to be well: once the doctor left, Hugh took Ada's hands and said, "Forgive me for speaking as I did. I was terrified—you were going to die, and blamed myself for forcing you to exert yourself. I couldn't abide without you!" But from the look in his eye, she suspected there was something he was hiding. Something she feared to learn. For some reason, she recalled Missus Dido's gossip about the courtesan who'd drowned herself.

Though Hugh had confessed to Ada of his past before their marriage, he'd offered no explanation for the suicide beyond a remorse-filled shrug.

Still, they pretended all was well, especially as November gave way to December, with all the festivities that corner of the year entailed. As sick as Ada had been, within four weeks she was nearly as she was before her collapse, though she still found spots of blood in unexpected places: on the edge of a lace collar, or inside the palms of her gloves. Once Ada was able to sit again, she'd watch children squeal as they pelted each other with snow in their corner of the Marais, taking solace in shop windows decorated with bright bows and candles, all evoking our Savior's birth. While she did her best to engage in the season, she found herself unable to banish her foreboding.

Yet there were consolations to be found.

Watkinson, to Ada's astonishment, sent by special parcel an array of jewelry that had belonged to her mother, Adelaide: emeralds, rubies, even a necklace of diamonds. He wrote, "Now that you are of age, they should be yours." Ada gave Hugh a walking stick carved of mulberry. "Magicians make wands of mulberry," she explained. Hugh delighted Ada with a spinet piano and a private dinner catered by her favorite restaurant. The dinner took place in a candlelit room inside a palace near the Louvre, where waiters left them in solitude once the food was served. As Ada lay in Hugh's arms while he hand-fed her prunes stuffed with fois gras and spoonfuls of *oeufs à la neige*, she remembered how wonderful it had been to love him before that day in Sèvres. She drank so much champagne that she recalled nothing more save that she'd dreamt of her parents for the first time ever. In her dream, Lucian and Adelaide were in the rose garden at Weald House. Her father was trying to say something Ada couldn't understand.

Christmas led into the New Year, and Hugh insisted Ada take voice lessons "to strengthen your lungs." He was busy too: his second book, *Cantos for Grown Children*, had been published several months earlier, which brought enough acclaim that he was emboldened to begin a new poem cycle now that his bird poems were finished. "This one will be even more ambitious, my love," he told her. "I'm thinking of using our story for inspiration." He also received a letter from a famed poet who shall remain nameless. He invited Hugh and Ada to visit him in the north of England.

"When?" Ada asked, excited; by then her foreboding over that day in Sèvres had become a scar that only aches in poor weather.

"This spring, once it's warm." Hugh looked up from his desk, where he'd been writing. "He writes we'd be very welcome."

Ada felt the entire world open beneath her feet. Had she ever lived in a manor house on the moors inhabited by ghosts? "What else did he say?"

"Read the letter for yourself. I've never received such praise! My head is spinning. Over there, in my bedside table."

Ada opened the drawer. She found two letters. The first was as Hugh described: an effusive letter of praise for his poems. The second was from a doctor specializing in lung conditions.

Monsieur de Bonne, the letter began. *I have read your letter detailing your wife's condition with great interest but acute despair* . . .

The doctor's words seeped into her like she'd been bit by a snake. The venom rushed through her veins, her muscles. Her heart. Her lungs. Suddenly Ada sensed the presence of those ghosts from Weald House. Her mother's calm hand on her shoulder. Her father's scarred hands amid the roses.

She was distracted from ghosts by the murmur of words. Hugh. He was sounding out the resonances of a poem.

> "I awake—I remember—I see—
> My *locus amoenus* lying beside me
> Again crowned by Roses
> And tamed by Ravens."

She sat up against the pillows, struggling for air.

Hugh turned from his desk. "How wan you look! Are you well?"

She held up the letter. He burst into sobs.

Once he'd contained himself, Hugh confessed the truth: the night of her collapse upon their return from Sèvres, Hugh had been informed by the attending doctor she would die if they remained together. "Your wife's consumption has advanced enough to require rest in a sunny climate," he'd said. "I recommend a sanitarium in Fiesole, outside of Florence. To hope for recovery is too much, but you may yet save her life if you cease your unfortunate connection." The doctor also included a list of rules drawn from the most modern medical studies. "If you wish for your wife's survival, I pray you mind them."

The first rule was that Ada must sleep on her back at a nearly upright incline, to avoid taxing her lungs. This would allow her blood to better irrigate from her heart. The second rule was that Ada was not to go outside unless accompanied by a nurse or a physician. The third rule was effective for the rare occasions Ada ventured out. She was to wear a heavy veil over her bonnet to avoid spreading her illness. When it came to meals, a fourth rule posited food must be served at room temperature. Like Goldilocks and the bears, her meals must not be too hot nor too cold, but just right. No matter that what Ada considered "just right" wasn't yet another blancmange, the eggy mixture pearled with sweat after sitting out for hours, or flavorless boiled meats. Raw fruit and vegetables were also forbidden, since they could sicken her system into collapse. Finally, emotional excesses and upsets were to be avoided as assiduously as uncooked fruits. "Marital relations and childbirth would be the undoing of her," Hugh had been warned.

Disbelieving this advice, he'd sought other opinions. Hence, the secret letter Ada found.

"I am a terrible, selfish man—a man who you loves you too much," Hugh confessed, his tears hot on her hands. "I deceived you, for I couldn't bear to leave you. Therefore you must leave me, Ada."

"Leave?" she said. "Never!"

"And yet . . ." Hugh's words trailed off.

"Yet what, darling?"

"I can't bear to say it, Ada. I won't say it."

"Why not?"

"I'm superstitious."

"Then you *must* say it."

Hugh looked up at last. "If you were to die, I wouldn't want to live."

His voice was nearly too soft to comprehend. Regardless, Ada pulled away as though a cold hand had been set on her shoulder.

That night as Ada was drifting off in bed, the memory of Lucian on the moors returned. Instead of his scarred hands among the Weald House roses, she imagined him decomposing beneath a cluster of crows after Adelaide's death. Then she knew: better she live apart from Hugh than he suffer her father's fate.

"I'm leaving," she whispered against his sleep-warmed neck. "I must."

To fund her unexpected journey to Italy, Ada sold some of her mother's jewels, sewing the remainder into the hem of her cape. They weighed down her steps as she traveled, but she did not truly leave Hugh behind. Four months after she'd arrived in Fiesole, Ada came across a book he'd authored displayed in the sanitarium's common room. Before she could stop herself, she'd opened it and read:

I awake—I remember—I see—
My locus amoenus *lying beside me . . .*

Her fingers curled around the book's leather binding, just as they'd once curled about Hugh's hand. Her tears stained the pages.

The sanitarium was a peaceful place with a view of the hills of Tuscany. By the time the first lilacs began to bloom, Ada was deemed improved enough that she was moved from the main building into a cottage flanked by poplars and pines. Improbably, it contained a parlor piano. The air agreed with her lungs. She began to take constitutionals in the sanitarium gardens. She'd saved her life—or so she thought.

One day while sitting in the garden with her nurse, Ada found an egg that must have fallen from its nest. The egg was still warm, the sepia-mottled shell miraculously uncracked. She set the egg inside a small box padded with a pair of velvet gloves Hugh had given her. A week later, a bone-white beak poked through the egg, revealing a tiny grotesque creature tufted with down.

Ada recognized the chick at first sight for what it was: a raven. Like her sparrow of long ago, she taught the raven to play with string and straw. She hand-fed it bread crumbs and seed. By late summer, the raven had transformed into a magnificent predator with grand plumage—far too wild to live inside. Though she knew she'd miss its company, Ada took it out into the garden to free it.

"Goodbye!" she said. "Godspeed!"

The raven returned the next morning, tapping on the window nearest her bed with its beak. Its talons were bloodied.

Ada didn't take this as a sign. Not yet.

Ada was alone playing the piano the day the knock arrived. It was just after dawn on a sultry August morning, the sort of day when it seems impossible to believe winter will ever return. Her nurse had left with breakfast, and Ada had been practicing the adagio from Beethoven's Hammerklavier sonata.

Just as she'd arrived at the mournful final chord, the knock had sounded. She opened the door.

A tall man stood on her threshold, silhouetted by brilliant sun. Though he was several feet away, she made out a familiar scent. He smelled like roses and fir trees. Like Weald House, where her parents had met their ends.

It can't be, she thought. She folded her arms over her bosom; she was still barefoot in her nightdress.

The man stepped toward her, emerging from the light. Hugh—but how different he was from when she'd last seen him! He looked wearier than when they'd parted six months earlier in Paris. New wrinkles crested his forehead. The hair at his temples had gone bone white.

He held a brass cage bearing a pair of white doves.

"I brought you a gift," he said.

He set the cage at her bare feet. The raven swooped down from its perch to land beside the cage, managing to unhitch the door. The doves hopped out and fluttered to the table, where a loaf of bread had been left out to grow stale. They pecked delicately at it.

"You came," Ada said, unable to turn from her husband's gaze. "You shouldn't have."

"I tried to stay away. I couldn't."

"I'll be the ruin of you," Ada said, tears leaking from her eyes.

Hugh kissed the moisture from her cheeks. "We'll ruin each other then."

And then he whispered for some time into her ear—words that shall never be revealed by any living being. Once he'd finished, he offered her his hands.

Ada hesitated only a moment before she took them.

Just as she had that night at Herne Bay when he came to her room, she rubbed her thumb along the heart of his palm.

Three times. Once for each forbidden word.

Hugh collapsed sobbing to the floor before her feet, pressing his lips against her hands, the tip of his tongue tasting the salty skin between her fingers. A strange peace fell on Ada, a relief even. It was the sort of relief you'd feel upon coming to the end of a long journey when you're tired and hungry and lonely. Even if she wasn't where she'd expected, at last she'd arrived.

Somehow she fell onto the floor into his arms and was kissing him, and his mouth was on hers, and then they were on her bed with the linens twisting about their limbs, her nightdress raised above her thighs.

As they lay together, the doves swooped above their bodies, their feathers rising like souls returning to heaven.

II.

Alas, Ada's joy would soon be replaced by sorrow, Mr. Highstead.

Immediately after their reunion, Ada left the sanitarium against her doctor's advisement. Hugh insisted they find a similar environment for her health. Remembering Ada's beloved book of fairy tales, he suggested the Black Forest, where they could live alone amid nature. Hugh found a cottage deep in the woods, where the trees grew so thick that little sun fell. Rose brambles trailed along the window ledges, and sparrows nested in the eaves. The cottage reminded Ada of Weald House, though it was much smaller. It had belonged to a sheep herder who'd recently expired from old age. His widow could no longer bear to live there, but neither could she bear to sell the place. The house was covered in cobwebs and inhabited by feral cats. They mewed as they rubbed against Ada's ankles, desperate for milk and attention.

"The cats are included with the cottage. They're good mousers, though your doves may not like them," the widow said, shoving a tabby and her kittens off the kitchen table. "I must warn this is not a good place to be in winter. You could freeze to death if the snow gets too deep. Better to stay in the village. No one will find you here."

"But that's what we want," Hugh said. "To never be found."

Once the landlady left, they fell into each other arms and onto the bed.

"This shall be our *locus amoenus*," Hugh said.

"Forever," Ada responded.

Ada and Hugh. Hugh and Ada. Surely things would return as they were. They didn't. Just as the oak trees finished turning color, Ada began to sicken in a manner different than any she'd ever experienced.

At first the illness was such that she discounted it. "I'll be better soon," she told Hugh, ignoring the piano he'd had delivered to their cottage. This illness was different than last time, when she'd collapsed in the restaurant. She spent her days lying in bed too dizzy to stand. Food rarely passed her lips. She refused doctors. And then the vomiting began. Sometimes she spent all day curled over a bowl, unable to move lest her stomach clench anew. If that wasn't awful enough, the vomiting spurred fits of coughing, leaving Ada depleted of air as well as nourishment.

Hugh was so foolish that he never recognized the evidence before him. Nor did Ada, who accepted the illness as a mark of unavoidable fate. Still, Hugh cared for Ada in his way. He slept on the floor so he wouldn't wake her should he need to relieve himself in the night. He found homes for the cats, who spent more time yowling than hunting mice. He brought her birds from the forest: sparrows, swallows, a wren. They joined the raven and the doves in that sordid cottage. Their songs replaced the ones she no longer played on the piano.

As Hugh set the birds inside their makeshift cages, Ada knew he was trying to capture her soul in the same way he'd planned the glass chapel for his family.

"Remain with me," he'd whisper when he thought her asleep. "Never leave."

Ada began to dream of being entrapped by glass.

By the time Christmas arrived, the cottage was surrounded in snow up to Hugh's knees and Ada hadn't eaten in days. Though there was a blizzard underway, Hugh said, "I don't care what you want. I'm going for a doctor." He walked off on foot all the way to the village two miles away. He was so distracted he wore a wool frock coat instead of the fur one Ada had given him.

Some time later the door opened. Ada heard Hugh exclaim as he stomped his feet of snow, "Forgive me for not introducing myself, Herr Doktor—you have been so kind, so good to come so far on a snowy night with a stranger. My name is Hugh de Bonne . . . my wife is here. Take this candle. I keep the light dim so she may rest."

Ada saw the doctor was barely past twenty, but she was too sick to care. She allowed him to take her hand. To place his cold instruments against her bare flesh. Had she ever taken pleasure in Hugh's caresses? In love? Now everything felt a torment. She squeezed her eyes shut, wishing it was over already. No matter how she moved, her body brought anguish: the curdling stomach, the gasping lungs. The woozy head and aching limbs.

She heard:

"How long has she been in this state, Herr de Bonne?"

"Six weeks, though her illness progressed gradually. At first we thought the food disagreed with her. She's already delicate—cold weather does not agree with her—but she's grown much worse."

"What are her symptoms?"

"She vomits. She cannot eat. She barely sips tea. She cannot stand for dizziness. I fear . . . I fear . . ."

Ada opened her eyes. She was to have a baby—and she'd die. She'd known it as soon as the doctor questioned her. Instead of the quiet acceptance she'd expected, an anguished fury rose. It wasn't enough for Death to take her. He'd take her child as well. Two as one. And then none.

What will it feel to be dead? Ada thought. Anything must be better than this: the torment of illness. The anticipation of loss. To know she'd never hear the laughter of her own child. Never feel the sun on her skin again. Never watch spring return.

She stared out the window. Snow. It was still falling. Everything was white, as though nothing were there. Nothing.

Perhaps that's what death was like. Like nothing.

And then none . . .

* * *

"And then none . . ."

Isabelle's words drifted into silence. Robert looked up from the journal, waiting.

"What happened next, Miss Lowell?"

"I-I find myself unable to continue." She wiped her eyes against her sleeves. "I'm sorry, Mr. Highstead."

Robert resisted the urge to set his hands on her shoulders. To comfort her. "Let me finish your story," he said, his heart breaking for her. "I'll write it for you."

Just as he had with his Ovid biography, he'd use what he hypothesized. This time he wouldn't be wrong.

Robert wrote:

> *But Ada didn't die, to Hugh's surprise and relief. Instead she strengthened as her pregnancy progressed. For the first time, Ada began to hope. By the time she'd reached full term in May, she was back to playing her piano. It was as well, for it was the rainiest spring they'd ever seen. They spent days inside, entwined in each other's arms, feeling their baby kick. "A girl. I know it," Hugh said. "I want to name her Mathilde, after my mother."*

The baby came in the dead of night, just as a thunderstorm began. Ada woke with her nightdress soaked in water. It wasn't from rain.

Hugh ran for the doctor. By the time they'd made it safely back to the cottage in the woods, Ada's hands were bloody. "What took you so long?" she wept. "Now all is lost." Her poor body ached like she'd been torn apart by wolves.

They buried the baby on the first dry day after her arrival. Ada wouldn't meet Hugh's gaze to witness his tear-swollen eyes. It was his fault. Hadn't he brought them to this accursed place, where their only child had been born dead?

Soon two months had passed. Inside the cottage in the heart of the Black Forest, Ada paced in front of the ash-covered fireplace on a day when Hugh had gone to the village. "I never want to see you again," she wrote in Hugh's journal on the same page where he'd sketched the glass chapel. She gathered the remainder of Adelaide's jewels. She freed the raven and the doves.

When Hugh returned to the cottage that night, Ada was gone.

III.

Once Robert finished writing, he'd stood from his chair and closed the journal. He offered it to Isabelle after he trusted himself to speak. "You can't publish this. Nor does it prove your identity. But I suspect you already know this."

She hugged the journal against her chest. "You'll take Hugh's corpse when you leave?"

Robert nodded. "I promise you'll never hear of him again from me or my family. As for the pilgrims, I'll swear to your identity. I'll claim I'd forgotten meeting you as a child."

A teary smile. "That would be a lie, Mr. Highstead."

"Sometimes a lie is the most ethical course of action."

"True. If I'm not who I am, how could I know Ada's secrets?"

Robert was about to say, "You'd have to be Ada de Bonne herself." But then a new shuffle of footsteps sounded in the corridor outside the library.

An impatient rap on the door.

"I don't think it's Mrs. Chilvers this time," Robert said, his heart speeding. "Whoever it is, I'll turn them away."

"Too late." Isabelle shook her head. "I've no doubt it's Tamsin. She'll just come back."

Robert stared at the journal in Isabelle's hands. What would Tamsin do if she read what he'd just written in it?

Knock. Knock. Again. This time loud enough to make the library door shake.

Isabelle smoothed her hair, blew her nose. "I'm surprised she took so long. I was beginning to think she'd stolen Hugh's corpse from the stable." How calm she sounded. Relieved even. "Give me a moment."

Once she'd hidden the journal in a desk drawer, Robert opened the door.

Tamsin Douglas wasn't alone. Missus Dido paced behind her, her black cloak swaying like a shadow in the darkened corridor. Mrs. Chilvers bustled from the stairs in her nightdress. "Don't blame me, Miss Isabelle—I've naught to do with this!" the housekeeper said, flailing her arms as though to take flight. "I tried to stop them. They forced their way in!" Owen and Grace shoved each other. "This is all your fault," Owen hissed at Grace. Grace hissed back, "You're the one fighting—"

"Please!" Robert said. "What's happened?"

"I'm glad to find you here, Mr. Highstead," Tamsin said, "for this concerns your family." She raised a piece of paper over her head. "Look! Can you believe it?" And she began to laugh, but it was a strange laughter, replete with exhaustion and relief. Robert's flesh prickled.

"What's so funny?" Grace said. "Did you call the constable on me?"

"Constable?" Mrs. Chilvers cried, looking as though she'd faint. "I can't bear this—I'm too old."

"No police," Missus Dido said, her face set in a manner Robert couldn't decipher. "Surely we can settle this—"

"I agree, no police!" Grace interrupted.

"Hush!" Owen snapped. "Whatever it is, let Miss Isabelle see it."

Once they'd entered the library, Tamsin held the paper before Robert's eyes. He recognized it as a document he'd witnessed too often these past three years. A death certificate.

His stomach dropped at the name set upon it.

Isabelle Ada Lowell.

"It's what it appears to be, Mr. Highstead," Tamsin said, pointing. "It even bears a seal."

"So it seems," Robert answered, his mouth dry. He glanced at Isabelle, whose back was pressed against the desk where she'd hidden the journal. He motioned her over.

"You should see this."

They read the remainder of the document together:

Date of Death: 7 November 1827—Telford, Shropshire
Cause of Death: Smallpox

"I can't explain it," Isabelle said, her fingers twining and twisting in their usual manner. "That's my name. But the certificate isn't for me. Another relation no doubt." Her gaze darted his way. A forced smile. "Mr. Highstead! Perhaps you can help—you know of our family history."

"You should leave!" Grace scolded Tamsin. "I know you're vexed with me, but let Miss Isabelle be!"

Robert shushed her. He looked up from the death certificate, his mouth dry. "How did you obtain this document, Mrs. Douglas?"

"I'm responsible," Missus Dido said, her eyes enormous behind her spectacles. "My solicitor located it this afternoon in Shrewsbury after discovering Ada's father's family had lived there years ago. It was most unexpected." She offered Isabelle a remorseful glance. "And unfortunate."

"Oh goodness," Grace muttered, looking as though she'd faint. "Is Miss Isabelle dead then?"

"No!" Isabelle cried. "That's another Isabelle Lowell. Not me."

Robert leaned toward the candle to better view the document. "If I recall correctly, Hugh's will is dated 1839. The death certificate is from 1829. Why would he leave an estate to a deceased relative?"

"Perhaps he was unaware of the death. It matters not—she's no proof of identity anyway." Tamsin snatched the certificate from Robert, her hands shaking. "Careful!"

Isabelle grasped Missus Dido by her shoulders. "Didn't we meet when I was a child? When I came home for school holidays?"

Missus Dido pulled away, grimacing. "It's been so long. My sight . . ."

"Look!" Isabelle drew out something small and metallic from her pocket; Robert immediately knew what it was. "If I wasn't Isabelle Lowell, how could I possess this? Surely you recognize this, Missus Dido."

"What is it?" Owen whispered.

Robert explained, "A painting of Ada's eye."

"How do we know the portrait is genuine?" Tamsin demanded. Yet she didn't hesitate grabbing the miniature to examine it, setting the death certificate on the table. "Hugh never wrote of this in his letters. My husband would have known."

"But Missus Dido should recognize it," Robert insisted. "Let her look." He called to Grace, "She needs more light. Get a lamp."

"I'll light it," Owen offered, drawing matches from his pocket.

Viewed beneath gaslight, the eye miniature was as different from the painting of Sida as chalk from cheese. Robert envisioned Ada sitting for the portrait after viewing Canterbury Cathedral with Hugh, the sun hidden behind clouds. How tiny the miniature was, no larger than the circumference of a robin's egg. He squinted to better view it. The iris of Ada's eye was grey. Similar to Isabelle's . . .

She must be her.

Before Robert could react, smoke twined up his nose. He was about to scold Owen for smoking in the library, but then Grace began to scream.

Flames. They licked along the table. The death certificate curled inside them, a twist of gold and ash.

"Fire!" Missus Dido shrieked, heading for the door. "We're all going to die!"

"We're not going to die," Robert said, smothering the flames with his jacket until all that remained was a charred tabletop.

Tamsin shoved Owen. "You purposefully set it!"

"'Twas an accident." He shrugged. "Suppose you've nothing now."

"Accident, my hat!" And then Tamsin punched Owen square in his jaw, just as Robert had earlier.

Owen staggered but he didn't fall, for Grace caught him. The look Owen gave her as she gathered him against her bosom to set her lips on his reminded Robert of angels singing. But there was scant chance for Owen to wallow in the kiss, for Isabelle swooned to the floor. Her blood-spotted handkerchief fell from her pocket.

"She needs a doctor!" Robert shouted as he reached for her.

IV.

Once Owen and Grace ran to fetch the doctor, Robert found himself holding the journal—Isabelle must have extracted it from the drawer when no one was looking. "Take it," she mouthed to Robert, her eyelids fluttering as she briefly met his gaze. "Keep it. Don't leave me." Immediately Tamsin and Missus Dido had crowded about them, shouting. Robert pushed them away and slipped the journal inside his jacket pocket.

"Leave her be!" he shouted to the pilgrims. "Go! Now!"

Once the room was cleared, Isabelle opened her eyes. She'd feigned her faint. Robert knew what else she was faking. Even so, her flesh was pallid, her breathing shallow. Was her deception real? Or reality a tool for deception?

"That death certificate," Robert prompted; surely she'd finally confess her identity. "It seems anyone who knows you is either dead or claims not to recall. You have no provenance. Only hearsay. And even with the death certificate burned—"

She shuddered as though stirring awake. "I never want to speak of that certificate again."

"You can't ignore it. I've sat here all these nights writing down your story. You must want me to know the truth."

"I am who I said, Mr. Highstead. There was another Isabelle Lowell. Another relation. I swear!"

Robert wouldn't challenge her. She seemed so fragile. So unwell. "Can you sit? I'll get you something to drink."

Isabelle nodded, docile as a child. Robert reached for a crystal decanter and goblet that was always kept on the fireplace mantel; it was filled with a burgundy-hued fluid. Port, from the scent of it—he recalled it from the first night he'd arrived at Weald House. (How long ago this seemed!) The ornate crystal always seemed out of place at Weald House, a last relic of Hugh and his love of fine things.

She drank heavily, the port dribbling down her chin. Once she finished, Robert asked, "Better?"

She nodded. "Better."

"The doctor should be here soon."

"No doctor can help me," she confessed. "You see, there's something else weighing me. Something I need to speak of."

Robert's heart began to pound. "Besides the death certificate?"

"Yes . . ." She muffled a cough, her lashes wet. "It's this. I know you're going to leave here now that I've finished my story. I know most likely I'll never see you again."

Her finger tapped the rim of the glass; Robert waited for her to continue.

"But that's not all that's bothering me—and there's so much! I-I was with Ada after she married. She never wrote me letters."

"I suspected as much," Robert said, his pulse speeding.

"It matters not, though. Not after that death certificate." Now she was sobbing in earnest.

Somehow he found himself stroking the slope of her shoulders to comfort her. Her bones felt as shallow as ice on a spring morning, and as fragile. She smelled of wine and soap.

"I don't know what you wrote in my journal, how you ended it," she said. "But I want you to know the truth."

His hands fell from her shoulders as she rose to stand before the fire. The flames flickered wildly, whipped by the wind hissing down the chimney, silhouetting her before his gaze. Perhaps it was exhaustion from the long day, or a trick of the light, but he had the sense that, while looking at Isabelle's shadow, Ada was standing beside her. Was it his yearning? Or something else?

Robert blinked several times to disperse the hallucination. The hallucination remained.

Ada seemed as much a presence as Sida had been these past three years. She looked just as Isabelle had described all those nights: her dark hair, her hollowed cheeks and luminous eyes, her clothing of fifteen years earlier with its flounces and flowers. Robert's sight blurred with light and color. Through this haze, he watched Ada playing the piano. Ada walking along the shore at Herne Bay. Ada examining an array of fossils. Finally, he saw Ada embrace Isabelle. But then something happened he could not have foreseen: Ada's form merged into Isabelle's body until only one woman remained. As the two became one, Robert had the sense he was watching a spirit enter a body instead of departing, unlike all those corpses he'd attended with his camera.

And at last she appeared whole to him—no illness, no suffering. Filled with life. Not death.

A looming joy rose in Robert, one he hadn't felt since his wife's return from the grave.

"You're her. Ada." He'd been right all along.

As soft as his voice was, Isabelle—or Ada, he reminded himself—flinched.

"Allow me to explain, Robert—"

He had no time to question her addressing him by his Christian name and all this might signify, for he drew as close as he could. Her mouth parted, her pupils dilated. He brushed her hair from her face, ignoring the vein pulsing at her temple, the air rushing from her parted lips. He stared at her, at the portrait of Ada across the room, then back again, envisioning the march of time spreading their toil across her features. *It must be*. And then he could no longer remain silent.

"You *are* Ada, aren't you? That's why you're avoiding the pilgrims. Because if they knew you still lived, they'd blame you for Hugh's disappearance and death. They'd accuse you of breaking his heart when you abandoned him after Mathilde's death. That's why you want me to write your book—to get rid of the pilgrims. To free yourself of your past. From Hugh."

After a moment, she gave a little nod.

"Yes. Yes, I'm Ada."

A strange smile overtook her lips. Somehow Robert found her eyes meeting his, just as he'd found himself clutching her hand. Her tongue, soft and pink, darted against her lips, as though they'd grown parched after a long night's sleep. How full and ripe her mouth was. How welcoming.

Their faces loomed closer until only a breath separated them. Now her scent of wine and soap mingled with moss and smoke. Her hand rose to caress his cheek. His stunned brain recited like a litany, *We are going to kiss. I am going to kiss Ada de Bonne . . .*

A gasp caught his ears—a gasp Ada seemed not to hear. Robert pulled away as though he'd singed his hands. He *knew* whose gasp he'd heard. Sida's.

He whirled around the room. "Where are you?"

Ada implored, "Who are you speaking to?"

A *ghost*, Robert wanted to say. *Like those you've been speaking of all these nights. Only mine is real. And I've betrayed her.*

"Where are you?" he begged. "Reveal yourself!"

"Here."

The voice was more a drift of wind than breath. It emerged from behind Robert.

He turned. The mirror above the fireplace. It reflected Sida standing beside Ada. Sida's face was pale and mournful above that eternal bloodstained blue silk dress. Her eyes were wet. All of Robert's love for her returned. All his guilt.

"I'm sorry," he cried, turning toward her. "So sorry!"

Sida dissolved into the wall as unexpectedly as she'd appeared, a whoosh of damp air rustling in her wake, the scent of smoke too. "Come back!"

Robert shouted. But before he could rush after his ghost wife, a glare of dazzling orange on the window caught his eye. It came from the direction of the stable house.

Ada saw it also. “How strange,” she said just as the clock struck midnight and the dog began to bark. “Can that be the sunrise already?”

The Ghost Bride

Excerpted from *The Weight of Air* by Hugh de Bonne, published 1835 by Chapman & Hall, London.

I walk solitary at midnight
Though not alone. My Bride
Follows with a tread so light
Like Crows aft their Stygian guide.
'Come with me,' I shall cry.
'Remain with me—or I will die.'

Alone, I turn to find her thus :
Her dark hair asunder with nested
Sparrow. Her shoulders artless
Yet garbed with Dove and Ibis.
'Come with me,' I did cry.
'Remain with me—or I shall die.'

Now my Bride walks before me in the night.
Still—I fear she might take flight.

*

I.

A beehive surrounded by briars will burn. A stable built of rotted wood and filled with hay will burn. A corpse embalmed in spirits of wine and arsenic will burn. But a house made of stone will not, especially if the wind is still. This was what Robert told himself as he watched the last of Hugh de Bonne become consumed by flames.

By the time Robert realized what the orange glare on the window indicated, the stench of smoke was overwhelming and Virgil's bark had grown into a howl that would have roused the dead from their graves.

"The stable house," Ada said. "It's on fire."

Her voice was oddly flat. But then the spell broke, and a sob escaped her lips as she rushed from the library. Robert ran downstairs after her, fearful what she'd do when confronted with the coffin of her deceased husband ablaze. She and Hugh once loved each other. Created a child together. Buried that child. And then lost each other. No matter their history, for Ada to witness Hugh's corpse destroyed in such a manner seemed a final cruelty. But he needn't worried: she'd gone to locate Mrs. Chilvers, who was safe in her bed, and Owen and Grace, who'd returned from the village without the doctor.

Outside the stable house, the flames shot even higher, for the hay loft caught fire. Robert covered Ada with his arms, protecting her from flying embers and fleeing cows and horses, who screeched as they scattered toward the woods. The air was thick with fog, which kept the flames from spreading to the main house. Shards of glass littered the walk; Robert recognized them as the broken remains of an oil lamp.

Before he could inform Ada of what he'd found, Grace and Owen staggered from the rose garden, their faces grey with ash, followed by Tamsin Douglas and Missus Dido.

"Oh sweet Jesus!" Tamsin screamed, her knees buckling. "Someone *do* something! Hugh's in there!"

She lurched toward the stable house, barely avoiding the falling embers. Missus Dido reached to stop her, but Tamsin slipped past her grasp, toward where the fire burned brightest.

Grace leapt and wrestled Tamsin to the ground. "No! It's too late, Mrs. Douglas!"

"Let me go! You can't possibly understand— "

"I *do* understand." Grace shook Tamsin's shoulders. "He's gone! Gone! Nothing can be done. You can't bring him back!" Whether she was referring to Hugh or Mrs. Douglas's son or husband, it didn't matter, Robert decided. For Grace was right: nothing could be done.

Soon after, Grace and Owen disappeared with the pilgrims. Robert and Ada watched in silence as the fire rose bright and hot. What more was there to say? He'd learned what he'd yearned to know; she'd confessed what she'd needed. As a result, Hugh was gone. So was Sida.

Nothing to be done.

Just after the fire reached its apex, they were joined by Mrs. Chilvers in her wrapper, who clutched her throat, and Owen and Grace, who clutched hands.

"Where'd you take Mrs. Douglas and Missus Dido?" Robert asked.

"The library," Grace said, her eyes swollen from smoke. "Didn't trust Mrs. Douglas alone. Had Missus Dido give her morphia to sleep. She's with her now—she'll keep her safe." She avoided Ada's gaze. "I fear Mrs. Douglas burned her hands when she fell. I'll fetch the doctor."

"Yet you didn't fetch the doctor earlier . . ." Robert addressed Owen, who was examining his cigarette. "It's fortunate the horses and cows weren't in the stable when the fire began."

Owen swallowed hard. "Nor was your camera box."

"I see. Where'd you take it?"

"The kitchen." He flicked his cigarette into a pile of leaves. "Well, you were leaving in the morning. 'Twas a miracle that I'd remembered."

"A miracle," Grace rejoined, whistling for the dog.

"No miracle," Ada said bitterly, hacking from the smoke.

Nothing to be done, Robert thought again.

The stable house smoldered through the night. Soon after dawn, the fog became a gentle rain that doused anything still burning. Once the embers settled, they crumbled to ash. By mid-afternoon, they'd dried enough that the wind carried them into the rose garden. The ashes were black as raven feathers.

"Don't play with those, Virgil!" Robert heard Grace scold. "Poison!"

Robert didn't see Ada the following day, which she'd spent recovering in her room, if he was to believe Mrs. Chilvers. Before he left Weald House, he searched for Sida everywhere. He didn't find her. Nor did he find her in Kent when he arrived at his family home.

He even dared walk by her uncle's cottage, in the unlikely case she'd returned there. In the ten days he'd been away, someone had hacked at the rose arbor and the fruit trees. They'd also torn out the herb and vegetable beds. The garden looked like a man who'd gone in for a haircut but ended up bald. The stench of horse manure and decaying leaves mingled with damp earth. "It's what it should be," Robert murmured. They were pruning and replanting for spring. Still, it was a shock, as though he'd come upon it gutted by flames.

He stood there staring at the garden for some time, yearning for a glimpse of Sida. Her blue gown fluttering against her limbs. Her dark hair about her cheeks.

She'll be in London. She'll understand once I explain about Ada. She'll remain with me.

This time he didn't believe it.

II.

Hugh's funeral was a subdued Saturday morning affair attended only by John, Robert, and their immediate household. "Best to keep things private," John said. Robert understood. At the last minute, John invited Hugh's solicitor, who came down from London for the day, but insisted on staying overnight. Awkwardness upon awkwardness, Robert thought, especially after he explained how Hugh's mortal remains had been incinerated during Robert's attempt to fulfill his last wishes. "You didn't have to take 'ashes to ashes' quite so literally, Mr. Highstead," was the solicitor's flabbergasted response. Still, John had managed to convince him to consider the terms of Hugh's bequest fulfilled, for nothing more could be done.

The pine box John had called into service for Hugh's coffin was empty save for a pile of the poet's books. Once John had learned the worst ("A stable fire! The house still stands? What the deuce, Robert . . ."), he'd rushed off to London, where he'd purchased every edition he could find of Hugh's published works, from juvenilia to *The Weight of Air* to *Cantos for Grown Children* to *The Lost History of Dreams.*

"The measure of a man's life is in his work," John explained.

"The measure of a man's life is in who he loves," Robert countered.

When John was busy fussing with his hounds, Robert slipped the journal bearing Ada's story into the coffin.

Still, some things remained as they had been before Robert's journey to Shropshire. Though he'd yet to return to his employment, he arranged for a mute clad in full mourning to accompany Hugh's coffin as they drove it to the family plot in Belvedere proper. He draped black crape over the mirrors to prevent Hugh's soul from lingering. Without a corpse to daguerreotype, Robert set his tripod beside Hugh's plot to record the funeral for history's sake.

Once the coffin had been lowered into the soil, and flowers dropped onto it, Robert settled himself behind his camera. Through the viewing glass, he saw his brother, who'd brought his dogs, and Hugh's solicitor, who scowled as a result. The remainder of their household chose to remain outside the composition save for their housekeeper, Mary, whose bulk filled much of the frame.

Once the composition was set, Robert took out the silver-coated copper plate that would become the daguerreotype. He'd already buffed it to a mirrorlike sheen. It was one of the plates he'd prepared to daguerreotype Hugh inside Ada's Folly—a plate that was never used.

A quick exposure to chemical fumes and the plate was ready. As Robert slid it inside the airtight box for exposure, his gaze wandered to the grave beside Hugh's. *Cressida Maya Highstead*, the slender granite headstone said. Someone had thought to weed around it.

Robert looked away. Best not to think of what was lost. But he did.

Come back to me. Please.

The camera mechanism felt to his hand like it usually did, yet somehow different. Colder. Stiffer. Perhaps it was his time away from it. He took off the lens cap with a flash of his palm. Though he'd carefully framed the composition, Sida's grave stone intersected one corner.

I love you. Only you.

Just as he finished counting down the exposure time, his stomach clenched, his sight blurred. The sour taint of acid choked his throat.

Before he could finish fixing the image, Robert packed everything away.

"I have to leave," he mouthed to John. "Now."

Back at his family home, Robert only made it as far as John's study, where he'd first encountered Hugh's corpse ten days earlier. After he vomited inside a half-empty coal scuttle, he collapsed onto the chaise that had belonged to his mother.

The memory of Sida's headstone returned. *She's really gone.*

Once he trusted himself to move, he grabbed a bottle of brandy from a shelf and a glass. He gagged down as much as he could stand, welcoming the burn against his mouth—alcohol was better than the taint of bile. He shut his eyes, yearning to forget.

Soon after, Robert felt a hand on his shoulder. John. He smelled vaguely of brandy himself.

"You fell asleep, brother of mine."

"It's been a long day."

"It's not even ten o'clock."

"I've been up since five." He eyed John warily. "Shouldn't you be with our guests?"

"You mean *guest*. Hugh's solicitor left. I don't think he appreciated our funeral service, but we did what we could," John said. "If you have that daguerreotype, I'll send it to him. It'll make amends for immolating Hugh's earthly remains."

Robert raised himself against the chaise, rubbing his brow. "I still need to varnish it. I'll bring it to him in London." *I'll find Sida there. I have to.*

"That reminds me. Did our Miss Isabelle Lowell ever explain why she wouldn't let you daguerreotype Hugh inside the glass chapel?"

A silence the length of a breath. In this silence, Robert felt the entirety of all that had occurred at Weald House before his departure.

"No," he said. He'd tell no one of Ada's story. Not even John.

Robert reached for his daguerreotype traveling case. It clattered like an alchemist's laboratory as he dragged it toward the door.

"I should leave. I've drunk enough of your brandy."

"So soon? I'd hoped you'd stay at least for lunch. I can arrange for a Bordeaux to compliment the brandy," John said, his pleading gaze belying his flippant tone. "I thought we could talk about Oxford. Perhaps it's time to reconsider your Ovid biography. Seems a shame to let it slide after your first book did so well. If you were to, I've something interesting. Letters Hugh wrote Father—Hugh's solicitor had sent them to me, though God knows how he obtained them. I glanced through them, but it's not the sort of thing I usually read. Perhaps they'd be useful for your book?"

"What does this have to do with Ovid?"

John shrugged. "Ovid disappeared. Hugh disappeared. Old is new and new is old."

"You surprise me."

"I'll take that as a yes then." John pulled the letters, which were tied in a thick black ribbon, from a drawer in his desk. "By the way you dropped something."

A glint of gold on the floor. The eye miniature. The one of Sida. It must have slipped from his pocket while he was packing his camera equipment.

Robert's stomach clenched anew. He pulled the eye minature into his fist, unable to look at it. Nevertheless, a deep shudder rose through his torso, starting from his stomach and rising to his throat. He felt as though he'd vomit again.

He clutched the miniature against his palm and slid to the ground.

"She's gone. She's really gone! Truly, utterly gone."

"Who?" John's tone was more bewildered than concerned.

"My wife. Sida." Robert's words came hard now. "I have no idea where she went. Only that I've lost her forever."

John said gently, "It's been over three years."

"I know. I know! But she's never left me. Not really—"

"You mean *you* never left her, Robert. Isn't that why you refused to speak to me? Abandoned your friends? Left Oxford?"

"You don't understand. I didn't love her as I should. Protect her as I should. And now I've betrayed her . . ." Robert looked up from the miniature, his breath shallow. "There was another woman."

The memory of Ada just before they'd nearly kissed returned. Her eyes, wide and startled, as if she'd been surprised by desire as much as he'd been.

"Cressida's dead. You're alive. How can you betray someone by living in this world?"

But there was more than this to Robert's grief. In that moment, Robert felt his past catching up with him from these past three years. Guilt rose like bile as he recalled all those stillborn babies he'd daguerreotyped, all those dead children and mothers. Those mourning fathers and left-behind siblings he'd comforted during his employment. The money he'd made from their bereavement, the catharsis he'd gleaned by capturing their loss on a silvered plate, as though this act would restore his wife to life . . .

"I never told you what happened the night she died, did I?"

John turned ashen. "I know what happened. Her uncle beat her. He'd beaten her before. It's an old story. A sad story. You did your best to stop him. There's nothing more you could have done."

"You're wrong. So very wrong." Now the words wouldn't stop coming no matter how Robert tried. "Her uncle found us together. In bed."

John's eyes widened. "I assume you weren't napping."

"We'd thought we were alone."

"Robert, you don't need to tell me—"

"But I do! I do! I want you to know the truth—no one else does. She'd thought he'd left with her aunt for the day—her aunt knew we'd planned to elope. There was no other way. Her uncle didn't believe I intended to marry her. Sida had said that would happen, that he'd call her a whore. A slut. He'd send her back to India."

"I understand," John said, taking Robert by his shoulders to calm him.

"No, you don't understand. You can't understand . . ." But Robert could confess no more. It was too sordid. Too painful. They were just about to leave for London to elope. Sida had taken a last look around the cottage to see if she'd forgotten anything. *"The only thing I'll miss is the garden,"* she'd said. *"Should I leave my uncle a note?"*

"Instead of a note, I should piss on his bed," Robert said. *"He'll understand the message."*

"I've a better idea, my sweet," Sida answered, giggling with nerves. *"Love, not hate. 'Remember, happy are those who dare courageously to defend what they love.'"*

Robert met her eyes. Robert understood.

As soon as they'd tumbled onto her uncle's bed, Robert's hands were on her breasts and her mouth was on his. *"One last time before we marry,"* he said, breaking from their kiss, excited by the danger; he'd already unbuttoned his trousers. *"One last time,"* she whispered, raising the hem of her blue silk dress. *"We'll be quick."* That had been the last he'd recalled before his head shattered with light and everything turned black . . .

Suddenly Robert found himself kicking his traveling case until he fell onto the floor beside it and he couldn't catch his breath. "She's gone. Truly gone!"

"Shush, brother of mine." And then his brother slid to the ground beside him, embracing Robert as he had after their mother died when they were boys and their father had been lost to grief.

But Robert couldn't take any comfort in his brother's compassion. He needed to find Sida before she was lost forever.

III.

Upon his arrival in London, Robert found the city covered by the densest fog he'd ever seen. Regardless, he ran from Euston Station to Clerkenwell, covering the mile and a half distance more quickly than he ever had; his chest stung from the cold, his sides ached though he'd left his daguerreotype equipment in Kent. With every breath, a silent refrain reverberated throughout his body. *I love you. Only you.* In Clerkenwell, the streets were just as they ever were: Back Hill, Eyre Street, Grays Inn Lane. He rushed past them until he found himself outside his boarding house.

Let her be here. Please.

Robert swung open the door, his nerves tingling. His landlady started like she'd seen a ghost; she was in her usual spot behind the bar, poring over an array of bills with a pencil. "Well then," she said once she recovered. "Mr. Robert Highstead, you're late with your rent—"

He ignored her shrill complaints to dash the four stories to his room. The door was open. He stared out the window at the fog veiling the roofs. It obscured the crows on the chimneys, his reflection on the window glass.

No Sida.

Robert turned once, twice around the room, ignoring the display of prepared silver plates, Sida's drawings, his books. His head felt light. His hands wrapped around Sida's miniature in the overcoat pocket. The painting felt more insubstantial than ever compared to Hugh's letters beside it. As insubstantial as his ghost wife.

She's gone. God help me.

He heard his landlady's heavy shuffle on the steps. "Aren't you the one, flouncing in without a word of explanation! I'd thought you'd abandoned us for good. Where's the tin you owe?" But there was no time to respond—already he was rushing down the stairs toward the pavement. He'd find her. He had to.

Outside the boarding house, the fog was heavier than before. In the short time he'd been indoors, it had turned from an ecru miasma some might consider picturesque to a threateningly tangible presence tinged with green. It stank of sulfur and was thick enough to obscure his hands. *Sida!* he felt like shouting into the dense void. But this wouldn't do. Even in the unlikely event of her hearing him, she'd probably flee. He couldn't blame her after what had happened with *her*. (Now he found he couldn't say Ada's true name. Nor could he refer to her as Isabelle. She was neither Ada nor Isabelle. Someone in between. Someone he must forget for the sake of his marriage.)

Robert whirled around Grays Inn Lane, his head pounding, his eyes straining. *Where could she be?* He felt unsteady. Disoriented. His memories of glimpsing St. Paul's Cathedral to the south on clear days seemed an impossible occurrence.

Just as he despaired, a shimmer of blue flashed before him. A set of dark eyes.

He held his breath, oscillating between trepidation and joy.

The figure of a slight Eurasian woman materialized before him. Robert knew her face as he knew his own. Instead of wearing her usual blood-splattered blue silk dress, Sida had changed into a smart navy day dress with matching bolero jacket. They'd been intended as her travel outfit for their journey to Oxford after their honeymoon. She'd spent weeks sewing it, inspired by an illustration she'd seen in a Paris magazine. She'd never gotten to wear it. The presence of the outfit disconcerted Robert more than her witnessing him with Ada, or her transforming into a raven. She was changing. Evolving. Or was he?

Just as he took a cautious step in her direction, Sida pivoted on her heel. She walked down narrow lanes toward Victoria Street. Robert lurked as close as he could. Despite the fog, he did not lose her. A quarter of a mile later, she turned a corner onto an alleyway off Newgate Street. Now he knew where she was going. St. Paul's Cathedral.

The fog had even managed to seep inside St. Paul's where Robert found Sida. He watched her float beneath the dome down the gilded nave of the cathedral. He followed silently, fearful of startling her. She paused to light a candle near the choir before continuing down the nave and through the Great West Door to the world beyond.

Once she turned toward Fleet Street, he'd given up guessing her destination. He trailed after her for what felt like a half hour. In Trafalgar Square, the eerie chatter of feral pigeons, horse-drawn carriages, bird-seed sellers, and footsteps echoed around the scaffolding surrounding the unfinished business of Nelson's Column. Unperturbed, Sida glided past the Mall. One turn later, she came to an abrupt stop in the middle of the pavement. The buildings looked familiar to Robert, but he couldn't remember why.

His steps slowed as he approached. How close she was! He could sense her coolness, her radiance, though it appeared dimmed like a mirror beneath tulle. Even so, for the first time in days, his stomach unclenched. She'd understand it was she he loved, not Ada. All would be set right. They'd never be parted.

Robert stretched his hand toward the crisp wool of her jacket shoulder. Toward her dark hair . . .

Sida melted into the fog as suddenly as she'd shown.

From the shift of weight, Robert's weak ankle gave way. He collapsed to a pavement splattered with bird droppings and let loose a string of expletives that would have made a fishmonger blush.

Once he recovered, he looked up. Through the misty air, he made out a cream-colored facade fronted by a curved portico. A discreet brass sign read: *The Union Hotel.*

Now he understood where she'd led him. The hotel where they'd spent the first and only night of their honeymoon.

His heart pounding, Robert pushed the heavy door open. He found himself inside an expansive lobby milling with humanity. His eyes stung with the sharp advent of light. The Union was just as he recalled from three years prior: the flocked red velvet wallpaper, the crystal-drenched chandeliers hissing with gas, the porters pushing brass carts towering with luggage, the upholstered chaises and chairs, the ringing of bells and clattering of teacups on saucers. At last he knew where to find his wife.

Robert smoothed his hair—he'd left his hat in Kent but at least he'd remembered his satchel—and approached the front desk. A pasty-faced woman of uncertain age stood behind a long marble counter before an array of keys. He didn't recall her from his previous stay.

She glanced up from the register at his approach. Her smile seemed weighed by reluctance. "May I help you, sir?"

"I'd like a room, please."

The woman glared over her lunettes, unimpressed by Robert's bird-soiled overcoat, his bare head. "Rooms are let after three o'clock. It's not even two—"

"I need the room *now*. If necessary, I'll pay for the extra day. Please."

There must have been desperation in Robert's mien, for she made a show of rustling through the register book. "Very well. You'll need to pay in advance."

Once he'd signed and paid, he asked, "Is room seventeen available?"

IV.

Sida wasn't in room seventeen. Nor was there any evidence of her. The hotel room was nicer than he recalled. He'd chosen well for their honeymoon—he'd wanted it to be special. It was also close to the National Gallery; he'd envisioned Sida taking pleasure in the art. Yet some things weren't as he remembered. Perhaps they'd redecorated in the years since, for he'd forgotten the scarlet damask curtains about the bed, the windowed alcove with the obscured view of Trafalgar Square. Nor did he remember the porcelain basin, or the gilded mirror above it.

Robert stared into the mirror. His heart sinking, he locked the door behind him, his head throbbing between the fog and the brandy. Whether Sida was ghost or madness, he didn't care. He loved her. Only her. She couldn't leave him.

"Come to me!" he cried into the empty room. "I love you. Only you!"

No answer.

She'll show. She has to.

He unpacked the eye miniature of Sida and set it on the nightstand, still unable to look at it. As for the letters John had given him, Robert couldn't decide what to do. Send them to Weald House? Destroy them? The only thing certain was he wouldn't read or write about Ada and Hugh de Bonne. Not after all he'd learned. For now, he pulled the packet from his pocket and placed it on the nightstand next to the eye miniature.

This done, he settled on the bed, the springs creaking, his chest heavy. At last, the exhaustion of the past week caught up with him. Though his stomach was rumbling, he didn't dare leave to get tea. Sleep could help. Perhaps Sida would show in the meantime.

Robert closed his eyes. But he couldn't sleep, for he was overcome by memories of that night over three years ago. The blow that had knocked him out. The shock when he'd regained consciousness and found Sida's uncle slamming his fists against her body. *"You'll never hurt her again,"* Robert had shouted, punching her uncle once he'd pulled Sida away. *"I'll keep her safe.*" Instead of going for the police, Sida had insisted on their eloping as planned. They'd even set scuffed shoes outside their hotel room so no one would know they'd just wed. "*I'm so happy,*" she'd said. "*Now I'm truly your wife. I'll love you forever.*" But she'd looked weak beyond the welts on her flesh, the bloody nose; her uncle had directed the whole of his fury on Sida, leaving Robert with nary a bruise save his head.

As soon as Robert settled her in bed, he'd rushed to get a doctor. It hadn't mattered.

"*How long did you leave your wife alone?*" the constable had asked after her death.

"*Just long enough to return with a physician. A half hour at most.*"

"*What happened upon your return?*"

"*She appeared to be sleeping. When she didn't stir, I called her name. It was then I noticed the blood on her lips. On her gown. She was having difficulty breathing.*" Out of delicacy, he'd omitted she'd dressed herself while he was gone; Robert suspected she'd felt so badly she'd decided to go for help before collapsing.

"*Mr. Highstead?*" This was the physician the hotel had recommended. "*I'm truly sorry. Sometimes these injuries are more serious than they first appear . . .*"

The memory faded. Robert drew a deep breath, his fingers brushing his beard. Suddenly he could no longer stand the hair on his face.

He forced himself from the bed, and found himself before the mirror. During his stay in Shropshire, mirrors had been a vehicle to seek his wife, not to address bodily requirements. He seemed a stranger to himself, with his rumpled hair that curled long about his forehead; his sensitive mouth; his fair skin that only burned in the sun; his exhausted eyes. Still, the allure of hope called: his gaze shifted to the void beyond the mirror.

No one there.

He shifted his eyes back: there he was again, a twenty-nine-year-old man with a beard, the scar at his left temple; his scab had finally fallen off, leaving a slender pale line in its wake. *Just like Hugh.* He examined the white in his beard and brow, which had increased during his time in Shropshire. Ada's long ivory hair flashed before him. Perhaps he'd be completely white by the time he reached her age.

You're tired. You need sleep. Tomorrow you'll decide what to do. Sida will return.

With a beard so grown in, it would be safer to go to a barber, but he was too impatient. He pulled out his shaving-tackle from his satchel—the soap, the brush, the strop and razor—and poured water into the basin. A subtle breeze caressed his neck in that old way.

Robert looked over his shoulder.

"Sida?"

His voice echoed in the room. His gaze lit on the letters, the miniature of her eye on the nightstand. The vacant space in the chair. The empty bed.

And yet if he closed his eyes, he could still feel her presence. Her soul.

Once he soaped his face he picked up the razor. His beard was so thick he'd need to be careful not to cut himself. Then, for reasons he didn't quite understand, he stared down at his hands still holding the razor. His over-washed skin was nearly healed, just chaffed where he'd punched Owen. In another week they'd be like new.

He turned his hands over. The veins on his wrists were bluish. His skin translucent . . .

The bed curtains rustled.

"*Robert . . .*"

Robert turned back to the mirror—and there at last his ghost wife stood.

Sida's face shimmered as though reflected in water instead of glass. She was still dressed in that outfit she'd never been able to wear while alive, looking as she ever did with her dark hair, her wide pragmatic mouth, her square jaw. Her kindness, her decency.

Robert set his razor down. For a moment he considered rushing to clasp Sida in his arms as he would have if she still lived. "*You're here!*" he'd cry, kissing her over and over. "*You didn't leave. You're here. You're here! Oh, how I searched for you—I went to Clerkenwell, St. Paul's, and so many other places we've been. I didn't dare call to you, so I followed you all over London. But the fog—it was so hard to see you, like a terrible dream. But you're here now, my sweet. You're here!*" And he'd take her hands and whirl her about the room as though they were children playing a circle game until everything would blur in a frenzy of red drapes, blue wool, and gold light. But he knew this wouldn't do with his ghost wife. Not after what happened with Ada.

He turned and approached her carefully after wiping the soap off his beard.

"I'm so glad I found you," he exhaled. "How you frightened me!"

"*Of course I'm here.*" She pointed down at her travel outfit, her tone hollow. "*I've no choice but to remain with you. I'm your wife.*"

The weight of her words drew the oxygen from Robert's lungs. *Ada. She hadn't forgotten.* "But it's you I love. Forever."

Sida shut her eyes so tightly that the delicate flesh at the corners crinkled. *"Forever . . . What about* her?"

How could he explain he'd been affected by Ada's return from the dead? That he hadn't intended betrayal? "You're the only one I love. You. Cressida Maya Highstead. My wife. Stay with me. I'll take care of you. Protect you. We'll be together always."

"It's not that, my sweet . . ."

"I understand. I betrayed you. I didn't defend you. Not enough."

Sida opened her eyes. They'd turned clear as glass. *"Happy are those who dare courageously to defend what they love,"* she replied, quoting his Ovid. *"You* did *defend me. But I didn't marry you for that—I married you because I love you. Because I wanted a life with you."*

"But it's my fault you're dead!"

Sida's face grew so ashen that she appeared to fade into the air. *"Robert, it's easy to look back and regret the past. What's hard is the future."* A sob interrupted her words. *"God help me, I wish I knew how to change things. To make them as they were."*

She began to weep so hard that she fell to the floor. Robert couldn't think what to say. He heard the omnibuses outside on Piccadilly Circus, the caw of birds beyond. The cries of street vendors. The shuffle of footsteps on the corridor beyond.

The sound of his heart.

And then, in a rush that felt like a blow, he saw Sida as she was, not as he wished her to be. His mourning had kept her suspended between life and death, like a raven he'd trapped in a cage—a raven that resembled the living in form only. But it wasn't just that. In a sense, he was in this cage too.

A troubling thought arose—one he couldn't bear to voice.

"There, my sweet," he said at last, his eyes wet too. "Don't weep."

He pulled Sida beside him on the bed—that same bed where she'd breathed her last—and gently spooned what remained of her. He smoothed the wool of her travel outfit, which was as ephemeral as her body. *"How tender you are,"* she murmured once she calmed. And then he knew what he must do.

"I've loved you from the moment I first beheld you," Robert said, his voice stronger than he felt. "I still remember the first time we met six years ago. You looked up at me from your sewing. That drawing of the dove beside you . . ."

"I loved you as soon as I saw you too."

Her voice lilted, like it once had. For a moment, he was back with her at that tailor shop, bathed in sunshine and possibilities. They hadn't wanted to leave each other, even when the time arrived for the shop to close. He'd said, "How hard it is to say goodbye. Let us bid farewell instead." All these years later, this hadn't changed.

He reached for her hand, grasping only wet air. He fought the urge to turn her toward him for a glimpse of her face. Yet he felt her body relax against him. Her hand loosen. And then he found her mouth searching for his, and his for hers for what he knew would be the last time.

As their lips met tentatively, and then hungrily, he sensed the years turn back yet leap forward. Robert imagined this same kiss as an old man, if Sida had lived long enough for their hair to turn grey and their skin wrinkle and grandchildren play at their feet. The kiss became the one they'd shared in the woods after she'd painted her eye, and the kiss exchanged after they'd wed. It became the kiss of sorrow Robert had set on her unresponsive brow before the coroner took her body away; he recalled her cooling flesh, her unseeing gaze. Finally, the kiss returned to the present, and Robert understood the kiss for what it was, though this knowledge made his hands clutch for hers and his eyes sting.

"Farewell, my sweet," he said.

And then he was alone with outstretched hands and empty arms.

V.

Robert lay there for some time on that richly appointed hotel bed just as he had the night of Sida's death. *She's gone.* This time, he had no doubt. Had he imagined her presence all these months? An unexpected answer came: *It doesn't matter.* As for what was next for him, his stomach ached from lack of food. It reminded him that while Sida might be spirit, he was decidedly human. Well, there was no longer any reason to remain there.

Robert buttoned his overcoat, raising the beaver collar against his neck though he didn't need it. The air already felt warmer, the air sweet with the start of spring, as if the world had entered the room to pull him back into it.

He turned to the nightstand to gather his belongings. He recalled there was a decent public house nearby. After he ate, he'd go to Clerkenwell. For now. He'd change into fresh clothes, leave Hugh's overcoat behind. Yet he found himself unable to quit the hotel. Not yet.

If it had been a month earlier, Robert would have daguerreotyped the room to record his last moments with Sida, just as he once daguerreotyped corpses to grant permanence to the past. But now, even if he had his camera with him, he couldn't do this. Not anymore. He looked around the room, taking in the overlarge bed with its gaudy curtains, the gilded mirror, the view of Trafalgar Square teeming with life. If she still lived, Sida would have drawn the room to give form to memory. And then he knew: he'd draw it too, as she once might have. Though he wasn't much of an artist, it would offer satisfaction.

Robert found hotel stationery and a pencil in the nightstand. He'd start by sketching the mirror in which he'd last viewed his wife. The mirror was the key to capturing her soul in the same way a daguerreotype captured memory. Yet once he picked up his pencil, his hands yearned for language instead of art. The urge felt similar to the one that had possessed him as he'd written his thwarted biography of Ovid, and while he'd transcribed Ada's words. But what to write?

Grace's words returned: "*It's easy to write about the past. Why not write of the future?*" In a way, she'd been right, flighty as she'd been. But for now, he'd start with the present.

He began, *My name is Robert Highstead.*

He bit the end of the pencil, the fog clearing from his head for what felt like the first time in three years.

I am twenty-nine years old. I was employed as a daguerreotypist, but no longer.

The paper felt welcoming beneath his hand, the pencil alive with a purpose he'd forgotten. He continued, propelled by a keening excitement. *I was a scholar. A historian. I loved—love,* he corrected on the otherwise pristine paper, *my wife, Cressida. She's now dead these past three years, rest her soul.*

His throat tightened, but he continued.

I am the cousin of Hugh de Bonne. The poet. He passed earlier this year. He was married to Ada de Bonne, who still lives.

And then: *I love Ada de Bonne.*

The words blinked up at him, unexpected.

Robert let the stationery sheet flutter to the carpet. His excitement soured into a strange angst. He dropped the pencil to the desk. Pushing aside the packet of letters, he grabbed the miniature of Sida, finally allowing himself to look at it for the first time since he'd left Weald House.

Ada's painted eye stared back at him.

He sank onto the bed, the springs of the mattress protesting. Cradled the miniature in his palms. His sight strained as he took in the eye with the finely arched brow, the dull flecks of gold in the iris.

It was impossible. He was hungry. Exhausted.

The miniature was small and cold and bright in his hand. Real.

Robert stared at the miniature. Ada's gaze confronted him. Somehow the miniatures must have become switched in the library. The near kiss they'd shared at Weald House was of that moment. Nothing more. A result of their nights together, those stories to untangle her past. Even he, a bereft husband, a failed historian, a daguerreotypist of the dead, understood this. If he closed his eyes, he could still see Ada during the last moments of her confession, when he'd at last teased the truth from her. Even with Hugh's corpse gone and the death certificate destroyed, he wondered how long until she'd be forced out from Weald House—a month, maybe two. Given her troubles with the pilgrims, he suspected she'd be more willing to lose Weald House than to confess she was Ada de Bonne. They'd destroy her.

He set the eye miniature down, breathing deeply to collect his emotions. He'd mail it to her, along with Hugh's last letters, as soon as he could. Perhaps she'd feel differently once she read them. They'd offer her the peace that had eluded all those years.

Go to her.

The words rose within him like they'd grown out of his very breath.

Go to her.

Yet when he imagined presenting himself to Ada, his anxiety flared. Would he encounter the Ada bright and sparkling with sparrows and light—*his* Ada, as he'd grown to think of her? Or the Ada who'd taunted him over the death of his wife and haggled with him over a story?

A bubble of laughter rose. The answer was obvious. Instead of mailing the eye miniature with the letters, he'd bring them to her. That would be his excuse to see her again.

He glanced at his pocket watch. Four o'clock. If he left now, he could be at Weald House by morning if he hired a coach from Shrewsbury.

He tucked the miniature of Ada's eye into his pocket. He grabbed his portmanteau, his shaving-tackle, his scarf, and finally, the packet of letters. The black ribbon securing them slipped from his fingers, scattering the letters onto the floor.

As soon as Robert saw Hugh's forceful handwriting he couldn't turn away.

VI.

16 December 1831

Dear Cousin Bertram—

It has been so long since we last corresponded—I trust this page of scribble finds its way to you without incident. Here is a small book of poems I've authored, which I hope will offer your family cheer this holiday season. I have been heartened by its reception, especially for the poem entitled "The Window of the Soul."*

My very Best to your Wife and Sons—
Yours in Contrition
I remain very truly

H. de Bonne

**Since the Chalk Farm "affair," I thought it prudent to remain from your family, as you suggested. I am deeply grateful my Life was not snuffed that day, and remain in debt to you and Felicity for your care after my duel. Be assured every step I take reminds me how I'd nearly lost my life—twelve years on, I still bear a limp and a scar. However, this is a scant price for Wisdom gained and Incarceration avoided.*

* * *

6 January 1832

My dear Bertram—

While I am grateful for your response to my unexpected letter, your words struck my corporal and etheric coil harshly—not because of any cruelty in your words, mind, but because of the dolorous news they relayed. Never did

I imagine Death casting his cold gaze on your household—especially not on an angel as your Felicity. Her kindness and discretion during the Chalk Farm affair will never be forgotten as long as I draw breath. (To think that one to whom I owe my life no longer lives—for once I am without words.)

I possess admiration that you've embraced the consolation of philosophy—such Faith in our Maker bears you credit. (I wish I possessed such!) Though it is true, as you write, that many were taken during the Asiatic cholera sickness, this Truth does not lessen your Loss. My deepest sympathies to Robert and John. I am grateful they were spared, and am affected by their motherless state. 'Tis a wound not to be wished on another.

May bright memory bring you warm comfort—
If ever you require my attendance, I remain yours
Most Faithfully
Your Cousin

Hugh

PS: No need to read my book—I know your mind slants toward Apollo rather than Dionysus. I simply hoped it would offer reassurance regarding my particulars. You were very kind to acknowledge my poems during such a time.

* * *

25 April 1834

Best and Kindest Cousin—

I've news that I know will surprise you—no, shock you—given my silence since our last correspondence. (Truth be told, I'm shocked myself.) I'll grant you a moment to prepare yourself:

I'm engaged to be married.

I know. I know—ever since the Chalk Farm affair, you'd thought such a thing impossible. Hadn't I declared myself espoused to Art rather than Love? Orpheus without his Eurydice? A Body without a Heart? How did such a miracle occur?

Once I explain my situation, you will understand—and, I hope, find yourself sympathetic to our wishes.

The woman I've chosen as my Eurydice is one Miss Ada Lowell of

Kynnersley on the Weald Moors in Shropshire. (Perhaps you have heard talk of her in Town? She had a brilliant Season two years ago replete with a portrait at the Royal Academy that caused quite the stir.) She has suffered losses, as I have—both her parents passed when she was a child. Hence, she possesses a soft compassion tempered by a sharp mind. She is also a musician of great talent, though of a delicate constitution that requires protection. She currently resides with a guardian who serves as a nurse of sorts. It is an unusual situation.

I know I am babbling like a schoolboy instead of a man in the full of life, but I must tell you of how I first met my Eurydice. Let me cast the scene for you, my Cousin, so you may comprehend the serendipitous collusion of Fate—

Imagine a moor crowned by a giant yew tree like something Odin would have hanged Himself from. Now imagine it teaming with Columba palumbus*—wood pigeons—mid-migration. Dozens. Hundreds. A thousand even. Finally imagine an angelic presence seated near this yew in a rose garden fallow with frost. Pale visaged like Isolde the Fair, with luminous eyes. A lithe figure gowned without the fraud of petticoats, attended by a sparrow she'd tamed by her own hand.*

Bertram, I loved her at first sight.

Now that Ada has promised me her hand, I am reborn. A new man. Cleansed of my past. Made pristine for an unexpected future.

There is one small issue. Alas, my Ada will not reach her majority until October this year, at which time she will be well settled. Hence, we need to wed in France—we have no desire to wait any longer than need be to join our Fates. In the meantime, may I trouble you for assistance? Fifty pounds should be sufficient—we also need to pay for her guardian to accompany us. (I have no desire for my bride to bear the stain of impropriety in our eagerness to be joined before Man and God.)

Do let me know as soon as you can. I hope your sons remain well. I think often of your Felicity—

Yours in a rush
Of gratitude and anticipation

Hugh

PS: I nearly forgot—you may address me at the Royal Pier Hotel, Herne Bay, Kent. Better yet, attend us here. We remain for ten more days whilst we arrange passports and visas and ferry bookings. It would be good to see you for the first time since the Chalk Farm affair (which now seems of another Age entirely. Indeed, I truly am a new man!).

* * *

9 May 1834

Dear Bertram—

I appreciate the funds, which I will repay soonest—you are Best Among Family. My new book will be published next month, which shall add to our resources, if I am to believe my Publisher. We are at present in Paris, but anticipate returning to England in the New Year.

Yours with all gratitude—

H. de Bonne (now blissful husband of Ada)

* * *

10 January 1836

Dear Bertram—

I can imagine your alarum at receiving such an unexpected and confusing missive from a stranger. (I assure you I have never met this Mrs. Serena Smith-Fingle of Chelsea.) Allow me to confirm what she wrote you: Yes, my wife is with child. Yes, she was unwell—hence, we'd consulted Dr. Engelsohn, whom I take to be Mrs. Smith-Fingle's brother—but Ada has improved since then. Yes, we have now taken residence in the Black Forest—hence, your letter arrived as intended. Yes, it is not the most hospitable of winter environments. Regardless, wherever Ada abides shall be my home. I shall never leave her, nor she me.

Wishing you a prosperous start to 1836—

I remain yours most sincerely—

Hugh

* * *

14 August 1836

Dear Bertram—

I've resisted answering your last letter as long as I could. I write with dolorous news: Ada is gone.

I can write nothing more of her Passing without the most exquisite Pain. How does one continue after such a Loss? How can it be that I still breathe, my Heart still beats? Forgive me—I know this is more than you expect from such a letter—but all one can do is to set our losses on paper in the feeble hope of excising them from Memory. I still dream every night of what happened. I cannot rid my mind of her—of my Responsibility. All I can do is write of the scene as I best recall. It will be a Grave Torment, but one I deserve.

The snow was still falling when the baby came, though it was early April. Despite the snow, yellow and purple crocuses flecked the muddy grounds surrounding the cottage, their petals pummeled by footsteps—such had been the doctor's rush to get to my beloved in time. If I close my eyes, I can still see Ada lying on a bed splattered with blood, her limbs splayed like a doll. Me weeping beside her. After a labor lasting four long days, our baby had arrived at last.

The baby's cry rang out, clear and strong and angry despite the cord that had been wrapped about her neck. I held the squalling, mewling bundle in my arms. "See?" I said to Ada. "Look how beautiful she is!"

Ada said nothing.

"Don't you want to take her?" I pressed.

"She's exhausted," Herr Doktor whispered. "Let her be."

"Where's Hugh?" Ada asked, her lovely singing voice gone from screaming. (How I weep to relay this!)

"Here, my love," I said, drawing closer, kissing her brow. "Look, our baby has your hands—her little finger is crooked, like yours. Shall we call her Mathilde after my mother? Or Adelaide, after yours?"

"A girl," Ada repeated dully. Blood spotted the edge of the coverlet closest to her mouth. Was it from her lungs or from the birth? (At this my heart truly sank.)

"Let her sleep," Herr Doktor said. "I'll return tomorrow. Your wife's body is weak but her spirit is strong."

The remainder of my story is even harder to set on this page. A day passed. Ada thrashed with fever; I dosed her with laudanum. Her fever broke two days later: I permitted myself Hope, fool that I was, especially when she slept at last.

When Ada next awakened, I rushed to her side kissing her face, her hands.

"You're still here," she said. "I'd thought you'd gone."

"No," I said. "I'll never leave you."

"Nor I you." And then my beloved Ada closed her eyes. She never opened them again.

Bertram, I can write no more—I shall never forgive myself for more than I can write here. But, as you know too well, to wed for Love is to wed Sorrow—

Until we meet in the Vale without Sorrow—

H. de B.

* * *

17 April 1838

Dear Bertram,

I must beg pardon for the brutal revelation of my last letter—I was wrong to write of Ada as I had. It was also wrong of me to take so long to answer you, setting you into worry. My excuse: this past year I have been hither and yon. Hence, your most recent correspondence only caught up to my Physical Being here in Paris (though I shan't remain here any longer). You see, I've arranged to have a glass chapel built in the woods near Weald House to house my wife's remains. A folly, if you will. It is my intention to join her there when my Sorrows have come to their inevitable End.

If you wish to help as you offered, Cousin, this I ask of you:

There is a young woman bearing the name of Isabelle Lowell who'd been traveling with us as my wife's companion. She and I have been estranged since Ada's passing for reasons too ugly to share. I do not anticipate any peace to be reached between us in this life. Therefore upon my death, I have arranged for a letter to be sent you from my solicitor regarding the details of my burial in the glass chapel. I ask that you, or a representative you trust, inform Isabelle of my final wishes, for a final bequest awaits her there.

If ever she bore any love for Ada, I pray she fulfill this.

In Eternal Gratitude—

Most Faithfully

Your Cousin

Hugh

PS: I apologize for my last letter's lack of clarity: yes, my daughter survived and thrives. That is all I shall write of the matter.

The Furies

Excerpted from the last poem by Hugh de Bonne, burned February 1850.

As he fled life for death, death for blame,
Fair Orpheus declaim'd as he wept :
'Hear me, illustrious Furies! O mighty nam'd
In Terror and Beauty that hath swept
My regret into a love so famed
That I shan't forget those who rent
Raiment to mourn Eurydice's descent.
Hear me O Alekto, Tisiphone,
But highest of all Megaera—
Too late I see my Responsibility.'

With Furies appeased, thus he sang :
'Now let Sparrows return; the Ravens too—
Let Oak envelope in its embrace—
Let Her be received back to Earth—
A *locus amoenus* for my Beloved's Soul.'

And lo! for first time, it is claim'd,
A never-known wonderment :
  The Furies' eyes grew true wet
  And sweet milk of Mercy lent.

*

I.

The last letter fell from Robert's hand to join the pile beside him. His thoughts of Sida were far away, along with his hunger and exhaustion and headache.

He rose from the bed. Nothing was as he believed. Ada was dead. Mathilde was born alive. Isabelle had been there with Ada and Hugh during their marriage; she'd misled Robert probably because she felt complicit in some way for Ada's death. Worst of all, he'd believed her. His skills as a historian had been outfoxed by her ability to spin a tale—he hadn't learned anything since his Oxford days. Yet what upset him most was how she'd held him hostage with her story, ensuring he wouldn't be able to reunite Hugh with Ada in the chapel. Isabelle was evil, a demon, a Circe. A fury. And now the darkness Robert had sensed within himself, which had arisen when he'd encountered Isabelle that first night at Weald House, rose anew, vile and foul and impossible to ignore. She'd tainted him. How could he have ever thought he loved her?

He grabbed the letters. Clutching them against his chest, Robert staggered out of the hotel room where his wife had lost her life. He tore down the stairs, stumbling as he swerved around the hotel lobby to avoid its inhabitants sitting laughing and drinking their elevenses tea. Everyone seemed foul and depraved, every single one of them: the debutante tittering with laughter as she flirted with a man old enough to be her father, the carmine-lipped dowager preening over her fan, the bald waiter sneering with sycophantic derision. Yet Robert understood it was only envy he felt, for they all possessed futures while all he had were regrets. He envisioned what they saw as he ran: a tall bearded man, his blood drained from his face, his hands clutching a handful of papers like he'd been poisoned. *Here is the poor man unfortunate enough to have his wife die on their wedding night. What a fool!* Not that anyone would say this, mind—it would require too much honesty. If there was one thing he'd learned over the past weeks, it was that the truth was only a fabric to be sewn into a garment to suit the wearer's fancy.

Robert didn't stop running even when he'd smashed against the doorman. "Rather early to be drinking, sir," the doorman smirked. Robert resisted the urge to punch him. Instead, he stumbled as his weak ankle gave way, granting the appearance of truth to the doorman's assumption.

Outside the Union Hotel, Robert's feet beat against the pavement as though he was chased. He ran down Cockspur Street toward Trafalgar Square. The cold air felt a slap. His chest heaved. His ankle stung. He wouldn't slow down.

Once he arrived at Trafalgar Square, he shoved aside the line of people waiting at the cab stand. He thrust money into the driver's hands.

"Euston Station as fast as you can."

There was only one place Robert could go. He had to get there immediately or he'd turn mad—if he wasn't mad already.

When the coach from Shrewsbury left Robert at the same crossroad where he'd first arrived less than two weeks earlier, it was well into the small hours of the morning.

Not even a slit of a moon lit the fields, for the sky was pissing with rain. *Would spring ever arrive here?* Even then Robert knew this was a strange question to ponder when your heart had been ripped from your chest, but there it was. Until he confronted Isabelle he'd be trapped in eternal winter, his mind tripping over Ada and Hugh's story of love and loss.

Despite the long journey and lack of sleep, Robert's fury gave him an energy he'd never felt. He lurched down the long road toward Weald House in the horizontal downpour. The water soaked his boots. Plastered his hair against his face. The only thing he cared to keep dry was Hugh's letters, which he'd set beneath his waistcoat. The words they contained were ones he'd use to free himself from Isabelle forever.

Sooner than he'd thought possible, Robert arrived at the iron gate. He yanked the handle, ignoring the slurry of ashes along the surface. The gate wouldn't budge. He climbed over its six-foot height, not caring when his ankle twinged.

Once he landed on the ground, he didn't go around to the kitchen door. Instead, he went to the front door, the one nearest the stairs to the library, where Isabelle slept most nights. He pounded on the door until his fists felt bruised.

No response. Not even the dog. He took to shouting. "Let me in!"

Several moments later, he was greeted by Isabelle Lowell in her wrapper, holding a solitary candle. No dog. No servants. Her hair was unbound, just as he'd seen it that day on the moors.

Not Ada.

She blinked several times as she took him in, her body blocking the door. Any illness she'd suffered from appeared gone; she'd probably feigned it like she had her collapse. A smile of welcome teased her lips, a softening. The smile faded as quickly as it had arrived, leaving her as wary as ever. And then he remembered: not only was he still wearing Hugh's mustard-colored overcoat, his beard had thickened in the four days he'd been away, making him appear more akin to his cousin than ever.

"Mr. Highstead. You're soaked with rain."

"This isn't the time to discuss the weather, Miss Lowell. I've come all the way from London."

"For me?" Her eyes widened. "Couldn't this wait until morning?"

"Let me in."

"Why should I?" Again Isabelle blinked, still blocking the door, her white hair loose around her shoulders, long and pale and lush. *Like Ada. Not Ada.* How coy she sounded! As though she thought he'd rushed all the way to Shropshire on a train and coach to press his suit like a callow Lothario.

"Open the fucking door already. Now."

Whether it was Robert's tone or his profanity, at last Isabelle acquiesced.

"You're dripping on the floor, Mr. Highstead," she said coolly. "If you're going to burst in here in the middle of the night, at least take off your coat. I've no one to clean up, for Mrs. Chilvers has gone to Shrewsbury to find someone to rebuild the stables and Grace and Owen ran off together to God knows where, probably to avoid accusations of arson. I can't even find the dog, who no doubt left with them—so much for loyalty of canines! But somehow I suspect you know all this already."

Why was she talking about servants and dogs at a time like this?

"You're not Ada de Bonne. You misled me. Who the hell are you?"

She looked at him askance. "You know who I am."

Robert grabbed her arm. "There's only one way to settle this. I want you to open Ada's Folly."

She gave a little laugh as she pulled away. "You still want to daguerreotype it?"

"No. I want you to open it because there's something in there for you. I don't know what it is or what it signifies, but that's why Hugh insisted I daguerreotype you inside it—because he wanted to make certain you'd find it. You suspect this too. That's why you refused to let me inside the chapel, why you've been so confusing with your damn story, and why you wanted me to believe you were Ada de Bonne. I don't claim to understand your motivation, but there it is."

Her face blanched beneath the candlelight. "That's enough. One more word and I'll scream until your ears burst."

"You won't scream because I know the truth."

"How do you know I'm not Ada?"

"Because after I returned to bury Hugh, do you know what I found?"

Now Isabelle looked truly fearful. "No."

Robert pulled out Hugh's letters from inside his waistcoat and threw them at her face. The papers scattered to the wet floor, visible evidence of her lost history.

"Within those documents," he continued, "I found a letter from Hugh to my father describing Ada's death."

She flinched, but to her credit, she didn't turn away.

"Is that all? If so, I'm going to bed. You can see yourself out."

"No, that's not all. We're going to open the chapel to find out what Hugh left you. Together. Now."

"I don't have the key. Grace stole it."

"I don't believe you."

She set the candle between them. "I lost it."

He sidestepped the candle. When she turned to flee, he grabbed a handful of her loose hair. "It's not like you to be so sloppy to lose something so precious."

"Let me go! You're hurting me!"

To Robert's horror, all the compassion he'd prided himself on while he'd daguerreotyped the dead was gone. He couldn't feel any empathy for her suffering, for her loss. But he couldn't turn back. Instead, Isabelle seemed to encompass everyone who'd thwarted him before and since Sida's death. "Get the key, Isabelle Lowell or whatever the hell your name is. You're naught but a liar— "

"That's not true!"

"It is! You even lied to me about Mathilde. She survived Ada's death."

Her voice grew small. "You know Mathilde is alive?"

Robert nodded.

"Was there anything in those letters stating her fate?"

"Only that she was born healthy."

"Oh."

For whatever reason, all defiance fled Isabelle; her shoulders slumped, her hands fell. She drew the key from beneath her wrapper, where it still hung about her neck on a black ribbon.

She handed the key to Robert as docile as a child. She lit a lantern, pulled on boots and then a cloak over her wrapper. The letters remained on the wet floor; he supposed they no longer mattered.

They walked to the chapel together in a silence broken only by the calls of crows and owls. The doves nesting must have been deeply asleep, for they didn't stir. By now the night was softening into the dense cobalt that precedes dawn, and the rain had become a fine mist. Isabelle didn't pull up the hood of her cloak, as if she could no longer be bothered to shield herself from the elements.

Once they arrived at the door of the chapel, she turned away, biting her lip. Her shoulders shuddered. Robert actually felt pity for her. She became the woman he'd thought he loved: the sparrow-clad vision he'd encountered on the moors during that moment of grace, the heartbroken mourner he'd nearly kissed in the library, the wife who'd lost her husband and child in a story he had yet to learn the end of. Not the cruel Scheherazade who'd tormented him with her tales and half-truths while his cousin lay unshriven before being consumed by flames.

And then Robert experienced something that surprised him more than his compassion: Isabelle's cold hand slipping into his.

"Open the door already," she said.

II.

When Robert was to think back upon the moment when he'd unlocked Ada's Folly for the first time since Hugh de Bonne built it nearly a dozen years earlier, he'd decide it felt anticlimactic, as many significant acts are. Just as when he'd married Sida after years of yearning, or when his first book had been published. After so much anticipation, the event couldn't possibly approach what he'd expected. However, in the case of Ada's Folly, it was what happened afterward that shocked most.

Isabelle lifted the lantern high with her free hand, the rain sizzling against its hot brass top. She turned her face from the desiccated roses nailed to the door. Robert couldn't help but glance at her. Her face seemed a mask he couldn't decipher. Again, he pitied her. He knew opening the glass chapel would cause her distress. He knew his words had upset her. Who was he to be so cruel? He considered turning back—his stomach tightened, his step slowed. He couldn't. In that moment, his need to learn what was in that chapel felt as tangible as the need for water and food.

The key slid into the lock like a knife through butter.

Robert pushed the door open. A rush of air hit his face. It bore the faint scent of pine. It set the lantern to flickering.

The chapel was colder than he'd have imagined, stilled and fetid from years of being locked. He took the lantern from Isabelle, his eyes straining to make out the contents of the chapel. His toes snagged against what felt to be moss or grass, and possibly stones; tree roots must have forced their way through the floor. The hour was still too early to see any of the stained glass. He made out only one certain thing: the chapel was empty save for a long alabaster marble bench inscribed with Ada's name. On it was an unsealed piece of paper folded into a square addressed to Isabelle. The ink was brown as a sparrow's wing.

He handed the letter to Isabelle. "Read it."

"I can't." She released his hand.

"Isabelle—"

She clamped her palm over his mouth. Before Robert could turn away, she ran her thumb across his scar. His lips. Just as Ada had done to Hugh that night in Herne Bay before they'd kissed for the first time.

"Ada," she said. "I'm Ada. Isn't that what you want?"

Robert pulled away, the letter forgotten. She couldn't be Ada—this was only a gambit to distract from Hugh's last letter. Yet he couldn't turn away. He cupped Isabelle's chin in his palms, tilting her face toward his. Stared into her eyes. A vein pulsed in the hollow of her throat.

But then he remembered who he was, and what he'd come to do.

"You're not Ada. Read the damn letter already—"

It was too late: Isabelle, or Ada, or whoever the hell she wanted him to believe, had covered his mouth with hers. Before he could push her away, she'd coiled her arms about his neck, drawing him against her.

Too stunned to turn away, his mind silenced.

To his surprise, he *liked* her kiss. Her kiss was different from Sida's—even in their most ardent moments, there was a delicacy about his wife that kept Robert from fully losing himself to protect her. Isabelle's lips were warm, demanding, yet softer than he'd ever expect, given the sharp words he'd heard spilling from them since he'd known her. And in that moment Robert learned something he never dared admit: that the separation between hate and love was hair-thin, and could flip like an hourglass, leaving nothing the same as it had been.

Robert's hands unclenched. The letter fluttered to the ground.

Shaking as though with fever, he drew her into his arms, pressing his lips against her wet hair, her neck, her cheeks, before returning to her mouth, which awaited his with a sigh. Her lips opened beneath his, her tongue meeting his without shame. There was an inevitability about their kiss. From their first meeting in the library, to all those nights where they'd tussled with stories and sentences, this is where their interactions had led them.

By then she'd blown out the lantern and pulled Hugh's sodden overcoat off his shoulders, setting the dry side up along the chapel floor. Before Robert could turn away, she'd pulled him down beside her onto it. "I love you," he thought he heard her whisper. "Only you." She draped her cloak over them to protect them from the cold. For whatever reason, this signified to his mind there was no turning back from what was about to happen. He, Robert Highstead, a historian unable to write a word after his wife's death; a son who'd rejected his family's income upon his wife's death; a husband whose wife had visited him as a ghost was going to commit sexual congress with a woman pretending to be someone who was, in all likelihood, dead. A woman who wasn't a ghost—a woman he suspected might even be a virgin.

Virgin or not, her lips felt like sun-warmed velvet, as though she was welcoming him home after a long journey. Somehow he'd opened her wrapper, freed her breasts from beneath her chemise. In the darkness, he brushed his fingers along her bared flesh; her skin was prickled with gooseflesh, the soft hairs standing upright. She drew his hand between her thighs, to the soft fur lining her cleft. Unlike Sida in that desperate ghostly encounter he'd dreamt of, she was solid, flesh, warm. She was also moist about her sex, wetter than he could have imagined. She desired him. This tipped Robert from the abstraction of desire into deep panic. She was *real.*

She whispered against his neck, "You know what to do."

"I can't." *Ada? Isabelle?* He stared at her, lying beneath him in the darkness.

Who was she?

"You can," she said. She pulled his shirt off, ripping his buttons, and bit his shoulder so hard he wondered if she'd drawn blood. For whatever reason, the pain shook him awake. He pulled her against him. In the dimness, her form seemed a shadow, a silhouette flickering with darkness beneath him. In that moment, she seemed to blur from Ada into Isabelle and then back again.

"You're not Ada," he said. "Who are you?"

She kissed him again, this time her tongue pressing into the deepest recesses of his mouth. Then it no longer mattered. Whoever she was, he wanted her. Only her.

She tasted sharp, like apples. Her hair was caressing against his cheek, fragrant with pine and flowers. Her fingers unbuttoned his trousers. She parted her thighs for him, pressing against him, her eyes shut tightly, her eyelids puckered. He was more aroused than he could remember. Robert pushed into her before he could change his mind. In all those nights while she'd told him stories of Ada de Bonne and her marriage and their loss, he'd never expected this to happen.

He couldn't stop himself. "I love you. I do."

"I . . . I love you too."

She turned her face from his kiss, tears spilling down her cheeks.

"Should I stop?" The question seemed ridiculous even as it left his mouth.

"No . . ." She reached up to cradle his head against her breasts. How warm they were! How soft! "I love you," she said again, this time forceful.

Making love with her was like swimming through a river laden with undercurrents. Her chemise kept tangling about his legs, the layers of lace and linen pulling him closer toward her. His overcoat and her cloak twisted about their bodies, wrapping them together as one. Yet this was a strange affirmation. Even had he wanted to, he couldn't have unwound his body from hers. They were entangled in a cocoon, a cave of warmth and fabric and flesh. It protected them from the cold floor prickling their bared limbs, the threat of their pasts pursuing them.

To avoid crushing her, Robert pulled her body against him, all that fabric still wrapped about them. He shifted his weight to turn onto his side. As they rolled, Hugh's final letter crinkled beneath their bodies, and she gave a little gasp that seemed to emerge from the back of her throat. He heard his breath but couldn't believe it was his, for it seemed so far away. But then her warmth surrounded him, so encompassing that he had the sense he was falling. She shuddered against him, biting his shoulder again to muffle her cry. And then he could hold back no more.

He collapsed against her, his body sweating beneath their clothes. Wherever or whatever had happened to Ada and Isabelle seemed far from what they'd just done. But he wouldn't speak of this now. There would be time to speak of this. Years even.

Once he'd untangled himself from her, he stroked her thick white hair—it had begun to dry from the rain in waves about her shoulders. By then the sun had risen, spilling through the stained glass, dappling the white marble chapel in vivid hues of red, green, and gold. She looked even more beautiful to him because of her cares and losses. She was a wonder. A miracle returned from sorrow, from death, just as he'd been.

"How you have suffered." He kissed her again. "I shall love you all the more for it."

She turned away, unable to meet his gaze. And then Robert remembered: Ada de Bonne was dead. So was Isabelle Lowell.

III.

"I'm sorry," he said. "So sorry."

Robert managed to sit up, rummaging for his clothing. He covered himself with the overcoat while buttoning his fly, speaking all the time to cover his disorientation. He felt light-headed.

"You're not Ada. Nor are you Isabelle." He asked yet again, "Who are you?"

This time she didn't avoid answering. "I had been Isabelle Lowell, Ada's niece. But after that death certificate . . ."

"How can this be?"

"It's like I said. There was another Isabelle. A different Isabelle . . ." She emitted a strangled laugh that sounded akin to a hiccup. "Not that it matters. When Tamsin Douglas has her way, I'll be turned out like the nameless woman I've become."

Unwilling to press her further, Robert stared at the floor, crawling with moss and ivy, while she smoothed her chemise, hiding her thighs from view. It was as if they'd never engaged in any intimacies. Never declared love. That she was as he'd found her when he'd pounded on her door pummeled by rain. Untouched. Unknown.

"Why?" he asked. "Why did you let me . . ."

Her eyes brimmed with tears. "That day in the church, I realized you believed I was Ada and you were in love with her. Though I knew I should correct you, I couldn't bring myself to. I never intended to mislead you, Robert, but this brought me such comfort. You see, whenever I spoke of myself in Ada's story, I felt so much sorrow. So much loss . . . As for just now—well, I'll say no more."

"I wish you'd told me. I feel a fool."

For confessing I love you. Had she meant it when she'd responded in kind? Best not to ask. Best to let her speak.

"You don't understand," she said. "I *loved* having Ada alive again, even if it was through your imagination. If she lived again, I could reclaim her. Then she'd leave me—"

Isabelle clasped her hand over her mouth.

Love stories are ghost stories in disguise.

This was what she'd said the first night of her story. She'd told him everything he'd needed to know, but he hadn't understood then. Now he did. *This* was what had drawn them together, what had tormented them. What had brought them to lie together in love and hate on the floor of a chapel crowned in glass.

Robert asked, "Like a ghost?"

He already knew her answer.

"You'll probably think me mad, Robert. I wasn't lying when I told you Ada's story. But she didn't tell me it while she lived . . ."

Robert's heart pounded against his ribs.

"I understand," he said carefully. "Is she here now?"

"Not now." A catch in her voice. "Yet always. Always."

A rush of wind hissed inside the chapel, a sound so loud that both Isabelle and Robert clamped their hands over their ears. The wind blew against the stained glass, setting a swirl of leaves skittering across the marble floor, up and around their feet. This same wind picked at Hugh's letter, tipping the letter over and over across the floor until it landed in Isabelle's lap.

Foreboding fell on Robert like a blow. "Don't open it." For reasons he could never understand—perhaps the same reasons that had led him to her poor haunted self—he knew whatever was in that letter could damn her. He also felt protective of her, loved her even in a way he couldn't explain.

It was too late: the letter slipped into her hands. It was comprised of only five lines.

If you must know your sister:
Mathilde Adelaide—
Care of M. Gautier, 19 rue Honore, Geneva.
If there is an Elysium beyond this vale of Sorrow,
I hope we shall meet there one day in Peace.

IV.

Isabelle folded the letter away. She settled on the bench inscribed with Ada's name, rocking herself back and forth like a child.

"How like Hugh to leave this here for me," she said at last.

Her voice sounded strangled and distant. Robert couldn't think what to say. How to respond. For some reason, he recalled Grace during that absurd tour of Hugh's study when he'd first arrived at Weald House. The memorized sentences she'd so blithely parroted without affect. *"It is difficult to speak of the many ladies whose hearts he broke in London and Paris. The duchess who drowned herself in the Seine. The unfortunate who indulged in too much gin after finding herself with child . . ."*

"You're Hugh's daughter." Robert stated this as the irrevocable fact it was.

Isabelle stopped rocking herself. Met his eyes.

This was all the affirmation Robert needed.

His heart pounding, he took a step toward her. "Why didn't you simply tell the truth? Tamsin and the pilgrims would have left you alone. They'd have no right to contest your inheritance. Why'd you claim to be Isabelle Lowell, whoever she was?"

"Because I had no name. None that I had proof of. No *true* name."

"No true name?" Robert shook his head. "This makes no sense. What happened to the real Isabelle Lowell? The one whose death certificate was found?"

She looked away, her cheeks wet. "It's as I told you—she was the other Isabelle. Another Isabelle. Another relation. A cousin to Ada through her father. One I'd never met before her death."

"So you both bear the same name. Yet you have no name." Robert couldn't stop his words from spilling forth. "Whoever you are and whatever name you bear, you knew Mathilde was alive all the time. That's why you returned to Weald House and remained all these years waiting for your father. Because you wanted to find your sister."

"My sister . . ." Now Isabelle was weeping in earnest. "All these years wasted. Waiting. And now *this* . . ." She shook Hugh's final letter like a flag. "He'd left it here for me. This was his coup de grâce. His revenge. He understood if I saw the chapel I'd understand how much he loved Ada. I'd no choice but to forgive him." She wrapped her arms around herself. "He's wrong! I won't forgive—I can't! He could have told me about Mathilde, or written your family of her, or included her address with that last poem I burned. But that would have been too simple. Too unsatisfying. Anyway, it's all his fault Ada's dead! I would have never left Ada if not for him. He forced me to abandon her. I could have protected her, convinced her to leave the Black Forest. She would have lived!"

"But why would he need your forgiveness? Why would he force you to leave Ada? Why would he abandon Mathilde? Why couldn't he acknowledge you as his daughter?"

"Why, why, why! You and your never-ending questions! Do they ever cease?" Isabelle pointed beside her on the bench, her eyes wide and glassy. "Sit, Robert, and I'll tell you everything—you'll know me better than anyone else who still lives. Then perhaps at last you'll leave me be in peace."

Robert sat. By then morning had arrived in earnest, spilling sunlight across the stained glass windows, revealing them at last in full. The windows featured innumerable birds captured mid-flight: doves, sparrows, ravens, starlings, and owls. They swirled around a central stained glass portrait of Ada with her sparrow, its composition similar to the oil painting in the library. The glass of Ada was framed by arches of ivory marble, branching up toward the sky, and swirling into curls of ivy. The combined effect was of a forest created of glass and stone. But Robert couldn't pay mind to this wonder so many had yearned so desperately to view. Instead, his attention compressed to Isabelle's ruddy, swollen lips—lips he had kissed only moments earlier. Lips that he now knew belonged to the eldest daughter of Hugh de Bonne—a daughter who bore no name save that of a deceased relative.

Syllables spilled from her mouth. These syllables became words, the words sentences. Sentences flowed into images. And then Robert no longer heard her voice. Nor did he see the stained glass surrounding them, or the soaring marble vaults, or the verdant greens twining about the chapel floor and walls. Instead, he was present with Ada and Hugh back in the Marais soon after they'd wed.

V.
The Last Day's Story

She'd been waiting outside their door when they'd returned from the opera that rainy May night. A girl they'd never seen before. A girl so thin she had no need for stays. A girl who looked younger than her fifteen years. A girl with wild auburn hair and grey eyes.

"Are you Hugh de Bonne?" the girl asked, speaking English with an East London accent.

"Who wants to know?" Hugh snapped; he'd nearly tripped over her on the stairs. He'd drunk too much cognac during intermission—Gluck wasn't his favorite. "Who the hell are you?"

"Shush, you're frightening her," Ada whispered.

"Well, she frightened me. Who are you then?"

"I-I'm uncertain, sir," the girl said. "I've had several names in my life: Jane, Mary, Nan. The last lady called me Margaret. Meg, if you will. Though that don't seem my true name either."

"Meg then." Ada offered her hands. "Come inside—"

"No," Hugh said. "We're not inviting a girl who doesn't know her own name into our home."

"It's raining. She's probably lost. Ill."

"I'm not lost. Nor am I ill," Meg answered. "I've been sent. If you're Hugh de Bonne, I've traveled all the way from London for good cause. Look, I've this from my mother."

Meg pulled from inside her cloak a tattered sheet of paper covered in sepia writing. The paper bore a poem dedicated to a certain Diana of the White Breasts, though this had been only one of her *noms d'amour*. (No self-respecting whore with ambition used her Christian name; in addition to Diana of the White Breasts, she was known as the Venus of Chiswick and Hecate Blacknight.) When Hugh had last encountered Diana a dozen years prior, she'd thrown a gin bottle at his head after he'd told her to sell the poem to provide for an accident of birth. *"You should be grateful. I don't owe you anything, not even a poem. You've no proof she's mine,"* he'd protested. *"She's grey eyes. Mine are hazel."* Diana had retorted, *"But my eyes are grey, you idiot! Look at her hair! Her chin!*

She's your very image! If you shan't take her, I'll dump your daughter in the Thames."

"Oh," Hugh said. His walking stick slid from his hand as he slumped to the steps. "I think I need another cognac."

At this, Ada stole another look at Meg's bright auburn hair and understood. A shock of raw joy rose in her.

Meg spent an uncomfortable night on the parlor chairs in Hugh's study after relating her secret history: the doss-house where Diana had abandoned her when she'd turned two, the lone poem she'd been left as proof of Hugh's paternity; how she'd been passed from proprietor to proprietor to earn her keep as a maid-of-all-work once Diana had been found dead of a disease respectable people didn't acknowledge. Meg's last missus, who'd been *very* fond of poetry, had uncovered Hugh's location from his publisher. She decided it cost less to send Meg to Paris than to keep her—especially after she caught her husband peeping on Meg unclad in the bath. (After that, Meg's name became "the poet's bastard.")

That night as she twisted on the bony wood chairs, Meg's sharp ears made out hushed words from the other side of the door.

"She has to leave." Hugh's tone was firm. "In the morning."

Ada's voice cracked. "She needs a mother."

"She *had* a mother. A whore. I won't shame you with my indiscretions, Ada. I'll send her to school."

"My cousin died at school. A girl named Isabelle. She was a Lowell, like my father. How I loved her! Had she lived, she'd now be this girl's age . . ."

A long pause.

"Is that why you're weeping?"

"No . . . Yes." A rustle of pillows. "Isabelle was only nine when she passed of smallpox. One of my guardians had insisted on sending her away. The missionary. I'll never forgive him."

"So we'll send the girl somewhere else."

Meg clenched her hands over her ears and squeezed her eyes tight. Wherever "somewhere else" was, she didn't want to find out.

In the morning, Ada's eyes were red. Hugh's brow was furrowed.

Meg sank to her knees before Ada. "Don't send me away. Please. I promise not to cause you shame."

Ada caressed her shoulder. "The parents' shame is not the child's fault."

"But I want to forget my past. To have a new life. You can call me Isabelle after your cousin. Like I'd returned from school."

Ada and Hugh exchanged glances. And then, before Hugh could intervene, Ada embraced Meg.

"I cannot have children," she'd whispered, *"but I can have her."*

Later that day Hugh anointed the girl's forehead with flat champagne. "I dub thee Isabelle Lowell, henceforth niece of Ada and Hugh de Bonne." Then, in a low voice, "Pray never address me as father."

Afterward, Hugh destroyed the poem that had served as Isabelle's proof of paternity.

At first they'd been happy.

Ada immediately began Isabelle's education, for the girl could barely read and write. Turned out life in a doss-house wasn't conducive for book learning; Isabelle struggled with what most children would have been taught years earlier. Regardless, Ada introduced her to the classics—Ovid, Homer, and Virgil—as well as to Wilhelm's beloved fairy tales. However, music was another story: Isabelle took to the keyboard as though she'd been born to it. Within months she and Ada were working their way through four-handed arrangements of Bach and Mozart. As for Hugh, his appreciation of Isabelle eventually outweighed his resentment. Isabelle was quick-witted, slow to complain, and grateful for whatever scraps of affection were thrown her way. If she was indeed his blood as she appeared to be, she was more credit than curse.

But even the happiest of times cannot last. When Ada's consumption flared anew after that day in Sévres, Isabelle insisted she accompany Ada to the sanitarium in Fiesole. She'd already lost one mother; she couldn't bear to lose Ada too, whom she'd adored at first sight. Though Ada initially demurred Isabelle's offer, she was secretly relieved.

"So you both are to leave me?" Hugh asked; he hadn't thought ahead to what would become of Isabelle in Ada's absence.

"I'll watch over her," Isabelle promised. And she had. She'd been with Ada in the sanitarium as winter snow turned to spring rain, and spring rain to summer blossoms. She'd witnessed Ada's tears when she'd found Hugh's new book of poetry, and helped her nurse the raven chick into adulthood.

But even Isabelle had not anticipated the raven's return after they'd freed it that August day. It seemed an omen. But of what?

Two days after the raven's return, Hugh arrived at the sanitarium bearing a pair of doves in a gilded cage.

A month later, the three of them were living in the Black Forest in a cottage filled with birds.

By the time the first snow arrived, Ada was sicker than she'd ever been.

VI.

The snow fell anew. By then it was late December, an hour after Doctor Engelsohn had informed Ada of her unexpected pregnancy. "*There is something else sickening her,*" he'd warned Hugh before he'd departed. "*You must leave here as soon as the snow allows.*" The birds had all fled their cages; Hugh had freed them, convinced the end was near for his wife. Only the raven remained, perched high on a rafter hidden in shadows.

Isabelle did not notice the birds were gone when she'd burst inside after accompanying the doctor through the snow. She'd never seen Ada so poorly, not even in the sanitarium. It terrified her.

"I took the doctor to the village," Isabelle said. "All the way to the churchyard. He seemed to think I was your maid. Feeling better, Aunt?"

Ada and Hugh exchanged looks.

Isabelle's heart began to race, thinking of the doctor's warning she'd overheard—Ada must be even sicker than she'd feared. When the opportunity arose, Isabelle hadn't been able to stop herself from speaking of Bertram Highstead and his sons. He'd send them funds to return home. Hadn't Hugh bragged the Highsteads were his only living relatives? That he'd helped them elope? Isabelle was no fool. She'd seen how things had grown tight of late. Ada wasn't meant to be living in the midst of a dark wood with her delicate health. It would be better to settle at Weald House with its rose garden, dove cote, and mysterious histories she'd learned from Ada. She'd be Weald House's new Isabelle. The Isabelle returned from death. Not the abandoned daughter of a whore.

Wind rattled the shutters. The raven cawed.

"The medicine helped. I even drank some broth," Ada answered. Her smile appeared strained. "I'm going to have a baby in the spring, my beauty."

Isabelle had to sit, for she was dizzy.

I cannot have children, but I can have her.

"That's why the doctor said we should return to England," Isabelle said after a long moment. "Thank goodness it's not consumption—I was so worried! I think the doctor is right. That would be safest." She forced herself to add, "I'll have a brother or sister then. A blessing." Yet something else scratched inside Isabelle. Something she couldn't—no, wouldn't—name.

The raven shifted on the rafter. A sole black feather fluttered to the floor. Beneath candlelight it shimmered a dark watery green.

Hugh said, "How was your walk? Do you think it will snow much longer?"

That night, Isabelle wept herself to sleep. In the morning she realized it wasn't because she feared Ada dying. It was because she feared the baby living.

Two weeks after the New Year, most of the snow had melted. Hugh left Isabelle and Ada alone for two days. The raven accompanied him, abandoning the cottage for a forest of fir and spruce. "Take care of Ada," Hugh had told Isabelle. Of course Isabelle would take care of Ada. She loved her more than she'd imagined possible. Hadn't Ada taught her to play piano? Shown her the only affection she'd ever known? Isabelle should cherish this time alone with her. Soon she'd have a brother or a sister. (What would it be like to have a sibling? There had been other children at the doss-house. They'd either ridiculed or ignored Isabelle.)

Yet when Ada had felt too weary to rise, Isabelle had forgotten to bring her tea. She practiced piano scales when Ada was trying to sleep. For the first time ever, Ada snapped at her. "It's my fault," Isabelle had said when Ada complained her head ached. "I'm so sorry." Deep inside she wasn't.

When Hugh returned, he refused to reveal where he'd gone. "A surprise," was all he'd say, frowning.

Isabelle grew dizzy again. It had to do with the baby. Maybe they were going to leave the Black Forest after all. Or maybe it had to do with her. Had Ada complained?

"Did you take good care of Ada?" he asked Isabelle.

"I-I tried my best." Isabelle flushed, feeling he'd seen inside her soul.

That night, Isabelle saw Hugh whisper to Ada. Caress her belly.

Isabelle bit the flesh inside her mouth until she tasted blood.

"Get up," Hugh whispered. "Now."

A month later the raven watched Hugh try to wake Isabelle from sleep. The girl had stayed up late with Ada, forcing herself to discuss baby names. *"If it's a girl, you could name her Mathilde, after Uncle Hugh's mother. Or Adelaide, after yours . . ."* Isabelle was anxious to make amends; she'd spilled tea on the baby's layette and left sheet music on the floor where Ada might have slipped. When Hugh scolded Isabelle, she'd claimed they'd been accidents. But were they really?

"Isabelle, get up," Hugh said again, jostling her shoulder. There was a rare edge to his tone. "No time to waste."

Isabelle forced her eyes open at last. The sky was violet with the promise of dawn, watery with fog. She thought it must be very early, far earlier than she usually woke. Once her sight adjusted to the gloom, she saw Hugh holding a knapsack she'd never seen before. It was tight and round and full. It reminded Isabelle of Ada's womb; her stomach had swollen alarmingly of late, like a tick bloated with blood. The baby would be big.

Isabelle pulled herself up from her pallet. "Aunt Ada isn't sick again?"

Hugh offered a crooked smile. His skin looked greyish, like he'd aged overnight. "We need to go to the village. Not for the doctor."

"So early?"

"Yes."

Isabelle dressed in silence. Hugh told her not to kiss Ada goodbye to avoid waking her.

Hugh was silent as they walked, the remaining snow sloshing against Isabelle's boots—it had been a cold March. How different the trees looked in half-light, emerging from the fog! Isabelle never went into the forest when it was like this; it felt too much like being swaddled in cotton. Yet its allure was not lost on her. The firs, so tall and fragrant, especially reminded Isabelle of those months when it had just been the two of them at the sanitarium. Her eyes filled, yearning for days past. Isabelle's fingers on the keyboard. Ada guiding her through the notes. *"How fast you learn, my beauty! You've a true gift."* The Beethoven sonata. The C major. Ada had promised to teach it to her . . .

"Does she need medicine then?" Isabelle asked while they walked. Her toe snagged a rock hidden beneath leaves. Her stomach rumbled. She wished she'd insisted on breakfast before they'd left.

"No, Isabeauty," he teased. Ada's usual nickname for Isabelle was "my beauty"; the English for *belle* was "beauty." Hugh in his usual teasing way had made a portmanteau of it.

"We're fetching the doctor after all?"

"My brain is too sleepy to answer questions." Hugh refused to meet her eyes; Isabelle wondered if he was still angry over the tea-stained layette. "Trust me, this is a nice surprise. It's for the best."

Isabelle's hands clenched inside her muff. She'd learned early on that when someone said "it's for the best" they meant "it's not what you want."

She matched Hugh's silence while they walked. His uncommon reticence made her heart race. After a quarter hour of this, she began to wonder whether he'd forgotten her presence—he'd been so preoccupied of late. Sometimes she found him weeping when he didn't know she was there, but he was prone to drama just as Ada was to stoicism. Maybe he wasn't happy about the baby after all.

Or maybe he's had enough of you and wants you gone.

She snuck a glance from beneath her bonnet, imagining Hugh a stranger leading her to her doom, rather than the reluctant father fond of puns and puzzles. Her dark fancies vanished when he handed her a knot of hard brown bread spread with sweet butter.

"I'd forgotten I'd brought this for you," he said, his tone solicitous. "You must be starving. Forgive me."

Isabelle ate. Guilt did funny things to a mind. Her mood lifted.

About a mile down the hill the fog cleared, the trees turned spare with deforestation. The village came into view, with dark wooden roofs laced with thick grey smoke, tainting the pure morning air. Isabelle wrinkled her nose. The smoke stank of dung. She was glad she'd eaten. Otherwise her stomach wouldn't have been able to take it.

"We're here," was all Hugh said. He pointed his walking stick toward the village square in the valley, anemic sun glinting off the brass tip.

Isabelle followed him down the hill toward the village square. The raven must have spied prey, for it took off shrieking back into the forest; months later, Isabelle would consider this as much an omen as its return to the sanitarium had been.

She glanced at the church tower laden with medieval black letter. Seven in the morning. Isabelle yawned. The square was unnaturally empty—no sullen women wearing red pom-pomed *bollenhuts* on their heads, no industrious men dressed in thick wool *lederhosen*.

"What are we waiting for?" Isabelle asked. The nape of her neck prickled.

Hugh scanned the square, his mouth tight. "She must not have arrived."

Isabelle's foreboding spread from her neck to the tips of her fingers.

The silence was interrupted by a horse's whinny. Isabelle's eyes darted toward it. She saw a gleam of black wood, a crest of gold, on the edge of the square. Closer examination revealed an ebony carriage, partially obscured behind the remnant of a wooden military fortification.

Hugh said, "Come."

He grasped the soft flesh of Isabelle's arm. She winced as he led her toward the carriage.

And then all was made clear.

A grey-haired lady emerged from the black carriage. She was dressed in a fur-lined cape. She approached Hugh as though she was pressed for time. They spoke quickly in French. Their tone was too low for Isabelle to follow their conversation.

After several minutes of whispers, the lady offered Isabelle a supercilious smile. "You wrote she's been playing less than two years. Is she really that talented?"

"Extremely," Hugh responded, smiling. "Her talent is wasted here. My wife, a gifted musician herself, has taught her all she can. That's why we were so eager for you to come."

Isabelle immediately knew what was about to happen. She'd be leaving. Alone.

"No," Isabelle cried. "No. I won't go!"

She turned and ran back toward the forest. Toward Ada.

Hugh grabbed her more swiftly than she'd have expected.

"Let me go!" she screamed. "I'm sorry! So sorry!"

"It's a fine music conservatory," Hugh soothed. "The best in Brussels. I've made sure of it. One of the few for ladies. This lady will accompany you. She's been paid generously to keep you safe."

"You just want to be rid of me!"

Hugh's arms tightened about her. "Don't you want to become a better pianist? It's just for a few months. Just until the baby's born and settled."

Isabelle stopped struggling.

"You promise to send for me immediately?"

"I promise, Isabeauty."

No matter. Isabelle never saw Ada alive again.

Three months after Isabelle had left Ada, Hugh wrote: *Nothing could be done for Ada or our baby. The baby was born with her cord about her neck. I gave her the name of Mathilde Adelaide. It was quite distressing. For now, it's best you stay at the conservatory. I'll write when I'm settled anew.*

Isabelle's tears soaked the letter.

But something could have been done, she thought. *If I hadn't been jealous, I wouldn't have been sent away. I could have forced Ada to leave the Black Forest. I could have protected her. She and my sister might have lived.*

Six months after Isabelle had left Ada, Hugh still hadn't written since his last letter. Isabelle discovered her second white hair amid the red. It was the day after she mastered the slow movement of the Beethoven Sonata in C major, the one Ada was going to teach her. "*Don't be confused by the key signature*," Ada had said. "*Remember that's where you'll find your sorrow.*"

She'd been right.

Nine months after Isabelle had left Ada, Hugh could not be found. One cold night when Isabelle was combing her nearly white hair and mopping her eyes before bed—she still wept regularly—she heard a soft female voice drift behind her.

"Black bombazine for you, my beauty. You need wear it only for me."

The voice was barely more than a whisper. Isabelle recognized it.

She whirled about. She saw no one. She decided she was mad with guilt.

Isabelle slept with her candle burning.

The following night Isabelle heard skirts rustling inside her room—the same stiff taffeta as the peach dress Hugh had bought Ada in Calais.

"Aunt?" she called, rising from her bed. "Are you there?"

"Why are you crying, my beauty?"

"Because I miss you," Isabelle whispered. "Because I love you. Because there's nothing I can do for you. Because . . ."

If I hadn't been so jealous, you and my sister might have lived.

"Is that all?" Ada gave off a maidenish giggle; her scent was fetid, like leaves after an autumn rain.

"Yes," Isabelle lied. "Where are you?"

"Step toward the mirror."

Isabelle's sight strained. After some minutes, Ada's face appeared faint in the glass beyond. Isabelle's eyes prickled with moisture. How beautiful she was, even after death.

"Well, there's one last thing you can do for me. Promise?"

"Promise. Tell me. I'll do it."

"I want to know how my baby is faring."

"Mathilde?" Isabelle asked. "Is she a ghost too?"

But Ada was already gone.

VII.

The following night, Isabelle wrote Dr. Engelsohn regarding the circumstances of Ada's passing. As soon as the doctor answered, Isabelle left Brussels though her only valuable was Ada's wedding ring, a deathbed bequest Hugh had sent. She sold it.

It took Isabelle over a year to find Hugh. She couldn't imagine him returning to Weald House after Ada's death, so she retraced the places they'd gone after they'd left Paris. When Isabelle finally arrived in the Black Forest, she found the little cottage abandoned by bird and human. The sanitarium in Fiesole, where Ada had hoped to recover her health, was inhabited by another consumptive, this one thinner and frailer than Ada at her worst. She suspected Hugh had returned to the Marais, to the rooms where she'd first come to him and Ada; he'd probably be ensconced there writing tearstained poems. By then Isabelle had run out of funds, but she wouldn't turn back. The memory of Ada in the mirror wouldn't let her.

Isabelle traveled on foot. She watched the forest darken into a summer so sultry that the sun singed the leaves into a growth no light could penetrate. Then autumn came, and the leaves dried brown and tumbled into the air before settling and crumbling underfoot. That year the ground frosted early in October as she traveled through the winter to Freiburg, Strasbourg, Avricourt, and beyond, tramping and stumbling toward Paris. Whenever she'd arrive at a town, she'd take in sewing or offer piano lessons until she had enough to continue. Neither brought much coin.

It was spring by the time Isabelle reached Paris, six months after Hugh had published *The Lost History of Dreams*, but she barely noticed the flowers blooming, the earth ripening. She'd seen the book everywhere during her travels. Isabelle immediately understood it was about Ada—how could it not be? In Germany it was titled *Die verlorene Geschichte der Träume*, in France *L'Histoire Perdue de Rêves*. Ada's death had made Hugh more famous than anyone had a right to be. A biography claimed Mathilde had died at birth, unlike what Dr. Engelsohn had written. This only strengthened Isabelle's resolve.

Once she arrived in Paris, she learned she'd been right: Hugh had returned, but he'd already left. His landlady in the Marais reported no sign of a child during his stay. However, he'd left an address on the rue de Rivoli near the Tuileries.

When Isabelle arrived at the address, she found herself before the door of the grandest hotel she'd ever seen: tall mirrors, marble floors, hushed voices, ceilings like a cathedral. Hugh was no longer the impoverished poet Ada had married. He was the bereft widower, the sorrowful father, the tragic poet beloved by literati.

At first the *maître d'hôtel* wouldn't allow her in. "Monsieur de Bonne is not to be disturbed." Isabelle refused to be turned away. "Please," she begged. "I'm his niece. I've traveled far to find him." He laughed, flicking his finger at her. "That's what they all say, mademoiselle." Isabelle didn't understand then, but she didn't question.

On the top floor, she found the door open to Hugh's suite, the largest one in the entire hotel; she later learned a duchess had paid for it after reading *The Lost History of Dreams* upon her husband's death. The foyer had a bronze fountain. Beyond the fountain, which had goldfish the size of a child's fist swimming in it, there was a Louis XIV dining table with crystal vases of roses so dark a red they were nearly black. Abandoned platters of caviar and half-eaten lobsters. Beside those, petit fours and melting ice. Half-empty wine bottles.

The windows were shuttered. The air stank of oleaginous food. Rank sweat.

When no one responded to Isabelle's knock, she made her way into the foyer and through the reception room. Past the fountain with those ridiculous goldfish, the white satin chaise, which was stained with what looked to be red wine. Her boot sent a bottle skittering across the black-and-white checkered marble floor.

"Hello?" she called, her voice tremulous. "Bonjour?"

No answer came.

Her heart pounded. What if she'd happened into the wrong chamber?

She arrived at the bedroom, where one of the double doors was ajar. Inside was a grand four-poster, the satin sheets rumpled. And then she saw the back of Hugh's head. She knew it was him—the rumpled curls of his auburn hair, the arrogant tilt of his head. He wasn't in the bed. He was seated with his back toward her, his legs akimbo on a chair all gilded in gold, like something the Sun King would have reigned from.

"It's me. Isabelle," she said, her voice echoing against the marble floors, those high ceilings. "I don't know how to say this, Hugh"—by then she'd fallen into calling him Hugh in her mind instead of Uncle or Father—"but I know you lied about my sister's death. Where is she?"

And then she could say no more, for she was weeping. Any anger she felt about Mathilde had flown away, like those birds from the Black Forest cottage. How could she blame him? He was probably as wrecked as she'd been by Ada's death.

Isabelle fell before him on that marble floor stinking of waste in that suite, which cost more for a night than most people made in a year. That's when she saw *her.*

Isabelle knew what the woman was as soon as she saw her. The woman's yellow curls were an even more unnatural shade than her red satin gown. Her hands were covered in black lace mitts. They rested on Hugh's hips.

Her head was settled between his thighs. Hugh was moaning, unable to even note Isabelle's presence. Insensate.

Isabelle must have made some sound—a gasp, or a catch of her throat, or a scream—for he pushed the prostitute away, laughing, laughing. The prostitute protested, "*Vous voulez qu'elle nous joigne? Vous devez payer plus pour ca.*" And then she thrust out her purse for payment in anticipation of Isabelle joining their intimacies. "*Non, non,*" Hugh answered the wretched being. "*C'est seulement ma fille. Ma fille qui revient de l'enfer.*" Only my daughter returned from hell.

He turned his attention to Isabelle. "*Mon dieu*, you look rough. I almost didn't recognize you with your hair so white. Like Marie Antoinette in prison. No one would know you as my blood now."

Isabelle couldn't think what to say. The prostitute rose to leave. Hugh fumbled with his trousers. Isabelle averted her gaze so she couldn't see him, her father, exposed. But she couldn't avoid smelling him. He stank of drink. Of decay. Hugh always wore beautiful clothing, which he had sewn special after he'd gained success. Isabelle recalled his dark green frock coat from that day in Sévres—it was this coat he now wore. She could smell he'd pissed it like a baby. He was nothing at all as Isabelle recalled, or the man Ada loved. The skin around his eyes had sagged, ageing him a decade. His beard had grown in long over his handsome face, making him look more wolf than man. He must have just eaten, for there were sauces drizzling down his beard. Crumbs along his collar. His beautiful green frock coat all wrinkled and ruined, like he'd been sleeping in it for days.

Once he'd settled himself, Isabelle handed him Dr. Engelsohn's letter. "What did you do with my sister?"

He thrust the letter back at Isabelle. "Burn it. Better no one should know."

"But now *I* know."

He turned from Isabelle's stare. "I don't care."

"But I do. You must tell me where Mathilde is. Ada would want me to know."

He laughed. "I can tell you where Ada is. I fed her remains to birds so she might fly. She'd like that, don't you think?"

Isabelle was without words.

"You know, I knew you'd be coming here," he said, turning eerily calm. He set his hands on her shoulders. "I knew it was only a matter of time once you read that book."

Isabelle understood too well what he meant. *The Lost History of Dreams.* Still, her face must have shown skepticism, for he said:

"Ah, but you don't believe me. How do you think I got all this?" His arm swept around the room of that fancy hotel suite, so gilded and garish and vulgar. "All paid for by Parnassus because of that wretched book of poems my wife inspired. Who knew grief could be so profitable?"

Isabelle felt her heart crack. "How can you jest about this?"

"I'm not, Isabeauty. Did you know those poems are meant to mimic the architecture of a chapel? They rise from the earth toward the heavens. And the chapel is meant to be like a poem—well, a cycle of poems anyway. Cantos, if you will. It'll take less than a year to build. Just as well to work on it since I haven't been able to pen a damn word save for shit verses since I finished that book. I'm as dry as a whore's notch."

"Chapel?" Did he mean writing or building one? Between his chatter of cantos and whores, how dull Isabelle felt! She recalled that sketch after he'd taken Ada to Sèvres, the chapel for his missing family.

"Yes. Like this, Isabelle."

Hugh pulled out a long roll of paper from beneath his chair. His hands shook from drink as he unfurled it.

"See? A chapel like a poem. And with stained glass too. A *locus amoenus*. Even better than a poem! I've arranged for the glass and hired workers. They're already building it. It will be the most beautiful place that ever was." His voice caressed her ears in his old way. "Did you know I first gained the idea for it when I visited Canterbury with Ada well before you entered our lives? I knew I'd marry her even then. I wanted the chapel to be as transcendent as she was. A home for her soul. A permanent record of our love, since I thought we'd never have children . . ."

At this, Isabelle's distress began to rise. *Never have children.* What about herself? Didn't she count?

Isabelle grabbed Hugh by his shoulders. "Where is Mathilde? Tell me!"

Hugh shrugged her off. He stumbled from his throne to uncork another bottle of wine. Isabelle felt invisible, as though she were a ghost herself. Was she dreaming? Did she breathe? She touched her face, stared at her hands, to convince herself she was awake.

"You've been crying," Hugh said, as if starting from a trance.

"Of course I'm crying! I loved Ada like a mother. And now she's gone. And you . . . I never expected to find you in this state."

"Neither did I." He gestured with a wide, wild sweep of his arm at the drawings of the chapel, the fancy hotel room, the marble floor, the prostitute slinking toward the gilded door. "Well, at least my wife has proven herself useful for something beyond sorrow. What about you with your music? After all, if she'd never gotten with child, you'd never have gone to conservatory. Did you ever think to be grateful for that?"

With those words Isabelle lost herself. She hit Hugh's jaw. She hit him so hard that her palms stung like they'd been burned. She'd come all that way, searching for him, hoping to find Mathilde, seeking absolution for her jealousy, for agreeing to piano lessons over remaining with Ada. Over a year of traveling across Europe alone to find Hugh—she, a young girl with no prospects, no money. She'd sewn linens, worked in kitchens, scrubbed floors, begged. And then she'd discovered her father with a whore's mouth around his genitals. A whore like her mother had been.

"*Merde!* Why the hell did you do that?" Hugh shouted; she'd struck him so hard that blood trickled from his mouth. He dabbed it with a lacy handkerchief, cloying with perfume from some woman. This further enraged her.

Isabelle kicked his plans for the chapel across the room. "Because it was always about your poetry. Your inspiration," she cried. "And now you're using her for your art with that glass chapel! Mathilde too—that's why you gave her up, so you'd have another loss to weep over."

"You little bastard!" He grabbed Isabelle by her shoulders. Her neck. His hands tightened. "Don't you understand? You *had* to leave, Isabelle—Ada said as much. Don't believe me? It's true! You lived through her. You never drew a breath you did not think of her, worshipping her like she was the fucking Madonna descended to earth. Like I, your own flesh and blood, didn't matter. You don't even call me Father—"

"You'd told me not to. Please, you're hurting me!"

"Not that it matters—Ada is gone. She's really gone. Not even our baby resembled her—she had red hair, like me. Like you used to. Nothing like Ada. God help me . . ."

Now Hugh was weeping so hard he had no choice but to release Isabelle. She collapsed to the floor, gasping and clutching her throat.

"God forgive me," he said, reaching to help her up. "Forgive me, Isa-beauty. I'm so sorry. I shouldn't have done that . . . I'm sorry. So sorry! I know you didn't mean to say what you did. I loved her so. I know you did too—"

She slapped his hand away. "Fie on you! You never loved Ada! Not like I did!"

"That's not true! I loved her more than life. More than death—I couldn't live without her." His tone turned odd, unlike anything Isabelle had ever heard of him. "We had a plan."

Isabelle grew cold. "What sort of plan?"

"Laudanum. Drowning. Hanging. Does it matter? I promised her we'd never be parted." He forced a laugh, but it came out like a sob turned sour. "You don't believe me, Isabelle? Remember when I came to her that day in Fiesole? When she tried to turn me away, and oh! how I begged her to let me stay? After she'd sent you away, I told her that she was my soul and I hers. That it went against natural order for us to live apart, for we were each other's *locus amoenus*. And she took me in her arms, and oh! how she took me! Isabelle, it was like that spring morning when I first met her beneath the yew tree—the wood pigeons, her poor sparrow, the beauty . . .

"Before we'd taken our fill of each other, I remember lying there in her arms, listening to the rise and fall of her chest, the mortality rasping inside her lungs. I thought, 'If we have nothing more than this, I shall know I have lived more than most men. I shall ask God for no more.' And then I whispered to her, 'If I remain with you, your life will end, but I cannot bear for us to be apart. Therefore, I shall die with you.'"

"You said this?" Isabelle shuddered. She'd had no idea.

"I did, Isabeauty. I told her she should not be afraid of death, for we'd be together always. I promised when the time came I'd hold her in my arms, kiss her, lie with her even as she breathed her last. And then I'd join her afterward. That they'd find our bodies entwined, so we'd be buried as one. For to know a love such as ours was enough for a life." He broke off. "You're shocked, aren't you?"

Isabelle forced herself to speak. "That's why you sent me to music school and gave Mathilde away. Because you planned to commit suicide when Ada died." It had never been about her jealousy.

He forced a nod. "Laudanum seemed easiest. She thought so too, and swore if I didn't join her, she'd haunt me. That she'd never leave . . ."

Isabelle recalled her vision of Ada in the mirror. "Did she come back to you?"

". . . But the poems, they kept coming. I couldn't stop them. And they were unlike anything I'd ever written. They possessed me. You must believe I couldn't turn away from them. I just couldn't. And it was *her* doing! Her death—"

Isabelle interrupted, "You must tell me! Did she come back to you?"

"You really want to know?"

"Yes. Yes, I do, Father."

Father. How strange the title felt on her tongue.

Hugh leaned in close. The stench of wine, of sex, on him made Isabelle gag.

"No," he said at last.

And then through sobs and shouts he related the strangest tale Isabelle had ever heard: of how he'd traveled everywhere in search of Ada; from sea to mountain; from country to city, oftentimes disguising himself to avoid interaction with humanity. He attended séances held by charlatans who stole his money and his hope. He ingested opium with strangers under bridges. He even went to church to take communion but was turned away by a priest who thought he'd come to steal silver.

"Not once did I glimpse her," Hugh concluded, his cheeks wet. "Not once. Here's the sorry truth, Isabelle. There is nothing after death. Nothing! Only rot and regret." Then he wiped his eyes and offered Isabelle his hand anew, as though he'd forgotten he'd tried to strangle her. "Did I hurt you, child? Forgive me. Pray forgive me . . ."

Isabelle couldn't forgive. She wouldn't forgive. Her recollection of leaving the Black Forest, of Hugh sending her to go to music school so he could let Ada and their baby die without her awareness, returned fresh as the morning it occurred. She felt her sorrow twist to anger, her anger to fury, and her fury grow until it expanded beyond that hotel room. Beyond Paris, to the sky.

"You forced me to leave her!" she shouted, balling her hands into fists. "I never would have otherwise! And she died because I left her—if I'd been there, I'd have protected her, I'd have given my sister a home, I would have talked her out of your stupid pact! And now Ada is gone, Mathilde is gone. She's gone! Really gone! All is gone!"

Isabelle punched him again. And again. She hadn't known she possessed such strength. Hugh's nose was bleeding, his cheek swelling.

"Where did you take Mathilde? Tell me!"

Hugh arched a brow, laughing. "I appear to have misplaced her."

In that moment, if Isabelle had had a knife, she probably would have stabbed him. Then she realized how wrong she'd been—begging would work better than accusations.

She fell to her knees before him. Wrapped her arms around his ankles.

"Please, Father. Tell me where Mathilde is. For Ada's sake. For mine. I'll raise her as my own. It's the least I can do. You need never see her, if that's what you want. Please."

Hugh slumped back down in that throne chair, his wine and bloody nose forgotten. "I won't ever tell you, Isabelle. I can't! It's too late. Too late for Ada, for me, for everything. Better Mathilde grow up without knowing her wretched history. To not bear responsibility for her mother's death and her father's ruination. It's the least I can give her, my poor daughter, a life unburdened of her past."

"But if you don't tell me, I'll never forgive you," Isabelle whimpered. "I won't forgive you for keeping Mathilde from me. Nor shall I forgive you for Ada's death. How can you live with that?"

"Such youth. Such certainty . . ." He caressed Isabelle's hair, his hands unexpectedly gentle. "I know it's hard for you to imagine, but you will forgive me, Isabeauty. Not immediately, but in time. Once you go inside the glass chapel, you'll have no choice. You'll understand how much I loved Ada, and that we weren't meant to be parted. That I was right to let Mathilde go . . . The chapel will make amends for everything. All will be set right. You'll see."

With this, Isabelle couldn't bear her father's touch. His stench.

She released his ankles and stood.

"I promise you this, Hugh," she said, her voice ragged. "I will never step foot inside that chapel. Ever. Not even if my life was dependent upon it. Not even if I was without shelter in this world, and was starving. This I swear upon all I hold dear."

"Then I suppose we're done, Isabelle."

He rose at last from that ridiculous gold throne. Reached anew for his bottle of wine, and took a deep gulp.

He spat the contents of his mouth onto the floor in front of Isabelle.

"Go," he said.

VIII.

"I never saw my father again," Isabelle concluded. "When I returned to the hotel the following morning to try to change his mind, he'd already left for God knows where. At first I wondered if he'd killed himself. Then

I decided he'd gone to Weald House to build the glass chapel. I was right, but I was so destitute that by the time I had the funds to leave France, he'd already disappeared. And now he's dead.

"And that, Robert, is the whole of my story, and the whole of my suffering. Once I learned of Hugh's death, I knew I needed Ada's story preserved to honor her memory, which you've now written, or some version of it . . . but then it no longer seemed to matter. While I spoke, I understood I yearned for something more."

Revenge.

The word hung between them, bitter as rue.

Robert said nothing. What words could he offer to undo the acts of so many years earlier, which had led to so much sorrow, so much remorse? All he could do was sit on Ada's marble bench in her chapel—a chapel he now knew had been built by Hugh out of guilt instead of love—and set his head between his hands. It was hard to recall any life beyond what he'd experienced that morning: him seated there, Isabelle kneeling before him, Hugh's last letter on the bench. How heavy his skull felt, so thick, so dense! The lack of sleep, the emotion, even the scent of sex lingering about the folds of his clothes made the air feel still. Frozen. In all his years as a historian and a daguerreotypist of the dead, he'd never heard such a saga. Repulsion rose in him tainted by compassion, a conundrum of sour and sweet. No wonder Hugh sought to destroy himself. No wonder he'd given up Mathilde. No wonder Isabelle refused to allow Hugh to be buried beside Ada. No wonder Hugh had needed to leave Mathilde's address and lock it inside a chapel of glass.

"I had no idea," Robert said at last. "I'm so sorry."

"Sorry . . ." Isabelle gave a strangled laugh. "Not as sorry as I am. To think what I wanted was here all along. I feel such a fool! So stupid!"

"You couldn't have known."

"But I should have suspected, Robert." Her voice dropped. "You see, every year on the anniversary of Mathilde's birth, Hugh sent me a key. Year after year. Package after package. Key after key. Each exactly the same. *To Miss Isabelle Lowell, Weald House*, he'd write, so damn confident I hadn't yet gone inside the chapel. That I was still here waiting for him to show, to tell me where he'd taken my sister. And I was. I was! Every year, I'd open them, praying he'd at last sent Mathilde's address. Afterward I'd burn, bury, or toss the packages down the well to spite him. It mattered not. The packages still came."

This Robert had not expected.

"Sometimes they'd be postmarked from the Alps. Others from France. Another from Germany. Each year a new location. If that wasn't enough, he had to get your family involved by sending you here." She looked up at last from her clasped hands, her eyes dark pools of exhaustion. "I even thought to destroy the chapel. I tried to throw a rock through the glass, but I couldn't do it. I just couldn't."

"But that's in the past," Robert said. "At last you know where Mathilde is—she's now old enough to bear her history. I'll help you go to her. I want to."

With this, he found himself drawing closer to her. Yearning for her.

"Because of what just happened between us?" She shook her head, laughing oddly. "I don't need your pity. I can go to my sister alone, thank you."

"No. Because I want to be with you."

The words took Robert by surprise, but there they were. His willingness to admit this truth went beyond the intimacies they'd shared in the chapel, or the story she'd told him all those nights.

"You don't want me, Robert. You want Ada. Her story."

"No," he said. "I want you."

Isabelle's eyes widened; he thought he spied a warmth in their depths. "What about your wife? Your ever-lasting mourning?"

"I'm alive. She's dead." His throat tightened as he said this.

She brushed a tendril of hair from his scarred temple. "You'd be a fool. I'm like Hugh. I don't know how to love. Only to destroy."

"That's a risk I'm willing to take."

Her eyes grew wet. "But you don't even know my true name. Nor do I."

"Be who you want to be. If you say you're Isabelle Lowell, that's enough."

To prove his suit, Robert found his fingers searching for Ada's miniature in his pocket. He'd give it to her. Prove that it was *she* he loved, not Ada. Instead of the miniature, he felt something cold and hard atop it. Something the size of a chestnut.

The rock Tamsin tried to throw at Grace—he'd forgotten it was there.

Before Robert could pull either miniature or rock from his pocket, Isabelle rose from the bench. A dove nesting in the eaves flew past her shoulder to settle on the bench. Though she offered her hand to help Robert stand, any tenderness he'd sensed seemed firmly locked away.

"We should leave," she said, releasing his hand once he was upright. "It must be well after nine. Once word gets out the chapel has been unlocked,

Tamsin will be here—I can't bear to see her gloat." Her gaze swept over the moss, the reeds breaking through the floor, the forest carved of marble. The sun was now high enough to set the chapel windows ablaze: the bounding glass birds, the ivy, the twisting roses, the sparrows, the raven. As beautiful as the chapel was, now that he knew her story, it seemed a necropolis forged from regret and memory. Just as his life had been these three years. "I should have sold it when I had the chance . . ."

Isabelle's words trailed into silence once her gaze reached the stained glass window bearing Ada's portrait. Then, to Robert's wonder, she recited:

> "As the Poet waited 'neath domed glass
> Whilst the clocks chimed forlorn for noon
> His fists stopping those who might trespass
> With dreaded words he dared impugn . . .
> Then he cried : 'Break the glass, but not to plunder!
> Let Eurydice rest protected from her foe
> On a bed of diamonds—a chimera of wonder—
> A home for—'"

She broke off as a second dove landed beside her feet.

"A home for her soul," Robert finished; he'd memorized the poem after hearing Tamsin recite it outside Ada's Folly that day.

A home about to be invaded. Lost.

Isabelle swiped at her eyes. "God help me, despite everything I can't bear to think of the pilgrims here. At least I'll be gone for good."

Robert couldn't respond, for his mind was racing like a horse toward a broken fence. He stared at the glass, trying to capture it to memory as he'd once captured light and shadow with his camera.

A riot of blues, reds, and greens spilled across the white marble tracery, across the floor and along the carved trees. The glass portrait of Ada seemed intensified too, as though it was imbued with a soul, like Hugh had written. Robert imagined the chapel overtaken by time and nature, just as it seemed destined when he first viewed it. The white marble walls crumbling beneath ivy. The arms of the forest jutting past the clear glass dome. The windows choked by vines and nests. Birds clustered amid fissures. Foxes hiding in crevices. Moss crawling up arches. The earth reclaiming Ada's Folly for its own . . .

"Now let Sparrows return; the Ravens too—
Let Oak envelope in its embrace—
Let Her be received back to Earth—"

The words emerged from within Robert like a prayer, though he had no idea where they came from. Now this could never be. Instead, hordes of pilgrims would arrive to weep at the stained glass of Ada. Faint before it. Deposit offerings of raven feathers and blood-red roses, which would rot on Ada's bench. Couples would request to be wed there. Mourning widows would weep. The pilgrims would give way to curiosity seekers arriving from as far as London and Paris, each queuing to pay sixpence a tour. Who'd lead the tours, now that Grace and Owen were gone? Perhaps it would be Tamsin Douglas once she recovered from the fire, or even Mrs. Chilvers; Robert couldn't envision Missus Dido's involvement, given her disdain for the pilgrims. Though that hadn't stopped her joining forces with Tamsin when it came to that death certificate.

Robert pressed his eyes shut, unable to stop the thoughts pummeling him. This time, instead of his wistful march of nature's dominance, he viewed a darker fate unfold for Ada's Folly:

Caravans of carriages arriving at the coach stand.

A wider road built to accommodate them.

The willows near the chapel chopped for a footpath.

Ivy trampled around the doorway.

Muddy footprints on the marble floor.

The torrent of newspaper articles.

Books. Scholarly articles.

Hawkers along the path.

Watercolors for sale.

Daguerreotypes.

Hysteria.

Noise.

Chaos.

Loss . . .

"No," Robert said, opening his eyes. "No."

Isabelle frowned at his outburst. "No?"

"No."

His hand jabbed in his pocket. The rock inside it was small. Dense. Jagged. Just the shape to break glass. To banish ghosts.

"Here," he said, pressing the rock into Isabelle's reluctant hand. "If you're not going to do it, I will."

"Do what?" Her hand was shaking. Was it fear? Excitement? Her forehead furrowed. But then, like Adelaide and Lucian decades before he'd planted those rosebushes, Isabelle met Robert's gaze. Isabelle understood.

"We must hurry," she said, squeezing Robert's hand. She even smiled. "Now."

The rock made a small hole in the window closest to them but didn't penetrate through to the milky glass protecting it from the outside world. "What else can we throw?" she asked. Robert pointed to rubble on the floor, where a thick tree root had forced its way through marble tiles. Isabelle laughed as she gathered the shards in her arms, piling them atop Ada's bench, her movement swift and strong. What other surprises did she hold?

Her voice rang out:

"As the Poet waited 'neath domed glass
Whilst the clocks chimed forlorn for noon . . ."

Robert threw the second stone, which shattered the whole of a window showcasing a large glass raven. The third cracked a gathering of sparrows.

He shouted in reply:

"His fists stopping those who might trespass
With dreaded words he dared impugn . . ."

They ran back and forth, gleeful as children, fearful they'd miss a window. Their boots scraped on shards of glass, which crumbled beneath their weight. Isabelle's laughter resounded, loud and hearty. As the windows shattered, colored glass rained above their heads. Robert clutched her against his chest, covering her head beneath his overcoat. She didn't pull away, not even when a flush of doves materialized before their faces.

A cold breeze, the scent of pine, wafted through the chapel as their voices traveled into the forest:

"Then he cried : 'Break the glass, but not to plunder!
Let Eurydice rest protected from her foe
On a bed of diamonds—a chimera of wonder . . ."

Soon only one stained glass window remained, the central panel bearing Ada's portrait with her sparrow. Isabelle wrapped her cloak around her forearm and smashed its base with a triumphant yell. As the portrait collapsed and fell, a giant wind hissed and Robert envisioned Ada's soul released into the ethers of memory—perhaps Hugh was there too, at last at peace.

But there was no time to mull this, for there was one last threat: the clear glass dome Robert had climbed that first night. The dome arched like a soap bubble over the skeletal remains of Ada's Folly, its otherwise pristine surface marred by a spiderweb of cracks near the ledge.

Isabelle pointed up. "What to do?"

Before Robert could answer, a giant tremble shook the ground as the chapel walls shifted beneath the dome's weight.

His heart pounded like a drum. They needed to find cover. Now.

But the dome did not collapse. Instead, something far more unexpected occurred. An unearthly cry spread across the moors as dozens—no *hundreds*—of doves emerged from the eaves beneath the dome. The wind roared through what remained of the chapel walls, scattering more doves in its wake. He raised his arms to protect Isabelle. The doves grew thicker still. They appeared a blinding mass of life. An elemental force. In that moment, they felt more threatening than anything he'd ever imagined. Worse than a glass dome shattering above his head. More terrible than the renewed loss of his soul to sorrow.

"Come! Against me!"

Robert had to shout to be heard—the air was filled with the rush of air, the blur of feathers.

He threw the overcoat onto the floor just as the glass dome cracked. A single fracture was enough to do a dozen's work. It joined with the fissures already present to spread across the dome. Isabelle tensed, and Robert screamed for cover, but the dome did not shatter; Hugh had reinforced the dome with thin ribs of steel. The metal glittered like diamonds beneath the sun. No matter—there were other threats to consider.

The doves continued to come. Thick. Relentless. By the time the first dove landed on Robert's shoulder, he'd grabbed Isabelle's arm. He pulled her against him. Down onto his coat. He awaited her protest, but she only drew her cloak over them. Shards of glass pricked their flesh through the wool.

The din of wings grew louder. Brighter. Stronger. A shower of lavender-hued petals rained from the blossoming willows, dappling their faces, their hair. Robert shut his eyes. Held his breath. He imagined what the doves might see: a man and a woman beneath a cloak covered in flowers, curled on a bed of glass.

He felt Isabelle's hand creep toward his. Her touch was surprisingly warm. He held his breath further still.

"Open your eyes," she said, twining her fingers into his. "Look up."

Robert looked up just as her thumb pressed against the heart of his palm. Three times.

The doves rose toward the sky like souls returning to heaven.

Acknowledgments

The Lost History of Dreams was born from an actual dream I had several years ago. In it, I witnessed a young woman arguing with a gentleman over an inheritance in a shabby room lit only by a fireplace. Both were dressed in mid-Victorian clothing. When I woke, I had no idea what the dream was about, or who the couple might have been. Regardless, I found myself turning the dream over in my mind, unable to forget it.

The novel you have just finished reading is the result of that fragment of a dream, and the support of many people and institutions. Though it feels an impossible task to express the depth of my gratitude to everyone involved in the writing and publishing of *The Lost History of Dreams*, I shall try my best.

First off, I owe my biggest debt to my literary agent, Michelle Brower, who took on *The Lost History of Dreams* when it was little more than a one-page synopsis. Michelle saw the potential in this novel long before I did and has been there all along, bolstering me with her enthusiasm, dedication, and willingness to spend hours brainstorming the tangle of Robert and Isabelle's story via emails and "summits" involving strong coffee and French pastries. I'm especially elated that Michelle found the perfect editor for *The Lost History of Dreams* in Tara Parsons, whose sharp-eyed brilliance and love of my manuscript transformed it into the book you now hold in your hands. I am also grateful to the entire Atria team, especially Trish Todd, who took over the reins from Tara with enthusiasm and aplomb; her assistant, Kaitlin Olson, marketing whiz Isabel DaSilva, and publicist Megan Rudloff. In addition, Isabella Betita kept production running smoothly, and art director Cherlynne Li commissioned Jarrod Taylor's stunning cover design depicting Sida's first appearance in my novel.

Though Michelle, Tara, and Trish served as fairy goddess-mothers to *The Lost History of Dreams*, I received invaluable assistance from the following institutions. The Virginia Center for the Creative Arts provided me with a residency fellowship during the crucial period when I was finishing my first draft. I'm grateful to Karen Dionne, Christopher Graham, and Robert Goolrick at the Salt Cay Writers Retreat, where I presented the first scene from *The Lost History of Dreams* for the first time ever. The Highlights Foundation offered a quiet cabin and delectable meals when I was chin-deep in revisions. On the craft end, National Novel Writing Month, better known as NaNoWriMo, turned me from an author who makes illustrated books into an author who writes novels. I'm also indebted to the Sackett Street Writers' Workshop, where I workshopped my fiction with Heather Aimee Fisher-O'Neill, whose life-changing advice transformed my career. Another debt of appreciation goes to Emily Kramer and Kate Piggot of LitWrap, who facilitated a Poets & Writers works-in-progress reading grant for *The Lost History of Dreams*. My colleagues at the Historical Novel Society, especially Nancy Bilyeau, Christopher Gortner, and Mary Sharratt, provided encouragement and friendship over many conferences and confabs.

The research for *The Lost History of Dreams* included two trips to England, where I walked the paths trod by Robert and Isabelle, and a trip to Herne Bay, Paris, and nearby Sèvres, where I followed in Ada and Hugh's wake. Another research trip took me to Rochester, New York, where Eric Wilder of *Spine Magazine* escorted me to the George Eastman Museum and listened patiently while I enthused over daguerreotype plate formats and antique cameras. In addition, the George Eastman Museum's photographic processes video series granted me a deeper understanding of the mechanics of Robert's work as a daguerreotypist.

Closer to home, Courtney Walsh of the Stevens Institute of Technology in Hoboken was the librarian friend every author yearns to have. Courtney assisted with researching the details of post-mortem photography, consumptives, and nineteenth-century pre- and post-natal medical care. From a twenty-first century first-world standpoint, where sterile medical practices and readily available antibiotics are taken for granted, it's shocking to consider how often premature death befell our nineteenth-century counterparts, especially in regards to infants and children; in England, the average life expectancy at birth in 1851 was 41.9 years for females and 39.9 for males (source: UK Office for National Statistics). Victorian mourning rituals helped the bereaved grieve, process the unimaginable, and take comfort in the promise of a celestial reunion on the other side of the veil; I've detailed some of these fascinating customs in *The Lost History of Dreams*, such as hiring a mute person to accompany a funeral procession and hanging fabric over mirrors to prevent trapping souls on the earthly plain. Louis Daguerre's 1839 invention of the daguerreotype, the first widely available method of photography, offered Victorians a new way to memorialize their dearly departed. According to Dr. Stanley B. Burns and Elizabeth A. Burns, authors of *Sleeping Beauty II: Grief, Bereavement in Memorial Photography American and European Traditions*, post-mortem photographs "were an unquestioned aspect of everyday life . . . They were taken with the same lack of self-consciousness with which today's photographer might document a party or prom."

The following books offered additional invaluable information about the art of post-mortem photography and daguerreotype creation: *Sleeping Beauty: Memorial Photography in America* by Stanley B. Burns; *Beyond the Dark Veil: Post Mortem and Mourning Photography from the Thanatos Archive* by Jack Mord; *A Full Description of the Daguerreotype Process: As Published by M. Daguerre* by Louis Daguerre; and *The Daguerreotype: Nineteenth-Century Technology and Modern Science* by M. Susan Barger and William B. White. Finally, Sheila M. Rothman's *Living in the Shadow of Death: Tuberculosis and the Social Experience of Illness in American History* helped me understand the lives of nineteenth-century consumptives beyond Gothic tropes, and *The Sèvres Porcelain Manufactory: Alexandre Brongniart and the Triumph of Art and Industry, 1800–1847* by the Bard Graduate Center for Studies in the Decorative Arts detailed the production of stained glass in Sèvres after the French Revolution.

On the writing end, I'm deeply thankful to the small army of beta readers who commented on my manuscript drafts with generous insight. They include Anne Clermont, Ellen Dreyer, Juli Craig Hilliard, Kristin Lambert, Stephanie Lehmann, Teralyn Pilgrim, Vicky Alvear Shecter, Erika Swyler, Anca Szilágyi, Kirsty Stonell Walker, and Karen Zuegner. Most of all, I send love and gratitude to my critique partners Julianne Douglas and Heather Webb, who were always there with excellent advice, word sprints, and the willingness to read yet another draft before yet another deadline.

My family remains a wellspring of love and support, especially my wonderful husband, Thomas Ross Miller, and wonderful daughter, Thea Miller, who endured several years of my coexisting in Robert and Isabelle's world with humor and fortitude, and my sister, Jennifer Johnson, who is ever-loyal and ever-wise. Finally, this book is dedicated to my father- and mother-in-law, Edward and Joyce Miller, who have blessed my life since I first met them nearly three decades ago. Though Joyce unexpectedly passed away in 2009, the memory of her loving kindness remains an intangible presence to all who knew and adored her.

About the Author

Kris Waldherr is an award-winning author, illustrator, and designer whose many books include *Bad Princess*, *Doomed Queens*, and *The Book of Goddesses*. She is a member of the Historical Novel Society, and her fiction has been awarded with fellowships by the Virginia Center for the Creative Arts and a reading grant by Poets & Writers. Kris Waldherr works and lives in Brooklyn in a Victorian-era house with her family. *The Lost History of Dreams* is her first novel.

The LOST HISTORY *of* DREAMS

KRIS WALDHERR

This reading group guide for **The Lost History of Dreams** *includes an introduction, discussion questions, ideas for enhancing your book club, and a Q&A with author* **Kris Waldherr**. *The suggested questions are intended to help your reading group find new and interesting angles and topics for discussion. We hope that these ideas will enrich your conversation and increase your enjoyment of the book.*

Introduction

Love stories are ghost stories in disguise. In this captivating debut novel in the Gothic tradition of *Wuthering Heights* and *The Thirteenth Tale*, a postmortem photographer unearths dark secrets of the past that may hold the key to his future. When famed Byronesque poet Hugh de Bonne is discovered dead of a heart attack in his bath, his cousin Robert Highstead, a historian turned postmortem photographer, is charged with a simple task: transport Hugh's remains for burial in a chapel alongside his beloved wife and muse, Ada. However, Ada's grief-stricken niece refuses to give Robert access to the chapel unless he agrees to her terms: write and publish Isabelle's story of Ada and Hugh's tragic marriage over the course of five nights. As the mystery of Ada and Hugh's relationship unfolds, so does the secret behind Robert's own doomed marriage to the fragile Sida and the origins of his morbid profession—a profession that leaves him seeing things he shouldn't from beyond the grave. Kris Waldherr effortlessly spins a sweeping and atmospheric Gothic mystery about love and loss that blurs the line between the past and the present, truth and fiction, and ultimately, life and death.

Topics & Questions for Discussion

1. The title of the novel, *The Lost History of Dreams*, is taken from the last book written by Hugh de Bonne, one of the characters in the story. What does the title mean to you? Which characters have lost dreams?

2. Supernatural beings, such as ghosts, are one of the main elements of a classic Gothic novel. How does the presence of ghosts change the reading experience? What do the ghosts in the novel represent to the characters? Are the readers meant to take the presence of spirits literally? Provide examples of how numerous characters are connected to the dead.

3. The novel opens with a quote from Ovid's *Metamorphoses*: "Eurydice, dying now a second time, uttered no complaint against her husband. What was there to complain of, but that she had been loved?" How is this sentiment expressed in the book?

4. Discuss how class is depicted in the novel, as well as the impact on those who don't follow societal norms of the time.

5. Weald House is used to convey a sense of place in the novel. How does the estate also function as a character? Provide examples of how the author represents the natural world in the story. How are the characters' lives changed by the presence of nature?

6. Discuss Waldherr's careful attention to the structure of the novel and how she uses poetry, letters, and stories to advance the narrative of *The Lost History of Dreams*. How do these techniques provide the reader with a deeper understanding of the characters?

7. What is Ada's role in the story and what is her power? How would you describe Ada's relationship and marriage to Hugh?

8. As the story unfolds, we learn that Isabelle Lowell may not be who she claims to be. What else do we learn about her? When did you start to suspect her real identity? Did the author leave clues along the way? Talk about how Isabelle challenges the preconceptions of women in nineteenth-century England.

9. What is Hugh's role in the novel? Is he a good man, a loving husband to Ada, or is he, as Isabelle accuses on page 290, "using her for [his] art"? What does the bequest of Ada's Folly symbolize to the various characters in the story? Do you agree with Robert and Isabelle's final decision regarding the chapel? Explain your answers.

10. Compare the characters of Robert and John. How does John serve as a foil to Robert? Who, if anyone, fills that role for Isabelle?

11. Analyze how the author uses Robert's profession as a postmortem photographer to challenge our perceptions of death and the grieving process. Why do you suppose Robert tells Grace the unvarnished truth about his occupation?

12. Compare and contrast Robert, Isabelle, and Tamsin's reactions to Hugh's death. In what way does his passing affect each of them personally?

13. On page 93, Isabelle says, "I believe love stories are ghost stories in disguise." Share your thoughts about love and whether you agree or disagree with Isabelle. What do Isabelle's beliefs regarding love reveal about her? Does your perspective of her character change over the course of the novel? Explain your answers.

14. Do you think Mathilde, who was "nothing like Ada" was able to break the Lowell family "curse" to find true happiness? Why or why not?

15. Discuss the ending of the novel. What are your thoughts about what occurred in the last chapter? Were you satisfied with what happened to the characters and how their stories concluded? If you could rewrite the ending, what might you have done differently?

Enhance Your Book Club

1. Make a list of the different birds mentioned in the novel and then take your book club bird-watching. Go here https://www.audubon.org/birding to begin exploring.

2. Daguerreotypes were the first successful form of photography and were created by Louis-Jacques-Mandé Daguerre. Discover more about the invention of photography and the daguerreotype process here: http://www.photohistory-sussex.co.uk/dagprocess.htm.

3. What combination of elements make a Gothic work? List ten characteristics of Gothic literature and note how many of those elements appear in *The Lost History of Dreams*. Then ask the members of your book club to name their favorite Gothic novel. Consider how those novels compare to the one you just read.

4. The epic poem *Metamorphoses* is considered Ovid's best-known work and was completed while the poet was in exile. What was the importance of Ovid to the characters of *The Lost History of Dreams*?

5. Hugh was fond of puns, puzzles, and scavenger hunts. When was the last time you went on a scavenger hunt? Head over to https://www.watsonadventures.com/whats-a-hunt/ for your first clue!

6. Visit the author's website (http://www.kriswaldherrbooks.com/site/) and discover more stories that celebrate art and words.

A Conversation with Kris Waldherr

What are some of your favorite Gothic tropes?

I've been enthralled with Gothic novels since I was a child—you can't imagine the fun I had playing with these tropes while writing *The Lost History of Dreams*! Though it's hard to choose the ones I like best, I'm especially fond of the trope of the haunted house on the moors. Another favorite is Gothic doubling—this is where two characters mirror each other, such as Jane Eyre and the madwoman in the attic or Rebecca and the second Mrs. de Winter. Finally, who can resist a forbidden love story involving a consumptive?

What research did you do for *The Lost History of Dreams*?

A lot! Besides consulting books about the history of daguerreotypes, post-mortem photography, and Victorian mourning traditions, I read biographies of the Romantic poets, such as Byron and Shelley, along with their poetry. Other subjects I researched: the treatment of consumptives in the nineteenth century (surprisingly they often managed to marry and have families in spite of the disease), prenatal and postnatal medical care, Eurasian women in Victorian society (more common than you'd expect, especially in London), and even the Gothic revival stained glass and the Sèvres Porcelain Manufactory. For additional authenticity, I looked at many daguerreotypes and photographs from the era when *The Lost History of Dreams* was set, along with prints and paintings depicting fashions and hairstyles. (Yes, the descriptions of Hugh's dandyish clothing are period appropriate. For example, men didn't have suits as we know them now, so for him to wear trousers that matched his frock coat was extremely fashion-forward.)

I traveled twice to England, where I walked the paths trod by Robert in London and Shropshire; the library in Wellington, the closest city to Kynnersley, was a treasure trove of archaic information about nineteenth-century inns, train routes, coach routes, maps, local wildlife, and more. For

Ada and Hugh's story, I traveled to Herne Bay, Paris, and nearby Sèvres, and consulted numerous period photographs and maps. Another research trip took me to Rochester, New York, to the George Eastman Museum to gain a greater understanding of daguerreotype plate formats and antique cameras. At one point I considered taking a course on daguerreotype creation there, but was unable to; instead I relied on the Eastman Museum's wonderful photographic processes video series to understand the chemistry and mechanics of Robert's occupation.

Finally, I studied the piano to get a sense of Ada's experience as a musician. I didn't get very far in my studies, but I did manage to peck my way through the andante of the Beethoven second sonata from his Third Opus. It helped that I already knew how to read music, and have played other musical instruments. One day I'll go back to it!

You began your career in publishing as a book designer and illustrator. Do you still illustrate and design books? Which do you prefer the most, illustration or writing?

These days, writing for certain. At this point in my publishing career, the challenge of writing a novel inspires me far more than illustrating or designing a book. Much as I love making beautiful books, fiction feels a richer and more immersive form of creativity. Writing a novel allows me to draw upon (no pun intended) everything I've learned so far in my life: psychology, history, literature, science, and so much more. But then again, I've spent many more years illustrating books than I have writing novels—perhaps it's a matter of balancing the scales before they tip back toward art.

That said, yes, I still illustrate and design books, but not nearly as often as I did before discovering the joys and challenges of novel writing. Frankly, much depends on the book I'm envisioning—if it needs art, I'll create it. My last illustrated book was *Bad Princess*, which was published in early 2018. The book ideas I have of late haven't required art so far.

You describe yourself as an "intuitive, nonlinear thinker." What does that mean? Describe your creative process.

I meant that ideas for my novels don't arrive in neat packages, where I immediately know the beginning, middle, and end of a story. Instead, they're spurred by flashes of images, snippets of dialogue, characters, and even dreams. These flashes come to me at unexpected and sometimes inconvenient times, such as when I'm taking a walk or washing dishes; just in case I always keep a notebook or phone nearby to write them down before I forget. (I always say that when the muses knock, you answer the door.) In my author acknowledgments, I've already described the dream that spurred the first scene I ever wrote in the novel, so here's another example: the title for *The Lost History of Dreams* came to me one morning when I was waking up; it took another year before I figured out what the accompanying story would be. Another inspiration was a painting I saw by Walton Ford in the Smithsonian of migrating pigeons lifting a tree limb (https://2.americanart.si.edu/exhibitions/online/birds/artists/ford/ford_bough.cfm); this led to the scene when Ada and Hugh first meet on the moors outside Weald House.

Over time, these notes reach critical mass. Then I'll organize them into an "inspiration" file, where they percolate until I get a sense of how everything connects—with *The Lost History of Dreams*, I had over twenty-five thousand words of notes before I began writing the novel itself. Once I'm ready to begin drafting in earnest, I'll arrange my notes like puzzle pieces until my story starts to make sense—as you might imagine, this can take time, but when it's "right" I can feel it in my gut. I also revise incessantly, which helps me unearth what my subconscious has in mind. It's not the most straightforward process, but I've come to accept it for what it is.

From a technical standpoint, I'm a big fan of Scrivener, where I can move scenes and notes around easily as I write. This also allows me to experiment with pacing and plot development, hold onto previous scene drafts, as well as keep track of character arcs and the like.

You make great use of the line "Every love story is a ghost story" from *The Pale King* by David Foster Wallace. What was it about that line that spoke to you?

It's such a rich quote, isn't it? I was deep into my first draft of *The Lost History of Dreams* when I came across the David Foster Wallace line. It was so perfect that I set it into my "inspiration" file—those seven words encapsulated so much of what I'd already written about Robert and Isabelle's respective ghostly relationships, where both haunted and haunter are constrained by love, memory, and guilt. Ultimately *The Lost History of Dreams* is intended as a love story about the power of forgiveness. Until Robert and Isabelle are able to forgive themselves for their inadvertent roles in the deaths of Sida and Ada, they remain trapped by their pasts much like Orpheus in the Underworld.

In the novel, Weald House is a prominent part of the story—does this house exist?

Weald House is a product of my imagination along with Ada's Folly. However, my description of the exterior of Weald House and the stable house where Isabelle sequesters Robert was based on buildings I encountered when I visited Kynnersley on the Weald Moors during my research. (Yes, Kynnersley is a real place in Shropshire. So are the Weald Moors.) The church and graveyard exist as described, along with the location of Missus Dido's cottage. So do the pathways, moors, and roads, which I suspect are slightly different than they were in 1850, though I did check them against period maps. It's a beautiful area of England.

Strangely enough, the name for Weald House came through happenstance. I'd originally named the house Wealt House because I thought it sounded mournful; I'd set it in Shropshire because of a documentary I'd watched on Victorian farms. After I discovered there was a Weald Moors in Shropshire, I shifted the house name accordingly. Later, when I finally visited Kynnersley, I found everything looked eerily close to how I'd described in my manuscript—a strange-but-true experience.

Which writers and illustrators have influenced your work?

The Lost History of Dreams was definitely influenced by Diane Setterfield's *The Thirteenth Tale* and A. S. Byatt's *Possession*—I adore how Byatt used poems, letters, and archival documents to create stories within stories. Sarah Waters's novel *Fingersmith* spurred me to write historical fiction, and remains one of my favorite novels. Finally, how can I not include the Brontës? *Jane Eyre* is perhaps my favorite novel, and one I reread on a regular basis.

As an illustrator, I love the work of the Pre-Raphaelites and the early English book illustrators such as Edmund Dulac and Arthur Rackham, and the Scottish illustrator Jessie M. King. In terms of contemporary illustrators, I was fortunate to be mentored early in my career by Alan Lee, whom I consider one of the greatest illustrators working today. His watercolors for *The Lord of the Rings* and *The Mabinogion* are masterpieces.

What is your favorite part of the book creation process?

I love those initial flashes of inspiration, and experiencing how they come together—sometimes this can feel like magic itself. I also enjoy the revision process after I have a completed draft, when I know my characters and can see all the connections and themes begin to emerge.

What was the inspiration for Ada's Folly and the poetry of Hugh de Bonne?

Strangely enough, the initial inspiration for Ada's Folly was a newspaper article about a Paris apartment that hadn't been opened in seventy years (https://www.independent.co.uk/news/world/europe/revealed-eerie-new-images-show-forgotten-french-apartment-that-was-abandoned-at-the-outbreak-of-8613867.html). For some reason, this led to my imagining a glass chapel in the woods that had been locked since its creation years earlier; I wondered what might be found inside. From there, I read about Horace Walpole's Strawberry Hill (https://www.thecathedralstudios.com/conservation/strawberry-hill-house-twickenham/) and other architectural follies. I was also inspired by a photograph of an abandoned chapel in a French forest taken by Romain Veillon (https://www.dailymail.co.uk/travel/travel_news/article-3625995/Romain-Veillon-photographs-abandoned-buildings-world.html), which I used to envision the final scene of *The Lost History of Dreams.*

As for Hugh's poetry, Lord Byron and other poets of the Romantic era offered ample inspiration. I knew from the beginning that poems would be an important part of *The Lost History of Dreams.* Though I studied and wrote poetry in college, I don't consider myself a poet; I wrote the poems that make up Hugh's fictional oeuvre with much terror and trepidation. (Thank goodness for rhyming dictionaries!) Luckily, it was easier to compose poetry in Hugh's voice than my own. I also looked at poetry books printed in the nineteenth century to get a sense of the punctuation and typography, which wasn't standardized. Somehow this helped me envision what form Hugh's poems should take on the page, which in turn helped me figure out the structure they required.

You write books for adults and children. What are the differences between writing for adults or children? What are the similarities?

Whether you're writing for children or adults, a story is a story: you need setting, characters, plot, and themes to explore. However, my writing for children tends to have a snappier sentence structure and simpler vocabulary; I make certain to provide context for any references that might be above their age level. The narrative structure is also more linear for a children's book than for an adult novel (at least the ones I write!). Each requires a different mind-set. I also take far longer writing my adult novels than I do my children's books.

Tell your readers what's next for you?

I currently have three novels underway, one for middle-grade readers and two for adults. Though both adult novels are historical fiction, the middle-grade novel is about a single mother and her daughter in modern Brooklyn—after writing *The Lost History of Dreams*, I desperately needed to write something that wouldn't involve years of historical research and emotionally tormented characters.

Now that I've finished the first draft of the middle-grade book, I'm letting it simmer as I turn back to my adult novels. The first of these is set during the Aesthetic art movement of the late nineteenth century—think absinthe, secrets, and decadence—while the second takes place a century earlier, and is intimidating me due to all the research involved. It's also darker than *Lost History*, and more overtly feminist and political. Interestingly, all three novels contain elements of mythology and folklore, like *The Lost History of Dreams*. As to which one will be published next, I suppose whichever one reaches the finish line first!